In

DREAMS
AWAKE

In

DREAMS AWAKE

JOE HOFFMAN

ARPress
45 Dan Road Suite 36
Canton MA 02021

Hotline: 1(800) 220-7660
Fax: 1(855) 752-6001

Ordering Information:
Quantity sales. Special discounts are available on quantity purchases by corporations, associations, and others. For details, contact the publisher at the address above.

Printed in the United States of America.

ISBN-13:   Paperback   979-8-89389-691-6
                eBook   979-8-89389-692-3

Library of Congress Control Number: 2024923819

1

. . . .

AS TOM JORDAN STOOD BAREFOOT in the surf, he couldn't remember exactly how long the nightmares had tormented him. It hadn't been that long since the Presque Isle incident, but he didn't think he had any mental scars. And ever since Alex came on the scene, life seemed to be at an all time high. So what, he thought to himself, is my problem? He knew he would have to get to the bottom of this and quick. In a couple of days Alex's daughter and granddaughters were to arrive and that would be a new experience for Tom.

He stood for awhile in the pounding surf trying to maintain his balance against the angry waves. It was ironic that the surf was so rough this morning. It was as if the ocean was imitating the way he felt. The evening would develop so wonderfully and passionately only to end with his falling fast asleep and entering an encompassing nightmare. Despite his fight to wake himself or reach out to Alex on the other side of the bed, his energy was wasted. He found he could not escape the grip that the nightmares had on him. Once he did manage to wake up, he stayed awake for fear of being imprisoned again by the ghosts that visited him in the night.

This morning was different, however. Tom could not find that peace the surf always afforded him, and could not be rescued from the torment of the night before. So in essence he was just staring off into the gray wet horizon of the morning sky trying to come to grips with this feeling that had taken over his every waking hour. He couldn't explain it and it was beginning to scare him. As the waves churned up the beach sand, Tom could identify with the grays and dirty browns that were making up his morning. The peace that every morning brought had failed him.

Turning away from the beach he threw Rocky his fetching tool while thinking, 'if I play my cards right maybe I can sneak in a nap before work'. As he and Rocky started to the house they got a panoramic view of the depressing horizontal gray in the reflection of the backside of the house. It was completely enclosed in glass.

They were greeted by Alex who hollered out the kitchen window in a mocking tone, "If you don't get out of that water you're gonna be shark bait. And that little dog, too!"

At this Rocky dropped his toy and gave out a condescending bark toward Alex who was coming down the back porch steps.

"Don't you sass me, you little furball!" Alex said as she reached and scruffed up the fur around his ears.

She walked a few more steps and, meeting Tom, gave him a good morning kiss.

"So how are the two men in my life this morning?" she asked while she playfully pulled Rocky's tail. "How was your night, Tommy?"

"Good," answered Tom. "Why do you ask?"

"Oh, no reason really, I was just concerned. You seem a little restless when you sleep. And with the stories you tell, I could write a book," Alex said as they reached the house. "If you ever need to talk, remember I'm here for you."

Tom stopped dead in his tracks as if a bolt of lightening hit him. That is what the person in the dream says, he recalled to himself. Why would Alex say that?

"Tom! Come on, honey, or your eggs will get cold," Alex said unaware of the effect her statement had made on him.

He hesitated at the stairs to let Rocky in and then closed the door behind him. Alex poured him a cup of coffee as he sat down. Rocky took up his position at the beggar's area next to her.

He was just about resigned to tell her about the dreams when the phone rang. Thinking from the context of the conversation that it must be her daughter, he drifted off to his own thoughts while he watched Alex admirably.

This woman he had only met six months ago had become the greatest thing that ever happened to him. He was blessed and he knew it. In all his wildest dreams he could never fathom that someone as wonderful as Alex could come into his life. He sometimes thought that something this good would not last. It only happened in the movies- never to someone like him or someone his age.

Tom Jordan was a middle-aged man with brown hair that had an intermittent tint of gray, making him more distinguished. He stood six feet, two inches tall and had square shoulders and a level jaw made of good German stock. He was slim yet he wasn't skinny. He took great care of himself but wasn't excessively muscular. He was a quiet, private man, a trait he acquired from all the years of living alone. He never had a crossword to say about anyone and he always had a smile on his face. He was always eager to help any lost stranger he chanced on in the airport concourse.

He was a fantastic pilot who learned his trade in the U.S. Air Force and was as proud of that as he was of the education that went along with it. He was a bachelor who had the usual scars of relationships that went south and eventually gave up looking for a wife or even a steady girlfriend. When he was in the air he found his true love; solace. There was no pain, disappointment or broken promises in the air. He found the tranquility he searched for and the wall it built for what he protected himself against when he was flying. Somewhat sad for a man like him, he would often say to himself, but it served him well and he had grown accustomed to that type of cloistered existence. He enjoyed his own company.

He lived in peace with Rocky, a yellow lab who moved in with Tom after he washed out of guide-dog school. He and Rocky were quite a pair. They had a language all their own and both respected the other's space.

Everything in Tom's life was comfortably plain until the day he met Alexandra Sanders. And nothing was ever the same after that. That day Aurora Airlines and Tom Jordan would always remember as the worst day in their lives except that no one was killed. It would take investigators at least five months of sifting through tons and tons of rubble to find that a disgruntled housewife placed a chemical potion in a bottle of after-shave. This in turn ignited a major fire in the cargo hold when the aircraft was about two hours over the Atlantic Ocean.

Because an alert flight attendant noticed that the galley floor was a little warm, Tom Jordan went down into the cargo hold to find that a fire was indeed becoming out of control. Since this model of 747 had no fire control system in the cargo hold it didn't take long for flight 409 to become an emergency, a bona-fide Mayday.

Although Captain Tom Jordan was a well-trained pilot, on that day he earned his keep and his reputation as a man you could call on in a clutch. He was originally a B-52 bomber pilot during the Vietnam conflict and had moved on to the SR-71 Blackbird to finish out his career. He had, over the years, developed a keen sense of getting out of tight spots with little or nothing to work with. Those many trips over the Chinese coast when they knew he was there only added to his ability to deal with immediate conflict and the enormous stress that comes with it.

With all the training Tom had had in his career, the Presque Isle flight was definitely a final exam to test his skill. There was to be no passing or failing grade-only life or death. But for Tom, the Presque Isle flight was more of a reward than a test. For it was during this flight that he would begin his relationship with Alex Sanders, even if there would be a great deal of turmoil to cut through first.

Alex Sanders was a forty- four-year-old divorcée who had come to Aurora Airlines after the Eastern Airlines breakup. She was tall for a lady of her descent. She was five feet, eleven inches in height and had sandy to light blond hair. She had long slender legs and a beautiful figure to match. Her smile would melt even the hardest of hearts. Alex had an air about her that tended to keep strangers at bay, as if in the presence of royalty, but deep inside she was as open and friendly as she was beautiful. When she spoke you knew she had culture. She never minced words or put on airs. When she walked it appeared she was used to modeling as nothing got out of line. Alex was every bit as classy as she looked.

Prior to the break-up of Eastern, Alex was in the pilot upgrade program to become a pilot. When they broke up the airline she was put back to square one and this time without a job or a husband, and with a daughter who blamed her for her father's demise as a pilot.

Ed Drummond who had also come to Aurora from Eastern had an acquaintance with Alex and her husband inasmuch as he was their chief pilot. It was Ed who came into the pilot's lavatory and found Captain

Pete Sanders drunk and passed out sleeping on the bathroom floor twenty minutes prior to his next scheduled flight. Therefore, there was no love lost between her and Drummond.

Alex's daughter Chris refused to accept the fact that Alex couldn't have done more to help her father keep his job. Chris knew her father had an occasional beer, but that didn't warrant Alex deserting him. This was a fight that had plagued their relationship for quite some time.

It wasn't until her daughter learned a hard lesson from her own husband's drinking. Then she realized it wasn't Alex's fault that her father was fired, anymore than it was her fault that her husband was fired after he was found asleep in the employee washroom of his workplace.

The very day that Alex met Tom and the day of the fire, Alex and Chris had talked at length about a reconciliation between them and getting on with their lives, with no more unresolved differences.

It had been some time since Alex had seen her grandchildren. For over a year the girls were growing up around her and she could do nothing to prevent Chris's unyielding refusal to let her see them. It was tearing her apart but she had to go on. She had to make a living and lately, working only part time as a fill in, it was kind of hard to make end's meet. She did, however, do all right taking care of herself financially. She was willing to stretch her finances if it meant helping her daughter.

It was obvious that since Chris left her husband she couldn't possibly make it without Alex. However, Alex, being the loving and understanding mother, forgave the formality of money and the "I told you so" attitude and welcomed them with open arms. There were two things Alex knew in her heart. One, she loved her daughter and granddaughters and two; she loved Tom Jordan. She knew she could make them both happy.

To Tom, Alex was the blueprint of what the Almighty must have wanted when he planned the Garden of Eden. She was the sunshine he didn't realize was missing until she came into his life. And how he went all these years without her he would never know. But one thing was for certain; he would never want to go through life without her.

The very way Alex came into his life was as bizarre as her very presence. One day Tom was caught in a relationship he wasn't sure he wanted to build, yet could see no way out of, and the next he was in paradise. However, this time it was with a different woman.

Who could have known that the flight attendants' strike would have produced the end result it did even to the point of Caroline, Tom's full time co-pilot calling in sick from her co-pilot's seat, which in turn led to Alex being placed in the right seat next to Tom. The rest as they say, is history, and Tom had no complaints.

The flight to Paris was in its own right a new experience. The two new friends were just getting to know each other when three hours into the flight an on board fire forced the aircraft to turn around and head back to the mainland. They had gone from friends to two professionals who had to work together to insure their own survival. Flight 409 barely made it into Presque Isle, Maine, before being completely destroyed by the flames that had turned them around.

To say the relationship between Alex Sanders and Tom Jordan underwent a baptism of fire is an understatement. It did, however, burn an everlasting love into their hearts for each other which was growing stronger every day.

Was it the loneliness they had lived with for so long or the intense love that was fueled by their mortality? The answer was only to be found in the heart. But, from that day forward they live a romantic, passionate and respectful existence together under the same roof. Nevermore to want for the love they both so badly needed and were denied! Nevermore to be lonely and to work in a profession which did not forgive mistakes! They began a new life that day and never looked back.

As she sat across from him eating her breakfast and talking with her daughter, Tom kept his gaze fixed on her. He saw the very essence of beauty in the way she smiled and expressed herself. Her hands were perfectly manicured; her hair was perfectly kept. She dressed neatly and was always presentable. Tom constantly wondered how she could look so fresh even when she was on the go.

Due to the circumstances surrounding their meeting, there really wasn't a courtship before their relationship became intimate. Her lovemaking was a mirror image of the way she lived, and. in Tom's word- incredible. They would make love like newlyweds and because of the courtship issue they would lie together and talk of their plans, their wants, and the things about each one of them that made the other happy.

Alex finished her conversation with her daughter and said to Tom, "You don't know how lucky you are. My daughter is coming a day earlier than expected."

"That's nice," said Tom.

"Yeah, except for the mutt! He goes to the garage," returned Alex, trying not to laugh. "I don't want that flea bitten mongrel humping my granddaughter every time she bends over to pick up her Barbie."

"Excuse me!" Tom said defensively as Rocky let out a muted growl "If he goes to the garage, so do I."

"Isn't that precious," said Alex. "Well I'll just have to put on another blanket while you're gone, I guess."

At this Rocky left the kitchen and headed at a trot in the direction of the bedrooms.

"Where's he going?" Alex asked. "I hope I didn't hurt his feelings."

"I'd say that you did hurt his feelings and he is probably going to clean his teeth on the new shoes you bought yesterday," Tom replied with a serious tone. "That's where I'd be headed if I were him."

"You're kidding, right?" said Alex. "Thomas, you better be joking!"

He just looked at her with that blank empty look on his face as they both heard the bedroom door creak and Rocky enter it with a full head of steam like a dog on a mission.

Alex jumped from her chair and in one motion removed her slipper and tore after Rocky in a full sprint hollering at him something about the wrath of God and his scrawny hide.

Tom just sat back and laughed at the two of them running through the house. It was very comical really. She, a grown woman, was chasing a cantankerous dog with a shiny new shoe in his mouth through the house. It was one of those Kodak moments that don't happen every day. It was something to see.

Before long the chase had ended and Alex once again secured her shoe and returned it to the bedroom tightly shutting the door. She then returned to the table, out of breath and said in a very casual tone, "How's your breakfast, sweetheart?"

That was all it took. Tom blurted out laughing hysterically and Rocky stood down the hallway and barked with a big grin on his face.

Alex just sat there shaking her head and said, "Uh-huh, that's all right, just keep it up you two. Remember who's doing the cooking around here. Who knows what can fall into your plates? Never underestimate a woman who was denied the last word."

They sat quietly for a few moments when Alex broke the silence saying, "Well now that I'm finished making a complete fool of myself, do you still love me?"

"Yes I do, my dear," Tom replied, "and your little dog, too."

From the back of the hall came another muffled bark from Rocky as he said that.

What he never told Alex was that when he first got Rocky, he was trained to bark quietly when anyone said "Dog". He was originally trained for a seeing- eye dog but developed a "personality" unlike the rest of the dogs in the class. So, Rocky got a D+ on his final exam and was sentenced to live with an old bachelor in a beach house on the gulf coast of Somerset, Texas. Rocky could live with that.

"What's on your agenda today?" asked Alex.

"I've been asked to stay on stand-by for an afternoon flight if the pilot calls in sick," answered Tom. "Bob Reynolds is having some back troubles."

"I hear it's from rolling around with that little preppy during layovers," returned Alex.

"Not my business, honey," answered Tom. "I told them I'd be here if they needed me."

"Well, I have to go to the grocery store and stock up on some items before my daughter gets into town," said Alex. "Why don't you get some sleep? Maybe with me gone you can get a little rest. I'll be gone a couple of hours so set your alarm. There is something we need to talk about when I get back though, okay?"

Tom shook his head affirmatively and began helping Alex clean up the table. They kidded each other while flicking one another with the dishtowel until Rocky came upon the scene and got it from both sides. Off he ran through the house headed for the closed bedroom door.

"That dog reminds me of you, Thomas," said Alex. "Always has his mouth open with his tongue hanging out and breathing heavy. Of course you smell a little better!"

"Okay Alex, keep it up!" Tom said as he walked toward the bedroom door. "Hey, dog, how about some nice French shoe leather to chew on while Alex does the dishes?"

Following that attack on Alex, a great battle of strength and agility broke out in front of the bedroom door over who would escape victorious with the shoe. After the scuffle quieted down the three of them ended up in bed and Rocky was soon shooed away and the door was again closed, this time from the inside.

"God, I love that dog!" Alex said.

"And that dog shore do love you, too!" answered Tom with a southern accent.

Alex woke a short time later and was very quiet so as not to wake Tom, slid away unnoticed to the garage and off to the grocery store. Rocky walked back into the bedroom and took up his spot on the bed next to Tom.

2

. . . .

TOM LOOKED AT HIS WATCH and noticed that he had been in the air for over five hours and was well over the Chinese coast. He set the stopwatch and his slide rule to calibrate the onboard cameras to begin their sweep of the designated area. He had been here before and although he loved the flying, it was deadly boring. The landscape didn't change much at this altitude. Everything was either a deep rich green or a contrasting muddy brown. An occasional rice plantation would send a sliver of reflecting light off a rice paddy, but for that the scenery remained unchanged.

The onboard camera- ready alarm made a single "beep", meaning it was armed and ready. With that Tom looked again at his watch and counted down the last thirty seconds and then activated the cameras.

Transmitting the code for cameras to the onboard voice recorder he just routinely sat back and let the camera do its thing.

His imagination began to drift ahead to the week he was planning to spend with John Beck when the silence was broken by an annoying shrill alarm. Jerking himself alert Tom looked down at the radar-warning screen and at the dreaded light flashing "missile warning!"

He turned his attention to the camera, which had his auto- pilot locked for another twenty seconds until the camera finished its sweep. He next turned his radar to "track mode" and attempted a quick estimate of how long the missile would take to reach him. Tom had what looked like a ten second window of escape.

As he anxiously watched the camera clock tick down, he could hear the audible alarm on the radar warning get louder. Tom placed his one hand on the stick and his other hand on the throttle, ready to launch the SR-71 into a hard right dive with full afterburner as soon as the camera released his auto- pilot. He had come too far to override the system and pull out only to come back again and try later. And now that they knew he was here they would be waiting for him. As the clock ticked down to zero the camera light turned off and the auto- pilot indicator light went off. Tom forced the throttle to "afterburner" and put the Blackbird spy plane in a radical four-G dive.

"Video sweep complete, taking evasive action from missile attack!" Tom said to the voice recorder.

Taking a hard right turn at 70,000 feet takes a bit of puckering on the part of an SR-71 pilot and Tom was at full pucker by this time and could actually make visual contact with the missile. He would continue on this course to about 50,000 feet while watching the missile on his radar screen. He would pass in the opposite direction on the right side of the missile where it could not detect the engine's exhaust heat. The missile would become confused and eventually run out of fuel, or so was the plan.

When he had put five miles between himself and the heat-seeking missile he began climbing to 70,000 feet when a second alarm went off in the cockpit meaning there were now two missiles after him. And to add insult to injury the first missile had turned.

"We're off and running!" Tom said to the voice recorder. For that is exactly what Tom was doing, running. The ground radar had him zeroed in; all Tom could do was outrun the missiles.

He puckered a little more and did another nosedive and then headed for the safety of the 100,000-foot range and some neutral air space. The radar said the first missile was gaining ground so he did some radar jamming techniques and more maneuvering to get away from the two missiles that he concluded were radar guided missiles and not heat seekers. Though these were a little more technologically advanced, they were still no match for the speed of the SR-71. However, they were gaining and he could not get a safe distance from them. The closer they got to him the more he evaded them but to no avail. Finally all Tom could do was put the jet into a suicide nosedive and head straight for the deck and make sure he did not pass out from the G force.

Tom continued on the dive to 8,500 feet, knowing it may take him 5,000 feet to bring the jet out of the downward thrust. He pulled back on the stick and the blackbird pulled steadily out and leveled off at 2,000 feet. He looked out the window and confirmed he was still over land and the radar was quiet. Tom began to climb back to a safe altitude when he heard a faint voice say, "I was there for you." Just then a third missile alarm went off followed by an explosion which rocked the whole aircraft. Tom jerked so hard that he rolled over the top of Rocky, fell out of bed and bounced off the floor. While still on his back he scooted over against the wall. He opened his eyes in time to see Rocky cower away from him and to hear the phone ringing.

Breathing so heavily and completely exhausted, Tom had to labor to get off the floor and answer the phone. It was Ed Drummond who asked, "What the heck you panting about?"

"I've been jogging," Tom answered his head still in a fog. "What's up?"

"Bob Reynolds still hasn't cleared himself for tonight's flight. Can you come in on stand-by?" returned Ed.

"Yeah, no problem. Let me freshen up a bit," said Tom. Hanging up the phone he sat on the floor bewildered and exhausted, and said to himself, 'My God, what was that? Just a dream, just a dream, it was only a dream. You're all right, you're all right. Breathe deep! Breathe! Breathe!'

He leaned against the wall and noticed that he was trembling. Still breathing a little heavy he began to perspire. Aware of the pain above his right eye, he was still too exhausted to move. After catching his breath and his bearings he went into the bathroom and looked in the mirror.

Noticing a slight bruise forming above his eye, Tom sat down in an attempt to regain his composure. The effects of the dream were so vivid that he thought he must have gone into a panic right before the phone woke him up. He definitely understood the feelings were related to fear or trauma. Rocky came back into the bathroom and sat next to him as if to tell him all was well.

He put his arms around the dog saying, "You've got to help me get through this before I go nuts!" Then he got up and began to get dressed for work.

3

. . . .

TOM FINISHED GETTING READY FOR the airport, and saying good-bye to Rocky headed out the door and to the car. Once in the driver's seat he lowered the sun visor to look in the mirror and examine his now throbbing cheekbone. A nice bruise was beginning to form and he needed a good excuse to reply to Alex's forthcoming cross-examination. He put on his sunglasses and headed out. As he drove the inclined driveway out to Sommers Street he couldn't help but gloat over his beautiful lawn. The place was beginning to reflect a woman's touch, ever since Alex came to live with him. She went about the womanly task of planting flowers here and there and even placed a few shrubs in strategic locations. She reminded Tom on every occasion that her hard work complemented his lawn and if he was lucky, Rocky would decline to mark the shrubs as his own territory and they would both stay out of the doghouse.

He had taken Alex out in the yard yesterday and tried to convince her that the lush green foliage she had the honor of standing barefoot in was imported from his mother's yard in Ohio. Tom also rambled on to say that he took great pain to transplant only the best Kentucky bluegrass by growing the grass from seed and then planting the harvested seedlings. Thus with the proper care and the nurturing of a baby did he arrive at the lush, thick carpet that she was now sinking her toes into.

Blinking her eyes and giving Tom that funny sheepish little grin she then turned her attention to his trusty companion Rocky, and said, "This is going to hurt me worse than it is you, but you two are in dire need of therapy." And saying this she drew with the speed of a gunfighter, the pistol grip of the garden hose and gave them both a good soaking while they fiercely retreated to the back yard. Rocky barked in agreement with Tom as he shouted out that a crazy woman was abusing them. Alex merely giggled and waved to the passersby on the sidewalk and went on with her hydro- therapy on her two most deserving patients.

Tom chuckled to himself briefly as he thought about yesterday when they spent the afternoon in the yard. He was grateful for all of the afternoons they spent together and hoped they would never end. He turned onto Sommer Street and headed for Highway 1 which would take him past NASA, where he spent a few years a long time ago. He had worked there as an astrophysicist and a pilot. That was one place Tom didn't fit in. He had trouble dealing with the egos and he was single without a family. That was an unacceptable social mistake to be single as well as open minded and happy. He began looking for other employment soon after he was hired in there. I should have listened to John Beck, he said to himself. He told me those people wouldn't accept me and I was too naïve to think someone wouldn't like me. He left NASA with so much animosity that he always recalled a Bible verse that reads, *if they do not welcome you, turn and leave, stop at the gate and shake the dust from your feet.* Tom always felt that they denied him his first love in life, to fly into outer space, but they could not deny him the hatred he felt for those people.

Soon he was headed into the Spanish district and drove past the adobe parish of a Catholic community, with its rich brown mud-like sand texture and its brightly adorned red tile roof. It was a sight to behold. This must be a new church, Tom thought as he approached the traffic light by the church. It was here that he felt a strange urge to stop. The church had immaculately manicured grass in an area where there was not a great deal of growth bearing sod, but was known for its dusty streets and hard unkempt clay yards. As he glanced over his shoulder toward the church he saw a priest waving and motioning to him to 'come here.' Tom glanced back to see the light change, but when he returned his gaze the priest was gone.

"Not this again!" Tom said aloud. He drove through the intersection with an undeniable feeling of emptiness and despair that he could not explain. As he approached the last intersection in the district, he looked up and saw a large billboard. It showed a picture of the priest that Tom had just seen in front of the Spanish church, and an advertisement that read, *I was there for you, will you be there for me?*

Suddenly, an old lady in a rusted Chevy pulled out in front of him causing him to stop abruptly. At this he pulled over to the berm of the road to collect himself. He could not take his eyes off the billboard. A car passed by, tooted its horn and waved to acknowledge that Tom was all right. This distracted his gaze from the billboard long enough to put his Mercedes back in gear and prepare to re-enter traffic. As he looked at the billboard one last time what he saw put him back into his seat. He was looking at a big "Tropicana orange juice" can and a slogan, which read, "it's not just for breakfast anymore." This unnerved Tom so much he shut off his car and got out and pretended to walk around his car looking for damage. He was beginning to shake and feel weak and exhausted. He looked back to where he saw the priest at the beautifully lawned adobe church, but only saw an old, run down, deserted mattress warehouse.

Tom walked around the car scared and confused and must have looked very distraught when the old lady in the rusty Chevy came back to check on him. He was so surprised to see her that he began to relax and feel comfortable. He talked briefly to her and assured her that he was all right and thanked her for stopping. Shortly they were both on their way.

Tom drove onto the freeway and his mind began to wander back to the sign and the dreams that he had been having. He was thinking about how calm the old lady had made him feel when she arrived. Her very, 'hello' put him at ease. Only a few minutes ago he was nervous, anxious and shaking. Now he was perfectly at peace. This is weird, he thought. I'm getting worse instead of better.

He was overcome with an urge to turn around and go home. He would let Drummond find someone else to fly today. If he could be with Alex this would all go away. She would know what to do; she would know what to say. God, how he just wanted to go home.

Three miles from the airport exit, Tom's cell phone rang. It was Ed Drummond.

"Tom, I'm sorry!" said Ed. "I was hoping I could catch you before you left home."

"No problem, Ed," returned Tom. "Overtime is good whether on the road or in the air."

"Yeah, right," blurted Ed. "I've got your overtime. Really, Tom, Bob showed up so go on back home."

"Okay," replied Tom. "You'll get no argument from me. I've got things to do."

"How's Alex?" asked Ed. "You know, Tom, you owe me big time for fixing the two of you up, I could have put her in with that transvestite, Andy."

"She's fine, Ed. Thanks for asking," answered Tom. "You're right though, I do owe you big time."

"Are you all right? You're voice sounds a little strange," asked Ed.

"No, I'm great thanks," he said. "Even better now!"

"Okay, then," said Ed. "Just remember I was there for you."

When Ed said this Tom became very excited and uncomfortable.

"What did you say?" hollered Tom emotionally.

"I said there's only a few like her! What did you think I said?" answered Ed.

"Oh, nothing, I just got some static or something," returned Tom quickly as not to tip Ed onto his little problem. "I'll tell Alex you said hello."

Tom cradled the phone and began soul searching again.

I swear Ed said that, I heard him, Tom continued talking to himself. But I swear I saw the priest and the sign also and then I saw it again. Tom continued on with a battle of rationales, pro and con as he headed back home. This was weird and it wasn't fun anymore.

The closer Tom got to his house the more he felt he was being drawn to something. He couldn't quite put his finger on it, but he felt as if he needed to go to church. You should go back to church. Tom said to himself. Maybe you wouldn't be so darn wacky.

As he drove on, he began thinking of Alex again and his mind appeared to settle down a bit. A smile came on his face as he recollected all the pranks she pulled on him. Her facial expressions, her giggles, her cooking, the way she spoke of her grandchildren and her daughter! And the way she made him feel behind closed doors! Tom felt totally in love and could never figure out why the Almighty blessed him like this, but he was not about to complain. Life was good and it could only get better. Three miles from home, he thought he had better think of an excuse for this bruise. As he headed closer to home he looked out into the warm Texas sky. What a beautiful place to live and such a beautiful time to be alive. A tickle began to form in the pit of his stomach as he neared his home. The stress of the earlier moments had left him now and he was overcome with a kind of peace that only Alex could give him. It was that same peace that Alex had brought to all on Flight 409 that fateful day in Maine.

As he pulled into his driveway he could see Rocky sprinting across the lawn being chased by Alex and her trusty garden hose. The scene was set, Tom thought, it was going to be one of those evenings.

4

. . . .

THE LADY OF HIS DREAMS looked at him from across the yard and waved.

"Why aren't you at work?" she shouted. "How do you intend to keep me in the luxury to which I have grown accustomed?"

"Bob showed up after all and they sent me home," returned Tom. "They'll get no argument from me today. Too nice a day to spend at work. How was your trip to the grocery store?"

"Fruitful! Very fruitful," replied Alex as she approached him with a hug and a kiss. "How's that? Original, huh?"

"That's pretty good for a gal from Texas," responded Tom.

"Uh-huh, I hear you. What did you do to your eye, fall out of bed?" answered Alex.

"How did you know that?" he queried

"My ex-husband used to do that on occasion, but he had an excuse," she said in a caring fashion. "What's yours?"

"We'll talk about this later," answered Tom as he reached down and ruffled Rocky's fur. "I don't know exactly where to begin. So, what's for supper?"

"Supper!" exclaimed Alex. "No work, no eat! You and your little dog both."

Alex drew her trusty hose nozzle and he and Rocky took off for the beach behind the house where they chided her because her hose was too short for the job. She tugged on the hose as if to urge the water to arc further into the air and to soak those two worthy subjects into submission, but to no avail. She was, however, to have the last word.

"Did you say supper? Come here and get it!" screamed Alex with a sinister look in her eye.

Tom and Rocky, eventually through stealth, cunning and the fact that the phone rang, outlasted her and were able to return to the house through the garage. He was certainly impressed when he walked into the dining room and noticed she had set the table out on the balcony where the Gulf with its fantastic view was a favorite sight of hers. When they first took up their relationship, she was impressed with this sight and would sit and admire it for hours. It was a vision to behold to see Alex sitting, staring, and petting Rocky, and carrying on a conversation like they had been friends for years. That was one of those moments that he would always hold to his heart and never tell anyone.

She had even gone to the trouble of putting the hurricane globes on the candles so that the Gulf wind wouldn't blow out the romance of the evening. The table was adorned with Alex's favorite New Mexico style dinnerware and a matching brown tablecloth. She even went with the matching napkins. Tom was assured that a feast was coming. He remembered that she did say earlier that they needed to talk about the arrival of her daughter. Maybe that's what this is all about. Then again, maybe she just loves my darling self.

"Okay, I'll see you then," finished Alex as she hung up the phone. "Are you ready to eat, honey?"

"Yes ma'am, anytime," answered Tom. "Let me help you with that."

As he grabbed a hot dish from her and held the door open with the other hand he caught a glimpse of her hair through the golden Texas sun. The very rays of the sun seemed to radiate through a kaleidoscope of numerous shades of blonde hair. It also reflected off her skin and her inner beauty beamed outward like a painting exhibited by bright museum lights showing the highlights of a beautiful work of art.

Silhouetted against the background of the blue waters of the Gulf, she made a portrait of a very beautiful woman Tom was in love with and knew was in love with him. There could be nothing better in his life and he knew it. He had but to live it.

As the two of them sat down to supper there was a strange hush about. It was as if both had something to say but neither wanted to start the conversation. He sat patiently in his chair waiting for whatever it was she wanted to present with this wonderful dinner. He finally broke the ice.

"So, tell me, beautiful, how do I rate a dinner fit for a king?"

"You know, Tommy, I have to make some decisions soon. And I need your help," replied Alex with a troubled look on her face.

"Your husband didn't come back, did he?" chuckled Tom. "Rocky, be on the look out for an angry man with a gun. What troubles you, my dear?"

"My lease is up at the end of the month," she said. "Actually, I don't know what to do."

He waited patiently for what he expected the conversation to be. And although he didn't want to sound easy, he really didn't want her to leave. So he thought he would just shut up and listen.

"You're losing me, sweetheart," answered Tom to keep the conversation going.

As he looked up at her, he couldn't help but feel sorry for her. Obviously, there must be more troubling her than just the grandchildren coming to visit.

"What can be so important about your lease that troubles you so, Alex?" asked Tom.

"My daughter is coming a day early and she is not going back. She is leaving her husband and filing for divorce. She hasn't a job and he has managed to drink up their savings. She is in a bad way and is going to need my help. Obviously she is going to need a place to live. This is where my lease comes in," Alex went on with his full attention.

"You know I love you. And I'm thinking I would like to spend the rest of my life with you, but I have never asked your opinion on this," said Alex as she looked at her plate and not into Tom's eyes. "My daughter has two children and no money or a place to live. And right now I am the only hope she has in life. I know how that feels, Tommy, because the day I met you I was living day to day with very little hope. I had a place to stay and a part time job, but not a lot of hope for the future. You gave me that instantly. The second you shook my hand I knew everything was going to be all right. I thought there would be a price, but you never asked for anything, you were just there. What we went through on that day is what I call the dues someone has to pay for a gift they are given, and you and

I both paid some heavy dues for what we have. I've always felt you were a gift to me and I have always hoped I at least returned the favor. And I wouldn't trade it for anything, except my daughter's happiness. I know she is hurting and I know I can help her. It's myself I'm not so sure about right now. Since the first time we met I don't know what to say to you, Tommy, I can't even look you in the eye.

He looked across the table at the woman he loved and realized just how little he knew about her, or was it women in general? He knew he would have to be strong for her whatever was troubling her.

After a short pause, he said, "Alex, look at me, honey. What exactly are you getting at?"

"My daughter is coming tomorrow morning, a day earlier than planned. I'm thinking of putting her and the kids up in my apartment," explained Alex. "But it's not big enough for the four of us."

"I thought there were only three of them," replied Tom.

"That's correct, unless you count me," said Alex somberly.

"Is this your way of telling me that we are over? That you are leaving? Is that what this is all about?" asked Tom quite seriously.

"No, no, Tommy, not at all. I'm just trying to find out where I stand," replied Alex." You know, you have never really asked me to stay. I just kind of stayed over one night and never went home."

He looked over at Rocky in an attempt to break the serious mood of the conversation and said, "What do you think, Rock, should we keep her?"

Rocky's tail began to wag back and forth and he started to make a whining noise.

Tom looked over at Alex and said, "It's cool with him and it's necessary for me. We want you to stay."

He rose from his chair and went to her. Taking her softly by the arm he picked her up and hugged her. And placing his index under her chin he lifted her head until he looked right into her eyes.

"I've been a bachelor all my life and I'm not too sure how to say this. But, I have become so happy since you've been here that I don't even want to think what it would be without you. We are soul mates, there is no separating us. We were introduced to one another for one reason. We did what we had to do and our relationship was set in fire. We are destined to make each other happy forever. That is our reward, our gift to one another, together for all time, and time starts now and it never ends. Your problems are my problems. My home is your home, my life is for your life. That's what this is all about. The Almighty put us together and a little housing arrangement is not about to shake us up. So when your daughter comes we'll do all we can for her and let her live her own life. And all will be fine. We'll spoil the grandchildren, then send them back home. We will have the perfect life, and I'll take you to Ohio to meet my family.

He held her tightly in his arms. As he gazed out across the surf someone walking on the beach distracted him. Tom nearly swallowed his tongue when he recognized the person as the priest he saw at the old abandoned warehouse building downtown. The priest stood and smiled. He then held out his hands in a welcoming gesture and said, "We were there for you!"

Tom tried desperately to remain calm, but Alex sensed his change in body language and asked, "What is it honey?"

He looked at her and smiled and held her tight again. He glanced back to the beach to ascertain what exactly the priest was doing, but he was gone.

"What is it, honey?" asked Alex again. "Are you okay?"

"Yeah, sweetheart, I'm fine, really," he answered. "Let's go down to the beach."

Tom had a plan. He would go down to the beach and see the footprints of the priest and he would know he wasn't going nuts.

"Here, Tommy," returned Alex. "Don't forget your wine."

They walked down to the beach with their trusty dog bringing up the rear. Arm in arm they strolled like a couple of lovesick teenagers laughing and kissing as they walked through the sand, smelling the salt water and grimacing against the sand vapors the wind picked up and cast against their faces. Life was good. Their love was young but growing. Although Alex was a little more experienced at marriage than Tom, she never acted like he was a child when it came to loving and the way he cared for her.

When they reached the beach they took their shoes off and plopped down in the sand. Tom, ever the skeptic, looked about the beach in hopes of telltale signs of an intruder a short time ago.

"What are you rubber necking about, Tommy?" queried Alex. "You look like you're waiting on a train."

"What?" he said, "In this outfit?"

He acted as if he were adjusting his tie and took one more look over the beach and much to his disappointment saw no footprints Is there no end to this, he thought.

The two lovers sat on the sand talking; laughing and making plans for when the 'kids' came as they watched the sun begin to set.

Alex rose and said she needed to visit the ladies' room and would bring him more wine. Taking his glass, she made her exit to the house.

"All right, sucker, where are you?" he said to an empty beach. "I know you're out here, show yourself."

Tom shook his head and began to think he really was nuts when he looked over at Rocky and watched his hair stand on end. Jerking his attention to his right, he saw the priest standing about ten feet away. He just stood still and motionless against the wind staring blankly out over the ocean.

"What do you want?" asked Tom.

The priest turned his attention in Tom's direction but said nothing at first. What seemed like an eternity to him, was, however only seconds later.

The priest said, "We will need you soon. Remember that we were there for you, and now we call on you to be there for us. You will know when; the time is near"

Tom was unable to say anything in response. It was as if he were paralyzed and unable to do anything. All he knew was that there was a great feeling of peace about him. He had nothing but questions for the priest, but it was evident that the man would answer no questions today. He blinked a tear of fear from his eye and just that quickly, the priest was gone.

Tom glanced down at Rocky and saw that he was fast asleep. He knew only one person who could help him now as his peace turned to fear. Tom called on John Beck to come and help him again, to help him make some sense out of all this mayhem, but John Beck would not be talking today. He would have to deal with this alone.

As he fought to regain his composure, he heard the back door shut and was surprised Alex had returned so soon. He wiped his eyes and assured himself he would be all right. Relax, he thought, breathe deep.

Alex surprised him when she apologized for being gone so long.

"Drummond called and asked if you could call him back tomorrow," she said.

"Something about a dead head flight on your next three day trip to Paris. You overseas pilots are beginning to be spread pretty thin, I see."

"How long were you gone?" he asked.

"About fifteen minutes, I think. Did you fall asleep "she replied. "Here help me with this."

Tom turned his attention to her and noticed she had brought along a blanket, a fresh bottle of wine, and she was in her bathrobe. This could be interesting, he thought. We'll see if the priest comes back for this.

"What were you so deeply engrossed in when I saw you?" asked Alex. "You looked like you were in a trance."

"Alex, some despicable seagull had the unmitigated gall to take a dump on my beach," he said in a way that sent her into hysterics. "And what is worse, it looks like a Lake Erie Seagull; the foulest of the lot. What do you have hidden inside that robe? Is that for me?"

As she continued to giggle she opened her bathrobe and drew Tom in closer to her ordering Rocky to keep an eye out. They poured more wine knowing good and well that they were not interested in drinking it as they watched the sun set and held each other in a passionate embrace which would go well into the night.

"I tell you, Tommy, only you can find an artistic way to describe a seagull taking a crap. It makes one sorry they missed it," continued Alex giggling uncontrollably. "Get in here, you crazy devil, your dessert is getting cold."

As the two of them passionately embraced on the beach in unison with the waves, the troubles of the day passed away as a cloud threatening a sunny day moves along the horizon. They were with one another and the peace Tom so longed for earlier in the day was his to take in and enjoy. He always told Alex that when he was with her it reminded him of special times as a child. He would wake before sunrise at his grandmother's farm and listen to the birds tell their tales of chores to be done before the morning dew was gone and the sun would be at its peak. This, he thought to himself, was one of those times, as he lay on the beach watching darkness settle in, holding Alex tightly in his arms and listening to her breathe.

Eventually, the cool Texas gulf overcame the two of them and woke Alex out of her deep sleep. Rising to pick up the blanket and wineglasses she stopped dead in her tracks, dropped the blanket and glasses and said,

"I need a shower! Are you interested in joining me?" And off they went, running across the sand naked in the darkness into the warm welcoming waters of the Gulf. They stopped and hugged each other as the moon began to reflect its light off their glistening bodies.

Alex looked into Tom's eyes and said, "This is how life should be. This is how our life must always be. I will always love you and always be there for you, no matter what, no matter where. When we are apart we will always be together in our hearts and minds. We will never part. We are soul mates, you and I. Nothing can ever separate us." Then they strolled, hand in hand, back to the house, crawled into bed and fell fast asleep exhausted from their busy day.

5

. . . .

TOM BECAME ALERT AGAIN WHEN he felt the warm seawater on his chin. He jerked himself back into reality and heightened his grip on the aircraft seat he was using for a life jacket. Everywhere he looked there was carnage. Women and children were crying a hopeless moaning cry, one that would be heard from the mouth of someone miserable and exhausted. There was a putrid odor of aviation fuel about and a harrowing oil slick was visible fifty feet away. There were little flames about and it appeared that the children were all around a centralized area away from the fuel. Tom bobbed about in the water and looked helplessly at the women and children who were desperately clinging to life much like he was. He was afraid to leave the security of his life supporting aircraft seat for he knew he couldn't swim. How could he help those people without himself becoming a casualty?

He turned his body to the left to get a look in that direction and was paralyzed by a gripping burning pain in his back. Turning back he instilled in his mind that there was nothing he could do for the others. What is that language they were speaking? He was unfamiliar with it, unfamiliar with everything about this place. How did he get here? Where was Alex, she was just here? Where could she have gone?

He began to feel heavy with anxiety and exhaustion and could feel his grip weakening on the seat cushion. He began to slip farther into the water when he looked out across the desolate area and saw someone walking across the water toward him. At first all he could make out was a slender figure with long hair. He regained his grip on the seat and continued to gaze toward the figure approaching them.. All of a sudden he became aware of a great stillness on the water and of the shouting and crying. It was quiet as all looked toward the approaching figure. It has to be a mirage, Tom thought. I only know one person who walks on the water and if he shows up here we are all in a world of hurt.

As the figure approached it was plain that it was a man dressed in a blue robe with a red sash. He resembled a Spanish priest one would see in a Clint Eastwood movie and he looked familiar. He approached him and held out his hand. Taking Tom's hand in his and lifting him half way out of the water, he said, "Look around you; this is what the Father asks of you, to take care of the little ones. This is why you were brought to this place and put on this earth. Remember the Father was always there for you, now you are here for Him. Be strong, no harm will come to you. No harm will come to the one who answers the call of the Father. Again I say to you, it was He who was there for you, now it is you who are here for Him. Be strong."

The priest let loose of Tom's hand and began to fade as he walked away. As Tom began slipping once again into the water the pain began burning in his back. He attempted to turn around only to feel Rocky wiggle out from underneath him and scamper out into the hallway.

"Oh good!" said Alex. "You're awake. Come on, honey, breakfast is ready."

He looked about the room in total confusion as one would when he is totally lost. He looked left and then right and then left again staring aimlessly at Alex.

"Thomas, my boy, you get some good lovin' and it knocks you nuts," kidded Alex. "Come on, let's eat." She turned and made her way into the kitchen. "C'mon, mutt, you can have his waffles if he doesn't hurry up."

"I'm coming, I'm coming!" replied Tom. "Give a man time to collect himself. You touch my waffles, Rocky, and you're mink food."

As they sat down to breakfast he was still rattled by his dream, but he felt very well rested. He kept recalling what the priest said about no harm coming to him. But, what was it that he was to be ready for, that was going to happen soon? He was confused and yet relieved. He was still going to stop and see the priest on the way to work.

"So, how are you my dear?" asked Alex.

"I'll be fine once I wake up. I haven't slept that good in weeks," answered Tom. "Strange dream, though. That was a doozey."

"Have you ever thought about going to a counselor?" asked Alex. "It's possible you have delayed stress from the fire. Everybody is affected differently from something traumatic like that. And you took it all on the chin. You never know what evil lurks in the mind of a traumatized airline pilot."

She continued on, "I'm with you on this. I know someone or something is visiting you in the night. I can tell by listening to you. We can go together. No one needs to know."

"Go where?" Tom replied.

"To the shrink!" Alex answered.

"I don't need a shrink," he said.

"That's what my husband said," countered Alex. "The bottle was his therapy. I won't let that happen to you."

"I figure I have you to turn to, so I'll be fine," returned Tom.

"Yes, you do, Tommy," she agreed. "But, when you need me you won't listen to me. I'm thinking you need me now. I'll go with you if it's that bad, you don't have to face this alone."

Continuing on with the conversation, Tom was beginning to be a little scared that she thought he was already nuts.

"I don't think you're bonkers, Tommy," reported Alex. "I think there is something like a demon in you that will not come out on it's own. You still dream about the fire and you tell the tale every night in your sleep. So, something is definitely in your head trying to get out," she went on saying, "I can heal your physical ailments and needs. I can keep you warm and give you a shoulder when you get scared. But I can't help your mental health. I'm not qualified. And since you are my life now, we should seek professional help. And the airline doesn't have to know. And if they do, it's tough. You saved their bacon when you brought that airliner down without any crispy critters. Me included. They will accept it, believe me. Drummond owes you big time. Of course," Alex said in a semi-sarcastic tone, "they are probably still mad at you for letting your floozy girlfriend plug up the toilets."

Tom's head jerked to attention and he gave her a chilling stare.

"Oh no, you did not go there!" said Tom as he rose from his chair and leaned over toward her.

"Rocky, sick him!" she hollered. "Defend my honor! Kill. Kill."

But Rocky did not attack, he just stood alongside, wagging his tail and barking.

"That dog is just like you, Tommy," Alex harassed. "He just pants, eats and licks his nuts."

"Oh," replied Tom. "I don't recall any complaints last night."

"That was different," she said in self-defense. "Sometimes you get a burst of culture and impress me. Last night was such a time."

"I hear you," he said as he hugged her. "Don't forget who arouses in you those deep tremors and gives those satisfying back rubs on those cold Gulf evenings."

"Never!" replied Alex. "Don't you have to go to work? I hear Drummond calling. Speaking of him, he wants to see you today before your flight."

As Tom relaxed his grip around Alex's waist, he kissed her and headed for the bedroom to get ready for work.

6

. . . .

"COME ON BACK HERE AND let's eat before your breakfast gets cold. You have plenty of time to get ready for work," said Alex as she poured Tom's coffee. "You never answered me honey, how did you sleep? By the snoring I'd say quite well. My mother always said never bed down with a man who snores. I should have followed her good advice."

"Yes, you should have, my dear," Tom countered. "However, you must ask yourself this question. Had I followed my mother's advice, would I be graced daily with his suave humor, wit, disposition and intense undying love? I think not, my love. And," he went on. "Where would you find such a wonderfully kind, handsome, caring, cultured individual had you listened to your mother? Who would take care of you and shower you with the gifts to which you have become accustomed? Tell me, please, where is a man like me to be found?"

"The want ads, of course. Under 'Men Seeking Women'. Where do you think I found you?" answered Alex. "Eat your breakfast, honey."

He sat down to his breakfast while playfully muttering to himself about being abused and unappreciated and left for dead in the sea of love. She just sat down on the other end of the table with a smirk on her face knowing good and well she got one over on poor old Tom.

Back on a more serious note, she reminded him that her grandchildren were arriving in the afternoon so to be ready for a little change around here. She also reminded him that Drummond had called last evening, so be sure and see him before his flight took off.

He sat peacefully eating his breakfast, feeling the love of having a wonderful woman sitting across from him, and all in all he was happy.

She, on the other hand, thinking that maybe he wasn't really listening even though he had muttered a few strategic uhh-huh's threw in a curve .

"And also Drummond told me where the pound was so I don't have to worry anymore about the mutt humping little Carrie's leg."

Tom, while exercising exemplary self-control was indeed listening. However, that was the last straw. Being very subdued he put down his fork, picked up his napkin, placidly wiped his mouth, folded the napkin and putting it neatly alongside his plate, rose ever so slowly. By this time Rocky had figured out that he was the 'mutt' and he knew what the 'pound' was and he too was slowly rising to defend his honor.

Tom looked cunningly at her and said, "You hadn't oughta said that. He's got feelings, you know. I hope you realize this means war. I never thought you'd stoop that low to badmouth my dog."

Moving over to Alex, who by this time had a serious look of anticipation on her face, he put his hand on Rocky's head and said, "Kill!"

Tom playfully grabbed her in a bear hug and pulled her off her chair and onto the floor while shouting at Rocky to "get her!" Before long the two men had this poor ol' defenseless woman on the floor being assaulted by the man of her dreams and a long, pink, wet, dog tongue thrashing over her face. She was doomed.

After abusing her until she begged for mercy the two men ran off in the direction of the bedroom with her in hot pursuit wiping away the dog saliva all over her mouth. There was also a great deal of expletives uttered in the direction of Tom and his trusty friend. Alex saw the two of them lying on the bedroom floor in the triumphant grasp of fellowship one would display after winning a decisive battle in the trenches against the Huns. The only thing missing now was the champagne and cheese.

She caught up with her two victorious warriors and stood over them, but she was not to be taken seriously. Dog drool was everywhere about her and she was in no way able to carry the fight any further.

"All right, I'll give you that one," she said and made her way into the bathroom in search of a towel. "Yuk!"

As the two honeymooners went about the task of getting presentable and Tom finished getting ready for work he noticed he had time for two quick calls. He called his friend the priest at the church down the street. He used to be quite regular on Sundays before he took the Paris flight.

Nowadays he flew on every third Sunday and that cut into his church life. Now with Alex being a Presbyterian, he rarely went to the Catholic Church even though he was a member. Tom got a busy signal at the rectory and decided his friend must be in so he would stop on his way to the airport. The second call was to Drummond to see what his major malfunction was.

He advised Tom that Andy had gotten himself in some kind of trouble with a UFO report and Drummond needed Tom to sit in as Andy's representative. The airline was thinking of shipping Andy out as a section eight.

Andy was usually a stable pilot, but over the years had made many enemies with the top floor executives with his mouth and they were looking for a reason to be rid of him. None any more than Ed Drummond who had to listen to Andy tell him how during Ed's divorce he stepped in to take care of his wife's needs. Drummond never really forgave him for that one. Hanging up the phone Tom finished getting ready for work.

Finishing the task of tightening his tie Alex came alongside him. In a brushing fashion of cleaning dust off his jacket, she gave him a hug and a kiss and reminded him that the peace and quiet that he was used to would come to an abrupt end when he returned home from Paris.

Looking at Tom with her adorable eyes Alex said, "You know I owe you big time for this? My ex would never have allowed this to materialize. I probably would never see my daughter and grandchildren again once we separated."

"The least I could do for the woman I love," exclaimed Tom. "Besides, who else is better qualified to take care of the mutt?"

Hearing that, Rocky let out a little bark and the moment was once again filled with laughter.

"Okay, be careful, get some sleep and hurry home!" said Alex swatting him on the butt as he walked out the door.

"I'll do that," returned Tom. "Good luck and be careful driving. I'll see you soon."

7

. . . .

TOM CLOSED THE DOOR BEHIND him and got into his car. His next stop at the church was only a short distance away. As he left the driveway he couldn't help but think about what Alex had said a short time ago. She was correct. It would never be the same around the old house again. But it would be nice. All his life he had lived alone and was accountable only to himself. He always thought he was happy and content and neither wanted nor needed anything more or anyone else. He had Rocky and for friends he had Bob and Sharon. What more could anyone ask? 'How very wrong could I have been?' he thought as he drove down towards the church about a mile away,

For some reason he was taken aback by the beauty of the green lush lawns in the area. Although it was, for the most part, hot and dry, it was always so green. Given the dark gray of the concrete streets, this was indeed a colorful area. He had driven this way several hundred times in his trips back and forth to work and it never seemed to click as it did today. It reminded him of seeing something for the first time as if all the vibrant colors were trying to make an impression on its visitors.

Before he knew it, he was at the church, pulling into the driveway. Everything looked so bright. The dome at the entrance reflected the morning sun like a majestic torch announcing the coming of the Man Himself. His long time friend and short-term golf partner, Father Skip Harris, met him at the front door. They shook hands and exchanged pleasantries on the steps for quite some time, since the two friends had so much catching up to do. As they made their way into the hallway Rosa, Skip's housekeeper, and one of Tom's tenants, brought them a cold drink.

"I don't know where to start exactly," Tom began. "It all started a short time ago, but feels like an anchor around my neck that has pulled me for ages."

He began telling his friend about his dreams and the premonitions. He recalled to the priest how Alex never saw anything and there seemed to be a gap of lost time whenever these 'sightings' were taking place.

Father Harris began by questioning him about his health, drugs, alcohol as well as sleep and how many hours he was flying above the normal. The priest, also a clinical psychologist, weighed all his answers and agreed with him that there was nothing unusual in his lifestyle. Father Skip did make mention, however, about the change in Tom's sex life since he had teamed up with a roommate. The two friends continued to talk about things in Tom's life that may or may not cause any psychological abnormalities. So far all had gone Tom's way in the fact that the priest thought he was normal. Everything was well with him until Father Harris said,

"Unless He is calling you to serve in some way, shape or form."

"Why would you say that?" asked Tom nervously. "Serve who? How? What are you talking about?"

"Just relax!" Father Skip said as he tried to calm him down. "There is no need to be frightened here. Just relax. This is obviously a little more than an inconvenience, I would say, Tom. Am I correct?"

"The priest keeps telling me he was there for me and soon he will need me to be there for him!" Tom replied. "He scares the shit out of me. When I least expect it he's standing next to me. I drive down the street and he's standing there grinning at me. I tell you, this sucker is everywhere."

"When was the last time you saw him?" asked the priest.

"Yesterday," answered Tom.

"Did he say anything besides he needs you?"

"He said 'don't be afraid, no harm will come to you. Anyone who does the work of the Father shall not be harmed.' It was a dream, Skip, that's all it was," answered Tom who by now was quite stressed over the whole conversation and very ill at ease.

"Tell me about the dream," the priest asked. "While you're at it, sit back in your chair and relax."

"Don't you hypnotize me, I've got to go to work later on today," Tom interjected.

"No, no nothing like that," Father Skip said. "Just sit back and start from the beginning."

Tom leaned back in his chair and before talking, took a sip of his iced tea.

"I remember it all starting in the ocean. I was warm and I was clinging to a raft of some kind. I was slipping off the raft when I saw this figure walking across the water. But, somehow I knew it wasn't Jesus. It looked like Alex but as the figure came closer I could see it was the priest. I slid off the raft and was sinking because I was too tired to hang on. He came over to me and he grabbed my arm, but I couldn't feel it. I couldn't get over how sparkling, crystal blue the water was. The surface was smooth; there were no ripples. He took my arm and lifted me out of the water to my waist. That's when he started talking."

"What did he say?" Skip asked.

"He said, don't be afraid. You must be strong for the little children. The Father takes care of him who takes care of His children. Now be strong, the Father is with you. As He was there for you, now you must be there for Him." Tom concluded. "I looked around and there were hundreds of children floating in the water. Then Alex woke me up."

Father Skip looked at his friend for a long time as if trying to understand what he had told him. When he couldn't think of anything to say he broke the silence by asking, "How many times have you seen this guy and how many times did he talk to you?"

"The night before the dream I talked to him on the beach," replied Tom.

"What did he say?" asked Father Skip.

"He said we will be calling on you soon. As we were there for you, you will be there for us. But I was so convinced that he was there I even looked for footprints in the sand. He is that real when I see him."

"What is this 'there for you' stuff?" the priest asked. "What is he referring to?"

"I think it was the fire," Tom answered. "I never told anybody this, but right before I was to turn for a landing at Presque Isle, I saw John Beck sitting next to me. He told me I would be fine, but not to make any right turns because of the additional fuel tanks. How did John even know about those special tanks in the first place? Hell, he's been dead for seven years."

This caused Father Skip to sit upright in his chair.

"What do you mean he's been dead for seven years?" Skip asked quite surprised.

"He was killed in Fort Worth seven years ago," Tom answered. "I thought you knew that."

"Have you seen or talked to him since the fire?" the priest asked.

"No," Tom replied.

The priest began to rub his chin in a totally confused mood. Finally, once again he broke the silence.

"When do you fly again after today?" Skip asked.

"Tuesday," Tom replied.

"No, you've got to get sick," the priest said. "You've got to stay on the ground until I figure this thing out."

"I can't, Skip, I'm committed to my schedule and Drummond wants me to do a turn around Tuesday and get right back," Tom explained. "I won't even get my three days' rest in Paris. We're very short handed as it is. Besides if there is something to this, I couldn't run away from it if I tried. It would be like destiny or fate, whatever you shrinks call it."

"I only have one explanation," Skip said. "If you are called to do something for the Almighty you could well be told or warned in advance much like Joan of Arc, or Saint Francis. But to have signs like that in this present day is very unusual. However, that's not to say that it can't happen. I'm very uncomfortable with this, Tom; I'm going to consult some of my colleagues. The scary part is the water and all those kids. Can't you at least call off loony or something? Tell them you see UFO's or something."

"I see those a lot!" Tom said laughing as he rose from his chair to leave.

"Don't say that, Tom," Father Skip returned. "You're beginning to scare me"

"How do think I feel? This crap has been going on for quite a while," Tom said. "There is one good thing to all of this. The priest said I'd be all right, so I shouldn't have to worry about survival."

"Do you believe the priest?" Father Skip asked.

"Why not?" replied Tom. "What have I got to lose? The question is, do you believe Mulder?"

"Let me know if anything, or anybody shows up to talk with you," returned Father Skip. "I'll get back to you after I consult some of my more intellectual friends."

The two men shook hands and as Tom made his way to the door. Father Skip took one last opportunity to put in a plug for the Almighty and his church when he said, "Now that you know where the place is, can I expect to see you here on Sundays?"

"You remember now I'm living in sin with a Presbyterian," Tom replied jovially. "I'm not sure the Old Man up stairs would like that."

"I'll tell you what," replied the priest. "You bring her along and I'll set things right with the Old Man upstairs."

As the priest shook his head and crossed himself over the reference Tom made to the universal boss, he closed the door and Tom was on his way.

As he drove away from church he couldn't help but notice how good he felt. There's something about that church that always makes feel so good. The padre' is right, I'll have to come back there more often. I really feel good. Tom continued thinking to himself. We didn't come to any solid conclusions, but I still feel pretty good about myself and I don't feel afraid of the Spanish priest showing up anymore. Things are looking up. Now, all that's left is to go play union steward and see what kind of trouble Andy got himself into. Tom hit the on ramp and was on the freeway in minutes on his way to work. Life was good.

8

. . . .

TOM PULLED INTO THE PILOT'S parking lot at the airport and had a strange feeling of deja vue come over him. It reminded him of the day he met Alex. The sun was shining, the same gate guard met him, and as he looked ahead he could see his old friend, Bob Pearson waiting for him with a grin that could scare a grizzly bear.

This grin usually meant that a serious razzing was in order for him and that he better be ready with any kind of defense available.

"Well, hello, Tom, old boy," Bob started in. "I'm surprised to see that you still come around here. I figured you'd be up to your butt in alligators by now. Or were you and the airline able to come up with a compensation plan for all those toilets your girlfriend plugged up?"

"It's nice to see you too, Bob," Tom replied while extending his hand and returning a sheepish grin. "For the purpose of clarification I'd like to go on record as saying that she is not my girlfriend and I had nothing to do with the demise of the waste disposal system in this fine facility."

"You never change a bit, Thomas," remarked Bob. "You still have more bull than the fattened calf. You would have thought that fire would have cooked some of the BS out of you."

"Quite the contrary, my friend!" replied Tom with a laugh. "It only instilled in me a burning desire to never get too serious about anything that can't kill me."

After shaking Tom's hand, Bob changed his tone when he said, "I want to apologize that Meredith and I didn't get over to see you before you got released from the hospital. We were away and when we returned from our trip we heard about it. I just want you to know I didn't stiff you, we just didn't know."

"Not to worry," Tom said reassuringly to his friend. "I wasn't there that long and I knew you were away. After all I gave you the idea of going to that island where there are no phones and no news. Did you get her pregnant?"

"No, Tom, it was a purely bonding weekend," replied Bob. "Sex never entered into the equation."

"Maybe I should go along with you the next time," Tom said jovially. "I think you missed the point of the whole exercise. Anyone who spends a whole weekend in a cabin and sex doesn't enter into the topic of activities needs help. I'll give you an equation, buddy!"

"So tell me, how long were you off?" asked Bob.

"Thirty days," he answered. "No rest for the wicked. Once my back healed up, I was back in the saddle again."

As the two pilots made their way to their respective concourses, they continued to talk about the accident.

"Have you had any nightmares or phobias to deal with?" asked Bob.

"Well I don't look at a match the same way anymore," chided Tom. "And the fireplace just has a picture of flames, not the real thing. Other than that it had no effect on me at all."

"You know, Marion and your friend Alex are old friends," reported Bob. "She told me she saw her in the store the other day."

"You haven't met her yet, have you?" asked Tom.

"No, but I'll bet she is a darn shade better than that blond haired girl who roped you into plugging up the toilets," laughed Bob. "You realize that you will never live that down, don't you?"

"I'm beginning to see that very clearly," replied Tom.

"Do you see her anymore?" asked Bob.

"No!" said Tom.

"Have you talked with the NTSB yet?" queried Bob.

"No, I don't think they have anything yet," returned Tom. "Have you heard anything?"

"Meredith's brother says they have the accelerant figured out, they just have to put two and two together and they'll figure the rest of it out," said Bob knowledgeably. "Now how they will figure out who put it there is another story. But, that is what we pay them for. Well listen, this is where

I break off. I'll talk to you later. Don't be surprised if the Feds don't come and see you."

Waving good bye to Bob, he began thinking that it was strange he would hear about the progress of the investigation from one of his friends and not the source. As he entered by way of the pilot's entrance he was met by Andy who had a folder full of papers in his defense.

"I was worried about you," said Andy. "Drummond said you'd be here a long time ago."

"Drummond told me 9:00 a.m.," replied Tom. "It's only 8:30! What time do you have?"

"11:15!" answered Andy.

"Okay, tell me from the beginning," Tom said. "Exactly what happened here?"

"I got my ass buzzed by a UFO!" replied Andy in an excited manner.

"Not only did I see it, the controller saw it, asked me if I had any damage and did I want to officially declare it as a UFO?" Andy went on.

"Well since I had to do some course alterations and some quick turns, I said yes to cover myself if there were any injuries. So the controller said that he would log it as a UFO sighting and to advise if it returned and what the coordinates were so he could begin tracking."

"Then what?" asked Tom.

"So I continued on with the flight without any other problems. When I came back to Houston, the crew and all the people who saw it were standing around talking about it. The next thing I knew Drummond called me into his office and told me I was out of service pending a review of my mental status," Andy continued.

"Drummond said there is no such thing as a UFO and if I thought I saw one then my mental stability was in question. And then he said I would be advised of the findings of the investigation team. Then he just walked out the door and left me standing in his office. What a jerk!"

"Did the co-pilot see anything?" asked Tom.

"Well, unless he was blind, he couldn't miss it," answered Andy. "Like I said, even the passengers saw the bloody thing"

"Did they take a statement from him?" queried Tom.

"I don't know," returned Andy. "He was a fill in and I honestly don't even remember his name."

"Is there anything else you can tell me?" asked Tom as the two men left the pilot's lounge.

"Well you know as well as I do that Drummond is out to get me," stated Andy.

"But this is even low for him. I guess that I haven't given him a lot of breaks on my end either. I guess I have this coming but, for the record Tom, I never screwed his old lady. She wouldn't have anything to do with me. I just couldn't let the other pilots know I was turned down cold. I didn't know what else to say. I haven't really been too clean with you either as far as that goes. Hell, I know you're not queer just because you're not married. I didn't know what the hell I was saying. My mouth runs like a duck's ass, and some of these pilots believe anything. I guess I liked the attention. I damn sure don't get any at home. One thing I realize, although a little too late, is that I have been an ass hole for so long and now it has come back to bite me in the ass. All I can say is that I'm sorry for all the shit I've caused and I'm asking you to bail me out of this mess. I'll get my shit together. I'll clear this up with Drummond, I promise. I'm a good pilot, Tom. I'm just a dumb ass with a big mouth," finished Andy.

As they made their way down the hall to the conference room, Tom was taken by surprise at the complete about face of Andy, but was happy to see it, nonetheless. He didn't know it was Andy who started that rumor about him being gay. He knew he didn't particularly like Andy, but he just never could put his finger on why. To him Andy had always been a jerk and would always be a jerk. So, if this incident was going to transpose Andy into a decent human being, then Tom didn't want to stand in the way of progress. Andy needed his help and Tom was obliged to provide it.

As the two pilots arrived at the conference room Tom glanced at his watch. He had three hours before his flight took off. Opening the door for Andy, the two men made eye contact and with the nod of their heads, they were ready for battle. They were met by Ed Drummond, the airline's chief pilot, and another man in a black suit. Tom extended his hand to Ed who in turn extended his to Tom and, surprisingly, to Andy as well. As Tom began walking to the other side of the table to introduce himself to the man in the suit, he was cut off when the man said, "Sit down, Captain. We have a lot to cover and a short time to do it in."

This immediately put a burr under Tom's butt and the battle lines were drawn.

As the man started talking, Tom interrupted him.

"Who are you?" he asked callously.

"Who am I?" the man asked.

"Yes, you!" he replied sharply. "Who are you?"

"I am Mr. Sacks," the man replied attempting to clear his throat, "the airline's labor representative."

"Have you ever been to one of these hearings before?" Tom asked with a piercing gaze.

"Yes, several," the man replied nervously. "Why do you ask?"

"It is customary for all parties to be introduced before any hearing begins," Tom stated. "That's why."

"Oh, I see," Mr. Sacks said. "Let's get started, shall we?"

"Who are you, again?" asked Andy.

At this Tom pulled out a piece of paper resembling a document, and pointing to a spot on the paper made a gesture with his head to Andy as if he had some pertinent information on Mr. Sacks. At this Andy followed Tom's lead and just grinned.

"Do you have anything that you wish to say, Captain?" Mr. Sacks asked Andy.

"Say about what?" Tom asked.

"I'm talking to this gentleman," Mr. Sacks said to Tom.

"No, you're not," Tom fired back. "Because he's not talking to you. That why I'm here. You talk to him through me or this meeting is over. You haven't done one of these before, have you?"

"This isn't how the flight attendant's representative runs her meetings," Mr. Sacks replied in a nervous voice.

"Do we look like flight attendants to you, moron?" Tom fired back.

Being very unnerved, Mr. Sacks looked over to Drummond for help.

Tom kept the heat on Sacks. He demanded to know what the airline was charging his client with and what evidence they intended to show to substantiate their claim. It wasn't long before Ed Drummond broke in to quell the shit storm.

"Let's keep this civil, shall we?" Drummond asked.

"No!" Tom answered. "Civil is not an option. Didn't they teach your boy that in law school? Flight attendants, my ass! What the hell is your first name, dummy?"

Drummond stood quickly, held out his hands and asked Tom and Andy if they would excuse them a minute. With that Ed and Mr. Sacks left the room with collected papers in hand.

"Are you all right?" Tom said to Andy.

"Yeah, yeah I'm fine," answered Andy. "I've never taken part in one of these. I guess I'm a little nervous."

"Well, don't be," replied Tom. "I think this is about over. They don't have a case. Never did. They just weren't ready for you to jam it down their throats."

Tom took a sip from his glass of water and sat back in his chair. He didn't miss not being the union representative anymore. And this little exercise only firmly implanted that in his mind. He was not like this, not even close. He was all for a pilot doing his job and being responsible, but he would not tolerate someone stabbing one of his friends in the back. And he would never tolerate a stupid company lawyer. Not when so much of a pilot's career is his record and reputation.

A few minutes later Drummond came back into the room without Mr. Sacks. Ed sat down at his end of the table and began to search for the words that would end this to the advantage of all parties.

"What we have here, gentleman, is a statement that has gotten blown out of proportion." Drummond began. "We have a radar fix of a UFO. The controller saw it; and you saw it, Andy. You then reported it as such and it is on record as being seen. Now you are both aware of the NTSB's standing on the very word UFO over the airwaves. You are also aware that several of your passengers saw it and reported it to all the news agencies that would listen. This is where the problem lies. Such things do not exist in a free, safe society that is still consoling itself over 9-11. If this continues to get out, or if other pilots report UFO sightings, we are in trouble, both with the safety and confidence of our public and on a business end also. One thing we don't want is to have the Feds following us around trying to lie out of everything abnormal that we see up there and report on a daily basis. I've seen them before also, but I never had the balls that you had, Andy, to report them as they were. So, for the brass to tell me you have to go because you reported it is not going to cut it in my book. What I would ask is that in the future you refrain from using the term UFO. If the air traffic controller asks if that is what you see, tell him only that you either can't identify the object or deny even seeing it altogether. With the computerized flight data recorders we have at our disposal they can look it up on their radar screen memory system later if they want to. The air traffic controller was also given this same speech. He was however, one of the owner's grandsons trying to impress his colleagues in the tower. So a different avenue was taken on his behalf and I'm sure he understands the seriousness of the matter. But, please be careful not to use that verbiage anymore. Some day it may be as obvious as the nose on our faces, but until then let's be careful what we call these things. All the time that you were off will be paid to you, Andy, and yes, Tom, there is nothing on his record concerning this incident. I apologize for all the inconvenience caused by this. especially to you, Andy. I have never gone out of my way to give you an even break. It just got out of hand and I got it thrown in my lap. I knew I couldn't find a way out of this mess without ruining your career and that just wasn't going to happen today. I knew I could count on you as a pilot representative to bail me out, Tom, cover Andy's interest, and shut up that damn lawyer. I thank you both for the way you handled this. That's all I have," Ed said finishing his speech.

"Is that okay with you, Andy?" Tom asked.

"Yes." Andy replied simply. "About that other thing we talked about earlier, Tom. Can we straighten this out now also?"

"Andy would like to clear the air about a few things at this time, Ed," Tom said.

Andy went on with the same text he had talked over with Tom earlier. He apologized to Ed and once again to Tom for the things he said about them being bed partners. He admitted to Ed that he had been an ass for so long, he didn't know how else to hide his shortcomings. He finished by saying that this UFO business was the best thing that ever happened to him, for he finally realized that those men he thought were his friends actually thought he was an idiot. He found out that Ed and Tom, the two people he slandered the most, were the only two people who stood up for him during this incident and that is what changed him.

"I will strive everyday to do the best job I can," Andy concluded with a broken voice. "And I will tell all those people I spread the rumors to that I am full of shit. I assure you that this will never happen again."

Ed looked at Andy like an assuring father who had witnessed one of his children coming into manhood. Tom just looked at Andy in shock. Damn, Tom thought to himself, somebody has finally gotten to old Andy. Thank You Jesus! With that the three men shook hands and left the office.

Drummond shouted at Tom half way down the hall to call him before his flight took off. He waved affirmative and shaking Andy's hand one last time, bid him a good afternoon and turned down the corridor heading for lunch. Being a hard ass made him hungry.

9

• •

MAKING HIS WAY DOWN TO the Delta Concourse for lunch he ran into several employees he knew. One such employee gave Tom a sensation of trying not to laugh as he nodded a greeting to him. That was the man that his ex-flame Beth got into so much trouble during her mutiny when she convinced him to plug up the toilets. This is something that is still laughed about to this day. As always, Tom is the brunt of the laughter. It was a joke that Bob Pearson would never let die. It was quite funny none the less.

Two more hellos and who does Tom run into but Bob Pearson.

"You'll never guess who I just ran into!" exclaimed Bob like a child at Christmas. "The Rotor-Rooter man from Havana! God, it's a small world, isn't it? And to make maters worse, he was talking to the blond bombshell you used to take up with. This is going to be interesting. I thought you said they fired her."

"No, I guess not this time. Where did you see her so I can go the other way?"

"They were up by the washroom, not too far from the restaurant," Bob replied. "You're going to have to start eating at the competition's restaurant where nobody knows you."

"I guess you're right about that," returned Tom. "I was hoping to catch a meal at your house, but Miriam said you took too long in the shower this morning. So I'll just catch a burger."

"You have to remember, Tom, Miriam is spoiled. There is no food to be had in the house. I have to take her out for breakfast if I want fed," Bob joked.

As the two friends exchanged humorous embarrassments in the hall the passersby got quite a treat watching two grown men in pilots' uniforms laughing like school children. They shook hands and went off to work. Bob Pearson was from Canada and only saw Tom about once a week. They were old friends from way back who enjoyed getting caught up with one another each time they met. Tom made his way to the entrance of the Delta Concourse Restaurant and as he passed under the portrait of his friend, John Beck, he nodded a cordial greeting and went to wait in line for a seat. Gosh, how he hoped Bob was only kidding him about running into Beth. He had managed to dodge her for over six weeks now and he was in no mood to talk with her, let alone see her today.

Tom smiled appreciatively at the hostess as she led him to his seat.

"Thank You, Andrea," Tom said to the hostess. "Have you finished your classes at the university yet?"

"Two more weeks and I'm out of there," replied Andrea. "And I can't wait! Your waitress will be here shortly, Captain. It's nice to see you again."

"Thank you!" Tom replied courteously.

Lovely girl, Tom thought to himself. She has the prettiest smile. Nothing at all like her father. She was the daughter of Tom's Commanding Officer in Thailand. Tom hadn't seen him in years and Andrea never volunteered any information when Tom asked about him. So Tom left it alone.

"Coffee, Captain?" the young waitress asked.

"Yes, please," answered Tom.

As he was looking through the menu he recognized a familiar aroma lingering in the air. Trying very hard to thwart it from his mind he concentrated on the menu even more, but it was hopeless. He looked up from the menu only to see Beth Masters standing over him at the other end of the table. They were, as they say, an "item" not so very long ago. As a matter of fact they were together over nine months. Beth was as some would say quite overbearing and it was difficult for some of their friends to see what Tom saw in her. Beth Masters was a divorcee' with a little boy named Kevin. She was about six feet tall with a very clear complexion. She had medium length blond hair that she wore in a frizzy curl and had a high forehead. She had a radiant smile but she had small teeth. She had a pretty, however large, mouth and a pleasant voice. Most of her friends that hung around with Tom, liked him better, but made sure never to tell Beth that.

The day of the fire, she orchestrated a strike among the flight attendants, which involved incapacitating the whole concourse. Electricity, water, restaurant services and oh yes, she plugged up all the toilets. That was her way of making sure the airlines would listen to the demands of her flight attendants. She had just recently became the self appointed union steward. Her plans included the complete and unquestionable support of all the pilots and co-pilots. This is where Tom came into the picture. He was to convince the entire cockpit crew of every flight that they were to call in sick in support of the flight attendants. This would in turn shut down the airlines because if there were no pilots to fly the planes the flight attendants would get what they wanted. Also within the realm of dastardly deeds that Beth was capable of, she threatened to supply the pilots 'wives with all the information as to what attendant which pilot slept with when they were on those boring overnighters. This would occur only if the pilots were uncooperative or thought they weren't serious about going the distance to prove their point. There were to be no prisoners taken here. She knew the airlines could always find substitute flight attendants, but once the pilots stuck together the girls would have the bureaucratic machine by the grease fittings.

One of the main legal problems here was that the flight attendants' contract wasn't up for another year yet. Beth just thought she would expedite the next contract signing while the mood was good. Tom had told her time and again not to try this because it would only cause more trouble for the attendants as well as everyone else on the flight crews. But Beth would have none of this wishy-washy spineless attitude.

"It's time you pilots bucked up and showed where you loyalties are!" Beth would say.

No matter how much Tom pleaded she went ahead and began a real cluster. The worst part of it all was that Tom didn't think she would go through with it until it was too late. It was then that the brass expected Tom to put an end to it. Once the plan was put into motion there was no turning back. Beth was committed and the pilots weren't. No cockpit crews took sick in support of the flight attendants no matter who was sleeping with whom. The strike did cripple the services of the Aurora Airlines Concourse; however, everyone just went down to the Delta Concourse to use the toilets.

Once the dust settled and the disciplinary committees hashed it all out every flight attendant went back to work. The ladies did, however, get the repair bills for the bathrooms. And poor old Tom caught most of the flak for the whole operation since it was he who couldn't keep the reins on his girlfriend. That day ended the relationship between Tom and Beth. Tom couldn't be more grateful if he tried for the events that led to his freedom from her. Beth, on the other hand, had a different idea.

"Hello Tom," she said in a slightly sexy tone.

Reluctantly he mustered a semi-sincere greeting and went back to his menu.

"Aren't you going to ask me to sit down, Tom?" she asked.

"No!" replied Tom. "I'm expecting three more guests."

He never was a very good liar and Beth could see right through him on this one.

"You don't have three friends to eat with, Tom," Beth said in a demeaning manner as she pulled out her chair. "So, aren't you glad to see me?"

"Should I be?" he returned the sarcasm. "You seem to have a short memory," he went on, obviously not excited about seeing her again. "The last time we spoke you said if I wasn't for you, I was against you and you would not be bothered by anyone who was afraid to stand up against the company. Spineless, - I think is the word you used."

"Oh, come on, Tommy, you know I didn't mean it," Beth attempted to explain. "Besides that's all behind us now and it's time we got on with our lives again."

"I am getting on with my life," Tom answered. "I'm just getting on without you, that's all."

"You don't want to do that, Tom," she continued preaching. "We've been through too much together. We're a couple of lovers who have been out of touch for awhile, but it's time we straightened that out right now. We'll talk tonight over supper. Shall we say 7 - ish?"

"No, we shouldn't say 7- ish," he answered coldly.

"Thomas, I happen to know that you have taken up with a woman your own age," Beth began again. "I'm sure she can not keep up with you the way I can, let alone take care of you. I've also learned she's from Eastern. No good ever came from anyone at Eastern. So, let's quit this charade and get back to the way things were before."

"Things between us were never that great anyhow," Tom exclaimed. "If I remember correctly, if you didn't get your way life wasn't fun anymore. Just like that strike fiasco. Once I didn't follow your wishes, I wasn't wanted anymore. I was a fool once, but no more. Now if you will excuse me, I'm trying to eat my dinner and I'd rather not eat it with you!"

"This doesn't change anything. We are still a couple, and it's time you started acting like it." Beth was raising her voice now and drawing some attention.

"And you're right!" Tom snapped back. "That woman from Eastern is my age, but she is twice the woman you are. You can't even take care of yourself, you certainly are not taking care of me."

"What about Kevin?" Beth began to beg. "He misses you too. You two made a lot of plans together. What do I tell him?"

Tom wondered how long it would be before Beth brought her son into this conversation. It was just like her to use everything he liked about the relationship to get him back, but not any more. Badmouthing his love for Alex was the last straw. Rising from his seat Tom put two dollars on the table for his coffee and prepared to leave.

He looked at Beth and said, "Tell Kevin his mother is an idiot and better luck next time."

Tom left the restaurant still hungry. As he passed under the portrait of John Beck, he said to him, "You're right, John, she's still a bitch."

As he walked down the concourse attempting to calm down, he remembered he hadn't called Ed Drummond. Stopping off at the next white courtesy phone he found Ed was still in his office.

"I'm accepting favors, but I'm hungry," said Tom when Ed answered his phone. You buy lunch and I'll listen to everything you have to say."

"Okay, Tom, where?" asked Ed.

"Anywhere but Delta," returned Tom.

They agreed on a small off the wall restaurant and bar closer to Ed's office where the food was good and the crowds were small. Here the two could talk and not be tracked down by either a disgruntled girlfriend or an unhappy employee.

Tom arrived at the restaurant first and sitting down ordered a hamburger and fries and waited patiently for Ed.

When Ed arrived he extended his hand to Tom and said, "Thanks for covering Andy on that UFO crap. I knew that pencil neck lawyer would have his hands full. I was very surprised Andy apologized like he did. I wasn't ready for that. I may have to start liking him again - or not."

The two friends laughed hysterically for a few moments and then Ed ordered his lunch.

"So, tell me, Edward," Said Tom. "What's on your mind?"

"I've got a little proposition for you," replied Ed. "Are you ready?"

"Sock it to me," Tom answered and again they both broke into laughter like a couple of grammar school kids.

"I want you to pull a double for me on your next trip," replied Ed. "I'm short of pilots next week and I'd like for you to take your usual trip to Paris. Then I want you to deadhead back here and take another trip the next day. I figure you can sleep on the trip back. Your next trip will have an experienced co-pilot so you can relax on the way back. You can still catch a whole day off before you head back to Houston where I will give you an extra two days to recuperate. What do you think?"

"I'm not sure my butt can take that much sitting, "answered Tom. "Yeah, it's okay with me. As long as I don't have to fly with those Arabian pilots, you've got a deal."

"Anyone your heart desires," said Ed. "You just come on back and I will owe you big time."

"Big time is exactly what you'll pay," chided Tom. "We're talking double time and a half and two days more vacation."

"Don't push it," returned Ed. "Andy and I are on speaking terms again and he probably needs the money."

"Bastardo!!" shot back Tom.

As the two old friends laughed and talked about the old times their lunch break ended as Ed's pager told him he was wanted for more important things.

"Something else may be developing with me, Tom," Ed said. "If it materializes, I'd like for you to consider the chief pilot's position. You'd make a good one. You've got what it takes. We'll see what develops, and I'll get back to you on it."

The two friends parted company again, Ed to his office down the hall and Tom to his office in the sky. Tom was confused as to what Ed was talking about, because Ed wasn't old enough to retire but he'd figure it out later.

On the way down to the tarmac Tom stopped in the pilot's lounge to give Alex a call before she went after the grandchildren and her daughter. He wanted to say he was thinking about her and he missed her.

He couldn't help thinking how much she meant to him as he listened to the phone ring without being answered. He must be in love, he thought, for thinking about Alex brought a smile to his face. He decided he would call again later after his pre-flight check and before he took off for Paris.

Tom had been alone ever since he left the Air Force and began flying for Aurora. Sixteen years he and Rocky had shared the big beach house in Somerset on the Gulf of Mexico. And now with Alex joining them it was like a ray of sunshine that had been blocked by a large shade tree, coming through every window.

With the onset of Alex's daughter and two granddaughters the place would begin to hop. Old Rocky would have to make concessions, as would the girls. But, Tom thought, he and Rocky were going to have a lot of company for an awfully long time. They were both looking for a change, one that had been a long time in the making.

As Tom made his way to the tarmac Alex was making her way to the other end of the airport at the United terminal.

10

. . . .

A S THE TWO LITTLE GIRLS exited the plane and walked out to the boarding area they both spotted Alex, shrieked and took off on a dead run toward their grandmother nearly running down several elderly patrons traveling in a group.

Alex, just as excited to see her family, bent down on one knee and extended her arms to welcome her two favorite grandchildren back into her life.

"Grandma, Grandma!" the two little girls shouted out in unison. "You should've seen the big airplane we were on. It was huge!"

Alex looked up and saw her daughter come off the ramp.. She couldn't help but notice how she looked just like her father. She was beautiful, however not tall like Alex. She had a square jaw like her father but her walk was like Alex's. As they hugged, she couldn't help but notice a weakness in her hug, a sort of exhausted demeanor about her. She looked into Chris's eyes and her daughter started crying.

"It's all right now, it's all right," comforted Alex. "You're here now, everything will be all right. Everything will be just fine. You're all welcome here for as long as you like. You just need some rest and everything will be fine, you'll see."

"I know, Mom," said Chris, wiping her eyes." I'm just a little scared, that's all. I'm taking a big step and I don't think I can do it alone."

"You don't have to," answered Alex. "We are all in this together. Come on, let's go home. Speaking of home, you should see this place. My God, is it beautiful! Are you kids hungry? We can eat first. I also have to warn you about the dog"

With that the four ladies were together again as Alex, Chris, Carrie and Corrie left the airport and headed home to their new life.

11

THE SUSPENSE WAS TOO MUCH for Tom; he had to stop and call Alex to see if everything went well. He had checked on their flight and everything was on time. That's a plus, Tom thought. It would make everything just a little bit easier for her. The first conversation he and Alex ever had together was how she would do whatever she could to get back in touch with her family. Tom truly hoped and prayed that today would be the day that everything came to fruition. Alex truly deserved a break and Tom was all too anxious to help. She answered the telephone on her North Star system in her brand new van she was so proud of.

Knowing good and well who it was she answered, "Hello Tommy, you big hunk of man."

"Is this Pizza –Hut?" asked Tom mischievously.

"I've got your pizza, you big dummy," returned Alex. "Where are you?"

"Sitting on the tarmac, just about ready to board," Tom replied. "Did everything go all right?"

"Everything went perfectly," replied Alex, trying to control her excitement. "Say hi to Tommy, kids."

"Hi, Tommy!" came from three different voices.

"Hello, everyone, and welcome to Houston," replied Tom. "Rocky also says hi and told me he is looking forward to having some new people to sleep with. He hopes you don't mind fleas, he scratches a lot. But he said you can give him a bath and that will help a lot. I really can't wait to see you all. Welcome to our home. Your grandmother and I have waited a long time for this."

"Thank you, Tom," said Chris. "We're looking forward to meeting you too. You be careful today and we'll see you tomorrow."

"Okay, see you then," replied Tom. "Have a nice day and you girls be sure and give Rocky a hug and a kiss hello."

"Yuck!" the two girls sang out in unison. "I'm gonna puke."

"Give us a call before you land, and we'll come and pick you up," said Alex. "We'll let you buy us dinner for a ride home."

"Okay, I can do that," returned Tom. "See you then. Love you guys."

"I love you too, honey," answered Alex. "Bye-bye. Say good bye to Tom, everybody."

"Bye Tommy. Love you," was the reply.

Tom hung up the phone and finished the last of his pre-flight. He still had to meet his co-pilot.

As Tom made his way back up the ramp to meet his him he began to reminisce about the day he met Alex. A day not so unlike this one when he walked into the pilot's lounge and got a look at those legs. Tom had always been a leg man and Alex certainly had a set. The olden days brought a smile as he saw a young man walk out of the pilot's lounge desperately trying to carry his large chart case. That brought other memories to and he couldn't help himself any longer. He broke out in a fit of laughter as he looked down at the young pilot trying to maneuver that case.

"You don't have your car in there, do you?" Tom kidded the young man. "You know you only want the necessary charts in there, not two suits."

"It's my first day on an overseas flight," the young pilot disclosed. "I'm trying to make a good impression."

"I'm sure you'll do just fine," Tom said trying to build the man's confidence. "Who are you flying with?"

"Flight 232 to Paris," the pilot said. "Looking for a man named Tom Jordan."

"Never heard of him," Tom said. "But I think 232 boards down the hall there. Good luck."

"Thank you, sir," came the reply as the young man again fought with the heavy case.

Tom continued down the hall and decided to stop at the men's room. He didn't want the young man thinking he was tracking him down. He looked like he had enough self-esteem challenges for one day. That poor son-of a-gun, Tom thought. Every dog has his day. Go easy on him, girls, Tom said, referring to the flight attendants and the tricks they pull on new pilots.

12

. . . .

IT WASN'T LONG AFTER THEIR lunch break that Alex pulled into the drive at the house. Chris and the children just gawked at the house, the yard, and of course the Gulf. Upon exiting Alex took charge.

"Okay girls, these are your boundaries," Alex said as she pointed to four different directions. "No farther than the boat. Stay in the yard in the front. Stay away from the street. There are a lot of elderly people around here and they don't see very well. You see that red fence down there? No farther than that fence and if you swim too far in the water you'll end up in Mexico and that wouldn't be good. Other than that you can play anywhere you want. No one will bother you and you are perfectly safe in this neighborhood.

"Can we play house in the boat?" asked Carrie.

"Whose boat is that, Grandma?" asked Corrie.

"That's Tommy's boat," replied Alex. "And I don't think he'll mind if you play in it. But be sure you tell Mom or me when you do so we can unlock it and check it out

"Does all this belong to Tom, Mom?" asked Chris, somewhat amazed.

"Yes," replied Alex. "And all those duplexes up along the street."

"God, is he rich or something?" Chris asked.

"Yes! He's pretty well off," answered Alex. "Overseas pilots are paid quite well. He is quite the financial wizard, too."

"So, everybody," said Alex. "What do you think? Pretty neat, huh? Are you ready to see the house?"

The two girls screamed excitedly as they grabbed their suitcases and ran to the house only to stop when they heard Rocky bark.

Alex went to the door and hollered for Rocky to come and meet the girls. With a big tongue and a wagging tail he gave both girls a sloppy wet stroke and stopped to smell Chris.

"Say hi to your new playmates, Rocky," Alex said as she reached down to pet Rocky. "This is Tom's baby. He's a good dog. Say hi to Rocky, girls," Alex instructed the girls.

"Okay," said Alex excitedly. "Come on in. Welcome to your new home. You too, furball."

With that Rocky let out a bark and pushed his way in stepping on Corrie's foot.

"Ouch!" screamed Corrie. "Grandma, Rocky stepped on my foot."

"He does that a lot," replied Alex. "He doesn't mean anything by it, do you, dummy? He's just a klutz."

With that Rocky turned, barked twice and invited them all in his house.

13

. . . .

TOM RETURNED TO THE FLIGHT deck only to find that the girls had captured the new co-pilot and had him assuming the position as they went through the procedure.

"Having a cavity search, are we girls?" Tom asked. "What do we have here, an imposter? A stow away? Did we alert security?"

"We thought we'd take care of it ourselves, Captain," answered Ann. "You know how slow security is and ever since that Arab got in here, we are better off handling these things ourselves. We can get the truth out of this little runt as well as the Gestapo ever could. Sharon, get the cattle prod!"

"What is wrong with you people?" the poor young pilot screamed. "I told you who I am.. Why don't you believe me? I'm no Arab or German. I'm Keith Pitts. Check my wallet. I'm the co-pilot. You've got to believe me!"

"Give us five more minutes alone with him, Captain." replied Emily. "We'll get the truth out of him. Let's take his pants off. Where's that cattle prod?"

"No! No! Stop!" hollered young Keith in his defense. "I'm to meet with Captain Tom Jordan and fly to Paris with him. Honest, ask the Captain!"

About this time Emily couldn't hold back the tears of laughter, so she excused herself and went back to the galley. Ann was about out of self-control herself.

"It's your call, Captain, but I think he's a rat," reported Ann with a bit of a snicker. "I say we rough him up a bit. Attorney General Ashcroft said we had to be on the alert for terrorists."

"I don't know," said Tom. "Drummond said we might have some new blood in here today. But I think he said he was Puerto-Rican."

"My mother is half Puerto-Rican! Honest!" screamed Keith," and part Cherokee Indian."

"Why don't we let him down while we check it out?" said Tom. "If he's dirty we'll dump him out over the ocean."

"I still say give us five minutes with the little runt," said Ann.

"I don't know, he may be on the up and up after all," said Tom. "If you work him over he'll never be able to fly."

"All right, Captain," said Ann. "Have it your way. You're lucky the Captain came along, buster. Next time you come aboard unannounced you're fish food"

With that temporary parole the young co-pilot dropped his hands. When he turned around he was met by Ann and Emily who held out their hands and said, "Welcome to Flight 232." Then the whole flight deck roared with laughter over their indoctrination of the new co-pilot who still wasn't too sure where he was.

"You girls are getting more believable every time you do this," replied Tom. "I swear one of these days, Emily is going to take the prod to somebody."

"You mean this was all a joke?" asked First Officer Pitts while he attempted to pull himself together.

"We may get back to you later if we get bored," laughed Emily. "PMS runs rampant on this flight."

"My God, Captain!" the wide-eyed aviator queried. "Do you let those girls out alone in public like this?"

"Not without a trainer," replied Tom.

"Speaking of trainer, do you know where I can find Captain Jordan?" the young man asked.

"You're looking at him," Tom said. "I'm the guy responsible for letting those girls out of their chains," Tom extended his hand and said, "Glad to meet you, young man. I'm sure you'll not find this crew boring. Come on, we'll go meet the Gestapo, I mean the crew."

"No, no, that's all right!" replied First Officer Pitts. "I'll get with them in my own time."

"Surely you don't think they were serious, do you?" asked Tom

"You didn't see the look in that one girl's eyes!" answered Keith. "She wanted blood and she wasn't afraid to use that prod. No, sir, I'll just stay right here if it's all the same to you."

"Well, suit yourself," Tom said. "But they really are sweethearts."

"Yes, sir," said Keith. "They said Ma Barker was a wonderful mother, too."

"Well, First Officer Pitts," said Tom. "Shall we obtain clearance for a flight to Paris?"

And with that the two men settled into their routine of preparing Flight 232 for another day at the office, with a very skeptical co-pilot at the helm. As Tom began going over the indicator gauges and the checklist to record their readings the phone rang in the cockpit. Answering the phone, Tom heard Emily on the other end advising him that a pair of FBI Agents were in the boarding area and wanted a word with him. To add insult to injury, Emily conned Tom into telling First Officer Keith that they were here about him, and she was helping with the interrogation. She was on her way up front with the prod. Tom, never one to spoil a good joke, told First Officer Pitts that the FBI was talking to Emily about him, and they had put her in charge of guarding him until they could sort this thing out. She would be here directly and it would be to his advantage to cooperate with her during the interrogation With this latest invasion on First Officer Pitts' character, he simply rose from his seat, grabbed his chart case and began to exit the cockpit. He looked at Tom and said, "I looked forward to flying with you, Captain. However, before that radical masochist comes within one foot of me, I'm leaving."

Before Tom could stop the joke, Emily came in with a prod like device saying, "Where is the runt? I knew he was dirty! I want five minutes with him alone, Captain. I'll get it out of him this time"

Tom put out his hand in a protective motion and said. "I think we have carried this a little too far. I apologize, Keith. This is just how we welcome new troops. Some people don't take it as well as others do. Okay, I've got to talk with the FBI and I'll be right back. Go ahead and start, Keith. Emily, back to work with you now."

"Honestly, we were only kidding you, Officer Pitts, we'll give you a break," Emily said as she was walking out of the cockpit. Turning to Tom she said, "I would have loved to use this on the little runt anyhow just one time. What a wet blanket!"

"I'll talk to you later, " Tom said as he walked to the boarding area still a bit amused by Emily and her antics. Tom was convinced that she had lived an earlier life and served quite productively with the Gestapo. He was convinced that somewhere in her apartment was a portrait of Hitler himself pinning the Knights' Cross on her lapel.

When Tom made his way to the boarding area he was met by two FBI agents who, Tom thought, couldn't be more different if they tried. On the left was a mild mannered man named Agent Bob Dobbs. He stood about six feet tall and wore an ill fitting blue suit. He had a nice red pin striped shirt and a ghastly yellow pin striped tie. His hair was greasy and he needed a shave. However, he had a firm handshake and he was a remarkably friendly man Tom liked despite his first impression. His partner as women are sometimes described was absolutely beautiful. She was adorned in a black business suit and had auburn shoulder length hair and short - heeled shoes. She wore a white blouse and looked dangerously like Dana Scully. She had clear skin and made it seem a real pleasure to do business with her. Her name was Anne McCollough. However, unlike her male counterpart, Annie had cold hands. Agent Dobbs started the conversation.

"Is there somewhere we can talk, Captain?" Agent Dobbs asked.

In reply Tom looked at his watch and said, "I've got about fifteen minutes. How about right here?"

"This is fine, Captain," replied Agent McCollough.

Tom led the way over to some chairs in the boarding area and the two agents followed.

"We have some questions as well as some answers about the day your plane caught on fire," said Agent Dobbs. "We think the accelerant was carried in an after shave bottle which may have broken while on the plane. Can you shed any light on this?"

"Was it an Old Spice bottle, perhaps?" asked Tom.

"Yes, sir, exactly that," returned Agent McCollough.

"I smelled a putrid odor of Old Spice when a baggage cart passed by me coming back from the restaurant that day," stated Tom. "It was Old Spice, I'm sure of it."

The agents showed Tom a passport picture of a middle-aged man and asked if he recognized him.

"No," Tom said. "But, you must remember there were over six-hundred passengers on the plane that day. We were packed. I'm sorry. I really am."

"Captain," Agent Dobbs said. "We are nearly certain that the fire started in this man's suitcase. The bottle of after- shave had a heavy concentration of Aqua Regia in it. This is a fifty-fifty concentration of nitric and hydrochloric acids. It reacts violently with silks and some rayon. We believe it spilled in this man's suitcase onto his shirts and caused the fire. Our forensic lab is certain of it."

"I'm familiar with the compound known as Aqua-Regia, Agent Dobbs. Acid in an after shave bottle would do a number on someone's face, wouldn't it?" asked Tom.

"Yes it would, Captain," replied the tall brunette. "That is our other problem. Was the acid put there for a special reason and the fire was just an accident or did they think they could bring the plane down with that little bottle? Had it not broken, it would never had started burning in the first place."

"What can you tell me about this passenger?" Tom asked.

"Off the record?" Agent Dobbs replied.

"Of course, sir," Tom said.

"His wife is a chemist," returned Agent Dobbs. "We haven't talked to them yet, but now that we have talked to you, we are going on with the investigation."

"Can you keep me posted?" Tom asked.

"Oh yes, sir," Agent Dobbs said. "We'll keep you in the loop. We'll be talking again."

With that the three shook hands again and were on their separate ways. As Tom walked up the ramp he was overcome with an uneasy feeling about the whole deal. His face began itching when he thought of how bad that would hurt. Someone had an issue with this guy. Telling Tom that his wife was a chemist made the story all too easy to figure out. But deep inside Tom knew it wasn't funny and he was quite aware of how hard he was struggling to find inner peace since that day. He silently wished the same for that man's wife.

He was quite impressed that they could find evidence of any value on that plane. Before they all left Presque-Isle they looked at what was left of Flight 409. There was nothing left but a big cinder in a heap. Talking to the FBI agents about the fire brought back fond memories to Tom. When Agent Dobbs mentioned the after-shave lotion bottle Tom remembered that was when he and Alex were leaving the restaurant and that baggage cart nearly ran him down. The rest as they say is history. It's amazing, Tom thought to himself, how the smallest thing from your past could bring a smile to your face. Enough reminiscing, time to get back to work before Emily got out her prod and had a past life flashback about the good old days at Gestapo Headquarters.

"Have you the go ahead from the tower yet, young man?" Tom asked his first officer as he entered the cockpit and sat down.

"Ready when you are, sir," came the reply.

"All right, then," said Tom. "Let's head on out."

With that the large low riding tractor began pushing them from the ramp area and onto the taxiway entrance, and set in motion another trip to Paris, France, aboard Aurora Airlines Flight 232.

14

. . . .

"**O**KAY, YOU GUYS, DO YOU want to see your new bedrooms?" asked Alex as the girls were getting settled.

The answer was a very excited scream and cheers as Alex led the way down the hallway to the stairs. After getting them settled in their new rooms, Alex looked at her watch and shouted to the girls, "Hey, everybody, let's go outside and wave to Tom."

Sure enough! As the four of them walked out onto the beach a larger than life 747 flew over the house and dipped its wings just enough to notice as Alex and the girls waved back.

"See you tomorrow!" Alex hollered as she waved, and the girls followed suit right along with their grandmother. In a minute the plane was gone over the horizon. Alex stood motionless, shielding her eyes from the sun until the jumbo jet was out of sight and then turned to the girls, motioned them back into the house on a dead run to finish their unpacking.

"How do you know that was Tom, Grandma?" asked Carrie.

"Didn't you see him wave?" answered Alex. "Did you see the wings tip? That was Tom waving goodbye."

"Are you serious, Mother?" Chris asked.

"Oh, yes!" Alex returned shaking her head affirmatively.

As the four of them made their way up the beach to the house Alex would pause for a second and glance over her shoulder as if the 747 was going to turn around and pick her up and take her with them. With arms swinging in the wind a smile came across her face as she swept her hair back with both hands like a love struck teenager and then went into the house with the girls.

Chris just stood and stared at her mother. She could see the love she had in her heart for the man they had yet to meet. She was happy for her mother because she had earned it. Chris knew that she was responsible for the wrinkles on her mother's face. Her senseless bull headed attitude had ruined her marriage and nearly cost Chris her mother's friendship. Luckily Alex's compassion held things together. She had a lot of hurt to fix. She only hoped she knew how. This is what Chris needed Tom's help for. He loved Alex, and he knew her. He would know what to tell Chris needed to be done to repair the damage. Alex was eating this up. She couldn't be happier if she tried. She had the best of both worlds, her family back in her arms and living in the same house. In her heart she knew this was how it was supposed to be. She mourned silently for the time they had lost. But she refused to let that spoil today. Today was different and it would always be like this. It was like coming full circle, as they say, and she was starting over, starting over again with her family minus her alcoholic ex-husband, and with a new love in her life

Things were good. She would forever thank Almighty God for what he had done for her. After all those years of being left out in the cold, all the times that Chris listened to her father tell her to keep the children away from their evil grandmother, now they were together. Although Alex still struggled with the hurt Chris had caused her, she was ready to forgive and forget. It was time to pick up and move on and Alex had become quite good at that since she had left her husband some time ago.

She also knew that Tom was there for her, to help with the things that were unclear to her. She learned in the short time she had known him that he always knew the words to the song in her heart and he would sing them to her whenever she had forgotten them.

She had become quite independent over the years fending for herself with little or no income. She had always kept her sense of humor and her pride, refusing to be drug down to the level of her husband when the struggle for the affection of their only child and grandchildren began. But when she met Tom her walls collapsed and her hardened heart softened. She was in love and she knew the only way to get this man's heart was to let her guard down and live a little. She knew she was taking a hell of a gamble, but she felt Tom was worth it and she was right. Since she met

Tom all was forgotten and forgiven. She was alive again. Now all there was to do was get her girls back and life would be worth living again.

The very afternoon Alex met Tom was the day Alex's daughter called her and told her the story of what she'd been going through and that she wanted out. So in the sum of one day she met her true love, Tom, rekindled the future with her daughter and grandchildren, and nearly burned up in an airliner on the way to Paris. This was going to work, she could feel it.

15

· ·

ON THE OTHER SIDE OF the city, another story was taking place. Two people who didn't know Tom or Alex, but played a very important part in their lives were sitting across from each other having a late lunch. As the two of them traveled through a meaningless conversation about their day, it was quite obvious that their minds were on different topics.

Since it had leaked to the media that the FBI was investigating the burning of Flight 409, both had listened to the radio report, but had as yet not discussed it. Ashland Horton was still none the wiser about the after shave lotion being in his luggage and was afraid to say anything to Lauren because he wasn't supposed to be on that flight anyway.

Lauren, being a chemist and a pretty bright lady, knew exactly that the after shave lotion was in her husband's luggage because she put it there. She knew where Ashland was going even though he didn't know she knew anything different from what he told her. However, since the incident, as she called it, Ashland hadn't seen the woman and he had come home every night like the devoted husband he wanted her to think he was.

Lauren Horton knew that this was a secret that could never be told. What he thought she didn't know didn't hurt her at all and what she knew Ashland didn't know didn't hurt him. It would take a miracle for anyone to ever figure this out. Or so she thought, before she heard the morning news. Lauren thought this was a good a time to test the waters, so she started a conversation with Ashland on the subject.

"Isn't that something about that airliner that burned up a while ago?" Lauren queried her husband.

"What about it?" replied Ashland.

"Well, the news is saying that it came from a passenger's baggage," Lauren went on. "Gosh, I'd hate to be in his shoes when the police finally figure out whose luggage it was."

"That's why I never take those overseas flights, they're full of wackos," answered Ashland with conviction.

"Who told you it was an overseas flight?" Lauren cross-examined Ashland.

"The news did," said Ashland. "It was headed for Germany or England or some place like that and never made it. It crashed in the eastern U.S. someplace."

Oh, you're good, she thought. Attempting to get him to squirm and not having much luck she tried the oldest trick in the book.

"I heard some bleach blond talking in the grocery store this morning say that she was on that flight, and just listening to her gave me the creeps," Lauren was getting somewhere now and she continued on with the inquisition. "She said the FBI talked to all of those passengers before they returned to Houston. I hope they get to the bottom of it. I feel sorry for those people and what they went through."

"Yeah, me, too," replied Ashland. "But, I'd be more concerned for the person who put the bomb in that person's luggage. That's a felony. You're talking serious jail time here."

Ashland, who was still not getting the hint as to what she was getting at, was definitely getting to her. She never realized that if they could trace this back to Ashland's luggage, they could easily trace the chemicals to her. I have time, she thought; I'll figure an angle to this.

As the two of them sat at their table having lunch their world was about to change so dramatically; neither one them had the slightest idea what was ahead of them. The happiness that Lauren so desperately wanted was about to change for the worst.

As she rose to clear the table the doorbell rang. Going to the foyer, she opened the front door and was met by two cordial looking people.

"Hello!" the man said, "You must be Lauren Horton. I'm Agent Dobbs and this is my partner, Agent McCollough. We're from the FBI. We'd like to ask you a few questions. May we come in, please?"

As she stood there trying to get a grasp on what was happening all she could do was move aside and say, "Yes."

16

. . . .

AFTER MAKING SURE ALL THE flight attendants and the co-pilot made it to the hotel all right and were settled for the night, Tom got into his Cooper Mini and headed to the house that he had kept since taking this flight full time.

Since his flying hours were governed by days off between flights, he could not take three days at a time in a hotel. So when this became his full time flight schedule, he bought a house down the road from Paris in a small French city of LeMans, known for the car race which bears its name. Tom got a good deal on the house and was able to watch the race free from his roof. He was in hog heaven. He was so proud of his piece of French property that on his first flight with Alex he planned on showing it to her while they spent three days between flights. But since Flight 409 never made it to France, neither did Alex. So some day, he thought, some day I'll get her up here.

Tom's house resembled a Napoleanic era tenement house inasmuch as there were four buildings, or dwellings hooked together with the tall eaves and dormers separating the different areas of the family quarters that occupied the structure. The front of the building was uneventful, but the back of it complete with the garages had a curved architecture. The rear driveway was in a semi-circle as were the back porches of each dwelling. The main street was in a circle so the fronts of all the structures looked perfectly normal. All the windows were the pull out type that the French are famous for. They were the kind of long windows with flowing curtains and with no screens in them; they had all brass handles. Tom always felt classy within the walls of his French house. Life was good here. He couldn't wait to turn Alex loose on it. It was an interesting domicile and he owned the whole building. What he didn't live in he rented. He had it made and he knew it.

He found his neighbors friendly enough, however, he thought they were very laid back, for nothing seemed to excite them. It was as if they had all day just to cross the street.

In the building Tom owned, there were three family dwellings and one drug store and coffee shop combination. Sometimes the old lady that rented from Tom would stay overnight. She had a cot there and all the coffee she needed. Two newlyweds who loved Bach rented the other house. They would crank up the old master and the whole city block could hear them. It wouldn't be long before the police arrived to quell the concert and restore order to the area.

The last renter in the building was a bonafide survivor of the French Foreign Legion and their involvement in the Viet Nam campaign. He was disabled and he didn't say much. When Tom bought the building he was told about the man and his family. His youngest son Phillipe did most of the yard work and his father did all the maintenance. The government fed them since he was indeed a war veteran and although he was given a monthly rent stipend, the old landlord would give that back to him so he had some spending money.

When Tom bought the property they were afraid they would have to move, since he was an American. But the landlord and Tom agreed that the old man was a valuable asset to the building and the town. And so he became a permanent fixture in the building. Phillipe and his father took care of everything and Tom was grateful for it. The interesting thing about the whole complex was that when some one went on holiday, someone else would occupy the house while they were gone, a sort of subletting, if you will.

Phillipe would go to the airport with Tom and bring his car back instead of having it stolen from the airport parking lot like his two previous vehicles. Phillipe learned to drive when he was twelve and had taken care of Tom's car and his building ever since.

The majority of his neighbors were retired. They always talked about going on holiday. There were no vacations here, only holiday. The average age was probably sixty-five to seventy. They were different from the elderly retirees in Houston, for they seemed to be in no hurry. They had no where to go and forever to get there. He liked them and they liked him. Alex would fit in here. They would love her and she would certainly love them.

Tom finished cleaning up after supper and was ready for bed. A quick turn around and he was headed back to Houston. He would go to bed and dream of the woman he loved. Tomorrow he would be home with Alex and at the same time meet her daughter and grandchildren. That was the last thing that went through his mind as he fell fast asleep.

17

. . . .

L AUREN ROSE EARLY THE NEXT morning, being unable to sleep at all. The visit from the FBI was unnerving to say the least. She needed time to think. She needed time to figure out an alibi as to why she could not possibly have put that chemical in Ashland's after-shave. But being a chemist she knew all too well that the FBI were pretty smart and that nitric acid would lead right back to her. She wondered why the agents didn't come to her home with a search warrant. Had they done so they would have surely found the open bottle of the reagent in her basement cabinet. That would have settled it. Another mystery was where Ashland got a silk shirt. The Aqua-Regia would not have reacted on a cotton shirt like so many in his suitcase, but on a silk shirt it was an accident waiting to happen. Maybe I can take the acid to work and mix it with other bottles, she thought to herself. The bottle wasn't that big. She could sneak it in to the laboratory and dispose of it safely in the storage rack. Once it was mixed with another reagent of the same compound there would be no tracing it. Dumping the chemicals down her drain at home would be a little risky.

If she could pull that small little exercise off before the FBI came back to her house she would be in the clear. The more distance she could put between that acid and her home the better off she would be. She had already carefully disposed of the syringe, gloves and the shelf she mixed the compounds on; she merely needed to dispose of the acid. Lauren, at the time never ever considered disposing of the acid, but only the tools used in her diabolical scheme to get her husband back. Now it could ruin everything. She would fix this little oversight and then put everything right back on Ashland. She thought he had no idea why his suitcase burned up in the first place. With a little luck she would get the FBI off the luggage angle and back looking for a terrorist. There was that little problem of the acid residue sticking to the Old Spice bottle, however. That darn hydrochloric acid sticks to everything. She started the coffee and went down to the basement.

Tom rose a little later than he had planned. As he looked out the window to see what all the commotion was about he saw a division of Legionaries walking in a parade. With an excited rhythm about them they marched proudly around the corner and down the street, considering that they were all elderly retired soldiers. doing marching at this hour, Tom said.. He looked at the clock and noticed it was only eight a.m. He rose and put on a pair of cut off shorts and went outside to see what the big hoopla was all about. A small frail man stood proudly in his World War I vintage uniform and looking over at Tom shouted, "Very nice day to pay our respects to the General, don't you think, sir?"

Tom thought to himself that DeGaulle had died some time ago for crying out loud. They didn't dig his butt back up and bury him again, did they? And if they did, couldn't it have waited until the customary time of ten a.m.?

He stood and watched the parade wind down the street when the elderly gentleman in the uniform came over and said, "We gather every year to celebrate the old man's birthday.

"Whose birthday?" Tom asked somewhat clueless.

"Why, General DeGaulle's!" the old man replied. "Who else?"

After a moment of silence the old man looked at Tom and said, "You ain't from around here, are you, mister?"

He politely replied, "No, sir, I'm not. Have a nice day," and turned and walked back into the house.

He decided to get ready early since he had agreed with the flight attendants that they would take First Officer Pitts out to breakfast to mend some old wounds, so to speak, but Tom had to buy.

18

. . . .

AT TOM'S HOUSE IN HOUSTON, Carrie got out of bed first and ran into Alex's room complaining that Rocky slept on her pillow and he not only shed on her bed, but that he had horrible breath as well. Rocky took this in stride until Corrie asked Alex if they could chain him outside. That did not go over well at all and the barking began. Off Rocky went into Corrie's room to claim something to cover the damages.

"It doesn't take them long to make themselves at home, does it, Mom?" Chris said to Alex.

Alex looked at her for a minute and said finally, "I can't remember the last time you called me Mom."

"We've got a lot of catching up to do," replied Chris. "I hope it's not to late."

"It's never to late to start again," replied Alex. "As long as we love each other, God will see us through this."

"I didn't know you got religion, Mom," said Chris.

"I didn't either until the day I met Tom," she said. "If it wasn't for God I would never have met him. And I am convinced if it wasn't for God we all would have burned up in that airplane. So as they say, I'm a believer, baby."

"Where do you suppose God was when I was having my problems?" Chris asked her mother.

"Right alongside of you," she answered. "That's how you got here."

A silence fell over the two women when Alex started the conversation. "I learned with Tom that not everything is God's fault. Sometimes it just happens. What we do with it is what is important. Four hours after we met we were fighting for our very lives and the lives of all those passengers.

It wasn't God's fault that happened. But, I'm convinced God brought us together to pull it off and go on living. And neither Tom nor I will ever forget it. I didn't get religion, per say," Alex said. "I'm just blessed and I know where it came from. I am living in sin, you know."

"How do you feel about it now?" asked Chris. "Now that everything is back to normal, do you still feel blessed?"

"More now than when it happened," replied Alex. "Do you realize that in one twenty-four hour period I talked to you and we made plans to get back together? I also met the greatest man in the whole wide world, and damn near had to give it all away because we weren't sure if we were going to live or die. I have never had a day when I couldn't be happier one moment and sadder the next. Talk about coming full circle. I think God kept his part of the bargain. And if that's what it took for all this to come together then I think it was worth it."

"Can you teach me how to have your faith?" Chris asked.

"Yes!" answered Alex. "I'd be glad to."

Soon the conversation was interrupted by the girls screaming at the top of their lungs at Rocky who was running through the house with his newly acquired black and white teddy bear.

"Oh, yuk!" cried Corrie. "It's full of slobber. I'm going to puke."

"Everything will be just fine, girls,." said Alex. "No need to puke. Give me that bear before I take a newspaper to your bottom, young man."

Rocky persisted bravely until Alex rolled up the newspaper and then the bear was cheerfully returned. Off he scurried to play on the beach with the girls in hot pursuit.

"Breakfast in ten minutes," hollered Alex.

As the two of them started breakfast the phone rang. It was Ed Drummond.

"Hi Alex, Drummond here," said the voice on the other end of the line.

"Would you please remind Tom to give me a call when he gets back? Tomorrow's fine. I need to work out the fine print of this turn around he's going to do for me. Then he's all yours for the rest of the week."

"Yes, I'll remind him," said Alex. "Have a nice day." After a moment of holding her breath, Alex said, "Drummond!! I hate that guy."

With that, the conversation ended and the two ladies were off on another subject enjoying each other's company.

19

. . . .

TOM CAUGHT UP WITH HIS flight crew at the hotel as they planned and all sat down for breakfast. It was clear that there was an uneasy feeling with co-pilot Pitts and the rest of the crew. It looked pretty obvious that Emily was up to no good when she somehow managed to slip an old pair of hosiery in Pitts's pocket and then chided him on what was hanging out of his pocket.

The embarrassing part of the morning was not to be won by Emily; however, First Officer Pitts was to show his true colors.

While everyone was eating breakfast a man, one of questionable character, came into the restaurant crying hysterically that an American girl had used him for sex and had taken his wallet. He also complained about a sensation never before felt in his area of passion. The man came into the entrance of the restaurant and taking one look at Emily screamed, pointed and hollered that she was indeed the perpetrator and would someone please notify the authorities before this harlot escaped. Emily, who is usually not taken in by such trivial acts against her good name, just sat in the chair completely dumbfounded as everyone else just looked at this man of the street.

Ann began the questioning.

"Emily, tell me you did not sleep with this— this—gentleman?" examined Ann.

"I've never seen him before in my life!" added Emily defensively.

"I believe him," said Officer Pitts. "You have his glove sticking out of your pocket."

With this the street person let out a harrowing sob expressing that those gloves were the last thing his mother gave him before she left this earth. Since Emily had them in her possession, it only reinforced the burden of proof that this sultry harlot was indeed the woman who laid him and rolled him the previous evening leaving him to the mercy of the elements. Emily just sat there totally speechless, and by this time Ann was beginning to believe that Emily may have gotten some the night before, but had done a bad job of discarding the evidence.

"Do something, Captain!" Emily said. "Get this creature away from me!"

But Tom didn't know what to think. He didn't think Emily would get someone off the street, but she wasn't denying it either. This was getting a little dicey. Being compelled to come to the her aid, Tom was about to say there was some mistake when out of the blue in walked a French policeman.

"Here she is, Officer!" the man of the street hollered as he pointed at Emily with conviction. "Here is the tramp that has taken everything from me."

At this Tom stood up in Emily's defense.

"Excuse me, Officer!" exclaimed Tom. "There must be some mistake."

The officer held out his hand in a defensive nature and said to Tom, "Sit down, sir, this doesn't concern you."

"Oh, yes it does, Officer, we are all together here," replied Tom.

With this the officer unhooked the cover on his holster and looking at Tom said, "Perhaps I didn't make myself clear, sir. I said sit down."

Tom, feeling it his manly duty to stand up to the officer, pushed his chair into the table and said in a mocking tone, "Are you going to shoot me if I don't?"

With this Ann stood up and slamming her chair under the table said to the officer, "Yeah shoot me too, why don't you?"

Ann also had to go a step further when she hollered at the restaurant manager and said, "Hey, dummy, call the cops. I want this guy's supervisor down here right away."

However, the restaurant manager didn't move. He only stood by with a sheepish little grin.

"That's enough out of you, lady," replied the officer. "Any more of your lip and I'll haul you in, too.

Enough of this, I have work to do," said the policeman." I'm taking you in, lady, for sexual pleasures without permission and stealing of a family heirloom in the form of a pair of gloves from this wonderful French citizen. Stand up!"

Now normally, it is understood that a police officer in the performance of his duties is given the respect that he so richly deserves. This was not the case here. When the policeman took Emily by the arm and pulled out his handcuffs, Ann came to her aid with the speed and vengeance never before witnessed in the annals of modern times. She jumped on the policeman's back and put a chokehold around his neck and began to wrestle him to the ground. Tom completely shocked by her behavior, tried to subdue her. Emily got into the action by jumping on the street person and before he knew it there was an out and out brawl on the floor of the DeGaulle Hotel Restaurant.

There is nothing quite so funny as a grown American woman, a professional woman at that, attempting to beat the stuffing out of a French policeman who could not control his laughter, possibly because he was an imposter.

After Tom had managed to pull Ann off the policeman, Officer Pitts got Emily off the street person. However, Pitts, the policeman and the street person, who happened to be a waiter at this restaurant, and the restaurant manager were all laughing hysterically. Emily and Ann on the floor, and Tom on his knees, failed to understand what was so funny about the whole incident. The three of them realized that they were probably going to jail

And then the joke was out of the bag when the street person took off his raggedy coat and displayed underneath it a sharp black waiter's jacket. After he did this he walked over to Emily and said, "Give us a kiss."

Needless to say, the police officer extended a hand to Ann and Tom with a wide grin on his face, and said, "You Americans are so much fun." Both the officer and the waiter went over and shook Pitts's hand.

Pitts said to everyone, "I'd like you to meet a couple of my friends!"

"A couple of friends?" hollered Emily. "I hope they brought money for a funeral."

Emily headed over to Keith, but by the time she got there, Keith said, "Gotcha big time on that one."

That just melted Emily's heart. She stopped dead in her tracks and said, "Yes, I guess you did. I'm sorry about yesterday. I get a little too involved in those hazings, but, I got you big time yesterday, too."

"Yes, you did," said Keith, "but, never let the girl have the last word."

With that Emily and Keith hugged each other and all was well. But there was the issue of cleaning up the mess made by the American attack on that poor defenseless French policeman. So, before they left, they all pitched in and cleaned up the mess they had made.

When they left they all said their good- byes and walked out the door saying, "See you next week."

As they walked out with all the baggage and carts, Ann looked up at Tom and said, "Lucky for that cop you were there, I could have taken him easily."

Adding to that, Emily said, "I'll bet we'll have to find another place to eat breakfast from now on. Thanks, Keith!"

Tom just shook his head and couldn't wait to get in the car and get to the airport. He still couldn't get over what had just happened to him. Even Alex would not believe this one. As everyone piled into the airport courtesy van, Emily did have the last word.

"Keith," said Emily. "You have a date with the cattle prod." Then Emily kissed him on the cheek and said, "You are really going to get it."

Keith just made this satisfying moan one identifies with sex and once again they were all friends laughing it up and heading to work.

20

. . . .

LAUREN SAT DOWN TO BREAKFAST with a deep feeling of satisfaction that lady luck was on her side. It was raining and that meant that she could wear her long London Fog raincoat with the deep pockets. That bottle of acid would fit nicely in there and no one would be the wiser. Now she would just put the heat back on poor old Ashland.

Things were very nice for awhile after the airplane fire. But now he seemed to be back to his old self and since the visit from the FBI, she had him by the short hairs, and she knew it.

He sat across from her reading the morning paper. "You had better call the lawyer today and tell him about those FBI agents coming in here and questioning us about that airplane fire."

"What on earth for?" asked Lauren. "It's your suitcase on an airliner bound for Paris, France, that is all burned up. It's you they want. Call your own lawyer."

"I don't think you understand what's going on here!" exclaimed Ashland.

"No, you're wrong," said Lauren. "I know exactly what's going on here. Let me put it in black and white for you. You go to a seminar in Milwaukee, Madison, or some bullshit place like that, but your luggage shows up on an airplane in some boon dock town in Maine. Unfortunately, your luggage caught the plane on fire. What's worse is the FBI knows you were on that plane and they know it was your luggage that caused the fire. Therefore, unless you want to go to jail for causing that fire I suggest you call your lawyer and have him convince the FBI that someone else was on that plane and had your luggage, your ticket and your girlfriend sitting next to them!"

Ashland looked quickly at Lauren as if he wanted to scold her, but he was too appalled at the fact that she knew about Sandy. She looked at Ashland and with a slight twitch made a wrinkle in her forehead.

"Do you have something to say to me?" Lauren asked with the firmness of a judge.

"What girlfriend?" asked Ashland.

"Let's see," said Lauren. "I do believe her name is Sandy. You remember, that blond woman who everyone thinks poisoned her husband. I believe Winters is her last name. You've been screwing her for the better part of two years. Or at least you were until you burned that plane up. And if the FBI is talking to you, you can be sure they're talking to sweet, innocent Sandy. You know if you two were sitting together, your luggage was probably together. So, maybe you and Sandy should talk to your lawyer and figure a way to stay out of the pen."

Ashland just sat there and stared at his eggs trying desperately to think of something to bail himself out of this mess when the doorbell rang. The sound of the chimes sent a current of fear through him as Lauren rose to answer the door. In her mind she knew it was those two FBI agents returning to grill poor old Ashland about that suitcase. She was enjoying the poetic justice that was being served on poor old Ashland. That Winters bitch was next, she thought to herself.

When Lauren opened the door she was surprised to see that it wasn't the FBI at all. It was Sandy Winters.

21

· ·

THE FLIGHT BACK TO HOUSTON was going as smooth as usual. Tom and Keith sat in the cockpit and let the big bird fly itself. Emily had made more than her usual trips to bring Tom coffee. It was quite comical, Tom thought. I do believe Emily has fallen in love.

"I've got to tell you, Keith," said Tom. "When Ann jumped that cop I thought we were all going to jail. My whole life flashed in front of me. That was good. Really, that was good."

"Thank you," said Keith.

"Keith," said Tom.

"Yes, Captain," was the reply.

"Next time you get the prod," he said..

They once again burst out in a fit of laughter as it led to one story after another. It was beginning to appear that both men had found a new friend. The fun and laughter went on for some time when Tom had to excuse himself for a little leg stretch and fresh coffee.

"You got a handle on this lady?" Tom asked.

"I got her, Captain," Keith answered. "We' re going to try a few loops and rows to get acquainted. Send Emily up front here would you. I'm feeling kind of frisky."

"Oh, my God," said Tom. "That's all she needs. Please don't get her started."

As Tom went down to the galley he passed Emily on her way to the cockpit with coffee. Funny, Tom thought, Emily and Keith, what a fine couple they would make. When he reached the bottom of the stairs he ran into Ann who had a mischievous grin on her face.

"I think we have produced our first on board romance," said Tom.

"Really," replied Ann. "I think we had better check their shot records to make sure they're up to it. I'm not sure which one to worry about more. I thought Keith was too low key for Emily, but he certainly proved me wrong this morning."

"That was close," admitted Tom. "I thought we were going to jail for sure when you jumped on that guy's back."

"I meant what I said," Ann replied bravely. "I would have cleaned his clock if you hadn't stepped in to save him."

"I was more concerned with saving you, my dear," returned Tom.

"Maybe you'd like to go to the gym sometime," Ann said putting up her dukes. "Don't let this innocent yellow rose of Texas fool you, mister. I had four brothers and I held my own."

"I'm sure you did," he answered. "Thanks for the coffee."

Tom was enjoying the break from the cockpit, and he didn't want to disturb Keith and Emily, so he thought he would take a walk through the cabin and rub elbows. This was an exercise he learned from Alex. He never felt that comfortable with people, only with the aircraft. He always let the public relations to the co-pilot. Now since his co-pilot was busy trying to swoon a flight attendant he thought he would go himself.

As he passed through first class he noticed all save four were asleep. He also noticed they all had drunk their breakfast. The second class or coach area was a bubbling house of excitement. People were walking about, sitting on the armrests of the seats talking, laughing and just having a good time. The passengers would extend their hand in a greeting; some would just touch Tom's arm and wish him a good morning. It seemed to Tom that all made some type of physical contact. He even had his picture taken with a group of nuns on their way to Washington, D.C. All appeared to be very happy and no one had any complaints. When he reached the back of the airplane he walked by the elevator the same time Christine came out of it.

The sight of Christine set Tom back in his tracks. He wasn't ready for this and didn't know she was even on this flight. With the incident at the restaurant he didn't read the names of all the crew since they were in a hurry to leave. Not everyone on the crew list went to breakfast. Despite Tom's surprise, he settled his heart and relaxed enough to say hello and the usual formalities.

"I didn't think I would say anything. I'm just filling in and I was going to get back on another flight and go home," replied Christine.

"It's very nice to see you again," said Tom "How is everything?"

"Oh, I'm getting by for now," said Christine. "I take it a day at a time."

"Why don't you get out of that mess?" asked Tom.

"Where would I go, what would I do?" said Christine in an honest tone as if asking for advice.

Despite his willingness to help and offer assistance he reminded himself that he was now with Alex. He couldn't bring someone else into his home while she sorted out her problems. And besides that, he tried once before to sort things out with Christine and got burned. About five years ago, ten years after Tom left the Air Force and was flying with Aurora; he met Christine on a flight to San Francisco. He was filling in for a friend and he met Christine on one of those romantic spring mornings. They talked off and on during the flight and when the flight ended, they went out to dinner together. This started a relationship that had blossomed quickly and very happily. Both seemed to be comfortable with one another. Christine came to Houston when she could and Tom would catch up with her in San Francisco. He so liked San Francisco that there was talk of him transferring there and there even the talk of marriage.

Off and on throughout the relationship there surfaced another man whom Christine had been involved with for several years. One weekend Tom came to San Francisco to give Christine a surprise birthday dinner, but when she arrived home this other gentleman was with her. Tom, finding himself in a bad position retreated back to Houston and waited for her call. When she did call she was crying the blues, going on and on about being with someone for so long that it was hard to stop seeing him. He learned about a month later that they had moved in together. For several years Tom was fed tidbits of Christine and her live-in troubles in life. Although he believed he truly loved this woman he refused to get sucked in. He always felt he was an amateur when it came to love, but he wasn't going to be taken for a ride again. His heart was heavy for a long time after that and no one girl could bring him out of the state he was in. It was just one of those things that take time and Tom knew he had a lot of it. He retreated into being a bachelor for the rest of his life, grateful that he had loved even though he lost.

He hadn't seen her but a few times in the airport as she was passing through, but now he was face to face with her and he knew he was no good at this. If he listened to her he would fall for her all over again.

"It's nice to see you again," said Tom cordially. "Have a nice flight back to San Francisco."

And with that he turned and walked back up the aisle. Five years ago Tom would have walked to the ends of the earth for Christine. Such a long time had passed and even though his love for Alex was, in his mind unbreakable, he was sure that he was over Christine. Now, seeing her after all this time, Tom had to force himself to walk away and refuse to look back. And walk away he did. He had loved and lost. He was a better man because of it, but he wasn't stupid. He would never again let another human being do that to his feelings or to his life. He held his head up and walked to the cockpit. He greeted a few people, talking briefly, on his way back. Once he was back in his own little world, no one could bother him. The past was behind the locked door and that is where Tom chose to leave it. It was the future he dreamed about now. For the first time in his life since he left the Air Force life would be good. The past couldn't be helped, it could only serve as a reminder that all was not what God meant it to be. But, as Tom opened the cockpit door he was convinced that Alex was what God meant it to be. He was blessed and he knew it

22

. . . .

AFTER BREAKFAST THE GIRLS WERE very excited about how soon Tom would be home and they were becoming a little hyper.

"What do we call Tom, Grandma?" Corrie asked.

"Call him Tom," Alex answered.

"Can't we call him Grandpa?" inquired Carrie.

"Well, honey," replied Alex. "He's not your Grandfather. Grandpa Sanders is still your grandfather and he always will be. Tom is my friend and may someday be kind of like a grandfather, but for right now just call him Tom."

"Will we ever see Grandpa Sanders again?" asked Carrie.

"I don't know, honey," answered Alex. "I'm sure we will someday."

"Do you know where Dad is?" asked Chris.

"St. Thomas," answered Alex quietly as not to alert the children. "Or so he was the last time I heard from him asking for money."

"Do you hate him, Mother?" Chris asked.

"No, I don't hate him," replied Alex. "I'm more angry than anything else. To think we had a beautiful family and a good life and a future together and he threw it away on foolishness and booze. Someday I would just like to kick him in the ass and see if he is awake."

"So, I take it this Tom is a good man?" asked Chris.

"Tom is the most wonderful man I've ever met," replied Alex. "Never does a day go by that he doesn't do something to make me feel good and glad that I know him and love him. I wake up in the morning and I am happy. I look at him across this kitchen table and I know he would never hurt me. There is nothing that I could ever need that he couldn't get me or help me through. Just like you and the children. Tom helped me put this together. I look forward to everyday since I met him. I can't explain it really, but my heart knows the definition of what I'm trying to say."

"Something must be right between you two," said Chris. "I've never seen you this vibrant or healthy, for that matter. I just pray that we are welcome here, and I can't wait to meet him and see what kind of a man can do what he's done for my mother. I love him already and I haven't even met him yet."

Chris rose from the table and gave Alex a hug saying, "Thank you, Mother, for always being there for us. Even when I thought the problem was you; you never gave up on us. I hope you will be happy forever and Tom sounds like the guy to make it happen for you. Does he have any friends?"

The ladies released their grips on each other with a burst of laughter and went about cleaning up the breakfast dishes.

"You girls stay half way clean, please," shouted Chris out the kitchen window. "We're going to the airport soon to pick up Tom."

23

LAUREN MADE IT TO WORK at the regular time despite the visitor to their home. Although she debated sticking around to get caught up on the gossip, she chose to come to the office and let Ashland and Sandy figure out a way to stay out of the doghouse together.

She entered the laboratory and went immediately to the acid storage cabinet and returned the unused portion of the Aqua-Regia solution to the appropriate container. The anchor around her neck had been loosed; the only evidence that could connect her to the crime separated from her. As Lauren hung up her coat and was putting on her lab coat another chemist called her back into the laboratory.

"Lauren!" the voice said excitedly. "There are two FBI agents here to see you."

Agent Dobbs was just as impressed with Lauren Horton today as he was last night at her home. And why not, he thought to himself as he looked at her putting on her lab coat. She stood five feet, eleven inches tall and was wearing a tan skirt with a matching tan blouse and brown shoes. Her shoulder length brown hair shimmered in the lights of the laboratory. She was absolutely stunning, the kind of woman that makes you proud to be seen with. Add to that those gorgeous legs that held her beautiful torso in place and you had the Michaelangelo sculpture of all females, the standard by which all women should model themselves. The one character flaw that Dobbs could attach to her was her husband. Where, he thought to himself, did she find him?

Another time, another place and Dobbs would giver her his best shot. He knew he wasn't much to look at, but he knew how to treat a lady. Or maybe now was the time and this was the place. Why not, he thought to himself?

Lauren looked out through the laboratory corridor and had an evil thought. Mutt and Jeff, she thought to herself, this could be interesting, a worthy opponent.

"Well, well," said Lauren antagonistically. "To what do I owe this pleasure?"

"Good morning, Mrs. Horton," replied Agent Dobbs. "We're just following up on our discussion last evening."

"We didn't have a discussion last night," replied Lauren. "As I recall you suggested that since my husband's luggage was on the flight that he wasn't on, somehow he was responsible for burning it up. Now that-- is police work. As I also recall we just looked at you like you were on drugs and had absolutely no idea what you were talking about. Last night is still a mystery to me. Was it that discussion you were referring to?"

"We know your husband was on that flight, Mrs. Horton," returned Agent Dobbs. "And we are just following up leads as to what caused the fire. We explained all that to you last night."

"My husband said he wasn't on that flight. We explained that to you last night also," said Lauren coldly. "What makes you think I'm going to believe you over him? And please don't give me that bit about integrity. I find it difficult to accept that your pedophile mentor used that word to describe the values he was providing for the American people."

Lauren was holding her ground and she was feeling pretty good about herself. She knew Ashland was on that flight and she was fairly certain Agent Dobbs knew she knew. One thing Lauren had to give Dobbs credit for however. He could recognize that she was no dummy and he showed her no disrespect because she was a woman. Although she was certain she would beat Dobbs at his own game, she would not be vindictive toward him. She still wasn't crazy about the way he dressed, but she could work around that.

"Well, Mrs. Horton," said Dobbs. "We don't want to take up anymore of your time..."

"Then don't!" interjected Lauren before Dobbs could finish what he was saying, as she turned and walked into the laboratory.

"Wait a minute, Mrs. Horton!" Agent Dobbs said. "We'd like to look in your locker before we leave. It will only take a minute."

Lauren was ready for that little routine investigative procedure also. She was not going to be an easy day for Agent Dobbs.

"I trust you brought all the legal formalities with you," Lauren said holding out her hand to accept and read them.

"We can get a warrant if we have to!" said Agent Dobbs authoritatively. "However, when we return it won't be a friendly call."

"I have no interest in becoming your friend, Agent Dobbs," clarified Lauren. "If you want to inspect my locker, get a warrant."

"You really don't want us coming back, Mrs. Horton," refuted Agent Dobbs.

"What have I said to you, Agent Dobbs, that makes you think I'm afraid of you?" retorted Lauren. "I'm here all day. You should have no trouble in securing your warrant by then. Now, if you'll excuse me, I have work to do. And save your threats for someone who is easily impressed."

With that she turned and walked away picking up her clipboard of daily duties as she passed the desk. All her co-workers just stared in amazement at her. They wanted to clap at her standing up to those two agents. It wasn't unusual for the FBI to come into the laboratory and ask for tests. They usually were a bunch of stuffed shirts many of the employees thought had an attitude of superiority. Lauren had just taken care of the testosterone levels for today. Although she was certain they would return with their warrant, Lauren had won the first round and she would be ready for them by the next round. She had to be ready. She knew Agent Dobbs was a smart man. He did have a cute smile, she thought.

Agent Dobbs said no more to anyone at the laboratory. He merely withdrew without any scene or dramatic gesture. He was more convinced now than ever before that Lauren Horton had the inside track on how that acid got into that suitcase. Dobbs knew it might be necessary to look into the personal lives of the Hortons to see if he could dig up another lead to follow. There had to be a reason that someone was putting acid in her husband's after-shave. Revenge came to mind, or another form of crime of passion. I'll bet old man Horton was fooling around and the Mrs. wanted to get even, Dobbs thought to himself. I don't think I'd ever mess with her. And why would her husband want to cheat on someone so beautiful? All good questions, Dobbs thought to himself. I'll have the answers before long.

He knew he was on the right track. He also knew that deep inside he was smart and skilled at what he did. He knew he would never win an award from GQ in the fashion department, but he felt it gave him an unfair advantage. Looking like someone ought to take him to a clothing store and dress him made him look a little incompetent, but the opposite was true. It was the mistake that Lauren Horton would make to think that old Dobbs was a dummy, as did others in the past.

As Agent Dobbs and his partner got in the car, he looked back at the chemical corporation complex hoping to get a hunch which didn't come. He would go to the courthouse and get his warrant and return. He would do this because he had to if he wanted to keep Lauren Horton on her toes so she would make a mistake. He also had to save face, if you will, at the chemical laboratory and there was another reason Agent Dobbs was beginning to struggle with. For the first time in his career his judgment was betraying him. He was getting personally involved in this case. He was sure Lauren was the one he was looking for, but he was thinking more of protecting her than arresting her. He was beginning to like Lauren Horton. An occupational hazard, if you will.

24

. . . .

AS ALEX AND CHRIS GOT the children ready for their trip to the airport, Tom, the crew and the passengers were getting their first look at the American coastline.

Just then the onboard computer tweeted a signal telling the flight crew they had just been picked up by radar, and it confirmed their altitude at thirty-two thousand feet.

"Well I'll be darn!" said Tom in a fashion he knew would get a response from Keith.

"What's the matter, Captain?" Keith replied nervously.

"Oh nothing really," returned Tom. "Old man Phillips finally painted the roof on his chicken coop. Thank God, that was such an eyesore from here. I tell you, I was embarrassed to fly my passengers over his farm for fear we were promoting the riff-raff.

Tom didn't get much response out of First Officer Pitts until Ann came in to see if Tom wanted anymore coffee.

"Oh, Ann!" said Tom like a kid at Christmas. "Look, old man Phillips finally painted that chicken coop roof."

"No kidding!" said Ann knowing there was a joke here somewhere and she hadn't forgotten what Keith did to them in Paris. "Let me see. Move over, Tom."

He scooted out of the way and let Ann in his seat. She could have won an academy award for this performance.

"Oh my God! That is beautiful" she continued. "That looks great. Oh, thank God. That was an eyesore. It was embarrassing to have our passengers see that monument to the American farmer when we flew over it. Looked like the slums! He really did a good job. Keith did you see this?"

About this time she had Tom convinced that maybe he really did paint his roof, although you'd never see it from thirty thousand feet, even if he did do a great job.

"Well, listen you guys," said Ann. "I'd love to look at farms all day but I have to get back to work. Yeah, really, that's pretty. Good job, Farmer Jack"

Ann moved out of Tom's seat and to the back of the cockpit. It took a minute after Tom was making more comments about the roof, but Officer Pitts finally fell into the trap. Rising from his seat he leaned over Tom and said, "Chicken coop, I don't even see a farm."

"Gotcha big time!" Ann said with an evil giggle she lets out when she pulls off a good joke. And cracking Keith on the butt she repeated the phrase, "Big time!"

Tom began laughing and high fives were exchanged; the victory was consummated by an end zone dance usually reserved exclusively for pro football players.

"I think we should keep him, Tom," Ann said as she ruffled up his hair. "He's a keeper. Besides, Emily will never let you out of her sight."

"Sounds like a plan, Ann," replied Tom. "Shall we make our way down to Houston, Mister Pitts?"

"You want to see some chicken coops!" said Officer Pitts. "My grandmother has some the size of airports."

"Texas chickens?" Tom joked.

"Damn straight!" said Keith.

With that declaration Ann excused herself and went to prepare the cabin and crew for landing.

"Houston," radioed Officer Pitts. "This is Flight 232 Heavy, Over."

"232 Heavy, go ahead, this is Houston tower," came the reply of the air traffic controller.

"232 Heavy," returned Keith. "Request instructions for landing in your fair city."

"232 Heavy, maintain present course and heading. You may begin your descent by the preplanned glide path. You are clear for a straight in approach on runway 25 right. Welcome to Houston," instructed the tower.

"Copy, Houston: 25 Right," said Keith. "Hammer down, Captain."

This brought a quizzical look from Tom with the application of a wrinkled forehead.

"Just kidding," said Keith. "As we used to say in the Marine Corps, 'at your own good speed.'"

"Right!" said Tom, as the two began laughing again. "This is too much like fun."

As Tom and Keith made the final adjustments of the jumbo jet to bring her into Houston, the passengers and crew made ready for the squeal of the tires and the bump that comes when a jet touches the ground in landing.

"Okay," said Tom. "Put the glass on the arm rest and I'll show you how not to spill it."

"Okay, Captain, show me your stuff," said Keith.

As Tom lowered the jumbo jet onto the runway all that was heard was the squealing of the tires. As the shock absorbers bottomed out there could be felt no bump from the weight of the aircraft. He had landed the 747 without any overcompensation whatsoever and not one drop of water spilled.

"Captain, if I didn't see this first hand I never would have believed it could be done!" exclaimed Keith. "You're the best, Captain. Promise me you'll show me how to do that some day."

"Anytime, young grasshopper," replied Tom proudly.

"I've got your grasshopper, Captain," returned Keith.

"How vulgar you young people are today," said Tom. "No respect whatsoever for your elders."

As the two pilots slowed the jet and turned onto the apron and headed to the gate, he could see Alex and the girls on the observation deck. He sported them a wave that they saw and returned.

With the big jet safely locked down at the gate Tom and Keith shook hands and made plans for future flights since Tom once again didn't have a steady co-pilot.

Now with the introduction of Emily, he thought that Keith may well become a regular and fly with them on a full time basis, or so he hoped.

With the formalities of saying goodbye to the flight attendants Tom and Ann walked off the 747 to the gate and on home for a few days of much needed recovery time. They had both put in a great deal of overtime this month and were getting a little tired. Tom knew he had that thing to do for Ed Drummond and then he was going on vacation.

25

. . . .

ALEX COULDN'T WAIT FOR TOM to enter the gate area; she had Corrie and Carrie by the hands and they were running down the ramp to the open arms of Tom.

He caught Alex first and gave her a big hug and a kiss, then looked down at Carrie and said, "Why, Alex, who do we have here?"

This prompted the two girls to let out a shriek of excitement that could be heard around the whole concourse.

"Well, Tom, this is Carrie and this little darling is Corrie," replied Alex. "Children, say hi to Tom."

"Hi." came a shrieking reply from the two girls.

Tom bent down and hugged both girls and welcomed them.

"How do you like my little brother, Rocky?" Tom said to the girls.

"He's got bad breath," Carrie said.

"He's not your brother," said Corrie. "He's a dog."

Tom and Alex walked up the ramp hand in hand with a girl on each side of them until they reached the gate. Standing there in the gate area was a beautiful blond haired woman who had a striking resemblance to Alex with as wide a smile as one could have. He released the hands of Carrie and Alex and walked over to the lady hugging her for what seemed an eternity making sure she knew she was welcome.

"Tom," said Alex with her arm around him. "Let me proudly introduce you to my daughter, Chris. Chris, this lovely gentleman is Tom."

"I've heard so much about you," the two of them said in unison and began to laugh.

"Well, you're everything your mother said you were," said Tom in a praising manner. "And so are you two little cuties," he said as he hugged the girls again and picked them both up, one in each arm.

Looking back toward Chris, Tom said, "Has my lady showed you girls a good time?"

"I've never been happier in my life," said Chris. "Thank you, Tom. Thank you for this."

Chris hugged Tom, again as a tear flowed down her cheek.

"You are welcome here with us. Let our house be your house and let our love be your love. You needn't look any further to know you are where you belong," Tom said to Chris and then kissed her on the cheek. "Welcome home."

Tom was an old woman when it came to emotional issues, so when he saw Chris begin to cry, he knew he had to change the mood so he said, "I think someone promised me dinner today!.

Putting down the girls Tom took their hands in his and said, "I know just the place. Onward!"

The two girls just giggled as they began dancing and singing *"I'm off to see the wizard, the wonderful wizard of Oz.* Alex, grab my bag, would you please?"

A grown man and two little girls went bouncing down the hall without a care in the world. It didn't matter how many people stopped and looked at them, they danced all the way to the Delta Concourse restaurant.

And that is how the introductions took place. Everyone was very happy to meet Tom. And Alex just beamed with love for the way he made her girls feel. She had never seen her daughter and grandchildren act so happy after meeting a stranger. She was convinced more than ever that Tom was heaven sent. Just watching the way he made her girls feel she knew he was the greatest thing that ever happened to her. She loved Tom more than she ever realized. She cried right along with Chris when Tom and the girls went down the corridor singing and dancing like children. It was something to see.

Tom and the girls ran into Ed Drummond on the way down the hall and Tom stopped and introduced them.

"Edward, I'd like you to meet my two favorite ladies," said Tom. "This is Corrie and this is Carrie."

"How do you do?" Ed said with a burst of culture that Tom didn't know he had.

"Hello, Edward," said Carrie.

"Mom told us not to talk to strangers, Edward," replied Corrie.

That brought a burst of laughter from old crusty Ed Drummond that lit up the corridor.

"Call me, Tom," said Ed. "We're still on for that deadhead trip. It was nice meeting you, ladies. Bye-bye for now."

"Take care, Ed," said Tom. "I'll call you tomorrow."

The girls just stared at Ed as he walked away still laughing openly. To the girls he must have seemed like a giant.

Edward Drummond was a big man with broad shoulders and a big frame to carry all of him. He was easily six foot, four inches tall and about three hundred pounds. He had a rough exterior that appeared to be caused by weathering although he was rarely outdoors. His voice was as rough as his demeanor and he made no excuses for it. He was not a happy person. So when Corrie told him that they weren't allowed to talk to strangers and he let out a boisterous laugh everyone in the room was surprised. The events of Ed's life made him a very serious man who never seemed to find time to smile. He did his job well, but if it was possible for some pilots to take a cheap shot at him behind his back they usually did.

Ed and Tom became friends shortly after Ed came to Aurora Airlines, and had stayed friends ever since. When his son Chad overdosed on drugs and died, it was Tom who stood by him while his ex-wife blamed him. The death of his son separated him and his ex-wife and the other children a great distance. It was Tom's friendship that allowed him to see it through when everyone else fell apart. Tom made all the arrangements for the funeral and was by his side through it all. The only true friend Ed Drummond had was Tom Jordan and when he needed him Tom was there for him. That caring by Tom at Ed's time of need burned an everlasting friendship between them.

It was Ed Drummond who set up the flight schedule that joined Tom and Alex on that day that is now referred to as "the fire." He probably did it on purpose because he was always concerned that Tom didn't have a lady and he knew Alex from his previous job.

Alex on the other hand didn't like Ed Drummond. Although she knew it wasn't his fault that he caught her husband drunk and passed out in the pilot's washroom, she did expect some degree of compassion. She knew entirely too well the drinking problem her husband had, but like everyone else she hoped if there was no foul there was no harm. Her husband wasn't flying, after all. He was just sleeping. Ed Drummond the chief pilot of Eastern Airlines didn't see it that way, and Alex's husband was out the door before he sobered up. She always took offense to that and to this day never had a good word to say about Ed Drummond even thought she knew only two well that if it wasn't for him she would have never met Tom.

As Tom and the girls waved good-bye to Ed, Tom had an idea.

"Let's run in here and hide from Mom and Grandma," said Tom mischievously. "They'll never find us."

As Tom and the girls ducked into the restaurant, they were greeted by the hostess.

"Captain Jordan, who do we have here?" said the hostess.

"These are my two favorite girls, Carrie and Corrie," answered Tom. "Girls, say hi to Angela."

"Hi, Angela," said the girls in unison. We're hungry."

"Yeah, and we're hiding from our Mom, too," said Carrie.

"Oh, really!' said Angela. "Tom, these aren't stowaways, are they?"

Just about then the two women caught up with their escapees and all were seated for lunch.

"Thanks, Angela," said Tom. "We almost gave them the slip."

"Bye, Angela," said the girls.

"You three weren't trying to run away from us, were you?" said Alex with a serious look on her face.

"Tom made us do it!" spilled Corrie.

"I never did such a thing," retorted Tom in his defense. "Did I, Carrie?"

Carrie was definitely caught in the middle and chose to bite her bottom lip without answering.

As the five of them were looking at the menus Tom's old friend Beth Masters came by to say hello. Not receiving a warm welcome as was expected she mentioned to Tom in passing that some of the girls would like to sit down with him and discuss some options they were interested in for the next contract negotiations.

Tom knowing good and well what Beth was up too tried desperately to get rid of her before Alex stepped in. Alex on the same token was on her best behavior knowing how she felt about Beth. There was no love lost here by any means.

"I'm going on vacation next week," Tom answered. "Maybe you should see your union representative about these issues."

"He refuses to see us," said Beth." Maybe we can come over to your place when you're off next week."

"No, I don't think so," answered Tom. "I really don't want to get involved with any of your flight attendants' issues anymore. I called in a lot of favors and made a lot of deals for your girls and you blew it with that stunt of yours. Never again! See your union representative."

With that Beth looked at Tom as if to pierce his heart, but Tom looked away.

"Have a nice day, Beth," Tom said to expedite the matter. "Nice to see you again."

"You too," returned Beth. "I'll tell Kevin you said hi."

With that she walked away, however not fast enough for Alex. Beth made her exit with a little swing of her butt. She couldn't help but turn around to see if Tom noticed. Tom, being all too well aware of Beth's tricks, returned his gaze to his menu. This served two purposes. One; he didn't want Beth thinking he was still interested, and two he didn't want Alex catching him looking at another woman's butt.

"You were rude to her, Tom," said Corrie.

"Yes, I was," replied Tom. "I'm sorry."

The five of them sat at their table and had a lot of fun with the waitress. Every time she came to their table to get them something Tom and Carrie would work out a plot to get a smile out of her. It worked very well, since Tom was very good at getting a smile out of someone. Finally, it was Chris who had to settle the girls down so they would eat their lunch and head back home to go swimming with Tom and Rocky.

26

· ·

AGENT DOBBS MADE GOOD ON his promise to obtain a warrant and made his way back to Lauren's office to serve it.

As he cleared the security desk, he was met by Lauren dressed professionally in a white lab coat. She hadn't changed her clothes, he noted. This told him she had nothing to hide. She was stunning. And the more he was with her the more he was attracted to her. This was going to be difficult to say the least. Agent Dobbs was fairly sure Lauren had put the acid in that suitcase. Proving it without a confession, however, would be another issue. He was trying to get a grip on his priorities. Did he want to solve the crime or find a way to a have a relationship with his prime suspect? He was also fairly certain that Mrs. Horton was not happy at home and would be a wonderful lady to get to know better.

"Good afternoon, Mrs. Horton," Dobbs said while extending his hand in a gentlemanly fashion. "You're looking quite fetching this afternoon."

"Thank you, Agent Dobbs," returned Lauren. "You look quite handsome yourself. If I didn't know you were here to harass me, I'd think you were here to impress me."

Being a trained professional, Dobbs wasn't taken off guard by that statement. Instead he decided to capitalize on it.

"It is lunchtime, Mrs. Horton if you'd like to forego the search and have lunch instead," answered Dobbs.

"That would be nice, but only if you call me Lauren," she replied. "I can't take too much of that Mrs. Horton title. What is your first name again?"

"Bob," said Agent Dobbs.

"That's a nice first name," Lauren said as she extended her hand. "It's nice to meet you, Bob. Gosh, you have soft hands."

"Yes, it's an occupational hazard," replied Dobbs.

"I'm sure it could be a plus," returned Lauren. "If you get my meaning."

"No, Lauren, I'm not sure I do," replied Bob mischievously.

"I'll break it down for you later," said Lauren while laughing. "Come on inside with me, I need to take off my lab coat and get my jacket."

As the two of them walked into the laboratory they both felt very good about themselves. In a short time a short conversation seemed to liberate them and project an air of confidence never felt by the two of them professionally or socially. Bob Dobbs was a little shocked by Lauren's behavior and would certainly be careful not to be duped by her. He still had some soul searching in regard to the investigation. He was in no hurry to arrest Lauren so he was more in a hurry to get to know her. As it was the bureau had no leads into the case. All that was going on was Dobbs intuition and he had kept that to himself.

Agent Dobbs, being the perfect gentleman helped Lauren take off her lab coat and then helped her with her jacket. Lauren flinched when Dobbs touched her arm and was slightly embarrassed, fearing she had insulted him.

"I'm sorry," said Lauren quickly, "Chivalry is not something I'm used to."

"Someone as pleasant as you should be used to it, I would think," returned Agent Dobbs. "Maybe you hang around with the wrong crowd."

"And you'd like to change that?" said Lauren with a cynical tone. "Introducing me to the girls in D block, perhaps?"

"That's not what I'm saying," he replied as he straightened out Lauren's collar.

"Well, Agent Robert Dobbs, what exactly are you saying?" questioned Lauren. "What have they taught you at the academy about being a gentleman?"

"What I'm saying is that if you were my lady you would be showered with every courtesy I could give every chance I could give it," returned Dobbs.

"Thank you," she said. "I believe you. A girl could do much worse."

She looked into his eyes for the first time and their gazes locked. She put all her charm forward as she gave hin a very warm smile. Dobbs seeing a chance to comment on another facet of Lauren's beauty wasted no time.

"You have a beautiful smile, "said Bob.

"Thank you, Bob," replied Lauren admiringly, "I use it to lure prospective FBI Agents into bed."

Thinking this would trip him, she looked for his reaction but it appeared to have no effect whatsoever. She was indeed the one who was tripped up by his answer.

"Does it work?" Bob said.

"I don't know," Lauren said regrouping. "This is the first time I tried it."

As the two of them walked out of the lab and past the guardhouse they continued to chide each other as they worked on getting used to one another. Bob Dobbs could feel the attraction and was surprised how easygoing Lauren actually was. It was as if she rehearsed his return to the lab

Before he arrived here he was sure she was the culprit he sought. Her cold demeanor from their earlier meeting only reinforced that observation. When he saw her in the same clothes, he was forced to reconsider his opinion. Now that he had talked with her and saw the confidence she exhibited, he was more convinced that she would indeed be capable of doing anything she put her mind to and even the craftiest investigator would be taxed to prove it. However, Agent Dobbs thought to himself, she sure was a sweetheart and right now he didn't want to think of her possible implication in the demise of that jumbo jet. He just wanted to have a nice lunch.

He extended the courtesy of opening the door for her when she asked, "Where is your partner? I always thought everything was a twosome."

"Never over a dinner interrogation," Bob said laughing.

"That was good, Bob," replied Lauren. "You win the first one. That's the last one you're getting though."

As he got into the car and started the engine, Lauren looked at him and said, "Okay, tell me again. How did my dizzy husband burn up that airplane?"

27

. . . .

TOM AND THE REST OF the family arrived back at the house and he was immediately led away by the excited girls screaming about their sandcastle they wanted to show him. Out they ran to the beach where their past architectural achievement had since washed away. The disappointment showed heavily on their faces and it looked like Corrie was about to cry.

Tom knelt down to her eye level and said, "Don't cry, Corrie. Sandcastles are always here in the memory of the person who made them. The reason they wash away is that you have more ideas and memories than room on the beach. I can see in your heart the sandcastle that you made and it is beautiful. Come. Dry those tears and let's make another. Come on, Carrie."

Tom and the girls knelt down in the sand and began sculpting a castle that would have put the Hearst Castle to shame. Chris and Alex looked on from the kitchen window at the friend the girls and Tom, for that matter, had found.

"I wish he would have taken off his coat before he crawled into the sand," said Alex. "That will be fun to clean."

"I've never seen anything like it," returned Chris. "It's look like all three of them have found a new best friend."

It wasn't long before the girls grew tired of the sandcastle business and had Tom hand in hand wading in the ocean. They were asking him all kinds of questions that small children ask adults, thinking they know everything.

"What's over there?" Carrie would ask as she pointed to the south.

"South America," Tom answered.

"Are there little boys and girls there, Tom?" asked Corrie.

"Oh, yes, indeed," Tom answered. "There are little boys and girls everywhere."

"Do they have daddies?" asked Corrie.

"I'm sure that not all of them have daddies," Tom said trying to anticipate the questions that were coming knowing what their parental situation was. "Some of them die and some of them are somewhere else. It's a harder life there than it is here."

"Where do they go?" asked Corrie.

"Oh, some of them go to work a long way from home and some of them are in the Army. Places like that," replied Tom.

"Do they go to church over there?" asked Carrie.

"Oh, yes," said Tom. Being very gracious Carrie changed the subject about fathers.

"They have very nice churches there and quite a few of them also. They have processions in the street and big church parties. They have beautiful statues and big bull fights with little bulls. There are lots and lots of children for you to play with where you can make lots of friends. They have a Dairy-Queen on every corner and candy stores in the middle of the block.

Tom went on like this for a minute or so when Carrie finally interrupted him.

"No way!" shouted Carrie. "Mom said they don't have candy stores next to the Dairy Queens."

"Why, Carrie Louise," returned Tom. "How could you doubt me?"

"That's not her name," shouted Corrie.

"Why, Corrie Louella, it certainly is," answered Tom with a snicker.

"That's not her name!" answered Carrie.

Knowing good and well this game could go on for a long time, Tom stopped and said, "You remind me of two of my dearest friends, Clem and Clyde. I think I'll call you that since you girls can never remember."

When they arrived at the boat dock, Carrie resumed the questioning

"Tom?" said Carrie with a questionable air.

"Yes, honey," replied Tom.

"Can you be our daddy?".

Being a little surprised by the question, Tom held his breadth for a moment before he answered.

"Well, you have a daddy who loves you very much. I couldn't take his place. No one can ever take the place of your real dad."

"But he's not around anymore," said Carrie. "Mommy said he's gone."

"Yeah," said Carrie. "All he ever does is sleep. He never plays with us. He just drinks and sleeps and hollers at us to be quiet so he can sleep."

"That's why we had to leave the house and move into that house trailer," added Corrie.

"Mommy said he was sick and maybe someday he'll get better," said Carrie.

"Grandma said all we needed to do was go to church and pray for him," continued Corrie. "But Mommy said she didn't think that would help."

Tom realized he was caught in a situation he had no way out of. He didn't know what to say so he tried a long shot.

"I'm sure your father will get better again and you can all go to church together," said Tom.

"Will you take us to your church?" returned Carrie.

"Can you teach us about Jesus?" asked Corrie.

"Yes," answered Tom in a complete state of confusion.

Having to think quickly, Tom was relieved to come up with a good answer.

"We can all learn about Jesus at our church," said Tom. "How does that sound? And besides that my friend is a priest at our church and he can tell you about all the candy stores in South America. The ones next to the Dairy Queen."

With that Tom tickled Carrie and picked up Corrie to put her over the deck rope of the boat while Carrie squealed at the tickling that she was getting. Once all three of them were on the boat the girls took off screaming and running down the deck.

Realizing he wasn't getting any younger, he just stood still and let them run. His mind began to wonder how he was going to answer all their questions. How was he going to take the place of their father and grandfather and help them grow up with the advice that a parent would give if it were to come to that? Tom looked at their faces and could see they were having a good time and they liked him. He believed he could see in their eyes that they trusted him to be there for them. The trouble was that Tom didn't know if he was qualified. He knew there wasn't any training for parenthood, but he had absolutely no idea where to start.

He did, however, breathe a sigh of relief when his conscience told him that no one had asked him to. He was only asked a few questions that little girls ask. Tom felt a little better. He knew he was qualified to baby- sit with two beautiful little girls for awhile. He would enjoy their company and quit trying to figure them out. Off the three of them went to play for the remainder of the afternoon.

28

· ·

IN A REMOTE ROMANTIC LITTLE restaurant in rural Houston, Bob Dobbs and Lauren Horton sat down to a lunch for every reason but the satisfaction of hunger.

Lauren was still plying Dobbs for information he may have that she would attempt to convince him that he only thought he had. Dobbs on the other hand didn't really care about the events that officially led to this investigation in the first place. He wanted to be with Lauren and at this moment he was happy doing just that.

They sat at their table eating lunch and began to lighten up a bit. They were laughing and joking with each other as if they had been friends for years. On occasion they would remark about what they would do if they had more time to spend together.

Finally the joking mood became more serious when Lauren said, "Well, Bob. You know where I live. You know where I work, My number is in the book, and if I need you I'll just dial 911. How much simpler could our relationship get?"

He never replied to that, he just sat and took a sip of coffee out of an empty cup not knowing what to say. He liked what he heard; he just didn't have an answer.

She looked into his eyes and it was obvious what was happening. Lauren wasn't about to stop these feelings for the mere formality of fidelity. She liked what she saw when she looked at Bob Dobbs. A look of compassion, strength and love returned her gaze. She could read it in his eyes and she was certain she was right.

The silence was broken when his cell phone rang. It was his boss asking him when to expect him back. Bob gave him the usual policeman rabble about talking with several witnesses and told his boss it would all be in the report. He would check in with him at the end of the day. He said good-bye and closed the phone.

"Well, Robert," said Lauren, "How is your luncheon interrogation going so far?"

"As far as I can see, quite promising, "answered Dobbs.

"I must be getting back to the laboratory, "she said "You know how these government contracts are. I have so many poison cigars to make for our Cuban friend before the day is over. I'm taking off tomorrow afternoon. It would be nice if we could have lunch again and maybe spend the remainder of the day together. That is if there isn't too much crime that needs your immediate attention."

"Tomorrow afternoon would be fine," replied Dobbs. "I have only one stop to make and you can accompany me."

"Oh, really!" returned Lauren. "Where?"

"The airport," he replied, as he was picking up the check and helping her with her chair. "I need to exchange file notes with someone there about the interrogation of a suspected terrorist that didn't pan out. And also I need to identify the suspect by a photograph."

"You mean I get to see you in action first hand? Some real interrogation techniques?" asked Lauren mischievously. "The bright lights and the thumbscrews?"

"Those are antiquated nowadays," said Bob. "We use straight scopolamine on these important investigations."

"I can't wait," replied Lauren excitedly.

"I'll be dressed to impress," said Bob.

With that he and Lauren got in their car and headed back to the laboratory. There was the usual light discussion between friends until they pulled in. Then Lauren took Bob's hand and said, "Thank you very much. I'll see you tomorrow." Saying this, she affectionately squeezed his hand so there would be no mistaking the loving regard within it.

29

. . . .

O
N THE OTHER SIDE OF Houston, Lauren's husband, Ashland Horton, and his ex-girlfriend sat down in a much more subdued setting at the Hotel Texas to talk about the visit they received from Dobbs the day before. They both tried to hash over the events of that fateful day in New England, that day when the airplane, that was to take them into another life in another country suddenly turned around. Upon landing in some remote corner of Maine it burned up in a massive ball of flame and cloud of smoke, and with it their dreams of a life together. How this had all happened was still a mystery to them. But the issue of this Dobbs fellow asking them questions about Ashland's luggage was quite the quandary.

The other painful part of the puzzle was that Dobbs was asking him why his luggage burned up the airplane and he never saw his belongings again. He still didn't understand how his luggage burned up anything, let alone why, and what made them think it was his.

"That FBI guy said the fire started in my after shave bottle," reported Ashland. "Now, how could that be? You don't set fires in after shave bottles."

"Did he say how it started on fire?" asked Sandy.

"I don't think he knows," said Ashland. "That's probably why he's asking me. Like I have the solution!"

"Well, something had to start it," remarked Sandy. "If not something, then someone."

When she said that they both had a start as if gasping for a breath of air.

"You don't think she knew, do you?" asked Sandy, referring to Lauren.

"I don't see how," he said, "but she did mention us this morning over breakfast. So she must have known or found out shortly thereafter."

"I think she knew all along," remarked Sandy. "You're lucky she didn't tie you up in your sheets and light your butt on fire. Lucky for us she tried to burn the whole airplane up and we had a good pilot."

"You're not serious, are you?" said Ashland taken aback.

"Heaven's yes!" retorted Sandy. 'She's a mean one. She'd light both of our butts up and think nothing of it. I say we call that FBI agent and tell him all about it. I say we get her before she gets us."

"You can't be serious, Sandy!" he said, "I don't want my wife thrown in prison."

"I think your wife was planning on throwing us in a pine box and never looking back," she said. "I don't doubt it for a minute."

"How could she have known we were even together?" returned Ashland. "It's not like she has a life or any friends that could have told her."

"She's got something or someone out there who is giving her the 'whys and wheres'." answered Sandy. "Maybe you should consider moving in with me. You know, until we can be sure you're safe. You know I'd take good care of you. I'll have some friends of mine look into your wife and see what she's up to. Stay with me until we figure out what to do with her."

With those well-practiced feminine wiles Sandy reached over the table and took Ashland's hand in hers. She just stared timelessly into his eyes and tried to pick up what she had missed over the past six months. Ashland wasn't even paying attention to what she was saying. He had no idea what she was planning, but he remembered the lesson he learned the last time he was with her on the airplane. One was that she killed her first husband and two; he damned near got killed himself.

Surprised with his rush of intestinal fortitude herose from the table and said, "I don't think this is a good idea. I can't see you again."

With these words Ashland left Sandy Winters sitting in that hotel restaurant. And with his leaving, a saga ended in his life, which would probably save it. . He doubted seriously if Lauren would ever have him back. It was now obvious that she knew all along about him and Sandy. And although he didn't want to admit it, he was becoming convinced that if his luggage caused the fire in that airplane, it was Lauren who caused the fire, but why? Why do something so drastic nearly killing all those innocent people? It didn't make any sense. She could easily be a disgruntled housewife, but she was never violent and she was no where near menopause to be incited by PMS.

I could just explain what the situation was, he thought to himself. On the other hand maybe I should never mention it again and go on with life the best I can hoping that it was an accident that caused that fire. Let's not be hasty, he thought to himself. Let's stay away from Sandy Winters for the rest of my life and just wait a few weeks and see what happens with this FBI thing.

Ashland's concentration was broken by the sound of the transit bus as it slowed to pick him up. When the door opened, he stepped on the bus and found a seat. Drifting off again with his own thoughts he said to himself, don't worry…Lauren couldn't live without you.

30

. . . .

ALEX HOLLERED OUT THE WINDOW for Tom and the girls to come in for supper. The girls were reluctant to leave their newly acquired playground complete with a kitchen and all kinds of gadgets. Tom on the other hand thought supper was a gift from God. His new friends had completely worn him out. He was now convinced they had too much sugar in their diets.

As he entered the kitchen the abuse continued from Alex who jovially reprimanded him for getting sand in his uniform jacket. Tom, who took every advantage to get a clash going said, "You can't talk to me like that, I'm the Captain. Besides, it was Carries idea to lay it on the beach."

Both girls emphatically denied the accusations and he was left at the mercy of Alex who couldn't keep a straight face long enough to keep the inquisition alive. As they all sat down to eat Tom initiated the conversation only to be shushed by Carrie who was about to lead the prayer. Even Rocky had the good sense to bow his head. Alex gave him her favorite corrective look and Chris just smiled at him, noticing that he was indeed embarrassed. Once the prayer ended, Rocky took up a position next to Corrie and began whining and wagging his tail. With that the seating was complete and supper formally began.

"Mom," said Carrie. "Someone should tell Tom that we always pray before meals around here."

Tom had to bite his lip nearly drawing blood when he got a look from Corrie that showed her great disappointment with him at being a near heathen savage. The only one who would come to his aid was Chris when she said, "Well, girls, I'm sure he said grace before he came to the table and did so in his own way."

On that note Alex had to make her feelings known when she coughed, cleared her throat and wiped her mouth with her napkin.

Tom looked at Alex and gestured toward Chris saying, "Yeah, what she said. Remember, I'm the Captain."

The remainder of the meal went on with the usual bantering with Tom being the brunt of most of it. He took it in stride and by doing so made the family's first evening meal together one of peace, love and a clear atmosphere of security. Alex's girls knew they were safe, loved and welcomed here. It was, as they say, just what the doctor ordered. It was evident in the way Chris relaxed since she had been at the house and in the way she had taken to Tom since he was replacing her father as her confidant in her mother's eyes. He also was doing his part by just making them feel at home. This was something he specialized in and he was sparing no expense for Alex's girls. After supper ended he, Alex and Chris cleaned up the dishes while the girls took a bath and got ready for bed. Soon after that it was Tom's turn and then night was upon them. After the girls went to bed Chris and he finally had the chance to sit and just get acquainted. Tom was very impressed with her. She was well spoken and very courteous toward him. She also had a deep respect for her mother, and she had taught that to her children as well. They all had a mutual respect for one another no matter their ages.

Tom was certain Chris was a good mother. Despite the trials that she had gone through and the transition they were now undergoing with the pressures that accompanied those moves, she did not release them on her children. Although she had probably suffered some form of abuse at the hands of her alcoholic husband, she never let it go any farther. She had a demeanor about her that while it did not project that she was better than anyone else, did leave the impression that she would be someone to copy, someone like a classical actress of the silver screen. She reminded Tom of Greer Garson. He had seen a picture of her once hanging in the hallway of Louis Bromfield's home at Malabar Farms when he was a boy. For a young man of twelve, living in a rural town in Ohio, Tom could not imagine how Almighty God could bestow so much beauty on one lady as he gave to

Greer Garson. It confused Tom when he thought about how a man could turn to booze when he could turn to a good woman.

Chris was indeed a product of a good mother. She even acted a little like Alex in certain respects. They walked the same, laughed the same and ganged up on Tom with the same humorous vengeance every chance they got. Alex would make a remark about when Tom and Rocky stood side by side that Rocky looked a little smarter. Chris would interject by saying that Tom had a cuter butt with less sway; but she did notice that his breathing changed every time Alex came around. Of course, Alex would say that he was always in heat, which is what attributed to his breathing problem.

Tom, not to be outdone, would respond to that accusation by saying," That is what happens when one is surrounded by beautiful women." That would invariably get him a kiss from Alex as a reward and then all would be normal again.

Chris couldn't get over how easy- going Tom was. It surprised her that he had never married. Obviously, he wasn't gay, making him an easy prey for any woman who had something to offer. She was impressed how well he could take the humorous abuse Alex would give him and return it in the same breath. She could tell he loved her mother and that made her feel good. It was difficult to see her with another man, but she thought Tom was a good person for her and Chris could see the happiness in her eyes.

She thought that he was quite handsome and cultured for a pilot. Even though he has some gray in his hair he didn't look his age at all. She could also picture him with a much younger woman than her mother. He was the first easterner she had ever really sat down with and talked with.. She had a little trouble adjusting to the fact that he, unlike all Texans, did not wear cowboy boots. There were none to be found in the house. And with this she was surprised to see her mother in tennis shoes. Some of Ohio was rubbing off on her mother, she thought.

Chris loved listening to Tom talk of the days when he flew over China in a SR-71 while serving in the U.S. Air Force. All the stories outrunning the missiles were very exciting when he told them. Of course he would color the stories so it looked like the genius of the Air Force pilots were the only defense the world had during the cold war. She could see the gleam of pride in his eyes when he told these stories. She could also see the pain in those same eyes when he touched on his days as a bomber pilot in

Vietnam. The conversation went on for over two hours until both parties were assured they had been properly introduced. Chris was satisfied. She liked the man who loved her mother. Alex would be all right.

"Thank you for watching the girls this afternoon," said Chris. "It helped Mom and me get caught up a little."

"You've created a monster when you showed them they could play house on that boat," returned Alex.

"Well, why not?" said Tom, grinning from ear to ear. "You and I play doctor on it."

"All right!" retorted Alex. "That's enough out of you. Time for bed. Come on!

As Alex stood up to swat him on the shoulder, she was looking a shade brighter.

"Why, Mother!" said Chris, laughing. "I do believe you're blushing."

"Oh, are you going to get it now!" said Alex.

"That's the general idea," said Tom as he shielded himself from a second assault.

"You are absolutely impossible!" said Alex. "See how he is, Chris? Incorrigible! A typical male. Come with me, young man."

As he was led away by the arm he turned around and gave Chris a thumbs up. This prompted more laughing from Chris and only led to more embarrassment for Alex. In the bedroom she pushed him on the bed and while attempting to quiet her giggling she got Rocky barking in defense of Tom. Rocky jumped on the bed, straddled him like a grizzly bear protecting his booty, and barked at her. That woke up Carrie who came into the bedroom to see what the ruckus was. At this point Chris came in to rescue Carrie and all but one of the family was in the bedroom. Of course Tom had to ham it all up until finally Rocky tired of the exercise, and all visitors retreated to their own rooms. Rocky took up residence with Carrie.

After a few moments Alex had forgiven him his transgressions and was on the bed and in his arms.

"You know you're not right, don't you?" asked Alex. "But I love you and wouldn't have you any other way."

"I'm available for therapy right now if you're interested," replied Tom.

"You have to be quiet," said Alex. "The girls are right down the hall."

"Well, honey, you're the one who moans, groans, screams and carries on, not me!" returned Tom.

"That's it!" retorted Alex. "You're out of luck tonight," and over she rolled to the other side of the bed.

"Where's my dog?" asked Tom not to let the razzing end. "I can't sleep without my dog. He's the only one who understands me."

As he said this he rolled over closer to Alex and all was forgiven. The two lovers made love several times, well into the morning and afterwards they talked before finally falling asleep.

31

. . . .

AGENT DOBBS REACHED UP AND turned off the lamp at his desk. It had been a long, good day. He was already beginning to miss Lauren and was looking forward to seeing her again He was tired, but he wasn't going to take the time to get into bed tonight. He would stretch out in his recliner and sleep there as he had on several occasions.

Dobbs' plan was to call her tomorrow when she took off from the laboratory. He would pick her up, head for the airport where he would give another agent some paperwork that was too important to mail and then off to lunch and maybe a day at the park. Time would tell what the day would bring.

He thought of exactly how he was going to work Lauren into his life and out of the airliner fire investigation. He knew his partner, Agent McCollough, thought Lauren was good for the crime also. It may take some finessing on his part to clear her of a crime that she seemed obviously guilty of, but they didn't call him "Fox "for nothing. The worst case scenario would be if the bureau thought he deliberately covered up any investigation findings and then found out he had a thing for a suspect. He'd be lucky to get a job selling shoes after that.

He had a lot riding on this investigation. At first he thought he'd impress his superiors with an investigation that would be grounds for a promotion. He never bargained he would learn what he did from all his hard work. Now he faced another challenge, one that would take all the expertise he could muster. He expected to find a terrorist who had fallen from the cell and was trying to get back into the good graces of his leader. He never expected to find Lauren in the middle of all this.

Dobbs covered up his feet with an afghan and thought. He knew where there were a few terrorist cell dropouts in the area he could pin the fire on. Who knows, if enough terror cells got blamed for this and nothing panned out, no one would ever think that a fragile little wallflower like Lauren nearly succeeded in doing what a terrorist couldn't. She would be in the clear and he would go on chasing terrorists until he found some dumb ass who couldn't even lie his way out of a crime he didn't commit. It worked in the Lindbergh case, he thought to himself. Why couldn't it work here? He could get the name of some Arab living in Bonn, Germany, and pass his name around. He'd then get Interpol to snatch him up, run a little excessive interrogation program on his butt that he'd probably die from, and that would be the end of that. Dobbs would be a hero, he'd make section chief, and Lauren would be his wife. Life could not get better. With this Bob Dobbs drifted off to sleep to dream of his newfound love, Lauren Horton.

Lauren couldn't sleep. Her mind was too full of thoughts and plans for Agent Dobbs to relax enough. She rose and putting on her slippers went out in the living room and sat in her favorite rocker.

Her mind began to drift aimlessly through the events of the past year. Putting that acid mixture in Ashland's after-shave was an ingenious plan; however, even Ashland could screw up a perfect plan. To think that darn bottle broke and leaked all over the place catching his nylon shirts, which she didn't even know he owned, on fire causing an inferno which nearly cost everyone aboard their lives and completely incinerated a ten million-dollar airplane.

Lauren was fast becoming the wrong person to mess with. Even now the original plan had to be changed. At first all she wanted was to get her husband back. Now that he had appeared to settle down he still wasn't in any position for Lauren to take him back as her lover. He was still a woose, she thought. He was spineless when she learned about him and Sandy Winters and he was still spineless after that airline fire, the one he swears he was never on. She thought that maybe that kind of experience might put some hair on his balls, but she was wrong. He was still disgustingly bland.

Now Agent Dobbs was what Lauren called a man. He had class, was masculine and wasn't afraid to tell you how he felt. No matter how hard Lauren tried to get him upset that first morning at the laboratory, he held his ground. He did so in a mannerly fashion and Lauren felt strongly that if he were pushed far enough, he would cuff her, frisk her and drag her away. A woman would not rule him and he would only take so much grief before he used the patented Melvin Purvis arrest technique. She liked a man who was strong in his dealings with other people and Dobbs fit that bill to the letter. They had as yet to get intimate with one another, however, Lauren was sure that Bob Dobbs could do the dance with her in the most satisfying fashion.

Lauren began to think about the next day. She would do her very best to get Dobbs alone after they met with the FBI agent at the airport. There were some very nice and private hotels in the vicinity of the airport. She would wear her best blouse and skirt, both designed for easy access, and wear her best perfume. She would treat this as her first prom date with the captain of the football team. All the stops would be pulled for this special occasion.

Lauren was a little surprised with her attitude, but she liked it. For once she was going after something she wanted and she was sure he wanted her too. The more she thought of him the more her mind began to wander. Her rocking slowed to a stop and soon she was fast asleep.

32

. . . .

TOM ROLLED OVER IN BED and noticed it was only 7:00 a.m. The dog barking and children running down the hall woke him up. He soon heard Chris come to his aid when she told the girls to be quiet because Grandma and Tom were still asleep. He rolled over in bed for what he hoped would be several hours but was soon roused by Alex telling him breakfast was ready.

"I don't want any breakfast, honey," he said as he rolled back over in bed.

"Yes, you do!" replied Alex. "You have a busy day today. And after last night's exhibition you're going to need your strength."

She went over to the window and pulled the shades revealing a very beautiful sunny day.

"Don't forget you have to talk with Drummond today and you promised to take the girls so Chris and I can go shopping."

"I lied," Tom said in a sluggish tone.

"Too bad," said Alex. "You were already paid, remember?"

"You mean to tell me you were just using sex for favors?" he answered. "I thought you loved me."

"Maybe after we get back from the mall," replied Alex. "Let me re-evaluate my situation and then we'll talk."

"Come on, Tom!" hollered Carrie. "Your eggs are getting cold."

He lumbered out of bed, put on a pair of cut -off jeans and an Ohio State T-shirt, and staggered out to the table.

"So, I hear we had burglars in the house this morning, " he said, as he sat down. "That's what the watch dog was barking about, wasn't it?"

He looked around for an answer and everyone just sat there in dead silence waiting for Alex to sit down. When she did so, the girls began the prayer before meals and Tom was once again caught with his mouth open, forgetting the rule of no talking before prayer. He just put his face in his hands and glanced over at Chris with a smirk on his face meaning he was in for another lecture. She just shook her head and grinned back.

Once the prayer had ended, both Carrie and Corrie were ready to unload on Tom. Chris interrupted the girls saying, "Let's be nice to Tom, he isn't used to eating breakfast. In time he will do just fine."

The two girls just glared at him wishing they could have chastised him for his sin, but unfortunately Chris had cut off their intended lecture. Tom, not to be outdone, looked at the girls with a grin on his face and said, "Yeah, what she said."

Alex rose to get the coffee, and rapped Tom on the back of his head with the newspaper normally reserved for Rocky's bad dinner manners. This brought a round of applause from the girls, and again Chris had to come to Tom's rescue to settle the girls down.

"So, what's on your agenda for today, Tom?" asked Chris.

"Well, I thought I'd take these two ladies out on the town," he replied. "First I promised them a trip to my church to meet my dear friend, Father Harris. Then we are off to the airport to meet Ed and get this deadhead schedule straightened out and then back home for a nap."

"Wow!" returned Chris. "That sounds exciting. I wish I could meet your friend. You girls be sure and tell me all about him when you get home."

"Tom said he would show us the church too, Mom," said Carrie.

"Are you sure you want to do all this, Tom?" asked Chris. "They can be a handful at times."

"Of course, I do," answered Tom excitedly. "We've been talking about this since we met. We'll have fun. And besides, I'll spoil them rotten, fill them full of sugar and then turn them over to you and Granny Goodrich."

"That's Grandma!" hollered Corrie.

Chris just laughed aloud when Alex took the girls aside and began to get on poor, old Tom.

"You know you deserve everything you get here," said Chris. "You're as much an instigator as the kids are. I can't defend you anymore. You're on your own."

With that, he just put his chin in his hand and looking over at Chris, smiled and said, "Yep!"

The remainder of breakfast went without any more fan fare and soon the dishes were cleaned up and they were getting dressed for their travels of the day.

Tom changed his clothes, packed up the girls, gave kisses where expected and set off for a day of sightseeing.

"First stop is our church," said Tom as he pulled out of the driveway and onto Summers Street. As he cruised down the streets on the way to church he recalled the day he first saw the priest. As he passed by the old mattress warehouse it was nothing like it was that day. There was no green grass or lush lawns or brightly painted trims on the houses. Even the billboard still had the same torn and haggard Tropicana sign on it. Bringing all this to mind again confused him. He recalled how happy he was to talk to Father Harris about this and get a makeshift explanation about how he wasn't going crazy As they approached the church driveway, he saw the old car that nearly hit him on that day. And sure enough, Tom laughed to himself; the old girl had hit someone in the rear end right in the intersection. Things never change. As they turned into the driveway, they saw Father Harris walking across the lawn. Tom tapped on the car horn and pulled the car to a stop.

As the two girls left running, Tom interjected by saying, "Stranger!"

When the girls stopped running Tom said, "This is my friend over here. I have no idea who that man is."

"Good morning, Father Harris!" Tom said. "I'd like you to meet my two newfound friends. They and their mother are staying with us for awhile."

Father Harris bent down and took them both in his arms immediately making them feel welcome. After that he shook Tom's hand and said, "Would you like something cold to drink?" When all three answered affirmatively Rosario was off to the kitchen asking the girls if they would like to help. The three ladies went into the rectory to pour some cold drinks for what was promising to be a hot Texas day.

With the privacy the two men were now enjoying, Father Harris began the questioning.

"Tell me, Thomas, have you had any more dreams lately?"

"No!" Tom answered. "He seems to leave as quickly as he comes."

"Do you ever notice an odor or, for that matter, a fragrance?" the priest asked.

"No! Quite the contrary," was Tom's reply. "There is an absence of all sound, smells and time. The night I saw him on the beach it felt to me like a mere minute of time. Alex told me that she had been gone for fifteen minutes."

"I have done some research on the subject," began the priest. "Here is what I have found to date. Some people hear voices, but never see who is talking to them. Some people feel the presence of another being, one that they fear, because they have the feeling of being powerless in their presence. Some people see the orbs and opaque figures sometimes associated with cemeteries and then there is your type. Some people actually see a figure that looks natural, looks at them, talks to them and at times touches them. But the person who sees them is never able to answer why they didn't move toward the apparition. The research shows that the majority of your kind of people are powerless, just because they never even think of attempting to touch the being as part of an identification process. Another interesting tidbit is that your kind of person is always left in peace when the being leaves and there is never any confusion of what was said. Now that doesn't mean that they knew what the being was talking about, just that they knew what he said. This is very prevalent in places like some of the hotels in Gettysburg, Pennsylvania, and the Lincoln room at the White House."

"Did any of my type of people learn later what it was the being was trying to tell them?" asked Tom.

"Interesting that you would ask that," continued Father Harris. "In all but a few cases, there was an overall plan which dealt with rescuing someone from an upcoming disaster. For example there are those who were told in a dream to go visit their mother, only to find when they arrived she had just fallen down the stairs. There's also the man who got a call from an unknown source telling him that his ex-wife was having trouble with the furnace and electricity. When he arrived on the scene his ex-wife was ready to light a match in the dark to ascertain where all those horrible gas odors were coming from. The books are full of little bits of paranormal activity."

"So where does my particular case fit into the mold?" asked Tom.

"It would seem that you are being forewarned," he continued. "The fact that a priest is appearing to you and not an ordinary being is interesting. Also that he has come to you three times is very peculiar. It would appear to me that something big is going to happen and no matter what you do, you will not be able to escape it. You have been called. What you do when you are confronted with the problem is what will be the test."

"What about this business of no harm coming to me?" returned Tom.

"In all the cases I have read, the person called upon has always survived," he said with confidence. "Let that be your strength. You will survive as long as you do what the father calls you to do. However, this does not apply to someone who has been approached by a demon. They are more times than not, killed."

"You're beginning to scare the shorts off me, " replied Tom. "You realize that, don't you?"

"How do you think I feel?" said Father Harris. "I'm the one who has the inside track and I'll be the one left behind to answer all the questions."

As the two friends continued their conversation the silence was broken by the giggles of two little girls coming out of the rectory with a glass of iced tea in each hand.

"You don't think it has to do with them, do you?" Tom asked his friend.

Father Harris just shrugged his shoulders and shaking his head, said, "The Lord works in mysterious ways. This sounds like a bigger picture to me."

"Well if it is bigger potatoes, remember what the priest told me in case I don't come right back, okay? You will have to remember this conversation and stand in for me when things get rough. I don't even have a will."

"I understand," Father Harris said. "but you won't need a will, you are going to survive."

"That's what the other guy says!" he answered.

That was all that was said since the girls had returned very excited from their visit with the housekeeper and their tour of the church.

When the two girls delivered their drinks to Father Harris and Tom, they both took up a position on Tom's lap. They all talked and laughed with the fervent comfort being with friends brings. Soon, the earlier conversation of Tom's dilemma had all but been forgotten as they were having a delightful time with each other.

"I think you'll make a wonderful step grandfather, Tom," said Father Harris. "They do appear to put some of your lost youth back in you. You realize that soon we will have to discuss your marriage with Alexandra.. We can't be having a role model like you living in sin in front of these little girls."

"I wondered how long it was going to take you to get to that." answered Tom as Rosario started laughing.

"By the way," the priest asked. "Are they Catholic?"

"No," replied Tom, "Presbyterian."

"My God in Heaven!" replied the priest as he lurched in his seat. "Saints preserve us. Your work is cut out for you, my son. Your place in Heaven is guaranteed if you can bring her into the fold."

This brought a great deal of laughter from Tom and Rosario.

"What is so funny?" asked Corrie.

"We were just commenting on your old church and how happy we would be if you joined my church," said Tom.

"Can we all join your church?" asked Carrie.

"If you promise to sleep with Rocky every night you can," he replied.

"Oh yuck!" returned Carrie. "He's got bad breath and he farts in the middle of the night. No, thanks."

"Did you never hear the story of how the good Lord loves the beasts and children?" asked Father Harris.

"Yes, I did," said Carrie. "And never once did Jesus say anything about bad breath and farts."

"Your turn, Father," said Tom.

"Amen!" said Father Harris. "Let's have some more iced tea."

With that argument going to the girls, everyone rose from their seats and headed to the cool rectory.

"Those Presbyterians are a hard nut to crack," said Father Harris.

"Amen!" said Tom. "But they don't mind living in sin. I like that."

"We will touch on this more again later," he said. "They sure are a wonderful set of children, aren't they? Are things better now that they are with you?"

"Oh, yes," answered Tom. "Once Alex got her hands on them, everything was just roses."

"I sure would like to meet her someday," said Father Harris. "It would be better if I needed to talk to her over this other business if we were previously introduced."

"This dream business has you a little worried, doesn't it?" asked Tom as he put his hand on his friend's arm to hold him up for a minute while the girls ran ahead.

"Yes, Tom, it does," said the priest. "There is just too much detail here for this to be nothing. And there is just no way we can stop it."

"Are you a little more experienced in this area of the paranormal than you are letting on?" asked Tom.

"Do you know Mrs. Kentwillie, the short gray haired usher on Sunday?" asked Father Harris.

"Yes, I think I do, "he said.

"For months she dreamed of a boating accident involving the Statue of Liberty," said Father Harris. "Her brother was on that Staten Island Ferry that hit the dock last year in New York City."

"Dare I ask how he faired?" asked Tom.

"He didn't make it, " Father Harris said "However, this is a different set of phenomenon than what you're describing. But I still don't like it. You stay in close contact with me for a while until we can figure this out. And call me if there are any more dreams."

Tom nodded affirmatively and into the rectory they went. When they arrived there they were surprised to find that Father Harris had visitors so Tom and the girls said their good-byes and were soon off to the airport.

33

L AUREN HORTON HAD JUST FINISHED signing some testing results when she sat down at her desk and checked the time. Just as she did her secretary called and said, "That pesky FBI agent is here again and does he ever look good. I tell you, if you're just going to abuse him, send him my way."

"Thank you, Jan," returned Lauren.

Trying desperately not to look like an infatuated teenager, Lauren went out to the reception area and met the man she was awake most of the night dreaming about.

"Well, good morning, Agent Dobbs, "she said as she extended her hand. "What a pleasant surprise! You look a might dashing today, I must say."

As the two of them walked past Jan's desk, Lauren stopped and introduced her to him.

"Robert, this is my secretary, " said Lauren. "She would be most interested in any emotionally detached agents you may have running around the academy. She is especially fond of the Fox Mulder types."

As Bob extended his hand to Jan and told her how nice it was to meet her, Lauren gave Jan a mischievous wink so she would know they were only kidding her. After all pleasantries were exchanged the affectionate couple left for the day.

As they passed through all the security, Lauren said to Dobbs, "I have to put on my stern, put out face for the time being until we get out of here. You might try grabbing me by the hair and dragging me out cave man style while I kick and scream."

"You'd like that, wouldn't you?" Dobbs said. "The Melvin Purvis treatment. He was my hero and mentor, you understand."

"I'll just bet he was," said Lauren as she laughed lightly while passing the guard station.

"Keep a stiff upper lip, Bob," she cautioned. "You're the man here."

After they had cleared the last security checkpoint and were alongside Bob's car, they both had a good laugh at the expense of everyone else.

"Do you think we were coy enough for them?" he asked. "Do you think we fooled them?"

"Oh yeah," replied Lauren. "Like an iceberg in Miami. The old Elliot Ness fake out."

"Elliot used to do that?" asked Dobbs with a blank look on his face. "They never told us about that in the academy."

"Drive, please, Robert, " she said.

"Yes, ma'am," replied Dobbs. "First stop, the airport."

When the vehicle cleared the gate they were soon on the freeway and headed for the airport. He took this opportunity to begin the conversation.

"I had a heck of a time sleeping last night. I couldn't get you off my mind for love or money."

"I know what you mean," said Lauren. "Love and money has kept me awake many nights. Trying to find the one and winning the other has been quite a dilemma."

"Maybe we can work on that today, "said Dobbs.

"Excuse me, Robert, "she said, "I do believe you just suggested prostitution to a lady."

As he looked at her in shock, she used her feminine wiles cocking her head and giving him a mischievous grin "What kind of girl do you think I am?"

"No, no!" said Dobbs in his own defense. "I didn't mean that."

"Do you want it for free then?" asked Lauren. "In the presence of a lady you must express your intentions clearly. What would Mr. Purvis say about these lackluster tactics? I'll bet he would send you back to Mr. Hoover for a refresher course. Shame on you, Robert, talking like that to a tax paying Christian woman."

As he looked over at her he could see the smirk on her face. He thought he had misread her until she said in a soft, quiet sexy voice…"Gotcha".

"Don't do that to me," he said as he maneuvered the car around an erratic driver. "I thought you were serious."

"You need some work," she said as she laughed slightly." but I'll train you. You are much more fun than I earlier anticipated, much more sheltered. I thought you Hoover boys were brought up to speed on how to interrogate witnesses and talk maidens out of their pants."

"I do all right," he said.

"We'll see, " returned Lauren. "Now get back to the part where you couldn't get me off your mind last night. Here's the airport entrance ramp."

"Are you like this to all your friends?" Dobbs asked.

"I'm not sure, " she answered questioningly. "I never cared about someone like you before. You're new territory. Time will tell."

34

. . . .

LAUREN AND BOB PULLED INTO the airport the same time Tom and the girls did. Tom went in through the pilot's entrance and when they came to the security gate there was a new person there Tom had never seen.

"ID card, please," the young guard said. "What is your business here, sir?"

"I work here," replied Tom. "I'm a pilot."

"Then, why did you use this entrance, Captain?" queried the guard.

"Because this is the pilot's employee entrance," replied Tom.

"That's beside the point, Captain, " the guard answered.

As he and the girls sat in the car and looked in astonishment, the guard began walking around the car looking ever suspiciously at the undercarriage. After he finished his walk around, he stopped by the driver's side window. When he did this Tom thought he saw someone else standing in the guard office hidden beside the door.

The guard looked into the back seat of the car and said to him, "Can you vouch for those two stowaways, Captain? They look like Middle Easterners to me. Kind of shifty, if you know what I mean. They look like they're from the al-Qaeda School of dance.

Tom wasn't quite sure how to take this and he was about to become defensive when he thought he saw Bob Pearson beside the guard house door pulling another practical joke.

"Did Captain Pearson put you up to this, young man?"

"Yes, sir, he did," the guard answered as Bob Pearson came out grinning from ear to ear.

"My God, Tom!" Bob said. "The things you see without a gun. I was just trying to familiarize the new kid with the kind of riff-raff that comes through this gate. I was telling the boy here that you can't be too careful."

"I'll just bet you were," said Tom. "Does your lovely wife know you're on the loose?"

"The last time I saw the girl she was headed for the mall," replied Bob. "She's happy. Are those your two little girls from a stewardess?"

"Yeah, right," replied Tom. "No, these are Alex's granddaughters. Cute little shits, aren't they?"

"They sure are," Bob agreed. "They look a lot like you. Are you telling me straight? Where are you headed in those civilian clothes? Hell, Tom, I didn't know you had another change of clothes."

"I'm doing a deadhead trip for Drummond before I go on vacation. I'm coming in to get the final times and all that jazz, and then when this trip is over we are going on a boat trip. Who knows? I may retire and be a yacht bum the rest of my life," explained Tom.

"Well I'm off to the hotel to get a good night's sleep and then I'm going on vacation as well. Be safe, " said Bob as he patted the side of Tom's car.

"You also. "Tom waved to his friend. He always shows up in the most bizarre places, he thought. I wish I could spend more time with the Pearsons.

He found his usual parking space and after getting the girls out of the car they all walked hand in hand into the airport and up to Ed Drummond's office. There they met with his secretary, Sarah. Tom in his usual jovial mood said, "Oh, Moneypenney, what a bundle of sunshine you bring to a normal shaded day."

Sarah just looked at him with that usual female look of being unimpressed and said, "If you think you can come in here and fill me with lovely sonnets thinking those children will protect your virtue from aggressive assaults, you, sir, are sadly mistaken. Shall we go into the washroom a moment, Captain, and discuss this privately?"

Tom stood there with his eyes as wide open as he could get them to warn Sarah that Ed was standing in the doorway. She continued on her slow walk around her big desk wringing her hands and telling Tom that he can't hide behind those girls all his life, that someday she would catch him unprotected and then his butt and everything attached would be hers.

"Wow!" said Ed. "Those hormone tablets are making a monster out of you."

"You might consider a taut leash on her, sir," returned Tom. "You never cease to amaze me, Moneypenney."

The shock of Drummond standing there was a little more than Sarah could cope with. She became very embarrassed and immediately excused herself to the ladies' room.

"What have you done to that little wall flower of a woman?" asked Tom.

"I don't know, " said Ed. "She does drink a lot of bottled water. Maybe that's the secret. Hmm, I see that I will have to start monitoring her water from now on. Moneypenney, is it? That's good Tom, I like that. Come on in, you guys."

As the four of them left poor Miss Moneypenney alone and went into Ed's office, Lauren and Bob Dobbs had arrived at the gate looking for his contact.

"Looks like we're a little early," said Lauren. "Was that part of your tactics? Be here a little early and see if any bad guys show up?"

"It's all in the plan, my dear," said Dobbs. "All in the plan."

"Let's take a walk," said Lauren. "We just won't wander too far from the perimeter."

"Oh, you're good," he said.

As they began walking slowly down the hall, she took his hand in hers. Although Dobbs was genuinely surprised, he didn't retract his own hand; he only secured his grip.

"I need to know, Bob, where are we going with this?" asked Lauren. "Am I more to you than an airplane fire? Are you just with me because of my husband's luggage or are we looking at a real relationship here?"

"Is that what you think? That you are just a path to an end some where?" said Dobbs.

"That's what I'm trying to find out," she responded. "Please don't answer a question with a question. Honesty is important here. Do you have feelings for me or are you just trying to investigate a fire and you think I have the answer?"

"Both!" he answered. "At first I just needed to talk with you about this luggage business, but now I don't much care about that airplane. I thought I could handle this better, but I've discovered I only care for you. I didn't think someone like you could happen to someone like me. So now I'm in the middle of what I should do and what I want to do. The worst part of it is, I've figured out a way to do both.

"Explain, please!" returned Lauren.

"Let's just say for instance you know a little more than you are letting on." divined Dobbs. "Let's say that you put that acid in your husband's after-shave bottle because you knew he was sleeping with that Winters woman and you wanted it stopped. Now say that your plan was disfigurement and the very fact that the bottle broke was not your fault. Your intention was to hurt poor old Ashland and not the whole damn airplane. How am I doing?"

"That's an interesting story," replied Lauren. "Please go on."

"Okay, so now you have poor old Ashland getting on this airplane with this suitcase and this bottle of after-shave, which by the way, now becomes a weapon of terror, and off he goes with a one way ticket to Paris, France," Dobbs continues. "This in itself tells me that he isn't coming home again. Now I'm thinking why would anyone go all the way to Paris, France, to leave his wife and kids when all he has to do is go across town. No, my dear, Ashland had much more on his mind that a trip to a seminar that day. He was running away from someone or something. And that someone or something wanted to make sure he didn't make it back. I don't think that bottle of after-shave was the culprit. Any questions or comments before I go on?"

"What could Ashland have possibly done to make someone want to hurt him?" questioned Lauren.

"Well," he replied "One name that comes to mind is Samuel P. Winters. He and Sandy's husband were business partners as well as brothers and owned a great deal of property on the gulf that the great state of Texas gave to Sandy upon her husband's demise. Now the rumors say that Sandy killed the old man because he was beating her on occasion. However, if you interview the right people they will tell you that Sandy had every one of those beatings coming to her. So, if Sandy would happen to come to some great misfortune, our dear friend Samuel would be back on easy street where he was before Sandy took his half. And I've had the pleasure of meeting old Sam and I'd bet my badge he wouldn't hesitate for a minute to do Sandy in by some bizarre means that no one would ever imagine. However, I imagined it all along."

"You imagined what?"

Just at that time the FBI agent they were waiting for showed up and the conversation was ended abruptly.

"Dobbs, my boy, how are you this fine day?" said the agent. "Did you bring the dope on our friend, Smothers?"

"Right here you are, my boy," he said as he handed the agent the folder. "Everything you need."

As the agent looked through the material, he gave a mischievous chuckle and said, "Oh, you are the best, Robert, my boy. They will have to pipe sunshine to this poor bastard as deep as we're going to bury him."

Extending his hand to Dobbs he looked over at Lauren and said, "Don't ever cross old Bob here, he could find the fly that crapped on your counter top a year ago. They don't come any better. And you, my dear, are beautiful. Robert, you're holding out on me. Who is this lovely lady?"

Dobbs introduced Lauren to his friend and after a few cordial exchanges the agent was on his way and the two of them were left alone in the terminal. They walked quietly down the corridor hand in hand while Lauren tried to put together what it was that Dobbs was trying to explain to her. Not wanting to break the mood of the quiet attraction she had on him, he too walked quietly and let his feelings be transmitted through the pressure of his hand. The more he talked to her the more he was sure she had no idea the danger Ashland was in when he accompanied Sandy on that plane. He was also sure that she knew nothing of how he had staged that insurance pay off to himself and Sandy leaving nothing to her and the kids. Dobbs had done his homework on Ashland and Sandy and had gone through the paper trail they had left. The only thing that Ashland hadn't counted on was that the plane would never make it to France. When the plane turned around, his whole plan was shot. He would not become one of the pictures on the milk carton, lost for no one ever to find. He would not live the rest of his life in Paris under an assumed name where no one would ever be the wiser. He and Sandy with her money would not pass away with the sands of time where, before long, no one would even care. But once the plane turned around he was doomed and had a change of heart, thinking that divine intervention had interfered with his plans and set him on the path of righteousness.

But Sandy knew she could go on and start another plan. Dobbs was also certain that Sandy didn't suspect her brother in law of any ill feeling toward her. She was naïve enough to think everyone loved her and nobody would ever try to hurt her. But Dobbs knew better, He knew what caused that fire and he knew it wasn't Ashland's bottle of after-shave. He just used that as an excuse to get next to Ashland and Sandy. Yes it did catch on fire and yes it would have been just cause to turn the airplane around. But, Ashland's luggage was on the other side of the airplane in the depressurized cargo hold across from where the inferno had started, and there wouldn't have been enough oxygen to sustain a fire as basic as that. No, an incendiary device with a low oxygen accelerant, probably magnesium sulfate, caused the fire that brought down flight 409. This was the type that could be found at Samuel Winters Construction and Excavating Co., and was prepared by one of his expert workers, but left no trace on the ashes of an airplane that had been washed down by tons of water and foam. Only an expert Hoover trained man could find that residue and he would have to expect it to find it.

Dobbs could feel this in his gut and had hoped questioning Lauren would give him the answers he searched for. But, falling in love with her wasn't the answer he sought. Yet realizing that she knew nothing of Ashland's plans for leaving her and the kids forever told him that Lauren had been played by Ashland and Ashland had been played by Sandy. This told him that he could have a relationship with Lauren without the baggage of trying to hide her involvement with the demise of Flight 409.

He had figured it out. It had become quite clear to him this morning when the test results of Ashland's luggage came back negative for an accelerant and not capable of burning in an airtight environment. Lauren wasn't trying to kill Ashland, Samuel was trying to kill Sandy, and he blew it. He, Dobbs was sure, would try again. The only thing Dobbs wasn't sure of was how to tell Lauren what he knew. He would need a little help on that one, but he knew it would come to him.

"Are you taking me to a quiet place for more interrogation, Robert?" asked Lauren. "If you are confused about a suitable location I may be able to help."

The breaking of the silence startled him a little bit.

"Well, yes, my dear that is exactly what I had in mind," he said as he kissed her hand.

"You seem to be quite amorous this afternoon, Robert," she mentioned. "What has gotten into you?"

"Oh, nothing really," replied Bob. "Just being with you does that to me, I guess.

So tell me, Lauren, are you hungry?"

"No," she answered. "I just want to be alone with you, that's all. We can eat later."

"All right then," returned Dobbs. "Where to?"

"Come with me," she said as she tightened her grip on his hand. "I know just the place."

As the two of them made their way down the concourse who met them but a man who had two little girls in hand singing and spinning around like a family on holiday.

"Oh, my gosh!" said Dobbs "Look who's here."

Tom recognized Dobbs the same time Dobbs recognized him and both men waved at the same time.

"I was going to call you this afternoon," Dobbs said.

"Yeah, I'll bet. I get that a lot," said Tom. Seeing Lauren, he extended his hand and said, "Hello miss, Tom Jordan."

She gave Tom a cute smile surprised that a stranger would be that friendly and returned his handshake.

"My God, Agent Dobbs!" said Tom. "You've come to the mother lode for terrorists' investigation, haven't you? There are more Arabs here than in all of Afghanistan."

"Not really. We're just passing through," returned Dobbs.

"Lauren, this is Captain Tom Jordan," said Dobbs. "He was the Captain of the airliner that burned up. Are these your kids?"

"No, no! They're my girlfriend's granddaughters," replied Tom. "You remember Alex Sanders."

"Oh, yes, of course," returned Dobbs. "How is she? This is my friend, Lauren Horton."

Tom looked at her and gave her a very warm smile saying "I'm very pleased to meet you, Lauren. These two little girls are Carrie and Corrie."

"Hi, Lauren," they both said in unison.

"I'm going to feed them all kinds of sugar and give them back to their mother later on today," said Tom. "How is the investigation going?"

As Dobbs began filling Tom in on the investigation's latest findings, Lauren became filled with guilt. For the first time, there was a face attached to what she had done. There was someone else looking back at her in the mirror of reality that she had never seen or considered before. To make things worse, this face had made her feel immediately welcomed, and extended a friendship she knew would be as lasting as their lives. She would never see him again and not know who he was. A one in a million chance meeting had made him a part of her life. She would always know him as the man she nearly killed. And why does he have to be such a nice guy, she thought to herself. My God, he has a girlfriend and grandchildren and I nearly wiped him and six hundred other people off the face of the earth in a most horrific way. I can't deal with this. She nearly started to cry, but got hold of her emotions when Carrie said, "Do you have any children?"

Knowing she had never told Dobbs of her children, she said, "Why don't we go over here and sit down while those two talk?"

The three took a few steps and sat down by the wall as Tom and Dobbs talked more.

"Yes, I have two children," replied Lauren.

Her mind began to run wildly now as she thought of all those families that would have been affected had that plane crashed. What was she thinking when she planted that after-shave bottle in Ashland's bag? What had she done? In spite of the fire, she had never given any thought to anyone else or how her jealousy nearly killed them. Meeting Tom set off a chain of events she couldn't control. She wanted to apologize to Tom, but she knew she couldn't. She was alone with her guilt and there wasn't anyone who could take it from her. It was of her own making and she was stuck with it for a long, long time.

When it was clear that Tom and Dobbs had finished with their conversation, the girls stood up and walked toward them.

"Was anyone hurt in that fire, Captain?" Lauren asked.

"Fortunately, just myself," answered Tom. "I had some burns on my back from the material on the ceiling, but they're all healed now. We were very lucky that day. Those people in Presque Isle were the best around. Without them I don't think many of us would have made it out alive!"

"Have you ever been back there?" asked Lauren. "You know, to thank them for all they did?"

"No!" Tom replied. "Not as yet. I don't think I'm emotionally ready for that yet, but I'm sure one day I will be. Maybe at the one-year anniversary we can all get together and see one another again. It's really not something one would want to celebrate, if you know what I mean. We were very lucky. I'd like to leave it that way. Even though we all owe the people of Presque Isle a great deal of gratitude, it would be hard to go back there."

Lauren was beginning to feel a little better after talking to Tom, but the guilt was sweeping over her in waves and, luckily for her, Dobbs came to her rescue "Well, Captain, it was nice to see you again. I'll keep you posted on any new developments."

"Thank you," Tom said as he shook Dobbs hand. "Lauren, it was very nice to meet you as well," he said as he offered her his hand.

But she reached up and hugged him very tightly and whispered in his ear, "Thank you."

Lauren then hugged the girls, as they said their good byes and walked off in different directions. Dobbs noticed the emotional feelings that she was displaying, but chose to keep his comments to himself. He took her by the hand and said only, "I like Captain Jordan, he is a hell of a good guy. That man has nerves of steel."

As the two of them made their way out of the airport and through the parking lot, Lauren and Dobbs made no attempt to talk. Her silence told him that she felt responsible for the carnage brought on Flight 409 and Captain Jordan. But, as yet, he couldn't find a way to tell her she wasn't responsible. And then out of the clear blue, she asked him exactly what took place the day Flight 409 burned up on the runway at Presque Isle, Maine, and just that quickly he was given the chance to clear this up.

Dobbs began to tell her a story filled with bravery, heroes, a pilot's skill, and the refusal to go quietly without a fight. He told her how Captain Jordan and his flight crew found the fire burning in the cargo hold when they couldn't explain why the galley floor was becoming so hot. They wanted to come to Kennedy International Airport in New York, but the airport wouldn't allow them entry because of the risk of fire burning out of control in a heavily populated airport and sent them away on their own. They settled on a small airport in Presque Isle, Maine, which in no way could handle a 747 in peril, but it was all they had. All the passengers and crew had to help them was a small volunteer fire department that stood their ground as the burning jumbo jet landed and headed straight for them. How they held their ground so bravely when a large explosion blew off the tail section of the plane and sent it hurling down the runway in reverse was a mystery to Dobbs. And he explained to Lauren what it must have been like for all those people who were herded in front of the doors for an easy escape, all 612 of them. He then concluded by telling Lauren how Captain Jordan went back down the aisle after everyone was off only to find an old lady lying on the floor.

"He took her up in his arms, like a bride, " he said while positioning his hands to show what he meant. "And with his back on fire from burning debris from the ceiling, he jumped from the aircraft and slid down the chute with that lady still in his arms."

"How many people died?" asked Lauren.

"None!" he replied much to her surprise.

"No, my dear, it was a perfect example of what happens when people have their shit together and know exactly what they're doing. Thank God, they had the right pilot on board that day. I even heard an eyewitness say that the co-pilot stood at the bottom of the chute and screamed at the pilot."

"What did he say?" asked Lauren.

"What did she say," corrected Dobbs. "She said, 'come on you big dummy…jump'! And did you know the pilot and co-pilot had never met before that day? And they have been together ever since; intimately, I might add. As a matter of fact, those are her grandchildren."

Lauren looked at Dobbs and with tear- swelled eyes began to say something. He put his fingers over her mouth and said, "And that little bit of fire in Ashland's suitcase had nothing to do with it. The fire was set by an incendiary bomb located on the other side of the aircraft under an additional fuel tank. That's what caused the explosion that blew off the tail section when they landed."

The two friends got into the car, and Dobbs took her hands and said, "I'll tell you something and then we must never speak of this again.

Agreed? Sandy Winters' brother–in–law set that fire in an attempt to kill Sandy Winters. We knew that Ashland was with her because of the seat assignments. I needed to get next to Ashland so I could learn more about Sandy Winters. Not until this morning, when the lab reports came back did I know for sure that the propellant used in the devise was from the same batch tested at Sam Winter's construction site. It had a catalyst of magnesium sulfate in it because of the low oxygen content at 35,000 feet. The fire in Ashland's suitcase wouldn't burn above 12,000 feet. It would smolder and stink, but it would never have brought that airplane down."

"What does this Winters' guy have against my husband's girlfriend?" asked Lauren.

"Sandy Winters murdered her husband, Sam's brother, and took half of the family holdings," he explained. "He's a nasty character. He'll try again soon, believe me."

A silence fell as Lauren tried to sort all this out. Eventually she asked, "Were you ever going to tell me this?"

"Yes!" Dobbs said. "It was my answer to your question of whether I loved you or just wanted to get next to you for information against Sandy Winters. I never even suspected you of anything. I just knew I wanted to see you again, and I didn't know any other way to go about it. It may have been wrong, but I'm glad I did it and I would do it again if it brought me closer to you."

After a short pause he turned to her and said, "I've fallen in love with you and Melvin Purvis would roll over in his grave if he knew I used FBI time and funds to do it."

"I think Mister Purvis would understand," said Lauren smiling. "Pull in here, young man; this is our hotel."

Agent Dobbs did what he was told and turned into the driveway of the Ambassador Travel Lodge and said, "This is a pretty swanky place you have here, Lauren. To what do I owe this much luxury?"

"Nothing is too good for one of Mr. Purvis' men," answered Lauren.

As he opened the car door for her he took a glance around and noticed how pleasant and peaceful the surroundings were. Although they had just exited the concrete jungle of the freeway, it was apparent that the landscape had been well manicured and exhibited a deep lush greenery in the grass and bushes that surrounded the lodge. The trees even smelled good despite the hot Texas sun in full display over Houston this afternoon. One could even smell the yellow roses that Texas is so well known for in the lyrics of its state anthem. Bob was quite impressed. However, Lauren took it all in stride as if she expected it and would settle for nothing less. They made their way to the door.

As they entered the lodge the receptionist at the counter greeted them cheerfully saying, "Why, good afternoon, Doctor Horton. Your room is ready and the conference room is available should you need it later for anything."

As Bob looked at her in total amazement, Lauren smiled at the receptionist and cordially said, "Thank you, Al."

As she filled out the necessary registration forms, Dobbs became engrossed in the natural wood surroundings of the lodge. Although it had the usual big game trophy mounts hanging on the walls they were not a cheap imitation of an imported veneer. He recognized the wood as Philippine mahogany from the days he spent with his grandfather in his cabinet shop. He could nearly taste the odor that this type of wood left on his senses. It brought back memories of those days with his grandfather. Dobbs buried him shortly after his graduation from the academy. The elder Dobbs had daily rubbed elbows with Melvin Purvis as they fought the criminals from the roaring twenties era. His grandfather would be proud of him today, not only because of his becoming an agent, but also because he had taken a step in life that would seal his happiness.

As the two made their way down the hallway, their gait became a little slower and their heart rate became a little faster. Both in their own way wondered what the day would bring and how their lives would change. . Would this become a lasting relationship filled with love and passion that would go on well into their golden years or would it fizzle out and become just an experience between fools? Would Dobbs spend the rest of his life with a woman he fell so deeply and quickly in love with — a woman he felt had the vitality and ambition to make him a good wife? He knew he had the love and tenderness to give in return. Would she be the one he would be proud to call his own and spend the remainder of his days with? Would she be the woman that would make his life complete and would end his solitary confinement to loneliness? As he walked with her down the hallway he felt that he should be saying something, but he chose to be quiet and commit to memory the way he felt this very moment.

Lauren could feel the warmth of his hand as well as his pulse as they neared the room. Her mind raced with amorous thoughts of what was happening at this time in her life. She had never done anything like this before, but she in no way was regretting it. She felt good about the prospect of sharing this moment in time with Bob Dobbs. She was in love with this man and she knew in her own way she could trust him. She would show him without measure the extent of her love and was certain it would be enough to seal a lasting relationship. Lauren stopped at the door and put in the key opening it only a crack. She moved aside and let Dobbs open the door. They both entered the room as the door closed behind them with the certainty and privacy of the sound of a heavy latch. They were alone.

35

TOM AND THE GIRLS PULLED into the driveway directly behind Alex and Chris. He had to beep the horn and get the girls started, but it appeared it was Alex who was very excited. Upon embarking from the car, Alex came and giving him a hug and a kiss asked how his trip was to the airport. She recruited his help carrying in the groceries and it appeared she was genuinely excited about something.

"What, my dear, has put you in such a good mood?" Tom asked.

"Oh, nothing really," returned Alex. "I'm just happy to see you, that's all."

As the three adults made their way into the house Tom looked over at Chris who only grinned and shook her head. Once inside the house Carrie and Corrie both took up squatters' rights on the sofa and began to doze off. Looking at the two travelers Tom remarked, "That looks like a good idea. Call me when dinner is ready, would you, honey?"

"Not so fast, young man," said Alex. "I want to show you what I bought at the store today. Are the girls sleeping? This way, please."

With Chris giving Tom a sheepish little grin knowing good and well what her mother had in mind, the two lovers made their way down the hall to the bedroom.

"You two play nice now, you hear?" Chris said.

"Not a chance," said Alex.

When they arrived in the bedroom, Tom plopped down on the bed and covered up with a blanket thinking of going to sleep. .

"Thomas, Chris took me into a Victoria Secret store at the mall," said Alex. "Check this stuff out. You are one lucky devil. Pay attention. There is a test later."

Tom turned his attention to the lingerie exhibition on the other side of the room. As he watched her showing off all the neat evening attire that she bought to excite a new level of passion in him, he just marveled at the beauty of the woman he loved. He knew she didn't have to put on those sexy garments to excite an arousal in him. All she had to do was walk up close to him, and he was a dead man.

Alex would pull a garment out of the bag and go into a seminar over it. She would explain where it was made, who made it and the purpose of those little strings as if Tom didn't know. He listened haphazardly until she struck a cord when she asked, "Which one should I try on first?"

"All right!" he exclaimed. "Now we're talking. Here, let me help you with that."

As he rose from the bed he latched onto her and with one twist of his body pulled her onto the bed.

"Thomas, I have to try one on for you," she said anxiously.

"I'll do just fine with this outfit for the time being," he replied as they embraced on the bed.

"You are incorrigible, Thomas," she said. After all that shopping I did for you."

"Show me the rest later," said Tom, not letting her up. "Never tempt a man in the middle of the afternoon."

"You don't know what you're getting yourself into," said Alex.

"I'll take my chances," replied Tom laughing.

"Be quiet!" she said, "You'll wake the girls."

"No moaning!" he whispered.

That was the last of the conversational foreplay as they became one with each other. They would express their love until late in the afternoon when Tom finally drifted off to sleep and Alex rose to fix supper before the girls got up from their nap.

As she made her way down the hall fluffing up her hair, Chris asked, "What did he think? Did he like them?"

Patting away a yawn she said, "Yeah….yeah, he did." Laughing lightly she said, "Yeah, I'd say he was downright crazy about them. God, I love that man. I wonder sometimes where he learned to screw like that."

"What did you say?" asked Chris.

"Oh, nothing really," she said. "I'm just mumbling."

Shortly thereafter the girls got up and wanted to wake Tom up also so they had someone to play with, but Chris said no.

"Come sit down and tell your grandmother and me about your afternoon at Tom's church," Chris said.

The girls became excited and began telling the whole story of meeting the priest, his housekeeper, and Ed and his secretary. Carrie went on with the additional story of the gate guard and the crazy pilot with the big nose. They both told a story of big city tourism with all tactivities of a professional tour. Although their afternoon cookies and milk were gone their enthusiasm and stories were far from over.

Lauren and Dobbs began to unwind from their afternoon rendezvous and were still holding tightly to each other as they lay in bed. Although they both had places they should probably be, neither was in any hurry to leave. They had waited so long for this moment that it was not to be rushed.

Lauren looked at him and said, "What is to become of us in time?"

"Time starts now," answered Dobbs.

"Wait a minute, Robert," said Lauren. "That was on a Steve McQueen movie once. You can't say that.

"But you have to admit, it's romantic," he answered.

"Romantic, maybe a little bit," said Lauren. "Original, not even close. Robert, this relationship must be built on originality."

"I have original love for you," said Bob. "How's that?"

"I like that," she replied. "We can build on that."

"You're going to love me, Lauren Horton," he said.

"You're going to love me too, Bob Dobbs," returned Lauren.

And with that they embraced in a passionate grip and made love once again. They were not to be denied. They were in love and this day would carry them through the rest of their lives.

36

. . . .

WHEN SUPPER WAS READY AT the Jordan house Chris asked the girls if they would wake Tom.

As Alex walked up from the basement she saw the girls running through the hallway in the direction of the bedroom. "Where are they off to "she asked.

"I sent them to wake up Tom," said Chris.

"With her eyes opening up quite widely Alex screamed, "Wait, girls. Wait for me."

Looking back at Chris with a mischievous grin, Alex said, "I left him naked on the sheets."

"Wait for Grandma, girls!" Chris added.

Soon the whole family was at the bedroom door. Alex cracked it open and nodded that the coast was clear, and the girls were launched on top of him.

"Wake up, wake up!" they screamed as Rocky let out a few barks of his own. Soon Tom rolled over in bed and looking up at them just stared blankly into space.

"Is it morning already?" he asked as he grabbed the girls and Rocky in one large swoop pulling them all down on the bed.

"Give Corrie a kiss, Rock!" he said, and of course Rocky obeyed and lay a long pink tongue on the front of Corrie's face nearly lifting her off the bed.

"Oh yuck!" exclaimed Corrie. "I'm gonna puke."

To add insult to injury he then grabbed Carrie and said, "Get her, Rock!" But Carrie got loose, let out a harrowing scream, and headed down the hall with Rocky in hot pursuit.

Grinning from ear to ear claiming victory with the ruckus he had just caused, Tom looked up at Alex and Chris and said, "Pardon me, ladies, but you are in a naked man's bedroom. May I have some privacy, please?"

"You are so grounded," Chris said. "You know we had them pretty quiet for a little bit. You can take care of the after supper activities just for that."

After Chris walked out to rescue the girls from the dog, Alex looked at him and said, "Was that a good pre-nap or what?"

"You're the best, Alex," he said.

Looking at him most admirably, Alex said, "Come on, you big dummy, supper is ready."

After Tom collected himself and got dressed, he walked down the hall into the dining room and saw everyone already seated at the table waiting for him. Corrie still had the washcloth washing off her face. As he approached the table he saw Rocky on the living room floor and asked, "Isn't Rocky joining us for dinner tonight, ladies?'

"No!" said Corrie. "I'm gonna puke if he does."

Attempting to instigate anything he could, he bent down and put his arm around Corrie and at the same time motioned for Rocky to come over to the table. He looked at Corrie and said, "You don't want to hurt his feelings, do you? He's sensitive, you know. Here look at him; he's crying. Give her a kiss, Rock."

And before Corrie knew what was happening she got another pink tongue kiss from Rocky and the whole thing started all over again. At least now Corrie had her washcloth at the ready.

After everyone settled down and Tom was lectured from Carrie on the unhealthy conditions of a dog kissing someone after he cleans his bottom, it was time for the prayer.

Again Tom looked at Chris; winked, cleared his throat and began the prayer. Alex was proud of Tom's reverence for the reverence during the prayer. but it was short lived. After he was done he said, "And please, Lord, show Carrie and Corrie the love Rocky has for them, and thank-you for allowing us to share the day together. Amen. Anybody else need a kiss before Rocky starts eating?"

"Oh yuck! I'm gonna puke!" said Carrie and Corrie simultaneously.

"All right, girls, settle down," said Chris. "Mom, do you have a yardstick we can use on Tom; he is quite unruly after his nap. Where does he get such energy?"

"I have no idea," Alex replied clearing her throat.

"Did the girls tell you all the fun we had today?" he asked after the dinner meal had settled down.

"Yes, the girls told us they had quite a day with you," returned Chris.

"Who is the pilot at the gate with the big nose?" asked Alex.

"Bob Pearson," answered Tom. "He tried to get the gate guard to arrest Carrie because she looked like a terrorist. He had that new security guard looking under the car and everything. That Bob shows up in the darndest places."

"He sure had a big nose," remarked Carrie to everybody's humor.

"Where is he from?" asked Chris.

"Winnipeg," said Tom. "He flies for Air Canada."

"Speaking of Canada," said Chris. "We'd like to talk to you about a boat trip."

"You can't get there from here," answered Tom.

"Mom and I have come up with some wonderful vacation plans for a trip up the coast," returned Chris.

"You're talking about all of us, right?" asked Tom.

"Yes," she said. "Can we do that?"

"Of course," replied Tom. "We have ample room and we can carry enough supplies for two weeks before we have to dock and re-supply. Of course, Rocky will want to share his room with Carrie. Those two have a thing going, I think."

"Oh yuck!" said Carrie. "Rocky likes Corrie, not me."

"We were thinking about stopping at different ports and just looking around and leaving again; is that difficult?" asked Chris.

"No, not really," he answered. "What coast are you thinking about?"

"The West Coast," answered Chris.

"That's a nice trip," said Tom, "especially if we can get a good gulf wind. Will the girls be all right with the restricted space for that amount of time?"

"Well, that I'm not sure about right now," she said.

"Did you ask them?" he asked. "They seemed to be comfortable on it yesterday when they were aboard. I wonder if they'll get seasick. It would be nice if we could do a couple of day trips with them, but you're right, there isn't time."

Before long the supper dishes were set aside and charts and maps and supply checklists were spread over the table. The self-proclaimed masters of the sea were busy charting a course to ports of call spread out over the Gulf Coast. The girls had gone into the living room to watch a children's movie, and Rocky took up his spot on the floor for an after dinner nap. All was well on the night before Tom was to take his trip to Paris, deadhead back to Houston, and do another trip to Paris for Drummond. He would then pick up his trip home a day later and would begin his three-week vacation. It was agreed upon by most that it was a well-deserved vacation. If all worked out as well as these things usually did, they would be on the ocean in a matter of five days. Tom couldn't wait and became excited the more planning the three of them did,

37

. . . .

AS THE THREE ADULTS CONTINUED to make plans and put the necessary supplies on an order list, Bob Dobbs and Lauren rtom were making preparations for leaving the hotel and going home.

As they walked down the corridor to the exit, a completely different individual who nodded courteously and went on, greeted them.

"I was curious," said Bob. "How did you know that other man's name was Al?"

"I have all my affairs here," said Lauren.

"I can see you're not going to make this easy on me, are you?" said Dobbs.

"If I were easy," she said, "I wouldn't be worth it."

"How could you not be worth it?" he asked. "And exactly what is 'it'?"

"'It', my dear rough edged lover" answered Lauren. "Is what keeps you and me craving each other's touch for the remainder of our days. 'It' is what brings you home to my bed at night instead of going over to Melvin Purvis's' private cabin for Wednesday night poker. 'It' is what makes up the pieces of the puzzle to the picture of our life together. 'It' is everything! Any questions?"

"How did you know Purvis had a private cabin?" asked Dobbs.

"I saw it on a Pretty Boy Floyd movie," answered Lauren.

"That's incredible," he said. "What else do you know?"

"I know where there's a cabin owned by a friend of mine where we can spend the entire weekend, if you can get off," said Lauren quite to the surprise of Dobbs. "We've broken the ice, so to speak. It's time we spent some serious time together talking and working out the fine print. And, of course, there is always the necessary physical contact that comes with being a new couple. I can't think of a nicer place to get better acquainted. This cabin is nestled deep in the woods and will make for an excellent weekend."

"What about your husband?" asked Dobbs.

"If he is smart, he'll use the time wisely moving his belongings somewhere else, probably over to Sandy Winters house."

"I don't like asking you about your husband," said Dobbs. "If you don't mind I'll consider him a part of this relationship that is none of my business."

"Did I tell you I had two children?" she asked.

"You didn't have to," he said. "I saw the mess they left on your living room floor."

"They will probably be with us for a couple of years if you can deal with that," returned Lauren. "They're good kids, they just need a role model which their father definitely was not."

"I'll be there for them as much as I am there for you," said Bob.

"I believe you will be, Robert," she said. "I think we're going to make you very happy. Gracey will keep you in stitches. If it weren't for her I would have joined the convent. Stevey is a little backward but he'll come around. Of course, Gracey does her best to bring him around, but she has a different concept of where he should be sexually than he does, which is how we found out about his resistance to penicillin. But that is enough information for now."

As he moved to open Lauren's car door he thought he had heard it all, but it seemed he was in for an experience of a lifetime. He also felt it would take a lifetime to experience all of it, and that he felt good about. He closed the door after she sat down and soon they were on their way back to the laboratory parking lot.

Shortly before entering it, Lauren asked Dobbs, "What is the penalty for putting acid in you husband's after-shave?"

"No one will ever know, my dear," he promised. "Please don't put any in mine. I've been good."

"What is your next step?" asked Lauren.

"Tomorrow we will arrest Sam Winters for violation of the Homeland Security Act. That in turn will probably lead to the arrest of Sandy Winters for the murder of her husband. After that I will be ready for a weekend in the woods with my sweetheart. We FBI guys do this stuff all the time, you understand; usually before breakfast."

"You call me when you're done with all this stuff and I'll fix you breakfast," remarked Lauren.

"I might have a big appetite," commented Dobbs.

"I've got a big kitchen," she said. "Bring your pillow."

When they pulled into the parking lot, Lauren looked at him and said, "I had a wonderful day, Robert. Thank you. I can't begin to tell you what you have done for me today. I just hope in time I can show you my gratitude."

"I think the feelings are mutual," remarked Bob." I'll never forget today and I'll never forget you. I hope you and I can always show each other how grateful we are for each other. That would be a life worth living. One for each other."

A tear began to form in her eye, but Dobbs wiped it away and held her tightly for a moment.

"No tears!" he said. "Not for us."

"That was also from a Steve McQueen movie, Robert," chided Lauren. "I'll tell you what. This weekend, between sessions, we will watch some Steve McQueen movies so you quit stealing his lines."

"Whatever you say, dear," answered Bob.

"Call me after you bust those bad guys, okay?" Lauren said as she was leaving. "And be careful!"

With a wave they both went their own ways. Lauren went home to settle up with Ashland, and Bob went back to the office to settle up with Sam Winters before he had the chance to hurt someone else.

Agent Dobbs had always done his job without the slightest emotional involvement until today. When he saw how emotional she became on meeting Captain Jordan and his two grandchildren he had finally put faces on what he was investigating. He had never done that before. He actually felt sorry for Captain Jordan, even though his courage, skill, and knack for survival impressed him greatly. He was also angry at Sam Winters, who thought nothing at all of killing a great number of people just because he had a bone to pick with his sister-in-law. Dobbs would not allow emotional issues to cloud his judgment in this case. He would stay focused, sharp, on the edge, exactly where he had to be. This was the attitude that would bring him home to Lauren every night. It worked for his grandfather throughout his career, and it would work for him as well.

38

. . . .

TOM, ALEX AND CHRIS FINISHED the planning for their trip and decided it was about time to get to bed. Tom helped put the girls to bed and let Rocky out for his evening relief on the beach.

Saying good night to each other, the three adults went to bed. Alex, however, was still in the bathroom when Tom turned out all the lights, and as he went to the bedroom, he heard a whispering voice coming from the master bathroom. When he looked back around he saw her grinning from ear to ear with her head sticking out of the bathroom.

"Come here, I've something to show you," she said.

He turned around and as he arrived at the bathroom door, she reached up and pulled him in and closed the door.

"What do you think of this outfit?" Alex said.

"That's nice," he said. "I like it. Does it come off?"

"Well, of course, it comes off," she said. "But in due time. You're supposed to marvel in the beauty of the model. Didn't they teach you that in high school? So tell me, what do you think of it?"

"It's absolutely beautiful, Alex," replied Tom. "It only compliments your own beauty, my dear. And it can not be improved upon."

"Those afternoon pre-nap activities must be doing you some good, Thomas," she said. "You've never said those kinds of things to me before."

"Grab your bathrobe," said Tom. "We'll go out on the beach. I'll grab some wine and a blanket."

"Thomas, are you suggesting I go out in the sand in my new outfit?" asked Alex.

"Absolutely!" he said. "Trust me. You'll be fine."

She made her way into the bedroom to retrieve her bathrobe and out to the beach they went hand in hand to their favorite spot.

Tom put the wine and glasses down and spread the blanket out.

"There!" he said to Alex, "All the comforts of the Ritz Carlton. What do you think?"

"I like it," she answered. "Do those come off?" she asked him pointing to his swimming trunks.

"All in due time, my dear," said Tom. "All in due time."

Grabbing the wine and the glasses he sat down on the blanket and then helped Alex to her seat on the sand. Taking the cap off the bottle he poured her a glass of her favorite burgundy, and pouring one for himself laid down next to her and rested himself on his elbow.

"All right, beautiful," he said. "Whisper sweet nothings in my ear so I can show you my stuff."

"Well, you kind of put the kink in my plans here, Thomas," she said. "I was going to seduce you and attempt to talk you into something that would be good for me, but not necessarily good for you."

"Oh really!" said Tom. "What kind of shrewd scheme are you contemplating that would warrant that kind of a reward in advance?"

"Well, first you have to promise not to be mad about this," she said. "We kind of pulled it out of Corrie."

"Oh, you're talking about our visit with Drummond and his horny little secretary," divined Tom.

"Well, no, Thomas," she said amazed. "I was talking about the job offer he gave you. You'll have time to talk your way out of that secretary later."

"I didn't think Corrie knew what we were talking about," he answered.

"What exactly were you talking about?" asked Alex with a conniving tone.

"Oh, nothing," answered Tom.

"Don't you give me nothing, young man!" she demanded as he began to laugh. "This is serious business. Come on, Thomas, out with it."

"Old man Drummond offered me the chief pilot's job," relinquished Tom.

"Why?" said Alex. "Is he quitting?"

"Sounds like it," he said.

"Well what did you tell him?" she asked.

"Aren't you supposed to be seducing me right about now in an attempt to pull information out of me?" he asked.

"Thomas, I'm going to beat it out of you in a minute," reprimanded Alex.

"See! There you go!" chided Tom. "Always getting excited. I told him no."

"What?" she asked excitedly. "Why did you do that?"

"I don't want to stop flying," he reasoned. "Just because he offered me the chief pilot's job doesn't mean I'm going to stop doing what I love just to fly a desk. That's not for me."

"Would you do it for me?" asked Alex.

"That's not even fair, dear," answered Tom a little put out. "You know better than that."

"I'm sorry, I'm sorry!" she said. "I didn't mean that. It just slipped out. I'm just worried about you. You're not sleeping well. You talk in your sleep and I think you need a rest. You say things that make no sense at all. I think that's exhaustion and I think you need a rest. I love you and I'm worried about you is all. That desk never reaches any dangerous altitude. You and I could spend more time together if you were home every night."

"How do you know you will always be home nights when you return to flying?" asked Tom.

"I don't, honey," she said. "Don't be mad. But, if you're not flying, with my seniority I'll just have those short commuter trips no one else wants. And you know those are always home at night."

"How did we get on this subject?" he asked. "I thought you brought me out here to jump my bones."

"Well I did bring you here for that," said Alex. "But I thought we'd talk a little first."

Tom tried desperately to calm down and not feel like he was being manipulated. He lay flat on the sand and said, "I told him I'd think about it while I was on vacation, but I'm not too keen about the idea. What made you bring this up besides my dreams at night?"

"What dreams?" she said. "What are you dreaming about?"

"Well I just assume I'm dreaming," weaseled Tom. "You said I was talking in my sleep, I assume you have to be dreaming to do that."

"Is there something you're not telling me, young man?" grilled Alex. "You know how well schooled I am in dreams."

"No," he said, exasperatedly. "I'm just making conversation. I did dream Marilyn Monroe asked me if I wanted to see her white dress blow up over that grate last night, however."

"What did you say?" Alex asked.

"The alarm rang and I never got to finish the dream," he answered.

"Good answer!" said Alex. "May I have some more wine, please?"

"Certainly," he said while he poured the wine hoping the subject would change.

"We're not finished talking, are we?" she asked after he lay back down on the sand.

"If we change the subject," he answered.

"I'm just worried about you, Tom," said Alex. "I love you and I can worry about you if I choose to. You know the fire was number two for you."

"Number two?" he asked as if he didn't know what she was talking about.

"Yes! And you know darn well what I mean. Three times is a charm. That's not a good thing, you know."

"I thought it was nine," answered Tom as he yawned."

"That's lives, you big dummy," corrected Alex.

"Can't we just lie here in peace and quiet and you whisper sexy things in my ear and I'll grunt once in a while like they do on Roseanne?" he asked.

"No!" she said as she rolled over atop of him. "Not this time."

"Well I can see we're going to get a lot talked about like this," returned Tom.

"It's the only way I can keep your mind on the task at hand," she said as she maneuvered until Tom entered her. "That's better. Now then, where were we?"

"You were using sex to get what you want," he replied with a strain in his voice.

"There are certain tools that the good Lord gave us women to help get our point across," she said. "This is just one of them."

"You mean you have more of them than just this one?" .

"My techniques are endless, Tommy, my boy. Endless!" answered Alex.

With a quick overpowering move, he repositioned himself on top of her and said, "This is a better technique. Okay, go ahead I'm listening."

"Thomas, this is cheating," she said. "We weren't finished talking. You haven't heard the end of this, young man."

"We'll talk later, okay honey?" said Tom. "Let's take care of this discussion first, shall we?"

She just moaned a satisfactory response, the subject matter had changed and neither was complaining.

He had formed an addiction to making love with her on the beach. Alex shared the same passionate desires he did. They both were connected not only physically, but passionately and with an inner strength that told them both they were safe and secure in their own little world. It was a world where no one else even dared to enter or to interrupt. It was a world they both had formed with one another only a short time ago, and it grew stronger every day. It was nearly every day they reinforced their bond together so they only got better at it as they went on.

The two of them lay together on the beach as an occasional cool gulf breeze blew a little wet mist over them bringing them back to their senses from the romantic stupor they were in.

"That was nice," said Alex.

"It still is. Just be still and listen to the ocean."

"I'm freezing," she replied. "Take me in where it's warm."

He relinquished his favorite spot, position and activity on the beach to take Alex in the house where it was a little warmer. Once inside they began putting away the wine and cleaning up the glasses when Alex said to him with a grin, "You're pretty proud of yourself, aren't you? Seducing me in the sand where I can't get away. You know my butt gets imbedded in the sand, and you think I'm your little sex slave because I'm trapped there, don't you?"

He just looked at Alex smiling and said, "I love it when you talk dirty to me."

"We're not finished talking about this, young man," she continued. "As soon as we get back to bed I'm going to continue my argument."

"Go ahead," he said.

"No," returned Alex. "You're a typical man. You listen better flat on your back."

"Oh, that's nice," returned Tom. "I would have never said that to you. That was cold. After all we were to each other not even twenty minutes ago and this is how you act."

As soon as the glasses were cleaned the two of them went back to bed, and Alex started on him almost instantly when she said, "Lie down here and listen to me."

Being a normal man, he had to take this as an invitation for more bedroom bliss but was quickly calmed by Alex who laid her head on his shoulder and began talking to him about his accepting the job offer from Drummond.

They talked for a few more minutes when even she was too tired to keep up the discussion. About five minutes later they both fell fast asleep.

He was sleeping reasonably well, doing very little tossing and turning when he turned to his right side and tucked his pillow under his left arm. He found himself standing with Father Harris a level above everyone else and behind them as several people had gathered on the beach for what appeared to be some sort of ceremony. They seemed to be looking through a golden meshed curtain as the view was shrouded in a twilight glow. That glow was cast against a sea of blue that had no motion. The seagulls even stood by motionless.

"What are they doing?" asked Tom.

"They're saying goodbye," answered Father Harris.

"To whom?" he asked. "Saying goodbye to whom?"

"To you!" Father Harris said.

"I'm not gone," he remarked.. "I'm right here. Can't they see me?"

"No," said the priest. "You're not really here. You've gone somewhere else, but you will be back. You'll be gone for a short time and then you'll be home again with them when the Father is finished with you."

"Where did I go?" asked Tom.

"You went with the other priest. Remember what we talked about?" answered Father Harris.

"Am I there now?" he asked.

"Yes," said Father Harris.

"I don't see him anywhere. I don't think I'm with him. I don't think I can help him. I'm not what he thinks I am. Why can't he leave me alone?"

"Don't be reluctant to help the padre," said Father Harris. "The Father is never wrong on whom he calls for help. You will be his hero. You may be reluctant at first, but you will come around and be His hero. His reluctant hero maybe, but His hero nonetheless."

"What does he want?" asked Tom. "Why doesn't He tell me what He wants?"

"He will in time," said Father Harris. "When it is time you will know exactly what He wants, what is to be done, and how to do it. Remember the Father only calls on those He trusts to stand in for Him. You'll do just fine."

"Why are Alex and the girls crying if I'm coming back?" he asked. "They look so sad."

"They are sad now because they don't know you 're coming back," said Father Harris. "They will learn in time. They too are being called by the Father to be strong in your absence."

When Alex, Chris and the girls turned around and began to walk from the beach, Tom could see a large picture of himself and he could see the girls were crying.

"I can't bear to see them cry," he said. "I'm going down there and tell them everything will be all right."

When he tried to move forward, he found he couldn't move at all and he became frightened. Grabbing on to the priest he asked, "Why can't I move? Why can't I go to them?"

"Because you're not here," Father Harris explained. "You're with the other priest."

"What will happen to Alex and the girls?" Tom asked.

"They will be fine," said Father Harris. "I will take care of them until you come back. And besides their faith is strong. They will know the Father would not take you from them for long."

After a few moments of watching Alex, Chris, and the girls being consoled by the guests that had come to pay their respects, the two men started talking again.

"What are all those spots down there by the children?" asked Tom. "I can't make them out."

"Those are the hearts and spirits of children praying for you," explained Father Harris.

"Children?" he asked. "I don't have any children."

"Something tells me that this is all about children," said Father Harris. "A great deal of children."

As the vision of the memorial began to fade from them he and Father Harris turned and walked away. Tom turned around and Father Harris was gone. He found himself walking alone in a great abyss of blue. Becoming even more frightened he called to the priest but couldn't get an answer. He began thrashing and walking headlong into an immovable object.

Tom's thrashing and verbal utterance awoke Alex who turned over in bed and found him standing in the corner of the bedroom, shaking. He was uttering an unrecognizable jargon and moving to and fro as if he were caught in the corner.

She rose and went to him. Taking Tom by the arm she recognized that he was asleep and ever so carefully put him back in bed and covered him up. When she returned to bed she snuggled up next to him, he lifted his head and said, "I can't help the priest, I don't know what he wants. Why won't he leave me alone?" He lay his head back down on the pillow and didn't say anything else.

Putting her head down next to his, she thought to herself, may God give that man some peace, and she too fell fast asleep and began to dream. She walked out on the tarmac with Tom a short distance and thought how strange it was to do that. She had always waved good bye to him from the gate inside the terminal. There was even something more strange about this good-bye. As she waved to him she noticed that his trousers were very faded, even to the point of being bleached. He didn't have his uniform jacket on either. His tie was missing and so was his shirt. He had no shoes on and was dressed only in his T-shirt, which hung on him like a tent. His hair was plastered to his head and his face was without color. His eyes were sunken in and his skin was wrinkled and pruned. He walked weakly toward the cockpit in a bent over appearance. He resembled a dead man who had washed up on the beach from an ocean fishing accident.

He waved his hand in a gesture of good-bye and said weakly, "I'll be back soon. There is something I must do first. Remember I will always love you." And with that he was out of sight.

She stood there and tried to make sense of all that she had just seen when the bell tone that was ringing in her head woke her up Twisting quickly to see if Tom was actually alive she noticed he was gone. She could smell breakfast being cooked and the sound of his kidding the girls about kissing Rocky good morning, and just that quick she knew all was well. The dream had unnerved her and she tried desperately to regain her composure before going into the kitchen. She wiped away the tears brought on by the thought of Tom looking like that and the words he spoke to her both in bed and in her dream. She collected herself and made her way to the kitchen.

"Good morning, beautiful!" he said all excited. "Rocky, give Mom a kiss."

"Don't even think about it, furball!" exclaimed Alex as she reached down and ruffled Rocky's fur. "You, on the other hand, get over here."

After exchanging a kiss with him and covering a yawn, she asked, "How did you sleep?"

"Fine," he replied. "Weird dreams though. Carrie and Corrie were going to school and they both kissed Rocky goodbye."

"Oh, yuck!" said Corrie.

"Was that all?" asked Alex.

"Yeah, they wouldn't kiss anyone else" he said as he tickled Chris in the ribs and sent her squirming around him. "Just ol' furball."

"I meant the dream, dummy," returned Alex.

"That wasn't very nice," he said while hugging the girls. "I have feelings, you know."

"I'm sorry, Tom," she apologized. "But sometimes I can get more information out of Rocky than I can out of you."

"Something blue," said Tom. "Looking for someone in a blue room. It must be your cooking, honey."

"I think it's the job and that's what I wanted to talk to you about last night but you kept ducking away from me," she said.

"I wouldn't exactly call it ducking away from you," returned Tom. "Chris, let me tell you what she calls ducking away."

"Never mind, Thomas!" she said a little embarrassed.

"Why, Mother," said Chris knowing exactly what he was referring to. "Shame on you."

"Don't you hate that when it happens?" asked Chris.

"Oh no!" answered Tom. "As a matter of fact…"

"Enough, Thomas!" Alex said loudly as she swatted him on the butt with a serving spoon.

"Actually I'm not dodging the issue," he explained as they sat down to breakfast. "I just feel that any desk job when you're a pilot is a step toward grabbing the towel and throwing it in the ring. And I'm just not ready to do that yet. I've got many air miles to fly before I hang up my wings."

"I only asked you to think about it," replied Alex a little strongly. "I didn't say anything about hanging up your wings."

"Don't get upset, honey," he said when he realized there was more to this than met the eye and she was getting upset. "I'll think about it all this week until our vacation. I promise. I'm just messing with you."

"Can we talk about this before you leave today?" asked Alex as she fought back a tear.

Tom became very serious for a change and looking at her said, "Let's go talk right now. Would you guys excuse us for a moment?"

And with that, he took Alex by the hand with a suspect look. As the two of them walked into the living room they were joined by Rocky who felt he should be in on this family conversation. Once in the living room they sat down and Alex began once again about how she thought this was an excellent chance for him, and that she was upset because he was taking such a lackadaisical approach to something she thought was important. As he listened to her, it became very apparent that there was much more on her mind than this job offer. Finally he interrupted her and took her by the hand to break her concentration.

"Alex!" said Tom. "Calm down. What is going on here? This isn't like you to carry on like this. What's the matter, honey?"

She took a deep breath and said to him, "Don't sugar coat this so I feel better. You and I don't ever lie to each other, remember? What did you dream about last night?"

"Something about the beach," answered Tom. "Nothing big really."

"You were on the beach with the priest, weren't you?" asked Alex.

"Yes, there may have been a priest there," he said. "Father Harris, I think. Why, honey?"

"You dreamed about your funeral, didn't you?" she asked in a matter of fact tone which demanded he come clean on the subject.

After looking into Alex's eyes for a few minutes and remembering the promise the two of them made to each other, he had to tell the truth. He simply looked at her and shook his head affirmatively.

She rose from the love seat and closed the French doors, which led out into the kitchen. With the look in her eye he could feel there was definitely something wrong here, and he was about to be grilled.

"How long has this been going on?" asked Alex.

"All of the dreams or just the ones with the priest?" Tom asked as he rose from the love seat and walked over to the fireplace.

She took a moment to think and then said, "All the ones that deal with the priest, the missiles, or your funeral."

"About two months," he answered. "How did you know about the missiles?"

"When were you going to tell me about them?" asked Alex firmly.

"I wasn't," Tom replied. "I don't do that."

She was getting angry. She tried to keep her emotions in check, but she began to cry. He walked over to console her but she put her hands up and said, "Don't touch me."

He stopped in his tracks as she moved back to the love seat and sat down.

Putting her head in her hands she said, "I saw you dead last night. You were getting into the cockpit of some damned airplane, and you were dead. And now you have the balls to tell me you don't do that!"

"It was just a dream, Alex," Tom responded.

"For two months you have tossed and turned in your sleep, stood in the corner of the bedroom until I put you back to bed, talked to me in your sleep and all you can say is that it was just a dream! "She was beginning to holler when she remembered the girls in the next room. "What in the hell were you thinking? Did you think about getting help?"

"We talked about this kind of help once before," replied Tom. "I told you what I thought of it, what the policy, is and that I could handle it by myself."

"I don't call last night handling it!" said Alex in a louder tone than before.

"Just because you dreamed of my dying isn't my fault," he said.

"I'm not talking about my dream, dummy!" hollered Alex. "I'm talking about yours."

"Oh really!" said Tom, by now quite perturbed about being called a dummy." Let me get this straight. You presume to know all about my dreams and you think I can't handle them so, therefore, I'm a dummy. I think this conversation has ended."

At this point he began to leave the living room. As he did Chris came in and said, "I'm sorry to say this, it's none of my business, but we can hear you in the kitchen and I'm kind of concerned about the girls."

Tom walked past Alex to leave the room, and when he did he said to Chris, "I'm sorry. I'll talk to the girls." Opening the door he motioned to Rocky and they both exited..

"Did you ladies save me some breakfast?" he said as he sat back down with no intention of eating.

He looked over at Carrie and Corrie and said, "Don't worry about me and Grandma. We just had to talk about some things and sometimes grown ups get kind of loud. We don't mean to, but grown ups hate to admit when they're wrong and Grandma and I are both wrong. We still love each other and we love you guys very much. I'm sorry about that, we'll try not to do that again. Come on, give us a kiss."

After Tom smoothed it over with the kids, he poured himself another cup of coffee and looked desperately for a place to hide. He walked into the bathroom, sat on the commode seat and shut the door locking it from inside.

Chris shut the door behind him and stood in the living room with Alex and never said a word. Alex walked over to the window and stared out into the nothingness of the morning traffic going by.

She wiped her eyes and turned to Chris. "We made love three times yesterday. Three times, and today I just want to slap some sense in him and it isn't even his fault. It's just a dream but I got so angry with him over a dream I had. I don't know what my problem is, but since last night I'm afraid. And when I'm afraid I get angry. Something isn't right with him and he has no idea, but I can feel it."

"What happened last night, Mother?" asked Chris.

"I dreamed he was dead. He was getting on an airplane and he was dead. He looked right at me and said he'd be back soon, that there was something he had to do first. It was horrible. It was so real!"

"I think it would be good if you cleared this up before he left today,." said Chris.

"I don't think he'll let me within fifty feet of him anymore today," answered Alex. "I think I kind of blew the healing negotiations for now."

"Take him to the airport and don't take no for an answer," advised Chris.

"That's a good idea," said Alex. "You're a lifesaver. Thank you! Hang on before you open the door. Let me straighten myself up first and then I'll go talk to the girls."

After she made herself a little more presentable so the girls didn't see that she was crying she motioned to Chris to open the door and out to the kitchen they went.

When the two ladies went in, Corrie looked up sadly and said, "Tom is in the bathroom. He feels really, really bad."

"I know, honey, "said Alex. "Grandma is very sorry about that and is going to apologize to Tom, but first I wanted to talk to you girls. Please don't think that it is your fault that Grandma is mad. It's no one's fault, I just don't feel very good this morning. I'm very sorry. You know Tom and I love you guys very much and I'm very sorry about all of this."

After a brief moment the girls just looked at Alex who said, "You say he is in the bathroom?"

"Yes ma'am," said Corrie. "I think he was crying."

Carrie didn't say anything. She just sat with her head down and looked into her plate. Knowing that Carrie was around the fights that Chris and her husband had over his drinking Chris made a special stop and held Carrie for a moment until she was sure she was okay.

She looked up at Alex and said, "She'll be all right, she just deals with this a little differently."

When she said that, Alex also went over and hugged Carrie again and apologized to both girls. After that she motioned to Rocky and said quite strategically, "Come on, Rock, I'll bet you have to pee." With that she and Rocky walked out to the back yard away from the view of anyone inside.

Alex sat on a wrought iron bench that she and Tom had bought on a weekend getaway a few months ago and put under a shade tree. Rocky came up alongside her and while patting him on the shoulder, she said, "You know Tom better than any of us, Rocky. What is going on with him?"

Rocky leaned his head up against her and just sighed.

"Yeah, me either," she said as her eyes started to tear up again.

39

. . . .

ASHLAND HORTON HAD COLLECTED A pile of papers and was ready to head out the door to the office when the telephone rang. Standing by the phone he picked it up only to find Sandy Winters on the other end.

"Ashland," she said. "I need you to get over here right away. That crazy brother- in- law called and said if I don't turn over my ex-husband's holdings on the company he is turning you in to the FBI."

"What did you tell him?" asked Ashland.

"I told him to kiss my ass!" answered Sandy. "I'm not giving him jack shit."

Well, where is he now?" he asked

"He's on his way over here," was her response.. "I'm going to have something ready for him when he gets here."

"Don't do anything rash!" warned Ashland. "We didn't do anything to that old cranky bastard. We'll just send him on his way." "Yeah, right," returned Sandy. "Feet first. Hurry, baby."

Grabbing his coat he ran to the defense of the girlfriend he couldn't break free from. He would once again come to her aid in the hopes that whatever he hoped to find there would miraculously find him.

Robert Dobbs had assembled his team along with a member of the NTSB Task Force. They were in route to the construction site of Sam Winters to arrest him for terrorism of Flight 409 six months ago. When Dobbs saw Sam going at a great rate of speed in the opposite direction he put out a change of direction call to all units. He figured that Sam was probably headed over to Sandy's house so he made it an all points bulletin for any units in the area. This involved the Houston City Police as well. Dobbs was advised by the police that a 911 call had been dispatched to the address Dobbs gave them regarding a woman who feared for her life from a deranged broth-in-law who was coming to get her.

"That sounds like our boy," said Dobbs. "We'll have the whole bunch of them in one spot."

Once the turn around was completed and all units were speeding to that location, another radio call barked over the speaker advising that shots had been fired at that address.

With that announcement Dobbs decided to call Ashland Horton and make sure he wasn't part of this private shootout. Upon dialing the phone, having known the number by memory, he got Lauren on the other end.

"Good morning, beautiful," said Dobbs. "What a pleasant surprise! Hey, Lauren is Ashland home by any chance?"

"No, Robert," said Lauren. "He got a phone call and left here like his pants were on fire. Why?"

"There are problems over at Sandy Winters' house and I didn't want him in harm's way," replied Dobbs.

"If he got in harm's way maybe he might wake up, Bob," said Lauren. "Is that possible, do you think?"

"I'm afraid this time he may get himself killed," returned Bob. "We have a report of shots fired. Okay, honey, I have to get back to work. I love you. I'll talk to you later and fill you in on the dirt."

With that he hung up his cell phone and was turning onto the street to Sandy's house when the dispatcher reported more shots fired. The report said there was a shooter in the house and one in the front yard. This is getting interesting, Dobbs thought to himself. If they all kill themselves it will save me a lot of paperwork. That wasn't very nice, we have to remember Lauren's husband may be out here as well.

As his units rounded the curve from the north the police were approaching from the south. They all swarmed the place at once subduing Sam who was hiding behind his car with a gun in his hand and the barrel smoking and his assistant lying wounded beside him.

The other units surrounded the house only to hear Sandy screaming at the top of her lungs and still firing aimlessly in the direction of Sam's car.

His assistant, who Dobbs suspected of planting the devise on Flight 409, was lying on the ground with a serious gunshot wound to the abdomen.

Eventually Sandy ran out of ammunition and the police broke down the door to find Ashland hiding behind a chair in the corner. Although Dobbs found this to be comical, he was also glad he wasn't shot. He could call Lauren and tell her that she only needed to bring Ashland a clean pair of pants. At least he wasn't dumb enough to get himself shot for Sandy Winters.

Sandy was arrested for trying to kill Sam. Sam was arrested for trying to kill Sandy and for terrorism, and his assistant was arrested for both and drug trafficking. Once the assistant was drugged up for the pain, the police figured out who he was. Dobbs also charged him with violating the RICO Act. All in all it was a good day for law enforcement. Ashland was the only one who wasn't carried out or transported in shackles. However, with his accident he was allowed to use the bathroom to freshen up a bit.

Dobbs had two phone calls to make, one to Lauren who was still on her way to work, and the other to Captain Tom Jordan.

40

U PON LEARNING THAT ALEX HAD walked outside with Rocky, Tom took the opportunity to leave the protection of the bathroom and retreated to the bedroom to get dressed for work.

She was still sitting outside with Rocky when the telephone rang. This prompted her to head back in the house with Rocky who was only too happy to return to the air conditioning. Chris answered the phone and called for Tom. He came down the hallway to answer the call as Alex was coming into the kitchen. Their eyes met, not with the usual affection but with a glance that suggested distances between them..

He answered the phone with his usual greeting. "Yes?"

"Captain Jordan," said Dobbs. "This is Agent Dobbs. How are you today, sir?"

"Good, Agent Dobbs, thank you," said Tom. "How are you today, sir?"

"Well after this morning, I am very well, Captain," returned Dobbs.

The conversation went on as he explained to Tom how Sam Winters was apprehended and Sandy Winters was also arrested and charged with the murder of her husband. Dobbs went on to explain that it was Sam Winters and his partner who set the wheels in motion for the destruction of flight 409. Tom was asked to advise Alex that the two of them would be subpoenaed when the court case was put together. He thanked Tom for all the cooperation he had given during his investigation. He reiterated that he couldn't have done it without his help. They wished each other a good day and Tom hung up the phone and headed back to the bedroom hoping to get away before he had another confrontation with Alex.

As he turned around Alex stopped his retreat short when she asked, "Tom, do you have a minute?"

He stopped in the middle of his gait and turning his head slightly said, "That was the FBI. They caught the people who burned up our airplane. Kind of ironic, isn't it, Alex?" And with that he continued down the hall.. Alex, a little frustrated by his just walking away from her, immediately took the offensive.

"Thomas Jordan!" she said in a raised voice. "Don't you dare walk away from me!"

He stopped at that point and for the first time since he met her, he was angry with her. He felt very insulted that she would talk to him like that in his own house and in front of Chris and the children. Sadness came over him and settled in the pit of his stomach. His inner soul told him to walk away because the girls were still in the next room. Collecting himself quickly he merely continued down the hall and never said a word.

She was still in a mood to demand an answer and she started to walk after him, but Chris interrupted her saying, "Mom, you're out of line."

Alex turned and looked at Chris as if to scold her, but Chris stood firm and fixed her eyes on her. Alex turned completely around and said, "I know, but I can't let it end like this."

"That's exactly what you're going to do," said Chris calmly and quietly. "You're wrong, Mother. Tom doesn't deserve to be treated like this by someone who loves him. Let it go for now. Take him to the airport and talk then-- please, calm down."

Alex settled down a bit and she and Chris hugged in the middle of the kitchen.

"I did get the last word in though, didn't I?" remarked Alex as she wiped away her tears with a laugh. "That's more than I ever got from your father."

"Tom isn't dad," said Chris. "You owe him more than the last word."

"How can you love someone so much one minute and want to hurt him so bad the next?"

"I hear that happens a lot these days," answered Chris. "But you and Tom are old enough to know better."

"It was his fault, you know," said Alex.

"How do you figure that?" asked Chris.

"The woman is always right," she answered,

Tom had finished getting dressed and was sitting on a chair when there was a light knock on his door. Knowing it wouldn't be Alex by the tone of the knock, he went to the door and opening it a crack found Corrie. He opened the door and Corrie entered the room. He left the door ajar, as they sat down on the chair together and began to talk. Corrie was openly upset because of the argument. As the two of them continued to talk the conversation went from the argument to the boat trip they were planning and what would be the girls' part in all of this. He explained to Corrie how the only thing they should not do is wander off to the sides of the boat for fear of being washed overboard.

Corrie looked intently at Tom and hung on every word he said. It became apparent to him that he had made a new friend., one who would always be there for him and, he knew, it would be his pleasure to be there for her.

When Alex and Chris were finished talking Chris noticed that Corrie was not with Carrie watching morning television. Both ladies heard someone talking down the hall and surmised it was Tom and Corrie. Eventually Chris tapped on the door and interrupted them saying, "Corrie, why don't we finish the dishes and let Tom finish getting dressed?"

Corrie surprised her mother when she said, "No, thanks, Mom. I think I'll stay with Tom awhile longer."

Chris held the door open until finally he interjected saying; "We're talking right now. We'll be out in a minute."

With that Chris closed the door and returned to the kitchen reporting to Alex that the two of them were in the bedroom just talking like two old friends.

"It's kind of neat to see, really," said Chris. "No, Mother, you can not look."

Tom and Corrie continued their discussion until it was time for him to head for the airport. Getting his jacket out of the closet, Corrie asked, "Are you still mad at Grandma?"

"Oh no, honey," said Tom. "I was never mad at Grandma. We just got a little loud is all; you need not worry about it. I still love her."

"I love you, Tom," said Corrie with a serious look.

Yom got a little sentimental because no child ever told him that before. Taking Corrie up in his arms he said, "I love you, too. Give us a kiss."

Corrie hugged Tom and said, "If you need to we can talk more when you get home."

"That would be nice," replied Tom.

He put Corrie down and they left the bedroom as Corrie scurried down the hall to the living room to watch a movie with Carrie.

When he walked into the kitchen he saw Alex and Chris sitting at the kitchen table. Although he desperately hoped to get out of the house without being noticed he realized that was not going to happen. Alex had the car keys in her hand before he walked over to the pegboard to get them. Although he was reluctant to make conversation he found himself lost when Alex stood up. He said the first thing that came to mind so as not be rude and snobbish.

"Are you two going shopping again?"

"No," said Alex. "I'm going to take you to the airport."

"Why?" he asked. "I don't need a ride."

Expecting that he would react in this way she said very calmly, "I'd like to be alone with you for awhile so I can clear this up."

"Clear what up?" said Tom..

She didn't answer him but just remained standing .She held onto the keys even though Tom held out his hand for them.

Both were in a no budge situation and Tom could not compete with her for getting his own way. He lowered his hand and said, "Can't we do this some other time?"

"No!" replied Alex as she pushed her chair under the table. "We're not saying good-bye like this."

"I have to make a phone call first then, if you don't mind," he said. "It won't take but a moment."

Turning away from her, Tom walked past the kitchen phone and went into his study off the living room to call Father Harris. He had promised his friend he would keep him abreast of any new developments in the dream department. He dialed the number, but Father Harris was out of the office. He left a brief voice mail explaining his dream about his own memorial service in his back yard. He ended the recording by asking the priest that if something went wrong would he help Alex with all the particulars. Then Tom was a little more relaxed about the next few days and what they held for him. He was confident that if he could get back safe before vacation all would be fine. This nightmare in his life would be over. But as he hung up the phone he had a strange feeling that this wasn't over and he wasn't that confident he would make it for vacation this year. He was, however, feeling better about Alex and the girls having Father Harris looking out for them if he ran into harm's way.

He walked into the living room and kissed the girls goodbye. He then joined Alex and Chris in the kitchen expecting a nagging in stereo.

"You have a good trip and you remember to call us," said Chris giving him a hug. "Remember we all love you very much."

"I love you guys too," said Tom as he returned the hug.

Alex had returned from saying good bye to the girls and hugging Chris goodbye, she turned to Tom and said, "Are you ready, sweetheart?"

Tom knew from experience that wasn't a good sign. Once Alex had him in the car he was dead meat and he knew it. He was going to hold his own this time. He wasn't about to take any grief because she was having bad dreams. Join the club, he thought to himself.

Tom, not to let chivalry go by the wayside because of ill feelings, opened the car door for Alex. She looked radiant this morning, just like the day Tom met her. It brought back memories of six months ago when they met at the airport on that fateful day their relationship began.

When he sat down in his seat Alex smiled and said, "We haven't had the chance to drive to work together for a long time."

He just sat and stared out the windshield. Alex turned onto Sommers Street and soon they were on their way. Tom wondered how long it would take her to begin since she didn't waste time when she had something to say. She looked over at him but didn't say anything. It may have been obvious to her by the look on his face that he wasn't up to conversation. She would have to re-evaluate her approach before she began the conversation.

She was well aware that these were the first harsh words they had ever exchanged. And she had said those cross words, not Tom. She wanted to get her point across, but she knew she had been in the wrong. Although she knew he loved her deeply, he was not easy to talk to about issues he didn't want to talk about. A little hereditary bullheadedness crossed over in his genes, she thought. She also remembered that this man had never been anything less than wonderful, and that Chris was correct when she said he didn't need to be treated like this by people who loved him.

Alex heard their song on the radio, the one that was about how Tom felt about her. The song *nobody loves me like you do,* upset her and she pulled over into the driveway of a city park and stopped the car. Tom was aware that she was upset, but he chose to say nothing. It would be best to let her talk when she was ready. She took a Kleenex out of her purse and wiped her nose. "You know what? We have some time before you leave me for work, let's take a walk."

She exited the car before he even had his seatbelt off and walked to the front where she turned her back on him. Waiting for him to catch up she walked very slowly and held out her hand for him to take. Joining hands they walked very slowly still not speaking. Finally they came to a park bench and sat down. Taking both of his hands in hers she held them very tightly and began.

"You know what?" started Alex. "I've never loved anyone, not even my husband, as much as I love you. No one has ever been as good to me and my family as you have. And I don't think I have ever been as cruel as I was to you today. And do you know what else? The word sorry isn't going to get it this time. I know I hurt you deeply and I don't know what to say. I'm scared, Tommy. I'm scared to death that this dream will come true and you will never come back to me. I do this when I'm scared, I get nasty and now I've done it to you. So if you would just get a stick and beat me like a spoiled child all will be forgiven."

Tom just sat there and didn't say a word. He was hurt, but he had already gotten over it. He could tell Alex that all was well, but that wouldn't get it either. He searched for some thing to say, but he had no words. He was actually hurt enough that he might just let her stew over this for awhile, he thought to himself. When he looked at her it was obvious that the argument he expected to continue wasn't going to happen. She was upset and mad at herself for what she had said this morning.

Tom reached inside himself and offered this explanation to Alex, "Sometimes people say things they don't mean. Sometimes they say things they know will hurt someone because they are angry and they want satisfaction. Unfortunately, once it is said it can't be taken back. This, I believe, is where you are now. And as you can see, the speaker feels worse than the one spoken to. Therefore, I always say, never speak words that you won't have any trouble eating later."

Alex looked at Tom and listened intently to what he was saying because he had never said a corrective word to her before. She wanted him to give her hell so she would feel better, but he never raised his voice. Alex felt that it would be beneath him to holler, as she had done, not so long ago. She sat anxiously as he continued to talk about the argument. He was speaking his mind and she knew she had it coming.

"We brought your family into our home," continued Tom. "Yes, our home, a place where the girls wouldn't have to listen to people fight over useless issues they will remember for years, a place for Chris to live in peace and start over. What were you thinking? Do you think I am going to cower down because there is someone else in the house? I don't cower, especially in my own house. And there are things that you must get used to. If I say, I don't do that, it means I don't do that. It means that you aren't going to convince me with a stern look or a harsh order. I am not going to adjust my values to save our relationship. It doesn't work like that. There are things that you don't do either. I accept that. I don't question those things. That is what makes the person, Alex. That is who we are. Don't try to change me, it won't work. I have been with me longer than I have been with you and I have never had any- me- problems. If you have a problem with me then it is best I hear about it now. It takes too much time to be in love with you, I don't want to take any time fighting with you. I don't do that! And you won't do that either because I won't do it with you. Did you want to speak here for a minute?" Tom said to break the mood.

She laughed slightly as she wiped away some tears.

"You're right, you know," started Alex. "I thought if I said something in front of the girls you would give me anything I asked. That was wrong of me and I am truly sorry. It got out of hand and that was my fault. I didn't mean to call you a dummy and holler at you. I just didn't get my way and I didn't know what to do. I wanted you to say you would take Drummond's offer and I could forget those dreams and not worry about you any more, but you didn't play fair. I never expected you to say no."

"I didn't say no, Alex!" he replied. "I said I would think about it and we could talk about it while on vacation and make our decision then. Do you really think I would just pass over something as important as this? Hell, I know a gift horse when it bites me on the ass."

"You did pass over it, Tommy," said Alex. "You said it's like retirement and you weren't interested. That's why I got so angry with you, because it is a gift horse and you made it sound like it was for an old pilot. And you aren't a spring chicken any more, you know."

"I'm younger than you are," said Tom.

"Oh, you didn't go there!" said Alex as she went after a stick close by. "I wish I could beat some sense in you sometime, Tommy."

"There you go again!" he said. "Not everybody has the same feelings about things that you do. But you always want to change them into your way of thinking and it doesn't work."

"You know what I meant," said Alex.

"This time I do, but not always; not this morning I didn't," returned Tom. "I thought you really went off the deep end this morning. Ranting and raving over that crazy Drummond. You can hardly stand him anyhow and two hours ago you would have nominated him for mayor. So, I don't always know what you mean. But trying to bully me isn't going to convince me you're right. Now put down that stick before you hurt yourself."

Keeping the stick she approached him and put her arms around him. They held each other quietly as if time stood still and let them return to where they had left off last night. Back on the beach in each other's grasp, locked in a passionate grip that they had both hoped would never end. But like all the other lovers in the world, time would not wait and that was made very clear when Alex realized the time.

"Can you call in sick?" she asked. "We can get us a hotel room and not come out for days. I'll have you to myself and I won't be afraid. Call Drummond and tell him to go to hell. Tell him I have PMS and have tied you up. He can have you back when I'm done with you."

"What makes you think I would want to leave you for him in the first place?" he asked quietly. "Drummond is just an old friend. All that changed when I met you. You are my life now, not him. Not this job. A pilot is what I do for a living; it's not what I am. I am whatever it takes to be your man. That's all I really want anymore. You are all I want. You are all I need. I could give this up tomorrow and we could stay here with the girls and never be apart again. We have enough money and property to take us well into our nineties. We can be married and live happily ever after and never look back."

"You would give all that up for me?" Alex asked as she patted the wings on his jacket.

"In a heartbeat!" was his reply.

"Are you sure I'm worth it?" Alex asked quite sincerely.

"Absolutely," he replied.

She wrapped her arms around Tom and held him even tighter than before. She was surprised by what he was saying to her. She knew in her heart that he loved her, but she had no idea he loved her enough to give up the part of his life that made him whole.

"I never doubted you loved me," Alex said. "It's obvious in the way you make love to me and the way you treat me. But I had no idea you felt this deeply about me. I'm just a woman, Tom, nothing more, nothing less. I'm not sure if I deserve all this."

"You let me worry about that," he said." That's why I'm the captain."

In a half crying, half- laughing voice Alex said, "I love you, Captain Tom Jordan. I promise, no more bullying."

"I love you, too, Alex Sanders," Tom returned. "Always have! Always will."

With that the two of them exchanged a very romantic kiss found usually in the back seat of a teenager's car and then returned to the car to finish their trip to the airport.

Once inside Alex looked over at him and said, "I'm going to take good care of you Thomas. I'm going to make you so happy."

He smiled softly and said, "I'm going to hold you to that, Alex, my dear. I'm going to hold you to that. I thought by now Chris would be working on you to make an honest man out of me."

"Why, Tommy, a proposal on the way to work, how romantic!" said Alex. "As a matter of fact, Chris are I are going to make some plans while you're away this trip."

"I'll just bet you are," replied Tom and just shook his head. "Don't forget to invite my family."

With that Alex turned the car back onto the freeway and they were once again on their way to the airport.

41

. . . .

AGENT DOBBS COULDN'T WAIT ANY longer to tell Lauren about his morning of fighting crime As soon as he had the criminals booked in the city jail, he headed for the telephone.

Unfortunately he ran into Ashland Horton who needed a ride back to his car. All the other police officers were already gone so Dobbs thought it his civic duty to take Lauren's husband back to his car. This also gave Dobbs an excellent opportunity to get out of the office and officially go see Lauren and explain how the bandits were caught and that they would be bothering her no longer. It's beautiful when a plan comes together, Dobbs thought to himself.

"Are you ready to go, Mister Horton?" Dobbs asked Ashland..

"Yes," returned Ashland as he beat Dobbs to the car. "Yes, indeed."

Dobbs also thought it his duty to the taxpayers to get some more information out of Ashland. So he started a conversation with Lauren's husband about his being over to Sandy Winter's house. It was really very one sided as Ashland was reluctant to give any information to the FBI. Dobbs wasn't aware of the scheme that Ashland and Sandy had put together to get an extraordinary insurance indemnity payment. Of course he didn't really care, the Houston police would take care of that later.

It wasn't long and Dobbs and Ashland were back at the scene of the crime. It was too long a ride as far as Ashland was concerned, however, because he was very uncomfortable with the third degree that Dobbs was giving him. The inquisition was over eons ago, he thought to himself. Just let me get the hell out of here before Lauren finds out.

He thanked Dobbs for the ride and wasted no time getting into his car. It was all Dobbs could do not to bust out laughing as he watched him scurry to his car and to the security of his office. Now off to see Lauren, Dobbs thought, bubbling like a child with anticipation. She's not going to believe this.

The drive to Lauren's laboratory was about ten minutes via the freeway. Dobbs had to put on his serious professional face before he got to the gate so the guard did not suspect. He was led through the corridors to Lauren's work place where she was advised that she had company.

"Who's here?" asked Lauren.

"That FBI agent who was here the other day," answered a co-worker. "Go out there and tell him off again. We're right behind you."

"You girls think I should let him have it this time, do you?" she asked.

"Show that fascist no mercy, boss!" said another girl.

Soon Agent Dobbs came into the company of all those anguished women and with a smile extended his hand to Lauren.

"Good morning, Doctor Horton, how are you today?" asked Dobbs.

"I'm very well, Agent Dobbs, thank you," replied Lauren. "To what do we owe the pleasure of your visit?"

"Well I have an update for you about our conversation the other day," said Dobbs in an apprehensive tone.

"And why would that concern us, Agent Dobbs?" asked Lauren. "I'm sure you know we weren't impressed then, so why would we be now?"

"I came by to thank all of you for your cooperation and to tell you that we have the suspects in custody," replied Agent Dobbs holding his own despite the glares and mental abuse he was feeling.

Lauren couldn't control herself any longer, her emotions were running away with her, when she said, "Girls, would you excuse us? Agent Dobbs, could I talk to you privately for a moment?"

"Why, certainly, Doctor Horton," Dobbs replied.

They walked casually into Lauren's office and shut the door behind them. Lauren walked from behind Dobbs and taking him in her arms they hugged as tightly as a couple of teenagers.

"God, I missed you!" she said. "You have got to stop going home on me. I want no more of this 'missing you' business. You're not getting away from me this time."

"I don't like it either," said Dobbs. "But what else can we do right now?"

"Come home with me tonight," replied Lauren. "I'll send Ashland packing and introduce you to the kids. They'll love you. They'll love you as much as I do."

"What about their father?" asked Dobbs.

"They haven't had a father figure in years," she answered. "But I think you'll do nicely. Look at it this way. If they don't like you, they can always go live with their father."

"Can we talk about this some other time?" asked Dobbs.

"We don't have to talk about it at all if you don't want to," returned Lauren.

"Well," said Bob. "I'm off to fight crime."

"I thought you political types always got undressed in offices," said Lauren mischievously. "I heard something about a cigar once, I think."

"Not from my office," answered Dobbs.

The two of them kissed a while longer and before long Dobbs had to leave and go back to work. They made a date for supper at Lauren's house and soon they came out of the office. Several of the girls were still standing around when Dobbs said, "Well, ladies, it has been nice to see you all again. I hope to see you soon."

"I don't think you had better come back here again, sir," said Rachel. "I'd hate to see security get up in arms over your harassing Doctor Horton."

Dobbs chuckled to himself as Lauren interrupted.

"Agent Dobbs isn't harassing me, Rachel," said Lauren. "This visit was bona fide."

Lauren and Dobbs both laughed and Lauren extended her hand and said, "Have a very nice afternoon, Agent Dobbs. Please stop and see us again."

"And bring some single hunks with you!" another co-worker added. "A couple of Fox Mulder types would be nice."

"You better leave before they kidnap you as well," said Lauren.

With that they shook hands again and exchanged an amorous gaze. Smiling, Dobbs turned and walked away.

42

. . . .

TOM AND ALEX ARRIVED AT the airport gate and inserting her pass she drove to the lot.

They got out of the car and Tom went to the trunk and pulled out his chart case and overnight bag. When he closed the lid he found her standing directly in front of him.

"Did you want me to fit you in my bag, honey?" he asked.

"If it means I can go with you, of course I do," answered Alex and put her arms around him again.

"You believe me when I say I love you, don't you?" asked Alex.

"Of course I do," he said. "Why would you lie?"

"You know what I meant, Thomas," she answered. "I'm sorry about this morning. I don't know what I was thinking. I'd never forgive myself if something happened to you on this flight or any flight for that matter."

"Not to worry, my dear," said Tom. "I'll be fine. Be there and home before you know it. Come on, pucker up and give me a kiss. I've got to get going."

"Let me walk with you to the plane," she said. "Please?"

He felt the anxiety in her voice and looking into her eyes, he could see she was genuinely scared. Smiling a warm smile he picked up his bags and said, "That would be nice, honey."

He turned out his elbow making a place for her to put her hand and the two were off to the security checkpoint prior to entering the runway stairs.

"Will you be sure to call me when you know what flight you're bringing back?" asked Alex. "If I can meet you early maybe you can get some rest before you have to leave again."

"Rest, hell!" replied Tom. "You just want to get in my pants."

"A lady has to have a plan, Tommy," replied Alex as she hugged his arm with both hands. "And I always have a plan to get into your pants."

"I don't think that's fair when you use your body to get what you want," returned Tom.

"Welcome to married life," she said as they burst out laughing.

Soon they were at the security checkpoint and he put down his bags and kissed her good bye. He showed his pass and ID to the guard and was soon inside the turnstile that gave access to the apron where his jumbo jet was parked.

Looking back at her, he said, "In the words of your favorite actor and movie, I'll be right back. There is something I have to do first." Waving back at her, he turned and made his way to the aircraft.

She was shocked by that statement, and it took her a moment to wave back. That was what he had said to her in her dream last night, and when she looked at him she saw him in her dream waving back at her with that look of death. She shook her head and the vision was gone. Tom was walking toward the plane in his usual demeanor laughing and talking with the airframe mechanic assigned to his aircraft. Right before he boarded the stairs, he looked at Alex and hollered "I love you" and waved again. She waved back repeating the verse and Tom was soon out of sight. She turned and walked quickly away from the tarmac. She was so unnerved that the only thing she could think about was getting into the car and getting as far away as she could. Once she was home she would feel better and look for Tom's plane to fly over the house on his way to Paris. In a few minutes she was in the car and headed for the gate. She could see his airplane in the rear view mirror and once again she became scared. Thinking what he would do at a time like this she thought of a prayer, but couldn't remember the words. So to the best of her Presbyterian upbringing she said, "You take care of him for me. I've got a bad feeling about this one." And with that she pulled from the parking lot and onto the street. Soon she would be home.

43

. . . .

TOM STEPPED INTO HIS CLEAN fresh smelling 747 J Model and was at home in his office. He so loved this time of day when he was the only person aboard the jumbo jet and he could actually bond with her. He hadn't named this airplane as yet and he did feel a little odd about that. As he walked down the aisle he was filled with anticipation of what the future held. Although he and Alex had had their first fight, Tom felt good that they had broken the ground, so to speak, for marriage talks. It was the dawning of a new day and he was alone with his baby. Hope, he thought to himself. Hope would be a good name for his plane. He sat down in one of the passenger seats and just relaxed. He could smell the air fresheners and the cloth seats and the cleaner in the carpet. There was no greater smell than a clean untouched virgin airplane waiting on the tarmac to take people to their dreams. Yes, sir, he thought to himself, Hope will make a good name for you.

In a few minutes, Ann was at his side and touching him on the arm said, "Captain, how are you this morning? You're here bright and early.."

"I think I fell asleep," said Tom.

"Yes, you did," she replied. "You've been sleeping for a good twenty minutes."

"Hey!" said Tom. "I have a name for our lady."

"Really!" returned Ann. "Do tell."

"Hope," he said.

"Yeah! Hope works for me too. Good job Captain. How long have we been working on that?"

"Not long," defended Tom. "A couple of months maybe."

"Be sure you tell Charlie what you came up with so he can paint it on the front," she ordered.

"I'll get right on that, ma'am," he said as the remainder of the flight crew came aboard.

Tom noticed that his co-pilot, Officer Pitts, didn't board with the rest of the crew. He was concerned. Emily, Officer Pitts' latest flame boarded the plane with a grin from ear to ear when she was asked the whereabouts of Officer Pitts.

"He had to stop off at the chiropractor for a treatment. He fell out of bed. They just don't make them like they do in France," replied Emily.

Tom and Ann were completely taken in. He was convinced that Emily took him for a ride in her bed and God only knows what had happened to the dear boy.

"Well I suppose I had better find us a replacement," he said. "I'll be right back."

"And get me someone who can keep up if you know what I mean," said Emily.

About this time Tom and Ann were seeing no humor in this little exercise when he glanced over and locked gazes with Emily.

Ann walked over to her and said, "Where is he?"

About the time Ann was going to beat the answer out of Emily there was a great deal of commotion on the ramp into the first class section. As luck would have it, here came poor old Officer Pitts walking and stumbling up the ramp in a full body cast.

Tom and Ann had been known to put together a few good jokes in their day, but this was beyond the realm of funny. Both of them looked at one another in total shock and amazement.

"Help me into the cockpit, Captain," Keith hollered. "Let's get this show on the road. Emily, honey, did you make the reservations for the climb when we arrive?"

"All set, honey," Emily hollered back.

As Keith struggled up the aisle hitting everything with his casted arms Tom quickly went to his aid.

"No, Officer Pitts," he said. "You're in no shape for a plane ride today."

"What do you mean, Captain?" returned Keith jokingly. "I'm ready for some fun."

When he couldn't get through the door of the cockpit he turned around and with the finesse of a Hollywood actor said, "Take this cast from my being so I may serve my fellowman."

With that expression Keith started moaning and groaning horrifically and began to tear the cast from his arms, legs and torso much to the shock of everyone in the flight crew. Finally throughout all the painful squeals, Officer Pitts was free and the body cast lay on the floor beside him.. Tom and Ann looked at him in total disbelief while Emily and the other attendants just stood by with mischievous grins on their faces.

Officer Pitts, a true actor to the end, lay on the floor motionless with his eyes closed. As Tom and Ann looked on in near horror, he twitched ever so slightly, opened his eyes and motioned for Ann to bend down to his face. She got down on all fours and leaned close to his face to listen to him say his last words. When she got within range, he reached up, grabbed her face in his hands and in one swift motion pulled her lips to his and gave her a big juicy kiss.

Tom was in as much shock as Ann. Emily began giggling, as did the rest of the girls. It only added fuel to the fire when Keith said, "Gotcha. Big time."

Ann stood up, brushed herself off and said very calmly to Tom," Get that cattle prod Captain. Turn it up to max."

Turning her attention to Emily, Ann said, "You, young lady, are so grounded."

When Ann started to laugh everyone started laughing. It sounded like a party aboard Flight 232. The old salts at putting together a good joke had just been taken for a ride and they were handling it quite well.

"Well, Officer Pitts," said Tom. "If you're finished making a damn fool of yourself we have a plane to prep. I'll start the prep work, you clean up the mess."

Amid the laughs and back patting it was all back to work and business as usual as the crew of Flight 232 began prepping the jumbo jet for a flight to Paris, France.

When Tom and Keith entered the cockpit Keith looked at him with an evil grin and said, "You know, that Ann is a good kisser."

They exchanged laughs and all Tom could muster up was "No comment."

He noticed a little bruising on Keith's neck and being his usual inquisitive self asked Keith for the story. He went into a scenario that would make an old man feel like he missed the greatest sex of his life. Tom listened intently as Keith told the story of two days of pre-marital bliss with Emily and how they were talking about a future together. They were both definitely in love and youth was on their side. Keith talked of this past weekend not just the time spent in bed, but the whole overall weekend. He really threw Tom for a loop when he asked him if he would stand up for them in marriage. Keith explained how he had no father figure and he had liked Tom a great deal and considered him a friend and a mentor. Although Tom waited for the punch line from Keith, he was openly impressed by his offer.

"A father figure, you say," said Tom. "What makes you say that?"

"Outside of Emily, I don't have anyone," responded Keith. "I love Emily and I like you. I hope to fly with you until I move up. I know you wanted to fly with that brunette you're living with, but Drummond tells me I belong to you now. I hope you teach me a lot, because I don't intend to leave either one of you any time soon."

Tom was very interested in what Keith was saying. No one had ever said that to him before and he was very impressed. Knowing the kind of trickster Keith was he was very hesitant to open himself up or to get sucked in, so he just listened.

"Tell me, Captain," said Keith. "When are you and that cute little brunette going to tie the knot? I hear she is quite the dish."

"Yes, she is," replied Tom. "Let me log in the computer."

"Okay, I'll get the fuel truck info," said Keith. "He's here already. I'll be right back."

"Beware of Ann," replied Tom.

"I'll tell you what, Captain," said Keith. "There's nothing better than a good kisser and that Ann can kiss. I'll be sure to tell her you said hi."

"Yeah, you do that," Tom said.

When Keith walked out the cockpit door, Ann was walking in.

"I'll get you for that, young man," said Ann. And as Keith passed her she swatted him on the butt.

She handed Tom the weight figures for the food and drink carts.

"Keith tells me you're quite the kisser, Ann," said Tom. "You've been holding out on me all this time."

"Yes, I have, Captain," replied Ann. "I've always known one thing and that is although I'm not that passionate with my husband, I would never be able to let you go. So I've always enjoyed our friendship and known a love affair between us could never end without someone getting hurt. I've always respected our friendship and have always felt safe with you. On all those overnights we've been on over the years, I've never ever worried that one night you might want something more than my loyalty, although at times I wish you would have. You are a rare find, Thomas Jordan. You are truly a gentleman. Anyone who doesn't love you is a fool and I am no fool. I have always loved you, but in the way where our love doesn't involve any sexual relationship. Although it could very easily become passionate at any time, I would like to think that our love is one of respect and communication. You have never sidestepped me in what decisions were made during any emergencies and you have never undermined my authority with the flight attendants, and that kind of respect is very hard to find in this business."

Ann took up a position on the armrest of the right seat.

"I remember the day those damn German hi-jackers came on board and threatened to kill that blond haired woman. I had thought of coming to you in your hotel room when we landed in Paris that night. But I tell you I saw a side of you I didn't think was there, but thank God for all of us it was alive and well. You scared me, but you were also there for my girls and me and I've never loved you more. Those damn terrorists thought twice before they ever screwed with us again. But my point was that after the shooting stopped, the first thing you did was check and make sure we were all right. That was all I needed to know to realize we would be safe with you. You will never know how that felt. And the hi-jacking doesn't even hold a candle to the fire. That was more than anyone should have to endure in one lifetime, but you got us through it. I thought of coming to you that night also. It seems that each time I get up the nerve to come to you, something very tragic takes place. So I don't think the good Lord wants us together. I think He only wants us to work together. I think before I would fly with anyone else I would quit this business. I'll never find another you to work with, though maybe, just maybe, Alex. You and she are a lot alike. If you ever leave, I will sign on with her. All right, Tom," said Ann "Stand up and give me a hug."

Although Tom was a little surprised he stood up and took Ann in his arms. They hugged for what appeared to be a full minute when she looked up at him and kissed him on the lips. He, of course, returned the kiss and the two looked at each other for a second. Finally Ann and Tom separated and she said, "That Alex is a lucky lady, but you're lucky also. You two take care of each other. Thank you for listening, it was nice talking to you again. I'll be back when I have the total passenger load."

When Ann walked out the door Tom's head was spinning. My God, he thought to himself, what was that all about? As he thought a bit about his dream last night it was as if Ann and Alex had the same dream and an epitaph was being written. A eulogy from friends. It was making him very nervous. Although he had tried to forget the dream it was constantly reinforced by the argument he had with Alex. And now it sounded like Ann was involved somehow. This was too deep for him. He wanted to get to France and get this little extra work for Drummond finished so he could put this all behind him, but something just wouldn't let him. He continued putting data into the computer and hoped once again that his professional dedication would bale him out of another situation. He was at peace when he was working. The more data he entered into the computer the more he relaxed and didn't dwell on the things of last night or this morning. Before long he had all the necessary flight data entered. Now it was a matter of the computer accepting and committing it to memory. Shortly after Tom had completed this, Keith returned from his trip to obtain the fuel truck info.

"They filled us up with Ethel," said Keith. "Speaking of Ethel, how's that cute little lady you're sharing housekeeping chores with, Captain?"

"Quite well, thank you," answered Tom. "How did you hear about Alex?"

"Alex, is it?" asked Keith. "That's a pretty name. I hear you met her on the flight that caught on fire. Kind of strange, don't you think?"

"Why is that?" returned Tom.

"Well, you have a beautiful lady and you meet her for the first time." Keith went on. "You take her to Paris and tell her you'll be the jam on her bread and the next thing you know, the plane catches on fire. Didn't you think that was a little odd?"

"Maybe I got the bread a little too hot," he replied.

"I'm thinking something else got a little warm, Captain," said Keith.

Tom sat in his seat and didn't respond to this latest remark. He knew it was all in fun even if it was about Alex. After a short pause he looked over at Keith who still had an evil look on his face and again asked him what had happened to his neck. Keith became a little embarrassed and tried to pull his collar up to hide the mark.

"Now that looks like a heat of the moment act, Keith, my boy," he said. "Did Emily do that to you? Let me see, you may need medical attention."

Keith moved away from him as if he didn't want to be bothered while Tom just snickered.

"No, my son, the same heat that lights up my girl and me is not the same heat that burned up that plane; I can assure you of that," said Tom. "You didn't answer my question. How did you hear about Alex?"

"Ann told me," said Keith as he kept his distance from Tom's eye on his neck. "I asked her if you were married and she told me about your relationship. I think it's neat, Captain. Ann said she is a wonderful lady. Maybe I can meet her someday; especially if we're going to be flying together and all."

"Maybe you and Emily can come over for dinner someday," replied Tom. "Alex would love you. She already knows Emily."

"All right, Captain, it's a date," said Keith.

As the two men finished talking and finishing the preparations for the flight a knock came on the cockpit door. They could see that it was Emily.

"Well, hello, Emily," greeted Tom. "Keith and I were just talking about you."

"I hope it was all good, Captain," Emily replied as she gave Keith a big smile. "Ann wanted me to stop in and tell you she is ready to board the passengers."

"Okay," Tom replied smiling. "Thank you very much. Please tell Ann whenever she's ready."

With that Emily left the cockpit and Tom made a call to the ramp supervisor. Soon Ann brought up the weight and balance numbers and the ramp supervisor hooked up the tow bar to Flight 232.

"Things are going very smoothly today," Tom said to Keith. "Sometimes I get skeptical when things go like this."

"You're kidding, right?" he asked, looking at Tom in a strange sort of way.

"No, actually," said Tom. "I'm quite serious. I get funny if everything goes just right."

"Yeah, but isn't that the way things are supposed to go?" asked Keith. "I mean after all, we are professionals dealing with professionals. Why wouldn't everything go right as planned?"

"You're right," Tom replied. "I just feel better if there are a few ripples in the water, that's all. I never expect everyone to do everything just exactly right on a daily basis."

"How do you prevent mayhem then, Captain?" Keith asked.

"Well usually there is only one person who drops the ball." he explained. "Not a lot of damage is done that way. It's kind of a comfort zone, if you will."

"That's interesting, Captain," Keith exclaimed. "I would have thought you were a stickler for a smooth as silk attitude with no mistakes."

"Well, let's say no major mistakes," he said. "I never get too upset over small issues."

"That's really interesting." Keith said. "The other captains I've flown with have raised holy hell over the smallest little thing. I didn't dare say anything, but I thought who really gives a shit if a stew doesn't pull the curtain closed over the rear coat rack? So what! Adjust. And that's one thing that Ann said about you before that makes a lot of sense now. It didn't before, but now I understand what she meant."

"What was that?' he asked.

"She said nothing upsets you. Things roll off your back and you don't go off the deep end over ridiculous things." Keith answered. "She said I was to take lessons from you on how to be a good pilot and a good flight crew commander."

"Oh, really?" Tom asked with a snicker.

"Yeah, no shit." Keith replied. "Even Emily said you were the best she's ever flown with. She told me the day you caught a replacement flight attendant smoking in the crew's bathroom. Ann even said anybody else would have pitched her butt out the avionics bay door, but you told her not to let Alex see her do that and let it go at that. I think that's the kind of pilot I would want to be. I know there are issues that must be addressed, but there are ways to do it. That is what I want to learn."

"Well, you're right, Keith," Tom said as he looked at the telltale light that indicated the cargo bay door wasn't sealed. "That is an important part of you job also and I'll tell you my philosophy on that just as soon as I tell you we have our glitch for today. The cargo bay door isn't shut. Now I feel better; life is good."

Calling the ramp supervisor on the phone that hooks up to a receptacle under the nose of the plane, Tom advised them of the door that was ajar and soon the light went off.

"You should be good from here on out, Captain," the ramp supervisor advised. "Are you ready to start the engines?"

"Ten four, si,." Tom replied. "Are you ready to fire these babies up, Officer Pitts?"

"I was born ready, Captain," he replied confidently.

"That's what Emily said," responded Tom with a snicker.

As the two pilots coordinated with the ramp crew in starting the engines of the jumbo jet, the conversation returned to business. In about one and a half minutes all four engines were running and they were going over the checklist. Shortly the ramp supervisor motioned to Tom that they were ready to push him out onto the taxi area.

"Keith," said Tom. "Call back and make sure everybody is ready to roll."

"Yes sir," Keith replied.

As he was waiting for an answer from the back the ramp supervisor got on the phone.

"Sorry about that cargo bay door, Tom," the supervisor said. "It never helps being in a hurry."

Keith told Tom that Ann said all was in order and they were ready to go.

Tom thanked him and said to the ramp supervisor, "Not a problem. That's what we have warning lights for."

With that the ramp supervisor nodded to the tug operator and Flight 232 was on its way.

"To be a good captain, Officer Pitts, you have to have a level head and compassion in your heart," said Tom informatively. "Take for instance that cargo bay door. As long as you are doing your job you can catch little things like that. A ramp worker can only close and latch the door, he has no way of knowing if it's sealed; that's our job. It does no one any good, especially you if you let things piss you off. And as for flight attendants, never discipline one. That's Ann's job. Do your job and don't worry about the other man's. Life becomes very easy that way."

As the two finished talking the tow driver came and unhooked the bar from the front of the aircraft and disconnected the telephone hookup. The ramp supervisor gave Tom a thumbs up motion and saluted good bye to him. Tom returned the traditional salute and waited for the two workers to clear the engine's air intake.

"As long as they give you a salute, they like you," said Tom. "If they don't salute, you pissed them off. Jordan's law! Do not piss off the ramp supervisor"

Once the men had cleared the path of the jumbo jet Tom asked Keith to get the tower's permission to taxi out to the runway as he pushed the thrust levers forward to move the aircraft onto the taxiway.

"Flight two three two Heavy, you are clear to taxi to runway two nine right and await further instructions," came the voice over the cockpit radio.

"Two three two, Roger," answered Keith.

Tom added a little more pressure on the thrust levers and the jumbo jet began rolling down the taxiway.

"You remember your days as a marine pilot?" Tom asked. "Didn't they always tell you to be cool and assess the situation instead of panicking? Same plan here, you just have more time to think here that you do in a F-18 Tomcat."

"They always kept you on the edge," Keith responded. "They never let you fly the damn plane because you were too busy competing with everyone else. It wasn't fun anymore. If I'd show up for work in a body cast, they would have given me a Section Eight."

"As well they should have," returned Tom jokingly.

"You have to admit it, Captain," Keith replied. "That was good, even for an upstart like me. Hell, I even got a kiss from Ann for all my work."

"That was a classic, Officer Pitts," he said. "A true classic that will take some doing to beat, I assure you."

"Thank you, Captain," Keith said proudly.. "That means a lot coming from an old pro like you."

As they approached the end of the taxiway Tom again contacted the tower. By this time he assumed that the flight attendants would be finished with their briefing of the emergency exits and it was time for him to begin his welcome speech. When he completed thanking everyone for flying Aurora Airlines he cradled the phone and turned his attention to the runway.

"You want me to call out the markers and speed?" asked Keith.

"Roger that, young grasshopper," replied Tom.

"How far do you want to go?" Keith asked.

"How ever far one sixty-five knots takes us," Tom answered.

As they were waiting for the tower to clear them Keith kept up the conversation.

"We're not very heavy today, are we?' Keith asked as he put down the clipboard.

"No." returned Tom. "We are right in the lower range."

Just as he put more pressure on the brake peddle the tower called him giving clearance to take off.

"Two three two heavy," the air traffic controller said. "Sorry about the delay. You are clear for take off on runway two nine right. Have a nice day, sir."

"Thank you, tower," returned Tom. "You have a good day too."

With that exchange of words Tom put the thrust levers in maximum setting and advised the tower that two three two heavy is rolling.

After that Tom looked at Keith and said, "Power set."

With that, the two men's hands became joined on the thrust levers to hold them in maximum position, and the jumbo jet quickly gained speed with Keith calling out the speed and marker numbers.

"One hundred at eight," Keith called out. "One twenty. One forty at ten. One fifty coming up to twelve"

Tom took his hand off the thrust levers, as did Keith so he could put both hands on the controls. All of a sudden there was a loud boom on the right side of the aircraft. This in turn was followed by another loud boom that sent Keith in a panic.

"Explosion! Starboard side! Abort! Abort," Keith screamed.

And before Tom could react to his screaming, he reached down and jerked the thrust levers to idle causing the jumbo jet to nose down heavily and begin to slow. As Tom lunged forward in his seat the first thing he thought was that he was nearing the outer marker threshold where the runway ends. The next thought was getting Keith's hand off those controls. In an automatic and somewhat violent reaction, Tom screamed "No" and at the same time hit Keith with an open hand in a pushing motion on the shoulder, knocking his hand away from the thrust levers. In the same motion Tom slapped the thrust levers forward to maximum in an attempt to bring the jet back up to speed and quickly.

He again hollered at Keith shouting, "Get off the brakes," striking his legs as he hollered.

In an instant Keith regained his attention and jerking to reality put his hands on the controls. Tom again hollered at him shouting, "Hands off the wheel! Give me the speed and markers. Don't touch anything!"

He looked down at the speed gauge and noticed he had dropped down to one hundred and thirty-six knots. He then looked at the marker and saw that he was in the yellow caution sign area. In an instant he was crossing the outer marker paint. He was nearly out of runway.

"How fast, Keith?" Tom hollered. "Wake up, damnit! How fast?"

"One forty!" Keith finally replied. "One forty-five! One fifty!"

"Rotate!" Tom hollered. "Rotate now! Pull the wheel back. Help me, Keith! Pull the wheel back!"

He looked out the windshield and saw he was over the paint and nearly out of pavement. Talking silently to himself he said, "Come on, baby, get us out of this. Get up, baby, get up."

He looked at the red warning lights fast approaching the edge of the runway and then in an instant the lights were out of sight and under the nose of the aircraft as the jumbo jet lifted off at nearly a vertical ascent with an airspeed of one seventy-four.

"Let go of the wheel now, Keith," Tom said calmly. "Let me have it for now."

As Keith let go of the wheel Tom patted the dashboard of the jumbo jet and said, "Thank you, baby. Good girl."

As the jet continued to lift, Tom kept one hand on the wheel and the other forcefully pushing the thrust forward until he was sure they were out of danger. He looked over at Keith and said, "You all right, buddy? We're okay. Take a deep breath and relax. In through the mouth and out the nose. Just try to relax."

Before Tom could finish talking, the tower broke in asking him if everything was all right.

"We noticed you went a little far there, Captain. Is there a problem?" the air traffic controller asked.

"Negative, tower," Tom answered. "We blew two tires on the starboard side. It felt like they were on the same pod."

"Are you declaring an emergency, Captain?" the tower asked. "Do you want clearance to return?"

"Negative, tower," he answered. "Thank you. We'll advise DeGaulle Field and we'll deal with it there. We're light today, so we should be able to put it down on the back four. Once we're low on fuel we'll be in good shape as far as weight is concerned. I'd rather try this light."

"Copy that, Captain. We'll advise Paris of your situation. Advise if we can do more," the tower supervisor said. "We will inspect for debris and get back to you on that, sir."

"Roger," Tom replied. "Thank you, tower."

He hung up the mike and reached for the cabin phone to call Ann.

"Is everyone all right back there?" Tom asked.

"Yes, we're all okay back here," Ann said. "Things were a little dicey for awhile. Those were tires, I take it?"

"Yes, they were," answered Tom. "I counted two. How about you?"

"Yes!" she answered. "Damn, those thing were loud. Would you please make an announcement? Some of the passengers are a little rattled. Did you stall for a second there?"

"Not exactly," Tom said. "Okay, I'll talk to you later. I'll make an announcement. Thanks Ann."

"I'll be up to see you with coffee in about ten minutes," she said. "I'll talk to you then."

He reached down and switched the phone to the public address. As he did this he glanced over at Keith who was still breathing in through the mouth and out the nose.

"What the hell was that, Captain?" asked Keith. "What the hell was that explosion?"

"That explosion was two high pressure tires going out side by side. Quite a harrowing experience, isn't it? Hang on a minute; let me get this out."

"Ladies and gentleman, this is the captain," Tom began. "I'm sorry about that rough spot on takeoff, but what we experienced was two tires blowing out side by side. The ground crew will check out the runway and see if we have any leaks or damage caused by the tires, but I highly doubt it. We will continue on to Paris and advise the authorities there of our situation. By the time we get there we will be about fifty-two thousand pounds lighter from the fuel we've burned so the landing will be no problem at all. If there are any changes, I'll advise. Have a nice day and enjoy your flight."

Tom returned his attention to Keith who appeared to be regaining his composure. Reaching over and putting the jet in the auto pilot mode, he began talking to him..

"How are you doing now, tiger?" asked Tom.

"I really made a good impression on you that time, didn't I, Captain?" asked Keith.

"I would have done the same thing," said Tom.

"Bullshit, you would have," Keith returned. "I damn near ran us right off the runway. I don't know what I was thinking. I just panicked. I've never done that before. Hell, I've never been that scared before. It's a good thing you hit me or I would have driven us right into the ground."

Tom didn't say anything as Keith talked and after a short pause, Keith said, "I guess I'm not the hot shit I thought I was. I'm no different than a rookie in training."

He looked out the window and didn't say any more. Tom was thinking of the right thing to say, but he had to agree with Keith. He did damn near run them right into the ground. But since Tom was Keith's trainer and mentor he needed to find the right things to say. After some soul searching, he was rescued by a knock on the door. It was Ann.

"How about some fresh coffee?" Ann asked. "Keith do you drink coffee?"

"I'm not feeling much like coffee right now," he answered.

"Oh, heck, Keith," Ann returned. "Don't let a little flat tire put a damper on your day. Ask Tom. He had to clean out his pants the first time we blew out a tire. It happens to the best of us. Isn't that right, Tom?"

"Yes ma'am," Tom answered.

"I'll send Emily to cheer you up in a minute," Ann offered. "But you have to keep your clothes on, okay. I'll be back to talk to you. You guys need anything?"

"No thanks, Ann," Tom answered.

As Ann was turning to leave she kissed Keith on the cheek, turned to Tom and kissed her fingertips and placed them on his cheek.

Looking back at Keith, she said, "Sometime, someplace we are caught in a situation where we do a poor job at handling whatever it is. The trick and measure of what we are made of is how we get back up and face it. You'll get over this, won't he, Tom? And don't forget we are here to help you. That's what we're made of."

"Yes ma'am," Tom replied. With that Ann left the two pilots alone.

"This about ends my career, doesn't it, Captain?" Keith asked.

"Why do you say that?" Tom asked.

"Don't you have to report this on my performance reports?" he answered.

"I don't think you're responsible for flat tires," Tom said. "I think those just happen."

"You know what I mean, Captain," Keith returned.

"You know, Keith," Tom began. "Besides Ann being a good kisser, she is also a very smart lady. What she said about how you get back up and face what knocked you down is absolutely correct. These things can happen to you, and then they can happen to you again. The bad part of this business is that foul ups can kill you. That is why you always fly with an experienced pilot, someone who has, as Ann so politely put it, cleaned out his or her pants. Because of today you will never do that again. The next time you blow a tire, or two, maybe, all you'll say is, "oh shit," and you'll counter steer and get up as soon as you can. You'll never panic like this, I'm sure of it. That's why you have to let this go. Put it behind you and move on. You've got too much going for you to let this beat you. It happened, it's over and it's time to get to Paris and lie down with Emily again. These girls go through similar things like we do too. Their scenario is a little different, but they know what it is to be scared just like we do. So always remember to be there for them like Ann was for you and as I'm sure Emily will be when you go back and see her. I'm not interested in reporting this to anybody. I'm more interested in how you come back as a pilot and as a man and go on. We are all here to make sure you do. Someday you may have to be there for us and we'll be leaning on you pretty hard. End of lecture. Go see Emily, she's worried about you."

"Thank you, Captain," replied Keith. "Thank you."

"Keith?" he said.

"Yes, sir," returned Keith.

"The name is Tom." He extended his hand to Keith and from that day forward a true bond was set between two men living the same dream, to fly far, wide and often and to love their woman.

Shortly after Keith left the cockpit Ann entered and brought Tom another cup of coffee. He thanked her for the coffee and motioned for her to sit in the co-pilot's seat because he was receiving a call from Houston.

"Flight two three two heavy, this is Houston. Do you copy?" the tower supervisor said.

"Houston," answered Tom. "I read you loud and clear. Go ahead."

"Two three two heavy, Houston. We've checked the runway for debris and all we have is a great deal of tire fragments," the voice said. "There is no metal debris here on the ground or paint or fluids anywhere. You should be all right, Captain."

"Roger that, Houston," he replied. "Thank you for the update."

"Houston out," the voice said.

44

. . . .

CHRIS HAD GOTTEN UP AFTER taking a nap with the girls to find Alex in Tom's study looking at a picture of Tom in his Air Force flight suit headed out on a mission.

Alex looked up at her and said, "I've always loved this picture of him in his flight suit. He looks so gallant and dashing, ready for anything that comes his way, but at the same time he has that smile that is only Tom."

"How did your ride go?" asked Chris. "Did you get a chance to talk?"

"Yes, we did," Alex said in a serious tone. "You know what, I think it's the first time we have ever had a conversation that didn't lead to sex before the conversation was finished."

"Tell me all about it," pried Chris. "Be serious, Mother. How did it go?"

"It went well. We stopped down at the park and went for a short walk and talked it all out," said Alex.

"What exactly did you talk out, Mother?" Chris asked.

"Mostly the rotten way I handled the conversation in the first place," she admitted. "And we agreed never to start something like that again when there is someone else in the next room, like you or the girls. I never think he listens to me when I talk to him and I get upset. Sometimes, like today, I get very upset and I was wrong. He didn't pass me off like I was insane, he said he was really considering what Drummond offered him and was going to sit down and talk it over with me when he had more information. I just jumped to conclusions about how long he was taking to tell me. My schedule isn't always his."

"You know, Mother," began Chris. "It's obvious he loves you very much and I'm sure he listens to everything you have to say. He may not answer as fast as you want him to, but he listens. I think you and he are both very lucky and very much in love. You and he are slightly different in a few things, however. For example, you take things more seriously than he does. That's due to the differences in your lives, but I think he listens to you. The way he handles things is a little more laid back with less emphasis on immediacy. But I have to tell one thing. Even though he loves you, I don't think he's going to take a great deal of grief from you. So don't forget who you're talking to when you get mad at his answers."

"Yes, you're right," replied Alex. "I do go off the deep end sometime and forget to respect him. But we've always made up and gone on so far."

"I just mean don't take advantage of his good nature," Chris said.

"Do you know he mentioned something about getting married? she said.

"He did, really?" asked Chris.

"Yes," Alex replied. "I was telling him I was always worrying about him getting into trouble and maybe not coming home some day. So if he was to take Drummond up on his offer I knew he would be home every night. Then he said he didn't need any of this at all, that we had rental property and that the house and the boat and everything else were paid for, so we could go anywhere in the world together. He didn't need to fly anymore. Although a pilot is what he does for a living, it is not who he is. It was an interesting thing that he was saying. It was almost like he already had it worked out. He then said we could all just live together for the rest of our lives and be comfortable well into our nineties.

"Are you serious, Mother?" Chris asked.

"Yes, very," she replied.

"You're right in a strange sort of way," Chris divined. "It appears that he has worked this out in his mind a while ago. Maybe he's tired. Maybe he wants to get married and just love you for the rest of his life and never leave you anymore. It's possible he feels that way. You said yourself he's been flying for Aurora for fifteen years and he appears to be a financial wizard. Maybe he just wants to retire and spend the remainder of his days on the boat with you. That would be nice."

"Well, you may be right, Chris," she replied. "He said we would talk when he got back. That would be a wonderful surprise wouldn't it? I never really thought of it like that. I always figured we would both work and someday talk about retirement. I never even looked at it prior to that. Darn, Chris, I wish he were home right now. Did you ever want to just hold someone and never let him go? I don't mean take him to bed, but just be with him and keep him close to you? That's how I feel right now. I'm not going to be able to wait until he gets home this time, I'll be nuts."

"I'm sure he'll be here as soon as he can, Mother," Chris replied. "Doesn't he intend to be back tomorrow morning if he can get an early flight. I thought I heard him mention having lunch with the girls tomorrow."

"Oh, that will be nice," returned Alex. "Maybe I can have him to myself for about an hour."

"Mother, I thought he was coming back early to get some rest," Chris reminded her.

"Oh, I'm sure he'll get some rest," Alex said grinning. "Nothing like a nooner induced nap to keep a man happy."

"Mother, you're going to wear him out." Chris surmised.

"I really doubt if I'll wear him out," she said. "But I do like keeping him well broken in."

With that last remark the two ladies began laughing until one of the girls got up from her nap to see what all the commotion was.

45

. . . .

TOM AND HIS CREW WERE well into their flight to Paris and were two hours over the ocean. Four more hours of time over the water and then sightseeing over the French coast and they were home. Tom was beginning to regret wanting a perfect day to begin with a little glitch when he heard for the second time the long range radar make a light beeping sound. This sound would get increasingly louder the closer the object became to their aircraft at their three o'clock position. It was presently about forty miles away, the best Tom could estimate by the graph on the radar screen.

Shortly after the last estimate Tom made, Keith knocked on the cockpit door using the security knock and Tom opened the door. When he took up his seat next to the pilot, Tom looked up and said, "Don't get to comfortable; we've got visitors."

Although Tom pointed to the radar screen, Keith looked out the window.

"He's about thirty-eight miles out at three o'clock," said Tom.

"What's he doing?" Keith asked.

"I don't know yet, He may be lost or he may have lost his instruments and is picking up our transducer. I really don't know. But, we damn sure got to keep an eye on him."

"Has anybody called yet?" Keith asked nervously. "Who's out here, Madrid, right?" Keith was referring to the Trans-oceanic flight controller's station.

"Yeah, I think so," said Tom rather weakly. "No calls yet, they're probably too far away for a collision alarm at their station."

"Do you think it could be a UFO?" Keith asked.

"They're out there," Tom said, "It's just a little early in the season to spot one."

"Are you telling me those bastards have viewing seasons?" Keith demanded.

"Not exactly," Tom replied with a half laugh. "It's just that you usually don't see them this far north this time of the year. I'll bet that's not a UFO."

"What would make you say that, Captain?" Keith asked most seriously.

"Well it has been my experience that UFO's cover much more air space much more quickly than these people are," Tom explained.

"By your experience, Captain, are you telling me you've been here before?" Keith asked as he turned and looked at Tom.

"Many times," Tom said.

"I'm beginning to dislike this more and more," Keith replied. "I need to go see Emily. She will make all this go away."

As the two men laughed the beeping sound on the radar was getting louder. Tom reached down and put the radar on short range for a scan to avoid any unexpected surprises. A short time later he returned it to long range and it was obvious the object had closed the gap.

"Don't you think we should take some evasive action here, Captain?" Keith asked.

"The book says we call first," Tom said. "Let's do that now. If he gets within twenty miles, put the seatbelt sign on."

"Got it," he said.

Tom reached down and grabbed the company phone and made a call to Madrid. He explained what he had going on, what direction it was heading and the estimated speed. Tom awaited confirmation from Madrid on the status of the object.

After what appeared to be five minutes the Trans-oceanic controller advised Tom that it appeared to be Japan Air Flight Twenty-two thirty who had changed course due to weather over Asia. He did advise Tom they would make every effort to contact him to avert any problem. He also advised him he could take any evasive action he deemed necessary in the event they could not make contact. In turn Tom thanked him for all his assistance and turned his attention to Keith.

"What did they say?" Keith asked.

"They think it is a Japan Air Lines flight," Tom said with a smile waiting for Keith's reaction.

"Oh give me a freaking break," Keith hollered. "Them damn Japs couldn't fly a freaking kite and they're out here in a damn airplane. God help us all. Get us the hell out of here, Captain, before one of those slant eyed bastards tries to mate with us in flight."

After that outburst Tom was laughing hysterically at not only what Keith was saying, but also the way he was saying it.

"You go ahead and laugh, Captain!" Keith explained to Tom as a mentor. "Those damn slope heads will pull right up alongside of us and all you'll see is a bowl of rice and chopsticks. That silly son of a bitch is probably eating lunch right now."

As Tom continued to laugh at the synopsis Keith was giving him, Madrid station again broke in with an advisory.

"Two-three-two, heavy, Madrid station," the voice said. "Unable to make contact with airliner at your three o'clock. Recommend you take evasive action at this time. I have them at a speed of six-hundred forty knots and three miles away."

"Roger that, Madrid," Tom replied. "Turning right forty degrees to a heading of zero-six-zero and descending to thirty thousand feet. Will advise when we are clear."

"Call the back would you please, Keith?" asked Tom. "This may be a little dicey."

Tom took the controls in hand, disengaged the auto pilot and pushed the throttle levers forward to increase their airspeed. He then pushed forward on the yolk and turned slightly to put the jet in a gradual descend to avert the forward course of the Japanese airliner. This was done with so much precision that none of the passengers or crew felt it. After descending one thousand feet he then turned one hundred and eighty degrees to the right and was on a course directly opposite the Japanese airliner. He would watch his radar, which was now on short range tracking so when the airliner passed by them on their right he would turn one hundred and eighty degrees to the right and be behind them. After a short clearing observation Tom would then turn back on course to France.

Although this was a standard evasive maneuver, sometimes the unthinkable would happen. And in this case, in order to satisfy Tom's need for a glitch to make a day go smoothly, the Japanese airliner also turned with Tom. So now the airliner was above them and descending to meet Tom's altitude.

"That crazy Jap is locked on us, Captain!" Keith screamed. "How can he not see us? It's broad daylight, for God's sake!"

"I don't know," Tom replied. "Listen, let's go to terrorist mode and lose this crazy bastard."

"Madrid station," Tom called. "Basic evasion didn't work, going to radical."

"Roger that," the voice said. "They are one mile out, twelve o'clock high and descending rapidly.

By now the radar warning alarm was constantly whistling demanding your attention.

Tom told Keith to silence the alarm as he pushed the thrust levers farther for an even more exaggerated dive.

"I'm going down and right," he said to Keith.

"Down and right, roger," Keith repeated as he tightened his seat belt and shoulder harness.

As Tom turned the plane this time there was no mistaking that he was doing so. All the passengers as well as the crew knew that something was amiss.

Ann got on the public address system and reminded the passengers to please remain seated and be calm, the Captain was averting some unscheduled air traffic. She said that it was probably military air traffic on maneuvers away from their scheduled training routes and that there was nothing to worry about.

"We're damn near at seven hundred knots, Keith," Tom said. "Where is that crazy bastard?"

"Eight o'clock high at two miles west!" Keith replied. "I think we may have lost him."

"Let's bring her back to speed and course," Tom said. "Keep an eye on him."

With that Tom began to climb the aircraft without any throttle adjustment to slow down the airspeed. At the same time he began turning right to return to normal course behind the Japanese airliner. This had to be done very carefully so as not to stall the jumbo jet that was already feeling the strain of airframe stress. The radar collision warning alarm sounded as both Tom and Keith began jerking their heads around in search of the airplane.

Tom reached down and grabbed the cabin phone and pushed the button to call Ann.

"Ann, can you see that crazy bastard?" hollered Tom.

"He's on the right coming over our back," screamed Ann. "Go left, Tom! Left."

With Ann's directive Tom hollered, "Shit! Hang on," and dropping the phone he jerked the jumbo jet down and to the left. When the two pilots looked up they could see the Japanese airliner barely clear their fuselage roof as Tom continued into a downward plunge.

With that maneuver every warning alarm and voice went off. Soon the cockpit was filled with alarms and voices that said "Pull up…pull up."

"Thrust levers max, Keith!" Tom said. Help me keep the rudder from rolling us."

With that order, Keith pushed the thrust levers forward as far as they would go and held them there. He also placed his feet on the rudder pedals and locked his legs at the knees. As the turbines screamed, the jet responded to the delicate although radical demands Tom and Keith were putting on her.

"Can you see them?" Tom asked Keith.

"Yes, he's still headed North," Keith replied. "Do you need some help with her?"

"Help me bring her up slow and then we'll lock her down," Tom replied.

"Roger that, Captain."

As the two of them brought the aircraft back on course and slowed it down to the pre-scheduled speed all the alarms shut off and they were back on a smooth course. Tom reached over and turned on the autopilot. The aircraft made one last adjustment after Tom put it back into autopilot. This was due to the computer- generated information relayed to the gyroscope. Flight two-three two-heavy was out of trouble and once again on their way to Paris.

"The next time I tell you that I need a glitch, I want you to swiftly kick me in the ass," Tom said to Keith as he reset his seat.

He reached over and picked up the handset portion of the phone that he had dropped and rang Ann.

"I think we're all right now, he's headed North," said Tom. "Is everybody all right back there?"

"Yes, we're fine," Ann replied. "I think they were digging the loops and turns. Well, Captain, are you ready for a cup of coffee before your meal?"

"Yes, please, Ann," Tom responded. "That would be nice."

Tom hung up the phone and said, "Ann is coming up. I get the kiss this time."

Tom called Madrid station on the phone to advise them that they were out of the woods and then returned his attention to Keith who asked, "Tell me about your girlfriend. We got interrupted a little earlier and we were just getting into the exciting aspects of your relationship."

"Well." Tom began. "Her name is Alex".

46

. . . .

A GENT DOBBS LEFT HIS OFFICE that day a changed man. Not only was he in love with the woman of his dreams, but he was very confident he had made his grandfather very proud with the arrest of Sam Winters and the solving of the case of Flight four-zero-one. He had done a stellar job with his investigation and when he thought his judgment would be clouded by the introduction of Lauren Horton, he was able to work around it. He worked around it so well that he fell in love with Lauren Horton and had the most wonderful day in his life. He was not only certain that he made his grandfather proud, but he made himself proud as well.

Bob Dobbs loved Lauren Horton and he made no excuses about how and where he met her. His partner never made any comments about his involvement with a witness either. Dobbs was never informed by Agent McCollough that her husband was thrown over a car by her, searched, Mirandized, cuffed and thrown in the back of her cruiser before she became aware that it was all a big misunderstanding. He only resembled John Gotti due to his wavy hairstyle. They had been together for better that eight years now. The subject and the threats of police brutality only surface on the eve of their wedding anniversary. So Angie knew good and well that there are some good people out there who didn't work for the FBI. Dobbs and she had both found one.

Dobb's heart began to race as he pulled into Lauren's driveway. As he pulled his car to a stop he saw Ashland Horton being put in the back of a police car in handcuffs. The reign of terror of insurance fraud had run its course and Ashland had run out of luck. Dobbs had heard earlier this afternoon that the U.S. Marshall had a warrant for his arrest.

It became obvious that his most distant dream was quickly coming true. The day he met Lauren he could sense there was trouble between Ashland and her, and he entertained the idea of a future with her. He never believed it was possible, but how wrong he was. Although things moved very quickly, he and Lauren were okay with it and were handling it maturely. They had talked about her children and the part that Bob would play in their lives. There was the issue of Bob staying over night and the effect that may have on the children. They both agreed that Bob would be out the door before the children got up for school. Lauren decided that after she sat down with the children and Bob together, Dobbs would move in while the divorce procedures as well as Ashland's trial were taking place. But this would be something they talked out together; preferably tonight.

Dobbs crawled out of his car and was met by Lauren and Grace, her daughter.

Lauren approached and gave him a light kiss on the lips," Bob, I'd like you to meet my daughter, Grace."

"I hear you work for the Gestapo- I mean the FBI," Grace said. "Mom has told me quite a bit about you. It is nice to meet you."

"Thank you, Grace," Bob said. "It's very nice to meet you. Your mother has told me quite a bit about you as well."

Shortly after Bob and Grace exchanged pleasantries, Steve rode up on his bicycle.

"This illustrious gentleman is my brother, Steve," said Grace. "Did you talk to Sarah Allen today in study hall?" Grace asked as she tickled and then tackled Steve to the ground. "She told me you had a nice ass."

Steve broke from the clutches of Grace and regaining his composure came over to meet Bob.

"How do you do, sir?" Steve asked as he extended his hand.

"Very well, thank you," Dobbs said formally as he shook his hand.

Grace came to Lauren and began chiding her about the new man in her life.

"Show me that old timer kiss again, Mom," Grace said as Lauren turned toward her. "Did you learn that on the seniors 'channel. What's that called, AARP?"

"Bob, may I have your handcuffs, please?" Lauren asked.

"Yeah, right, Mom!" said Grace. "Shackle me into submission. It won't work. I won't break."

Bob Dobbs and Grace instantly hit it off as he laughed at the bantering back and forth between mother and daughter. She was everything Lauren said she was and Steve was just as docile as his mother described him to be. But Dobbs was convinced that these were two wonderful children. He felt bad for Steve, however. It was obvious that his father was never there for him. He knew in his heart that he would rectify that. Steve was docile due to a lack of fatherly intervention. Dobbs knew that the love he had for Lauren would easily extend to her children. He remembered all the love his grandfather gave him and how it was instrumental in developing his life. He would give the same love and attention and time to Steve in the hope of developing him a little further.

Dobbs knew that Ashland wasn't coming back for awhile so he was going to be the only father Steve was going to have. Grace was the kind of lady that had fended for herself and had clung to her mother for a long time. The relationship they had showed they were happy with one another and that Lauren had taken the time to be there for her. Lauren was a good mother even though Ashland did nothing to raise the children. They were together as a family due to her hard work. Steve was a little backward, Dobbs thought. But it wasn't something that couldn't be fixed.

Steve had picked himself up off the ground and as Dobbs looked out the corner of his eye he could see that Steve was looking him over. Dobbs being very careful not to miss an opportunity went over to him and said, "We have to stick together, you and me; or these women will be the death of us. We're going to get along just great."

"Don't let him fill your head with establishment bullshit, Steve," Grace rebelled. "The next thing you know they will take away your Internet and have you taking a bath every night before bed. You stick with me or we're doomed."

"Gracie Horton, I am going to find me a stick!" said Lauren. "You are terrible."

"I dare you, Mom," Grace hollered. "Shackle me then beat me while the neighbors watch. You'll be sitting next to Scott Peterson by daybreak."

Lauren just threw up her hands in despair and said, "See what I have to deal with day in and day out. It never ends. All right, Bob, this time I mean it. Give me your handcuffs."

Steve came over to Dobbs and said, "Are you staying for supper?"

"Yes, I think so," Bob said. "What are we having?"

"Bread and water." Grace hollered. "The standard establishment meal."

"Mom," asked Steve. "What are we having for supper?"

"You, Bob and me are having roast beef," Lauren answered. "Grace is having bread and water." With that exchange the four of them went into supper. Lauren couldn't help but notice Steve was right beside Bob. This could have been an answer to her prayer after all.

47

. . . .

WHILE CHRIS PUT THE FINISHING touches on supper the girls set the table and Alex excused herself and went out on the beach to have a cup of coffee. She looked toward the east and thought of Tom preparing to land in Paris soon. She also thought of the turn of the day as she looked up and felt the warmth of the Texas sun on her face. It was a day like the day she met Tom when she worried about the sun causing her to sweat and running her makeup. My God, she thought to herself, the things you recall to memory.

As she kept her face uplifted, she thought of how lucky and in love she was. Earlier this morning she had fought with the man she loved, and even in anger, she found him to be warm and compassionate. She knew she was blessed with his love and was proud to call him hers. She thought about life without Tom and a chill came over her body. She agreed with her heart that there would be no life without Tom. 'Now that I have loved him,' she thought aloud, 'I couldn't live without him.'

She lifted her cup to the heavens much like Tom did every morning and thanked God for him. Turning, she noticed that Rocky was standing next to her. Alex reached down and fluffed up his fur and said, "I was talking to our friend about Tom. Do you have anything to add? I always wondered what he found so pleasant out here. Now I see it all very clearly."

Alex continued her silent prayer to the heavens saying, "I was a lonesome old lady when You brought him to me. Ever since that day I have lived a life of perfect happiness. I know You sent him to me, I knew it the minute I met him. Only You could answer a prayer like that with someone like him. I thank you for him. I promise that I will never hurt him or be unfaithful to him. I will take care of him the remainder of his days. You will never regret entrusting his love and his life to me, I promise. Please take away all these fears and bring him home to me so I can take care of him like I promised. Please bring him home to me so we can continue to live our dream and I can fulfil my promise to you. Amen."

After finishing her prayer Alex brushed away a tear and turning around to walk up to the house she noticed an indentation in the sand the length of a human body. This could only have come when they made love in that spot last night. The memory brought a smile to her face and one last prayerful word. "Oh, yes Lord," said Alex. "I promise to keep him satisfied also. Now please bring him home."

Alex made her way to the house and got ready to eat supper. She wasn't fond of eating without Tom, but she would be all right with the girls there tonight. Turning one last time she looked out over the ocean. "Hurry, Tom!" was all she said.

48

• •

ALL RIGHT, CAPTAIN," KEITH BEGAN. "Tell me again how you're going to land this plane with two flat tires on the same pod."

Tom was preparing an answer when he looked over and noticed a nervous expression on his face. Being very careful not to make the problem worse for Keith, he tried to make light of the answer.

"It's a walk in the park, my dear boy," replied Tom.

"Humor me, please," Keith replied.

"Well," Tom began, "when we get one hundred miles out they will declare an emergency. So unless some poor sap has four blown tires we will get a priority approach. We will line up far in advance and get a straight in approach on the primary runway. Since we've been running our engines for over eight hours, we have burned up a lot of weight. So, I figure we are fifty-four thousand pounds lighter than when we left. We are going to land in such a way that we put all the weight on the back pods and drop forward in a slow and controlled manner. So! If we blow any more tires we will be able to stop quickly.

"What do you mean we are going to land in such a way?" asked Keith. "Go over that part again."

"We are going to land with about a forty-five degree angle," Tom explained. "The tail end will damn near drag on the concrete. The weight will be on the rear two pods. As we slow we will come down on the center pods and then quickly onto the front. Our weight should be evenly displaced. She'll make a lot of noise with the out of round vibrations, but we'll stop her quickly and crawl back to the gate. As I said, a walk in the park."

"You actually believe this old girl is going to let you put her down at a forty-five degree angle and mosey on down the runway with two flat tires?" Keith doubted.

"Yes." Tom replied. "Let me put it to you in a different way. Do you remember the first time you made love to Emily? How did you do it? Slow, soft and gentle. You did that so you she would come back a second time. It's the same here. Slowly, softly, gently."

"There is only one major difference that I can see, Captain," Keith added." When I made love with Emily the first time, she only weighed one-hundred and ten pounds," Keith stated. "Your girl here weighs one hundred and forty thousand pounds."

"Oh, what's a few pounds between lovers?" asked Tom. "When we're finished, we're going to convince our girl here that she is the homeliest high school junior dancing with the football captain at the senior prom."

This appeared to relax Keith a little bit and the conversation moved on to a different way of looking at aviation.

"How do you manage to compare flying a jumbo jet with making love and make it sound so good that one wants to get the airplane's phone number?" Keith asked. "Where do you come up with this shit?"

"That's why I'm the captain, young man," Tom replied. "That's why I'm the captain."

"We're one hundred and ten miles out, Captain," Keith reported.

"It won't be long now," said Tom. "Once in a while you have to dance with a lady before you get intimate. What do you say I teach you the waltz?"

"I wouldn't have it any other way, Captain," Keith replied.

"You're going to make a good captain, Keith," Tom surmised.

"What makes you say that, Captain?" Keith asked. "I'm close to messing my pants."

"Because we are in a serious situation and you are very aware of the danger," Tom said. "If you were making light of this, I would be worried. And always carry a spare pair of underwear just in case."

When the two them finished their discussion of erratic bowel displacement the tower at DeGaulle International Airport called and began the procedures for a straight in approach.

"Flight two-three-two heavy, do you copy, over?" the voice asked.

"This is two-three-two heavy, tower," Tom replied. "We read you loud and clear."

"Copy that, two-three-two. Maintain your glide path and continue on descent. Turn right to heading zero-two-zero and maintain that heading. That will be your vector for a straight in approach. We will be turning you over to the emergency landing coordinator. Turn your radio to one-two-five point six and await instructions. Good luck, two-three-two," the tower said and then signed off.

"They sound awfully serious over a flat tire, don't you think, Captain?" asked Keith.

"Yeah, they do," answered Tom. "It might have something to do with that Concorde accident a few months ago."

"Oh, thanks," Keith said. "I'm really feeling confident now. Hell, five minutes ago I had a handle on this. You better get out that underwear, Captain."

Tom began laughing again as Keith went on about being scared. He wasn't certain if Keith actually was uncomfortable or just kidding around. To be sure Tom thought he better test the waters, so to speak.

"Why don't you take the landing, Keith?" Tom said.

Keith didn't answer him.

"You all right, kid?" Tom asked.

"Yes sir, I'm fine," Keith replied. "This is something they don't teach you in the academy. I don't think I'm quite what you want for this landing, I'm afraid."

"You'll be fine," Tom said trying to cheer Keith up a little bit. "What would Emily think?"

Keith sat silently in his seat. Tom thought it was interesting that the jovial, confident, proud aviator who was just joking around about life in general, was now very reserved and quiet.

"What's the matter, Keith?" asked Tom. "It's not like you to get all worked up over something like this."

"Emily is the matter," Keith said. "You're right. It's hard to do your job when you fly with the woman you love. You haven't read my file have you, Captain?"

"Are you referring to that plane crash you were in a few years ago in the Marines?" Tom replied.

"Yes!" Keith said.

"That wasn't your fault, Keith," Tom said. "How the hell were you supposed to land a C-131 Hercules, fully loaded on a mud runway with two flat tires? I doubt if even Jesus would have attempted that one."

"Ten people eventually died in that one," Keith responded. "It was my fault."

"No! It wasn't your fault," Tom said emphatically. "Shit happens. Put it behind you, learn from it and move on."

"It's not that easy," Keith said. "They're dead because of me."

"You stow that shit, man," Tom said again, this time a little more aggressively than before." They're dead…

Just then the tower broke in again with new instructions for the jumbo jet. Trying to lower his voice a little Tom answered the tower and accepted the new directives for the landing. He also advised that he would be ready for final emergency landing instructions in five minutes.

Taking a deep breath he looked over at Keith who was staring out the window. Tom knew he had a troubled co-pilot on his hands at a time when he may need every ounce of his reserve. Tom had made light of the landing situation. Although he had no doubt that he could safely land this way, it was listed as a dangerous landing. De Gaulle Field knew it and that was why they were rolling out the emergency vehicles and putting Tom on an emergency channel.

Regaining his composure to address his friend, Tom said in a little more relaxed tone, "They are dead because it was an accident. It happens! Not every thing is your fault you know. You had over one hundred marines on that flight. Most of them walked away. The plane didn't explode and the way I understand it, you got it in the grass and slid to a safe stop. I think you did a hell of a job that day. And I'm sure all the survivors will agree with you. In this business, you never know what will happen. One minute all is good and the next minute you're asshole deep in alligators. You do what you can and move on. You have to let them go or they will eat you alive. You tell me the difference between people who die in a crash and the people you kill dropping bombs. What happened to you was an accident. Don't ever forget that."

Keith sat motionless in his seat for a moment and then turned to Tom and said, "It's amazing. One day you don't think about it and you think it's gone forever. And the next thing you know, something will set it all in motion again. I knew this morning was too good to be true when I woke up next to Emily. Okay, enough of that. What's next Captain?"

"Emily will always be there for you and so will I," Tom said. "We are all part of a team and we stick together. We stand by each other and we watch out for each other. So don't ever think you have to go through this alone. Don't even try it. It's too much. What do you say we land this thing and go see if Ann is passing out kisses."

"Sounds good!" said Keith. "Hammer down. You know, Captain, I think Ann would be interested in a little more than a kiss from you, if you get my meaning."

"Oh, really," Tom replied surprisingly. "What makes you think that?"

"Just an observation, young grasshopper," he replied. "That's why I'm the first officer."

"I've got your grasshopper," Tom replied with a smirk. "I'm going to give the passengers an update on our landing plans, okay?"

"Yeah," Keith said.

"You okay, bud?" Tom asked.

"Yeah," he returned.

Tom picked up the public address telephone and began his announcement about the landing that would take place in a few minutes.

"Ladies and gentlemen, this is the Captain speaking. I just wanted to keep you up to speed on that tire situation we had when we left Houston. When we land in Paris in about fifteen minutes, you will notice that there will be a great deal of emergency equipment on the scene. Please don't be alarmed by this, it is only a precaution. However, there will be a lot of it. Due to the tire situation we are going to land at an angle instead of flat like you are used to. This will put the weight on the back wheels and we won't use the flattened area. This is only a precaution also, but it takes away the chance of blowing out any more tires. The flight attendants will go through the landing instructions with you again. Please give them your undivided attention. Thank you for flying with us today and on behalf of myself, Officer Pitts and the crew, I'd like to welcome you to Paris."

"That was spiritual, Captain," Keith said.

"Thank you."

"Tom?" said Keith.

"Yes," he replied.

"Thank you," Keith said soberly.

"You're welcome," Tom said extending his hand, knowing only too well what Keith was referring to.

The tower contacted them again for the final approach on the emergency frequency and it was time to land after a trying day. Although Tom wanted to go to bed and get some sleephe knew he couldn't. He had to find a flight back to Houston to do that favor for Drummond. He hoped he could find a flight where he could get some sleep.

"Go ahead, tower," Tom responded. "Awaiting your instructions."

"Roger that, two-three-two," the tower voice said. "We understand you have two blow outs on the middle right pod. Confirm!"

"Affirmative," Tom replied.

"Ten-four, sir. We are standing by with emergency equipment on runway two nine right. Can you give me fuel and souls on board?" the tower asked.

Tom answered, "Three hundred eighty-eight passengers and crew; eight thousand pounds of fuel."

"Roger that," the tower replied. "Maintain speed and heading. Your glide path is good and your speed is good. Recommend you use thrust reversers and stop as soon as is safely possible. Fire and ambulance are standing by at marker six. You need not acknowledge any further transmissions."

"God, I wish they wouldn't say that," Keith said.

"You are now two miles out, two-three-two, check for wheels down and locked." .

"We've got three green, Captain," Keith reported.

"Thank you," Tom responded.

"Maintain glide path and speed, two-three-two. You are now one mile out."

After a few second delay Tom interrupted the tower and said, "Give me a hand with the wheel, will you please, in case we pitch when we touch?"

"Got it, Captain," Keith said

"You are now over the outer marker threshold," the tower said.

"Okay, Keith," said Tom. "When I say, now, we pull up on the yoke and set her down on the rear end."

"Got it, Captain," Keith replied nervously.

"Just like making love for the first time," Tom said. "Remember how smooth that was. We're going to do it one more time. Ready? Now!"

Tom and Keith pulled the yoke back in unison and the front of the aircraft went up like a kite as the rear of it settled down to a very low screeching sound.

"Okay, Keith," Tom said. "Let her down easy."

Keith and Tom pushed forward on the yoke slowly as the aircraft slowed and finally the aircraft settled on the pod with the blown tires. A rumbling noise was very audible through the whole aircraft when Tom said, "All the way down, now!"

Tom pushed the yoke forward all the way and the jumbo jet settled onto the front tires. With the rumbling noise very apparent, Tom pulled the thrust levers all the way back to the idle position and activated the thrust reversers. When he did this he pushed the thrust levers forward to slow the aircraft quickly and the jumbo jet responded. In a moment they were surrounded by emergency equipment as they came to a smooth stop.

Tom deactivated the thrust reversers and listened for them to "thump" their way back into position.

"Watch for the firemen on your side," Tom ordered.

"Got it, Captain," replied Keith.

In a moment there were ramp inspectors and firemen on the scene. One of the firemen sprayed a blast from a CO_2 fire extinguisher on the right pod as the ramp supervisor hooked up a telephone cord to the cockpit connection.

"Captain?" the supervisor said," You look good to taxi. Follow the truck and he'll take you direct."

"Roger," Tom replied.

As soon as the telephone wire was disconnected, Tom began to roll the jet to the gate area behind the lead- in truck.

He looked over at Keith and said, "Just like making love. Isn't it a beautiful thing? Good job, young grasshopper."

"Thank you, Tom," Keith said.

Reaching down and picking up the public address telephone he handed it to Keith.

"Welcome everyone to Paris, would you please?" Tom asked. "The temperature is forty-four degrees."

Keith took the telephone and graciously welcomed everyone to Paris. He gave a stellar performance, nothing less than you'd expect from a gifted orator. This made Tom laugh as he maneuvered the jumbo jet through the maze of shortcuts on the way to the gate. Before long they were secured and the passengers began to disembark. After Tom said good bye to Keith, who was headed out to see the sights with Emily, he and Ann did a walk through the aircraft before signing off on it and heading into the terminal themselves.

"How did you do with your visit with Keith?" Ann asked. "He was pretty upset about that when he talked with Emily?"

"He has some skeletons coming out of his closet that he needs to deal with." returned Tom. "Hopefully, the love of a good girl like Emily will do wonders for him."

"It's amazing," said Ann. "If the public only knew the skeletons in the closets of airline pilots. Would they fly or take the train? Does Alex take away your skeletons, Tom?"

"She's trying to deal with them as she goes along," Tom answered. "My problems are dreams; the nights are brutal. Last night was real bad and she heard me and we had our first argument because of it."

"May be you're burned out," Ann said. "You two are going on vacation soon, aren't you?"

"As soon as we get back from Paris on Wednesday, we're gone on the boat for about a month," answered Tom. "But there is a catch. We're taking Chris and the kids."

"Well, that will be nice," replied Ann. "I know if John and I go away alone for any time over a week we run out of ways to get along. So the kids will be a nice distraction for you."

"That's just it, I don't want a distraction," said Tom. "I want a vacation with Alex."

"Yeah, I get your point," said Ann. "Why don't we go get something to eat before you make arrangements for your trip home?"

"Sounds great! I'm hungry," Tom answered. "Let me check in here at the lounge and see if I can get a flight, and then we'll go and eat. That's so nice of you to hang out with me, Ann, this will be fun."

As Tom and Ann made their way into the pilot's lounge Tom was informed by the dispatcher that he had found him a ride on Korean Air Lines Flight four-zero-two-three, per request of Ed Drummond. He had about two hours before boarding and he would have him home by midnight. Tom thanked him for his help and he and Ann were off to lunch.

"That damn Drummond sure keeps an eye on you, doesn't he?" Ann asked.

"Yeah," Tom laughed. "He needs his noon flight to get off the ground. So he is taking a great interest in me right at the moment. It was nice of him to find me a ride though."

"The least that crusty old fart could do," Ann said.

"You and Alex both call him a crusty old fart," Tom said as he laughed. "Edward is so misunderstood."

"Yeah, right," Ann replied. "You got me feeling sorry for him already. He's got too much history with Alex and me."

"You too?" Tom remarked.

"Drummond married my husband's sister," Ann replied. "Chad was my nephew. He was a good kid."

"Yeah, I knew him," said Tom. "That wasn't Ed's fault, Ann."

"Did I tell you that you were buying?" Ann asked.

"No, I merely assumed," remarked Tom.

As the two of them entered the airport restaurant named after Charles DeGaulle himself, they were escorted to their seats.

As they were looking through the menus Ann said "Have you ever thought about marriage, Tom? Alex would be good for you."

"That's what she tells me, too." Tom remarked with a smirk. "Yes, we talked about it this morning as a matter of fact."

"I thought you were fighting this morning," Ann remarked.

"No, just a little heated discussion over an offer that Drummond made me," Tom explained.

"What kind of a deal did you make with the devil this time?" Ann asked.

"He offered me the chief pilot's position," Tom answered. "I think he's retiring soon."

"Well, I can certainly see why Alex would think that is a good thing," Ann remarked. "Can I be your secretary?"

"I'll see what I can do," Tom replied.

"So what were you arguing about?" Ann asked.

"I kind of played it down like I wasn't interested and she took it as a refusal to even consider the idea," he answered.

"Well, did you?" Ann asked.

"No," replied Tom. "I kind of like the idea myself. I could have a life. One with a wife, stepchildren and a couple of grandkids and be home every night. Make love on the beach all night long. Shucks, what more could anyone ask?"

The two friends continued their conversation through their dinner. When they finally finished eating, an airline representative came and introduced himself to Tom saying, "Captain Jordan, I have a seat for you on a Korean airline jet which is an embassy charter," said the young representative. "It leaves in thirty minutes. Have you home by eight at the latest."

"There you go, Tom," Ann remarked. "You can get home even earlier. Get yourself ready, I'll take care of this."

"We really must go, Captain," the representative advised. "They are ready to go."

Ann and Tom hugged good bye and exchanged pleasantries. Tom was off with the airline representative to find the Korean embassy charter flight and Ann made her way to a cab and the lonely hotel. As Ann was about to go out the door she turned and got one last glimpse of Tom walking away. She had a suspicion, call it women's intuition, that something just wasn't right about this as she watched Tom leaving. She turned and went out the door and hailed a cab.

49

· ·

TOM FOLLOWED THE MAN DOWN the corridor to the charter gates at the massive airport. It was not surprising to see motorized carts carrying passengers down the corridors here. This was the largest airport that Tom had ever been in, always bustling with activities and as many languages. It was like being within the operation of a major city. Through all the twists and turns the two men made, Tom was enjoying the tour. It was rare that he walked the halls of a major airport, only the immediate areas of where he was boarding. He saw a much different world here as he passed through these halls. It was a piece of God's world that he had never before experienced, but he was grateful for the opportunity. Entering a dimly lit corridor Tom and the airline representative stopped abruptly and the man pointed down the corridor saying tohim, "Three gates on your right, Korean flight two, two, three three."

Tom thanked the man for all his help and then continued down the corridor to the third gate where there was a very pleasant and beautiful Korean flight attendant with a very warm smile who asked, "Are you Captain Jordan?"

"Yes, I am," Tom responded.

"Welcome aboard, Captain," the attendant said as she extended her hand. "My name is Mylyn. We don't get many pilots from other airlines aboard our flight. You will be a pleasant addition. Did you see what kind of a flight this is before you agreed to take it?"

"No," Tom replied. "It was arranged through our office. Why?"

"Well, it's an embassy flight," Mylyn answered. "It's full of children and their parents. Gets a little loud sometimes. Were you hoping to get some sleep?"

"The thought had crossed my mind," Tom said.

"Well, come with me," Mylyn said, "and we'll see what we can do to find you a quiet spot for a nap."

As the two of them made their way down the ramp to the aircraft, Tom couldn't help but think of how pleasant Mylyn was. She was very slender but not skinny. She had a beautiful figure with long black glistening hair. She had a mellow face with eyes that invited you within her inner soul. Her long eyelashes complemented every aspect of her beauty. She was truly a remarkable woman. For Tom being from a foreign airline, he was amazed at how well he was treated. He had hoped that was because of his magnetic personality, but he knew that as tired as he was he must have looked anything but magnetic this afternoon. As they approached the door to the cabin, Tom could hear all the chatter going on. It sounded like a great multitude of children dueling over the best seat to watch Sesame Street. When Tom entered the cabin, the pilot met him. A pleasant looking tall thin man extended his hand and in broken English said, "Captain Jordan, welcome aboard. If there is anything you need, please don't hesitate to ask." And just as quickly, he turned and walked into the cockpit and closed the door behind him. Mylyn began introducing him to the other attendants in their native tongue. All Tom could do was shake their hands and nod his head saying hello to each of them. Mylyn led him to the rear of the coach where he found an empty window seat. She got him a blanket and a pillow.

"Thank you, Mylyn," Tom said. "That is such a pretty name."

"Thank you, Captain, "she returned. "It is such a pleasure to meet someone like you. You are so very kind. I'd like you to meet a fellow American."

As Tom looked up, he was met by a woman with fire red hair and a smile big enough for four people. Extending her hand, Tom rose from his seat and shook hands with her.

"Hi, I'm Irene."

"Tom Jordan," Tom said. "Nice to meet you. Are these your kids?"

"Well, kind of, yes," Irene answered to Tom's amazement as Mylyn laughed.

"I'm their nanny," Irene answered.

"To all of them?" Tom asked.

"Yes," Irene answered.

"You poor thing," Tom replied. "May the good Lord be with you, my dear."

With that Mylyn reached over and swatted Tom on the arm and began speaking again in Korean as she and Irene began laughing about something. Tom was none the wiser but he was convinced he was the subject of the joke.

As the laughing subsided Irene looked at Tom again and said, "Are we going to have fun with you today!" Looking back at Mylyn, they started laughing again.

Irene was a large woman. She was about six feet tall and had large shoulders and a large neck. She looked like someone who had worked hard most of her life. But with her red hair and a wonderful personality, she was quite an attractive woman.

As Tom settled in his seat he looked around and noticed there was nothing but children back in the coach section. He figured there had to be at least one hundred of the curtain climbers running about aimlessly up and down the aisles.

"Where are their parents?" he asked.

"Up in first class," Irene answered. "They stay up there and party while the children stay back here with me."

"That is your job?" Tom asked. "Is that what a nanny does?"

"Yes, sir," Irene answered with a shade of pride. "I wouldn't have it any other way."

"That's neat, Irene," he said. "You must be a very special lady to share your love with all these kids. That's amazing."

"Thank you, Captain," she returned. "I have been truly blessed."

Tom looked up at Mylyn who was still smiling and she merely nodded her head affirmatively and said, "These children are the ones who are blessed, Irene. Captain, may I get you something to drink?"

"No, thank you, Mylyn. I'm fine. Do you have any children?" he asked.

"No," Mylyn answered. "I've never married."

"Really!" Tom said in amazement. "I can't imagine either one of you two unmarried."

"Well," said Irene. "I don't see a ring on your finger either."

"I guess you have me there," he replied.

"Where are you from, Captain?" Mylyn asked.

"Ohio, originally," Tom answered. "But I fly out of Houston. How about you?"

"I was born in Tokyo, but have lived all my life in Seoul," she answered. "Irene was born in Gloucester, where the fishing boats are."

"No kidding!" Tom said.

"No kidding," Irene returned. "My father owned three fishing boats when I was a girl. I used to go out to sea with him during summer vacation."

"That is really cool," he said. "How did you end up here as a nanny?"

"Well, my father went out fishing one day and a storm came up," she said. "We waited for him for three weeks, but he never came back. So, after Mom took care of the outstanding debts from the insurance payments we went east; far east. I've been living in Seoul now for about twelve years."

"I'm sorry, Irene" Tom said. "That must have been very difficult for a little girl to handle."

"It was at first. We all stuck together as best we could until our mother got a job teaching in the American Embassy. After that it was all right. Then after I found this job I haven't looked back."

"Don't you get lonesome?" he asked.

'Oh, look around you, Captain," she answered. "I don't have time to get lonesome. See, I live right along with the children in the embassy."

"Do you ever get back to Gloucester?" asked Tom.

"No, none of the family is there anymore. We all went our own ways when we grew up. My mother has since remarried and lives in Maryland"

"You don't miss the good old U.S. of A?"

"No," replied Irene. "Seoul is my home now. Do you ever go back to Ohio?"

"Oh yes, at least once a year to see my brother, sisters and mother," Tom replied. "All my family lives there. The summers are better there than in Texas."

"My sister married a Navy man and lives in Minnesota," Mylyn added. "I've been there twice in the last three years. They get a lot of snow over there."

Tom hadn't as yet called Alex to tell her what time to expect him, so before they took off he wanted to do that. He excused himself from the conversation and made the call to Alex. At this time Mylyn and Irene went about the task of settling all the children in their seats. Alex had stepped out for a minute; Chris told him. He exchanged the information with her about the time and flight number and then bid her a pleasant day.

At this time the Captain came over the radio and said something in Korean and Mylyn and Irene settled everyone down. The tug began to push them out of the ramp area to the taxiway. Tom adjusted his pillow and put the blanket over his legs and closed his eyes. He was determined to get some rest on this trip if it killed him.

He noticed in his subconscious that the two engines on the right wing appeared to be a little out of synch with the ones on the left. It caused a slight vibration down the mainframe of the aircraft. Although he had never flown an Airbus 300, he was nearly certain that this wasn't normal. Wishing that he had talked to Alex before he left, a smile came on his face. He thanked Jesus for Alex and the girls and prayed for a much- needed nap. As the Airbus 300 headed down the runway, Tom drifted off to sleep.

50

. . . .

LAUREN, DOBBS AND THE CHILDREN cleared up the table and went out on the patio to finish the conversation they had begun at supper. They talked about the arrangements to see their father since his bail was refused because he was charged with a Federal crime. They had spent the majority of the supper hour talking about Dobbs being in their lives now. All seemed to be all right with that for the time being. Grace was happy to have Dobbs in her mother's life, because she could see the happiness that his presence brought her. There was a glow in Lauren's eye that she hadn't seen for years. Steve was acting like he had a newfound friend for life in Dobbs. Dobbs liked Steve as well. He saw a piece of himself in Steve at a younger age. But where he had his grandfather as a mentor in his youth, Steve had no one to pay any attention to him. His father had other priorities to tend to in his childhood days when a role model was important. Dobbs was confident that he could help the boy grow up responsibly. He would do it for his grandfather. He would do it for Lauren.

Grace enjoyed the bantering back and for with Dobbs as a method of play. She would antagonize him about the big brother establishment oppressing the youth and violating their freedoms. That was free will and the pursuit of happiness; of course. Grace had to alter that to the pursuit of sexual happiness in the local park.

Lauren tried her best to keep it to a friendly argument. Grace was a good challenge for Dobbs and by the time the evening was finished, Grace had him in a headlock on the grass screaming about her duty to stop oppression in American families by the dreaded infiltrating establishment.

As the children rose to go to bed, Grace turned to Dobbs and told him that since he had the least amount of seniority in the house he was expected to fix breakfast. Dobbs told her and Steve that he would not be staying overnight for a while. But he would be here for them if they needed him and he was always only a phone call away. So even though he would not be a permanent fixture here for now they could depend on him.

Of course Grace had to put in one last dig when she asked, "Does that mean you are just going to use my mother for sex?" Dobbs had to swallow deeply to avoid choking over that comment, but Lauren was quick on the scene with a swat and the wrestling match was on again. This time with Lauren in the middle swatting Grace on the bottom while Dobbs and Steve stood by and watched.

Soon the ruckus was broken up and the children went to bed. Lauren and Dobbs sat on the couch when she started the conversation that he knew was unavoidable.

"I thought we agreed you were staying here." Lauren began.

"I will, honey," he replied. "But let's do that part of our relationship a little slower. I'll stay over on the weekends to start with. Let the idea settle in with the kids a little more, or there is always plan B."

"Am I going to like plan B?" Lauren asked.

"I don't see why not," Bob replied.

"Okay, out with it," she said.

"We get into the habit of my getting up and out by, say, five thirty in the morning and I'm out before the kids get up. That way they don't find me here at seven."

"I'll tell you what," Lauren decided,. "Let's make it five fifteen and we'll have a quicky while the coffee is brewing."

"Okay, works for me," Bob said. "Well, why don't we go in and get that clock set?"

"Works for me," Lauren said. "I think it went well tonight. What do you think?"

"Well; after I turned on my charm and informed them of the rules, I think they all melted in my direction," Bob said.

"I wouldn't call getting wrestled onto the ground by a sixteen year old melting, honey," Lauren replied.

"That was a standard introductory procedure," Bob said. "All our agents use it with great success."

"You called that success?" Lauren asked. "It looked like hillbilly foreplay to me."

"Oh, you didn't go there!" Bob exclaimed. "That was a J. Edgar original."

"Show me again how it works," Lauren demanded. "Maybe I missed something the first time around."

With that challenge the two of them held each other and in the serenity of the night their spirits joined in intimate dedication to one another.

51

. . . .

ALEX, CHRIS, AND THE GIRLS decided to take in a movie on television before going off to bed. Alex would have an early up to get Tom in the morning. As the four of them watched the movie Chris asked quietly, "Did the divorce become final yet with you and Dad?"

"Yes," Alex returned. "Why do you ask?"

"I didn't think you ever heard from him. I didn't know you two ever got around to getting a divorce," Chris explained. "And I was wondering how you could marry Tom if you were still married to Dad. You have never really been too clear as to how you and Tom got to be a couple. I'm not sure what went on in your life when I was having my problems."

"I didn't ever talk with him again," Alex said. "I sent the papers to the man he was working for. Your father signed them, returned them and I filed them. It was all over but the cleaning out of my bank account to pay for all the damage he left behind. After the house was sold, I had two hundred dollars left to my name. I managed to get through this without killing my credit or filing bankruptcy. Once I got hired into Aurora, I got my apartment and I began to settle down a bit, but I was pretty angry in general. Not only with your father, but with myself as well. I just wanted to find him and kick him in the ass. I just wanted to ask him what the hell was he thinking to throw all this away."

"I had a pretty bad attitude, I'd go to work and no one wanted to fly with me. It didn't take long to have someone hitting on me and it didn't take me long to have the reputation of being a bitch. I got lonely pretty quickly, but I kept giving myself pep talks and in a couple months of crying myself to sleep, I began to pull myself out of it. But I was still a bitch. I did my job and I didn't have to say no to sex anymore, because nobody was asking anymore. I could do a complete round trip to Miami and eat dinner all by myself and not talk to anyone the whole day, only the necessary chit chat required to fly the plane."

Alex stopped talking when Carrie turned around as if to ask them what they were talking about. When Carrie turned back around she continued on.

"Then one day, Ed Drummond called me into his office. I figured he had enough complaints about me and I was going to be fired. I'll never forget this. He said, 'sit down, Miss Sanders'. And I am ready for his bullshit, let me tell you. But, I wasn't ready when he told me about Tom. He said there would be a pilot in the lounge that needed a co-pilot for a three-day trip to Paris. His name was Tom Jordan and he was a personal friend of his. Ed told me that Tom wouldn't try anything sexually. He apologized for all the problems I was having here, but he assured Tom would give me no trouble, since this was indeed my first overseas, overnight flight. As a matter of fact I would probably grow to like him. Ed said Tom was quite a character, but I would be completely safe with him, that I should relax and even give Tom a hard time for a change of pace if I wanted to. To let my hair down and live a little. So I said okay and went upstairs. All the time I was walking to the lounge, I ran into pilots that I had flown with and only a few of them even half nodded a greeting to me. But the longer I walked, the better I felt about this man I was going to fly with. And when I entered the lounge I was told Tom hadn't arrived as yet.

I remember when the lounge attendant told me it was Tom Jordan I was waiting for and he started to laugh. I asked him what was so funny. He asked me if I had ever flown with him before, did I even know him? I told him, no, of course not, and he started to laugh again. He went on to say that Tom Jordan was a crazy son-of-a-bitch and if I ever wanted to have fun with a person who can give it out as well as take it, it was Tom. He said, 'today is your lucky day, lady. You are going to have fun, Alex Sanders, so sit back and enjoy the ride. Now by this time I couldn't wait to meet him, but I was still a little skeptical because I still had a few issues. So I sat down in the chair and grabbed a magazine and just that quick Tom came in. The attendant at the window greeted Tom saying, 'well, good afternoon, Captain Jordan, how are you this fine day? 'And while he was doing this he was nodding his head in Tom's direction and grinning. Tom says, 'where do you get this good afternoon shit, Wally, have you been drinking again?' About this time Wally said,' here is the only person I could find gullible enough to fly with you today.' When Tom turned around our eyes met and he said to Wally,' I always did know you were good for something.' Then he walked over and introduced himself to me and I knew right away that we were going to be good friends. I never expected it to go this far, but I never expected the plane to catch on fire either. And Chris" Alex finished. "I've never been happier. All of a sudden I realized that all the crap I went through before that day was old. This was going to be different. I began living all over again. One day at a time to start with, but it didn't take long to fall in love with him; especially when I knew he loved me.

Tom helped me get over the financial pressures of the mess I was in and he got me squared away with the banks and creditors. He even showed me a way to beat the IRS out of the taxes I owed on the sale of the house. He never asked for anything in return, just to love him and let him love me. I wouldn't change anything in my life today. I hope you can find someone as nice as Tom is, because they don't get any better, even if they are men."

"He didn't ask you for anything, but weren't you two sleeping together by then?" Chris asked. "So weren't you paying him back just the same?"

"It wasn't like that, Chris." answered Alex. "Yes, we were sleeping together, but I had my apartment. I could come and go as I pleased. I just chose not to go. It was totally different with Tom. It was nothing like with your father. Tom is as different from him as night and day."

"Do you still love Dad?" Chris interjected.

"No, Chris," Alex answered, "not any more. I struggled with that when I first met Tom, but he helped me through that also."

"How so?" Chris asked.

"I was looking over some old bills one day and I started to cry. Tom came up to me and put his arms around me and told me that the life before us would always be there and it couldn't be replaced overnight. He said these things took time even if it was a bad situation. He told me to take all the time I needed that he would always be here, that his love for me was endless and would hold him until I returned. That afternoon I went back to the apartment and sat down, and in no time, I was just as lonely as those early days of living alone. When I finished crying I knew that I could not live without him. I shut off the light, locked the door and I haven't been back there since until right before you came home. I went in and aired the place out a bit. I don't hate your father, but that was a long time ago."

"I didn't mean that the way it came out," Chris apologized. "I honestly didn't know you were divorced yet. And you are right, Tom is a wonderful person. He just glows when you're around him. I can see why you love him so. He has an aura about him that welcomes everyone. He certainly has made me us feel very safe and welcome in the short time we have been here."

Chris looked down at the girls and commented to Alex that they were both fast asleep with Rocky's head on Corrie's shoulder and sleeping right along with them.

"Well, Mother," Chris said. "Let's call it a night. What time will Tom be in again?"

"Eight o'clock," Alex replied.

"How do you keep all this straight with all these time zones you go through?" Chris asked.

"You get used to it," Alex said as she reached down and woke the girls to get them to bed. "Right now Tom is six hours ahead of us."

Alex took Rocky outside before going to bed. She lit a cigarette and looked out over the ocean. Thinking about the night before she glanced at the spot where they had made love, but the wind had filled the indentation in the sand. Looking back out over the water Alex silently asked God to lean on Tom to take that job Drummond was offering him. It would be so nice, she thought to herself, not to go to bed without him anymore. Flicking her cigarette out she turned and headed for the house. It was late and she was tired.

Opening her dresser drawer to get her nightgown, she came across a piece of lingerie that she had just bought. It was one of the pieces she was attempting to model for Tom when his attention wandered to bigger and better things. Attached to the piece of sleepwear was a note that Tom left, which said, ' I like this one. Does it come in chocolate?'

Having a private laugh, Alex began to miss Tom not being there with her. She went into his closet and pulled out the shirt he had worn for a short time yesterday and put it on for bed instead of her nightgown. The shirt still had the scent of Tom's after-shave.

Her mind began to wander to the events of the day. She and Tom arguing that morning still had a haunting effect on her as she began to doze off to sleep. The last thing Alex did before she fell fast asleep was to ask God to bring him back to her and she promised never again to pick a fight with him. Thinking of the note on her lingerie brought a laugh to her heart. She rolled over in bed and ruffling Rocky's fur, she said, "Damn, I miss that crazy bastard."

52

· ·

TOM WAS AWAKENED FROM A nice nap when the aircraft hit a spot of turbulence and bounced his head against the window. As he raised his head for a quick look around Mylyn came by and said, "Sorry about that ride, Captain, you were sleeping so well. May I get you anything?"

"No, thanks, Mylyn," Tom answered. "I'm going back to sleep."

With that she reached over and tucked the blanket around his shoulders He thought again about calling Alex, but he was so tired he began to drift off to sleep despite the continuous vibration against the fuselage of the aircraft.

With Tom's last thought being about Alex he began dreaming about her. He dreamed about the earlier times in his life with Alex when they would sit for hours and talk until they were about to burst. He dreamed about all the walks they took on the beach and the places they would go on their days off from flying. They would talk about their dreams and plans and their lives today and in the future. The dreams kept changing each time Tom was jarred in his seat from the turbulence. Each time the setting was different. Each dream Alex seemed to be farther away from him. Although he was talking to Alex, she wasn't close enough to hear him.

Tom could feel himself swaying side to side and bouncing more in the turbulent ride, but he refused to wake up and interrupt his dream. Eventually the ride calmed down a bit and he found himself walking again with Alex down a long lane in a forest that he recognized as Mohican State Park not too far from where he grew up as a child. He could hear the wind blow and could smell the greenery and the blooming flowers found in the springtime. Alex had her jacket on and Tom noticed he was getting cold. He reached down to pull the blanket over his shoulders and returned to the scene in the forest.

Alex had walked away from him and he stood alone on the path that led in the woods. As he watched her walk away he could also see that another person joined her dressed in a dark robe with a purple sash. Tom recognized the person as the priest that had appeared to him in his earlier dreams and he became uncomfortable with the sight of the priest. As he looked hopelessly on he found himself reaching down to steady himself on a park bench. He couldn't imagine how Alex and the priest stood so still on the path when it was all he could do to keep from falling off the bench where he was sitting. As he watched, Alex and the priest walked toward him and he became afraid of the look on their faces. When she had reached him Alex held out her hand to Tom and tapping him on the shoulder said, "You must wake up, Tommy; it's time."

The priest came up to him and said, 'The Father needs you now. You must be strong, my son.'

Tom looked at Alex who pushed a little harder on his shoulder attempting to wake him up saying again, "Wake up honey, wake up, Captain, I need your help."

With that he awoke and the vision of Alex faded. He looked up and found Mylyn standing over him with a look of terror in her eyes. There was a great deal of commotion on board. Children were screaming and crying. Some of them were on the floor rolling side to side. The overhead compartments were opening and the contents were spilling out. Tom's senses were sharpened vividly when he got bounced against the fuselage again. It became very clear that they were in trouble.

"Help me with the children, Captain," Mylyn said. "We're going to crash."

He looked out the window and saw the trouble they were in. They were about three hundred feet above the surface of the ocean, rolling and pitching violently. The nose of the aircraft rose and fell like it was searching for good air to fly into.

Tom looked back at Mylyn who was crying and said, "Okay, what do you want me to do?"

"I don't know what to do, Captain!" Mylyn answered.

Tom took her head in his hands and said, "We're going to be all right. Follow the procedures. Let's get the children into their seats and tie them in," he said. "Two in a seat and tie them in together. Put them in the rear of the aircraft in case the front breaks off. Do it now! We have to secure this stuff from flying around. You get the junk, I'll get the kids. Get all the life rafts out and leave them in the aisle so we can get to them quickly."

Tom left his seat and began to feel the effects of the rolling aircraft. It was similar to standing on a roller coaster. Every step forward he took there was another child rolling down the aisle. He reached down and grabbed the child and putting him in a seat grabbed another child and strapped them in together with the other child. He grabbed the pillows that were lying about and put them between the children's heads.

Tom found Irene and told her to tell the kids to get into a seat and strap themselves in and hold onto a pillow. Irene barked out those orders in Korean and Tom moved forward to help the rest of the children that were still forward. He found children everywhere. Some were hiding under the seats or wedged in corners holding their teddy bears with their thumbs in their mouth. Tom reached under the seats and pulled them out putting them in a seat and fastening their seat belt and stuffing a pillow next to their bears. He remembered the vests under the seats and grabbing them put one on every child he had up front and pulled the cord that inflated the bright yellow vest. It would help, he thought. He knew they would need all the help they could get when they hit the water.

Tom hollered back at Irene and holding up a vest he got her, motioned that she should put them on the children. When he again looked out the window he noticed that they had lost more altitude. He could hear the engines scream against the demands on them, but they were not responding. At one point they dipped so far that the port side engine had stirred up some water vapor.

After about five minutes Tom looked back down the aisle way and it appeared that most of the children were in their seats. The other attendants had taken care of the rest of the children that he and Irene hadn't gotten to. That was good, he thought, but as he began to walk back to the rear of the cabin, the aircraft pitched and sent a food cart flying through the air. It came to rest right behind Tom and he reached up to secure it by laying it on its side. In doing this he could see hair and blood on the corner of the cart. He was able to push the cart into the vestibule, which leads to the first class galley. When he did that he looked into the first class section of the aircraft where all the adults were. There was a great deal of damage and the injuries were very apparent with the amount of screaming and bleeding among those passengers. There were all kinds of debris flying through the cabin inflicting injury on everyone it hit.

As Tom turned around, he found himself beginning to panic. The only word that came to his mind was Jesus…Jesus…Jesus. Over and over again he told himself to calm down. His mind began racing to the inevitable outcome. His thoughts settled somewhat and for a moment he regained control. He knew what he had to do. Being aware that this was an embassy flight there was probably not a suitable flight plan filed and with all the pitching and rolling they were doing they were probably well off any intended course. He fought his way to the rear of the aircraft to his flight bag.

Although he found his bag lying at the rear of the cabin, it appeared his things were intact. He reached in and found his compass and attempting to steady it as well as himself he concluded that they had started on a heading south-southwest at zero two zero degrees. He looked at his watch and noted they were four hours out of Paris. That would put them three hours over the ocean at probably six hundred fifty knots. Tom estimated that they were probably not too far off the coast of South America around the Tropic of Cancer. He made a few hurried notes and tried to get a final fix on their position when the plane dipped again and his compass crashed off the armrest breaking into pieces. He started to panic when his compass broke knowing all to well that the only chance they had of being rescued now lay in pieces on the floor of the aircraft.

Settle down, dammit, he said to himself. You've done this a hundred times. Do it once more, but for God's sake do it right. Settle down! Relax! Come on, Jesus, help me out here, work with me. Tom began to settle down despite the panic among the children and two of the Korean speaking attendants. He would do what he could for them in a minute. Taking into account the speed, the time in flight, and that the plane should have made a right turn forty-six minutes ago they should be on a heading of two four zero degrees heading due west until they turned again in two hours over the coast of Bermuda.

Tom stood by the window and looking out realized that this was going to be bad. The plane was still going at cruising speed. He looked around and calling again on his faith he cried out to the Lord hollering, "Help us out! We're in deep shit here."

Tom's prayer was answered when he realized that Alex could help if she knew where they were. He had to call Alex. Strapping himself in the seat so he could make a call he swiped his credit card and let it fall aimless to the floor as he heard a dial tone over the screams and tears.

Mylyn came by and Tom hollered out that he was giving their position, as best he knew it to be, to whomever was listening. As he dialed the phone the plane began to decelerate and lurch. The engines were stalling under the stress that was killing them. It seemed to take an eternity for the phone call to go through. When it did it rang its usual four times and the answering machine sequence started. Falling into despair at what seemed like another failed attempt to be saved Tom nearly hung up the phone when he realized that Alex would eventually hear the message. When the recording tone sounded he gave the performance of his life, giving all the information he had to Alex. He talked so fast and he knew his voice was filled with fear and despair, but it was unavoidable. There was no time to be professionally courteous. He knew she would understand his voice and would know what to do and who to contact. For the first time since he woke up he was no longer afraid. Before he hung up the phone he thought of how to say good bye, but all he could do was tell her he loved her. That would have to be enough for now.

Tom unhooked his seat belt and made one last ditch effort to insure that all the kids were in a seat and tightly strapped in. As he looked out the window again he could see that they were about fifty feet off the surface of the water going up and down uncontrollably. Tom noticed that the two port side engines were winding down. He attempted to get a fix on their speed, but with all the pitching and rolling it was hard to estimate. He knew one thing, however; they were going much too fast to attempt a landing on the surface of the ocean.

"Is there any way we can pull out of this?" Irene screamed.

"I don't think so!" Tom replied in a panicked response.

Tom looked back at Mylyn who had herself strapped in her seat and had a child on either side. All the kids were in a seat and all the vests were inflated. The screams and crying had subsided. It was if the children had no idea what was happening to them as the plane continued to fight violently lurching in the mist filled churning air.

Tom looked at Mylyn and Irene and gave them a thumb's up and nodded with a smile. He then moved back to his seat.

With the two port side engines out, the plane was beginning to yaw to starboard, but the pilot, in an attempt to compensate for the engine failure continued to turn the aircraft opposite the yaw instead of letting it circle into a landing approach. In doing so the plane began to yaw worse than before, popping the rivets which held the wing to the fuselage. The plane began to distort putting the starboard wingtip in the six o'clock position nearly touching water. When Tom saw that, he knew they were going to crash; there was no saving them. He took one last look out the window and, grabbing the three children he had with him, he put himself in the middle with the three of them against his chest, and buried their heads in a pillow.

Fear began to come over him once more as he continued to stare out the window, fear that he would vomit as he could no longer control the terror overcoming him as the jet came closer and closer to the water. He thought that this was it, but deep inside of him he wasn't ready to accept death. He knew the odds. He had been there before and he had walked away before. He was confident that he was going to walk away one more time. How many of these kids, he wondered, could he take with him. And then he remembered the dreams and the priest in them and he knew what the priest had been talking about. This was it. He was living the very warning he had been given. He was living his very own nightmare, the very test he was told he would survive. But how in the hell was anybody going to survive this? Where the hell was that priest now and how far behind him was Jesus? Reluctant, my ass, Tom thought to himself. I'm scared to death.

He continued to look out the window as that tickle of terror in the pit of his stomach began to encompass him. He fought back the urge to vomit, but he couldn't take his eye off the approaching ocean. Tom knew just how hard that water would be when they hit it. It resembled concrete and at this speed it would tear them up pretty bad. He knew being in the back would be to their advantage. They would probably break up and he, Mylyn, Irene and the kids might be thrown clear. It was a matter of how hard they hit and in what position they came to rest.

All the theories that Tom had learned over the years about the physics of an airliner crashing on the water at high speed were racing through his mind. That would soon come, he saw as he watched the water come ever closer. He took one deep breath and tightened his grip on the children as he felt the jet hit the water.

It crashed at a slight down angle making a horrific noise and causing it to bounce off the water like a rubber ball and tilt slightly tail up. The initial impact ripped the two engine cowlings off and sent them slamming against the side of the fuselage punching a hole in it. The G force caused severe pain at the location of the seatbelt designed to protect them. Being thrown through the air at that speed and change of direction was gut wrenching to say the least. Tom grimaced with pain as he was twisted and turned in every direction. Although he buried his head in the same pillows he held against his three children, he had to concentrate not to lose control of his head. Debris as well as blood and gray matter and facial parts flew through the air.

When the jet struck the water again it touched first at the cockpit and drove the nose of the aircraft into the water. When it did so, it tore the cockpit off the front of the aircraft and launched the remaining fuselage into the air in a spiral like spin. Had Tom looked forward he could have seen the sunlight coming down the aisle of the aircraft. There were some bodies flying down the aisle, but the centrifugal force of the spin threw them up to the ceiling as the jet rolled over on its back and sailed through the air. There was the noise of tearing metal as the force of the plane against the water began to rip it to pieces.

The aircraft rolled and tilted down one last time when it hit the water at the torn off first class section. It broke apart about twenty rows from the back of the cabin spitting out anything or anyone who wasn't tied down. Now all that was left was the tail section where Tom and the kids were. It floated in the air and for a moment all was quiet. He could hear the wind blowing through the cabin as the tail spiraled slowly in a clockwise position. Tom chanced a lift of his head from the pillow and looked out the window. With every rotation of the plane he could see bodies falling through the air and splashing into the water The G force had let up quite a bit and it reminded one of a roller coaster ride coming to a stop.

In a torturous, dismembering, violent, moment it was over. The tail section landed with a terrific thud and came to rest afloat on the water. For a moment time seemed to stand still. Tom released his grip on the children he had nestled against his chest. Although they were shaken up a little they were still alive. He stood up and looked around. He saw Irene remove the pillow from her head and look around. She too arose from her seat.

Tom walked to the aisle and quickly assessed the situation. He reached down and grabbed the life raft, inflated it and put it at the opening of the tail section. It appeared they would float for a little while. He turned around and touched one of the Korean flight attendants to get her attention. However, her blank, empty stare told it all. She was dead as were all the kids in her seat, their necks broken by the twisting motion and the shock wave of the jet's impact.

Tom quickly surveyed what remained of the tail section and found there was a great deal more damage in the front of the cabin than the rear. The majority of the children in the front along with both flight attendants were dead. Their motionless bodies, their unmoving eyes and the different position their heads were in, painted a grim picture of how swiftly death came to them as a result of the deadly effects of excessive, overpowering G force.

Tom moved to the rear of the cabin and began unbuckling the children. He asked Irene to tell them to stand still until he could get them on a raft. When he made his way to the back of the cabin he counted sixty-five children still alive. My God, he thought to himself, sixty-five out of one hundred and eight.

He began removing the seat cushions as he passed by them and gave one to every child. As he got to the back of the tail section he found the children with Mylyn were still strapped in. He went to them and unbuckling their seatbelt, realized that Mylyn was severely injured. She had lost a great deal of blood, but Tom couldn't figure out how since she had children on her lap.

Reaching down and taking her in his arms he attempted to move her, but she cried out in pain at the very touch of his hand on her back. When Tom reached behind her he felt a piece of a sharp object that had come through the back of the seat and through her. When the plane twisted it must have pulled it out leaving a large laceration completely through her torso.

Having to think quickly he grabbed a coat that was lying on the floor and put it behind her to slow the bleeding until he could get back to her. Looking at Irene he asked her to get every first aid kit and get the other raft up to the front. Once he had the children off he would come back for Mylyn because the plane was beginning to settle in the front and take on water.

"We don't have much time," Tom said. Get every kid in a cushion. Put the smallest ones in the life rafts. If they don't have a vest take one off a dead kid. If you need more cushions I'll get some more soon. I think we need to get off of here before it sinks. Let's get going and I'll come back for Mylyn.

"Do you know where we are?" Irene asked.

"Not exactly," he answered. "I think we're above South America and to the right of Bermuda. One thing for sure though. We're in warm water. That's got to be a plus."

Tom and Irene went about the task of securing each child in a life jacket that was once the seat cushion. With that and the vest on each child, they began leading them out of the aircraft and into the water.

"Tell them not to be scared, Irene," he ordered. "Tell them they will be safe, and if they do exactly what you tell them, they will be fine."

As Irene and Tom got the children out of the plane and into the water, it was Tom who was the most reluctant to get into the water. He had never learned to swim and now that was going to be a problem. He grabbed a second seat cushion and entered the water first.

He took the second life raft and inflated it, but it had a leak in it and only inflated part way. He reached into the raft pocket and pulled the emergency transponder and turned it on. It was dead. There were no batteries in the pack. The second raft, he was to soon learn, was the same way.

Tom reached out his hands to each child to help them get into the water. Once he and Irene had all sixty-five children in the water, he led them in an orderly fashion about fifty feet away from the tail section of the aircraft. He took the ropes off the sides of the life rafts and tied all the cushions together so no on would wander away. He now prepared to get Mylyn.

As he turned around from getting the children secured, he got his first look at the destruction of the aircraft and the carnage it left behind. There was debris everywhere. There were bodies or what passed as bodies or parts floating everywhere in the water. There was some moaning and groaning, but Tom couldn't really tell from where or from whom it was coming. As he swam back to the tail section bodies began bobbing up randomly. From what he could see the only ambulatory survivors were in the tail section with him. There didn't appear to be any survivors anywhere else.

There were a few surface fires burning, but nothing major like a moving oil slick burning and migrating across the water. Tom noticed as he looked at a man who was still hooked into his seat belt that he was wearing a belt. After he got Mylyn to safety, he would come back and get what he needed to keep his kids safe. He could make a floating raft of seat cushions to keep the kids out of the water. Sitting in ocean water for an extended amount of time would be very bad for them. And at this point he had no way of knowing just how long they would be here. It was obvious that the dead had no need for the cushions or their belts for that matter.

As he reached the tail section he pulled himself out of the water and walked toward Mylyn. She still hadn't moved from the spot Tom put her in, but he could see she was still alive. He greeted her saying, "It's a beautiful day out there. You don't want to stay cooped up in the house all day, do you? Come on outside with me and I'll get you some sun. We have some nice South American climate out there today, what do you say to that?"

Mylyn didn't say anything at all, she just sat there holding tightly to the cut on her abdomen. Tom attempted to remove her hand, but Mylyn wouldn't budge.

"Let me help you, Mylyn," Tom said. "I promise I won't hurt you. I wouldn't do anything like that, you know that, don't you? Just trust me and let me help you."

Mylyn grimaced with pain as she removed her hand and let him see what he could do.

He looked at a gaping hole that he was convinced passed completely through her body. Trying desperately not to show any emotion he said, "That's not so bad. We'll have you back in the air in no time."

Putting her hand back over her wound he grabbed some compress bandages from the first aid kit and kept talking as he attempted to look at her back.

"You can't believe how beautiful it is outside," he said. "Let me look at your back and we'll go out where it's nice. What do you say to that?"

Mylyn shook her head and leaned forward so Tom could dress the wound on her back. He took a compress bandage along with a Kotex that he got from someone's purse and applied it to her back. Since Mylyn was presently dry, he was able to secure that with a large adhesive bandage and then he turned his attention to her abdomen.

"Yeah, you're going to be all right. You're much too beautiful and strong to have a little cut get you down," encouraged Tom. "Okay, let me have your belly again."

Mylyn appeared to put all her trust in him as he fought to stop the bleeding in her abdomen. The injury was of a ripped organ that bled profusely once pressure was removed. Mylyn laid her hands on Tom's shoulders as he worked on her cut.

He kept talking to her as if they were old friends who finally had a chance to get caught up on gossip. He related it to talking to his mother when he saw her next month. They would talk for days just to get caught up where they left off. He rambled on about nothing just to keep Mylyn's attention off her injury. In about twenty minutes he had her wounds dressed although he knew it was only temporary. Unless they were found quickly, she didn't have a chance. The blood was black; it was coming from her liver.

Tom remembered that Aurora flights had a backboard in the rear of the cabin where spare coats are kept. He went back to the closet and was relieved to find exactly that. He also found some pain killing morphine in the medical safe and used Mylyn's key to open it. He remembered his captain's training and prepared the recommended dose for the amount of pain he had assessed she was experiencing

Walking back, he began his litany of chatter again when he said, "Look what I found. Your very own bed. It has a sleep number on it. Without her being aware of it he injected her with the morphine dose and began preparing to evacuate her from the cabin.

Tom took two seat cushions and tied the backboard onto them He then found several blankets and put them over the backboard for a makeshift mattress.

By the time he was done Mylyn was pretty much out of it so he ever so gently took her from her seat and laid her on the backboard. He added an extra cushion of a T-shirt for pressure against the wound on her back and moved her as gently as he could to the water.

Once Tom entered the water Mylyn looked at him and said, "Let me go, Captain. Let me go."

He had to fight back his tears when he said, "I can't. You're my date for this trip. I promised I would take care of you. Besides you're the only one who can speak the language and get us out of here. We're all in this for the long haul, I'm afraid."

Tom splashed water on his face to hide the fact that he was crying as he approached the others. By the time he got to Irene he regained his composure a bit and brought Mylyn over to her and said, "Hang onto her. I'm going to hook us all together with the belts these guys are wearing. If you have a better idea, I'd love to hear it. We might be able to make a big raft. You better have the children look away for awhile."

He went about the grizzly task of visiting everybody that had surfaced to see if there was anything he could use. Most of them had belts which was very helpful. Very few of them even had shoes on so their shoestrings were unavailable. Once he had what he needed or could find use for, he unlatched their seatbelt and took their cushion. In about an hour, he had secured twenty-six belts and forty cushions. He did manage to find about five yards of shoestrings. Returning to the children with all these things, he began building a makeshift raft. As he would work on the raft another donor would surface. He was more than happy for any donation he could get. In about four hours he had enough cushions to get all the children out of the water. He tied Mylyn on the end of the raft so he could tend to her easily. By the time he was finished getting the children out of the water he was exhausted. He tied himself off to Mylyn and relaxed for a few minutes. Soon he would have to go back into the tail section and find something for the kids to eat.

Thinking about getting help he looked at his watch, but it was gone. He was trying to determine if Alex had gotten the message yet.

"What time is it, Irene?" Tom asked.

53

ALEX AND CHRIS GOT OUT of bed the same time the next morning. Chris made coffee and asked Alex if she could hop into the shower first before the girls got out of bed. Alex agreed to that and calling to Rocky poured a cup of coffee and went outside with him to smoke a cigarette.

While she was out there, she heard the phone ring but decided not to run to catch up, thinking the machine would get it.

Alex was starting to pick up on some of Tom's habits when she caught herself talking to the Almighty just as he did every morning. Finishing her coffee and her cigarette, she turned to walk into the house. She looked back across the water as if she was talking to someone behind her and said, "I meant what I said about not picking fights anymore. Did you talk to him about Drummond's offer?"

With that exchange of words with the Almighty she went up to the house.

Corrie was awake when the telephone rang and was standing there when Tom left his message. Not being completely aware of what it meant she went to the shower just as Chris was getting out.

"Mommy, Tom called and he's in trouble," Corrie said. "You better come and listen to this."

Chris walked to the phone and pressed the message button. She listened in horror to what Tom was saying. She knew exactly what was happening and was overcome by a deep feeling of inadequacy. She turned and looked out the window and saw Alex coming toward the house.

"What does he mean, Mommy?" Corrie asked.

"I'm not sure, honey," Chris said.

"He was crying, Mommy," Corrie said. "He was upset like he was yesterday morning."

"I don't know, honey," Chris said. "I don't know what he means."

Alex entered with Rocky and looked at Chris and Corrie standing by the telephone.

"What's the matter with you two?" Alex asked. "You look like you lost your best friend."

Chris just looked at her mother and, in a most somber tone said, "Tom called. You better listen to this."

Alex finished pouring another cup of coffee and walked over to the telephone and pushed the recording button.

'Alex, this is Tom. Listen to me. I'm in a world of hurt here. We're going down, hard, in the ocean. I figure we are about three hours out over the ocean. Two hours at zero two zero degrees. Forty-six minutes at two four two degrees. I think we are northeast of South America and due east of Bermuda. We should be in the Tropic of Cancer, forty by twenty. We are in the middle of the ocean. I doubt if anyone knows where we are. This is an embassy flight. Alex, I need you to come and get me. We're going to hit hard. We're going too fast. I'm in deep shit here. We all are. You do what you can there and I'll do what I can on this end. I love you, Alex. Always have. I will get through this. But hurry, honey! Please hurry!'

There was no more, only the finality of a dial tone. Alex looked very serious as she played the message again. She had to listen intently to the words amid the screaming and background noises of terror. It was difficult to make out the coordinates since Tom's voice faded in and out. Alex wrote down the coordinates that Tom gave her and when it was finished she listened to it again. This time she lit a cigarette in the house. Chris and Corrie just stood by and kept out of the way. No one said a word.

She walked over to the counter and put cream and sugar in her coffee, even though she always drank it black. Looking out the window trying to collect her thoughts, she looked down at Rocky and said, "Do you think they are ready for us, boy?"

She walked back to the machine and took the tape out. She picked up the telephone and called the airport.

"Get me Ed Drummond!" she said. "This is an emergency!"

After waiting a minute for Drummond to come to the phone Alex began to show a break in her armor as a tear began to form in her eye.

She walked into Tom's office to pull herself together and emerged with the hand held phone when Drummond answered. Alex told him what Tom had said. They talked for a few minutes and both agreed they would personally take command of this situation. Drummond explained to her what Tom meant about this being an embassy flight. They also talked about the slim chance of getting NASA to turn a satellite around to view the northeastern sector of Bermuda. Drummond said he would call the French Air Force and put all Aurora executive flights on the water from the international sector where they would begin their search.

"We might have trouble getting the Koreans to believe that they even have a plane missing, no more that they keep track of their charters. We may get no where with these people," Drummond explained." If you can come here and take over the search from the operation's office, I think we have a better chance of getting through to these people. They don't like us telling them they screwed up."

"You let me do the talking!" Alex interjected. "The first son-of-a-bitch that tells me 'no' today is going to have an accident. I am going to make those little yellow bastards enthusiastic. They are going to understand what it means when I say—failure is not an option. This is not some NASA has been, this is Tom we're talking about here, and I'm in no mood for bullshit today. You get them together, and I'll be right there, Edward."

And with that Alex hung up the phone. Turning to Chris and Corrie she said, "I don't know when I'll be back. I'll keep you posted. This could take days. But I'll be home tonight no matter what."

"What can we do to help on this end?" Chris asked.

"Just pray for him," Alex said as she began to cry. "The phone will ring quite a bit when this gets public. Do what you can with that. If a Father Harris calls, fill him on everything. He is Tom's friend. He'll want to know. Tom told me to call him if I ever needed anything. That Tom is a tough bird; if we can get to him soon enough we may get him back in one piece. But if we get through this he is finished flying. This is his third strike. Take care of him also." Alex said as she looked at Rocky. "He knows when there is something wrong."

Giving Chris and Corrie a hug, Alex grabbed her car keys and looked back at Chris and nodded positively as if to give her some kind of hope in a situation even Alex feared was hopeless.

54

. . . .

TOM WAS ABLE TO REST for a little bit and decided to go back in the tail section and see what he could find to feed the children. As he swam back to the plane he realized that his trips here were limited. The tail section was sinking. Not totally, just sinking by the opening in the fuselage where it was torn off. The tail was beginning to stand upright. The emergency oxygen storage tanks were full enough to keep it afloat

When Tom entered the tail section he walked back to the spot where Mylyn was lying earlier and laid down to try to get some of his strength back. Being in the water and floating was already beginning to weigh on his endurance.

As he lay there on the seat he began to think back to the priest and his dreams and couldn't for the life of him understand what they had to do with what was happening now. He had gotten sixty-five kids out to safety and was able to build a raft to get them out of the water. Mylyn was in pretty bad shape, but there wasn't much more he could do about that.

Then his mind began to wander to the message he had left Alex and he realized the very thing he told her was indeed true. No one probably knew where they were. He gave her the coordinates based on his experience where they should have been had he been flying this plane. But he wasn't flying this plane and they were all over the place after he woke up. They could be anywhere. The very fact that there were no working transducers on board any of the rafts was a bad situation also. Even one transducer would attract any vessel, in the air or the sea.

What if there were sharks in the water? Tom only assumed they were in the Tropic of Cancer. The water was warm which was a good sign. Warm water breeds smaller sharks. He could feed them the dead if need be. What if there wasn't any food left on this tub? These children would begin to starve in about four days. He didn't think the kids would go along with eating their parents. They couldn't anyway; they would spoil in the heat in two days and begin to smell. He began to make a mental note of what he needed from this trip. The longer he sat in Mylyn's seat, the more he could see that the tail section was sinking.

He got up from his rest and began foraging through the rear galley for anything he could eat. About all he could find was syrup and jelly. Both had a high sugar content so he took all he could and put it in a plastic bag. There was very little food left on board. He came across some snacks such as pretzels and potato chips and some soggy cookies. Maybe, he thought, he could dry them in the sun. He only found a few bottles of water. He found an empty jug and filled it from the lavatory faucet. This was in no way enough food to feed sixty-five kids. Tom feared that the starvation scenario might start sooner than he imagined. He collected all he could salvage and went back to the raft. He would return soon and get all the blankets he could carry. Although they would be wet for awhile Tom thought that he could use them to protect the children from the mid-day sun.

As he returned to the raft past the debris field, he noticed that several more people had risen to the surface. The worst part of all this was that children were seeing the bodies randomly surface from all around them. Several of the children were crying in a strange tone. Irene told Tom that the word they used meant 'mommy' in English.

He tried desperately to get the children to look away as more bodies were surfacing from the first class area. These people were horribly disfigured and they were upsetting the children as they bobbed in the water only partially intact. It became obvious to Tom that the brunt of the crash was absorbed in the first class section of the aircraft. How horrible, however quick, death must have come to those. He said a prayer as he unhooked them and took their seats.

The best thing he could do at this time was to go to every floating body and remove all he could use from them. He took their belts, shoestrings and then eventually released their seat belts and took their cushions to build up the raft. In about a minute the body sank into the blue abyss of their lonely watery grave. Tom began doing that to all that surfaced. He felt if the children couldn't see it they were better off.

Most of the children just sat on their cushions and stared out over the ocean, apparently in a state of mild shock. He tried to get them to lie down and relax so they wouldn't build up an appetite. He went to the male children and made a special attempt to let them know he would care for them, but since he couldn't speak the language, he just talked with a hug, a kiss, and a pat on the back, or a look of encouragement. He asked Irene to talk to the children and tell them it wouldn't be long, even if Tom didn't believe it himself. Irene took care of the girls in much the same way.

It would be dark soon, he thought. The darkness would bring its own set of special problems, and Mylyn was getting worse. It was beginning to bother the children when she cried out for help. He gave her another morphine injection to help with the pain and quiet her down. Tom spent every available moment he had with her in an attempt to lessen her pain. But, he knew she was hurt too badly. Although he was ashamed of himself for thinking about this, he feared that if she bled into the water that would attract sharks. There was no way he could fight those bastards off. He could only feed them something else. He went after the blankets and tried to get some time to think things out. He was so tired.

55

ALEX PULLED INTO THE PARKING lot and was met by Ed Drummond and several other airline officials. One was the chief pilot of Korean Airlines.

Once the introductions were made they all went upstairs to a large conference room that was set up with grid maps, course maps, hemispherical charts, satellite charts and even the charts with the search plans already charted. Alex was relieved when she saw all that. This was the uphill battle she was afraid she would have to fight just to get started .It appeared that the legwork was done.

The chief pilot of Korean Airlines began the meeting saying that a listening station off the northern coast of Africa picked up a distress call. The caller identified that voice as a Korean male. He could not get exact coordinates from the voice locator, but he was able to identify it as an airliner in peril. He went on to say that the only aircraft that was flying at that time was an embassy flight, but there was no reliable flight plan filed for this. Why, he did not know. That was all the information he had. He apologized for this, but he reiterated that there wasn't a reliable flight plan followed, which would make it difficult to track the aircraft.

Next it was Alex's turn to address the group, but since she was only a pilot, Ed had to make the introduction.

"Good morning, everyone," Ed began. "First off I'd like to thank you for coming up to speed so quickly and getting organized for the search. The French already have search planes in the air in the coordinated area where Captain Jordan estimated they were."

"I'd like to introduce you to Alexandra Sanders. She is the lady that Captain Jordan called this morning and gave these coordinates. She is going to take over the efforts from our end. The company president has given her all the resources she requires and the authority to use what she will to secure the safe return of Captain Jordan and all the survivors. Having said that, let me introduce you to Captain Alexandra Sanders."

Alex stood up and began to address the crowd. This was something new to her and she was having a little trouble getting started. Ed saw the difficulty she was having, put his arm around her shoulders, and told her to be strong. She began addressing the assembly.

"Thank you, Ed. As you may or may not know I have a vested interest in Captain Jordan. We talked about marriage yesterday. We have been together about six months now and we were planning a lengthy cruise around the southern coast of Malibu in three days. So if anyone wondered why he called me, it is because we live together.

Okay, the last thing Tom gave were these coordinates. Since he flies this route about ten times a month, I figured he knew where he was. He did say that they were going very fast and were up and down quite a bit. So I'm thinking they strayed off course by as much as fifteen minutes. The last heading Tom gave me was the Tropic of Cancer. If there is any course alteration it was most likely south. I'm getting that because of the short wave locator off the northern tip of Africa. This is an interesting signal to receive from a short wave receiver. I think it would be a mistake to dismiss this as an amateur who doesn't know what he's doing. Presently we are trying to get NASA to reprogram a satellite over in that direction, but that is like pulling teeth. I think our best bet is search aircraft. We have also put out feelers to all marine traffic to be on the lookout. By the best of our deductions, they have been in the water a little over four hours. The Tropic of Cancer is four hours ahead of us, so we may be talking about darkness before long. We have no idea if there are sharks in that area either. We are waiting for several more reports concerning water conditions. So, to sum this all up, we are just beginning to get the search parties out and are waiting for initial reports. We will meet here again at four o'clock and see where we are. Please do not excuse any report as being futile. We must check everything out."

After her presentation Alex sat down. As the other members rose to leave, she realized that she was trembling. Many of the members of the committee came over and shook her hand giving her any encouragement they could. Most of them knew Tom and all had something good to say about him. One committee member even went so far to say that he wished Tom was with them today on the search, because he could find a needle in a haystack if it meant getting someone out of harm's way. All were very friendly towards Alex, but they all felt the same; a crash at sea was one of the worst things to deal with. It was the hardest to survive after the fact. They would do all they could as quickly as they could.

56

· ·

TOM ENTERED THE TAIL SECTION and salvaged everything he could find that wasn't bolted down. His heart leapt with enthusiasm when he found a flare gun with one flare already in it. He tucked that in the blankets and was ready for his trip back to the raft. He was hoping to get a few more cushions to tie together so he also could get out of the water for the night. As he left the tail section he had trouble getting out, as it was now nearly vertical. This would be his last trip for salvage; from now on they had to live with what they had.

Tom swam back into the raft area and couldn't help but notice the sunset. It was so full of radiance and beauty that it filled him with hope. He told Irene to have the children look at it, that it was a sign of good luck. He didn't know if it was or not but he thought it would pick up the spirits of the children.

"She's getting worse," Irene said of Mylyn. "How long can she hold out like that?"

"I don't know," Tom answered. "Have you got any ideas?"

"No," Irene said.

"I'll go see what I can do," he answered.

Leaving the raft area he swam slowly over to Mylyn, being careful not to stir up the water and move her. When Tom stopped he put his hand on her forehead to check her temperature and to calm her down.

"How are you feeling?" he asked.

She didn't say anything, but the pain on her face was evident. She moved her head back and forth in an attempt to distract herself from her discomfort. Tom put his hand under her head to steady it for a while. He lifted her head and rubbed the back of her neck to make her a little more comfortable. It appeared to help momentarily.

She opened her eyes and looking at him said, "Let me go, Captain. Just let me go."

"I can't do that, Mylyn," Tom replied, "you know I can't. Please don't ask me that. Let me make you comfortable."

"Give me the rest of the morphine," she said. "I don't want to live like this."

"You're going to be fine," he pleaded. "As soon as they get here we can get you to the hospital. Trust me. They'll be here soon."

Tom prepared another injection for Mylyn. It was only about a half-hour before her next scheduled one so he figured it couldn't hurt. It would at least quiet her down for awhile. He gave her the injection and stayed with her holding her head and talking to her until she fell asleep.

By his estimation he only had about one more day's worth of morphine. After that he couldn't control her pain. A feeling of helplessness began to shroud him as the darkness fell on the group of survivors. The feeling of helplessness only greatened when his attention was drawn to a noise. It was the tail section succumbing to the weight of the water and it stood straight up like the stern of a big ship about to sink.

Tom returned his attention to the children. Mylyn was quiet and for the most part the children were relaxed as well. He had distributed some of the food he was able to salvage to the children. Luckily for him the majority of the children had no appetite. He looked out over the horizon at the vapor trails the other jets coming and going from Paris were leaving, and despair began to creep over him. He knew they couldn't see them from that altitude, but he let it get to him that no one knew where they were, or no one was coming for them.

Tom began to get angry about the despair, but no matter what he did, he couldn't shake it off. The longer he looked, the more vapor trails he counted. He had to look away and put his energy on something else but worry. The water was reasonably still for an ocean, he thought to himself. He secured two more cushions from a surfacing casualty and made himself a bed. He was able to climb aboard it and lie down despite the weakness he felt in his back and legs. He was beginning to develop a slight pain in his lower back that he attributed to the violent twisting and turning of the aircraft when it crashed.

Lying flat on the makeshift raft was a comfortable relief after a long and tedious day. The last time he was in a bed he was lying with Alex. What a strange transition this was. What he wouldn't give to be back in her arms at this very moment. The last thought Tom had as he slipped off to sleep was Alex. She was their only hope of survival. Tom knew they were screwed unless she could find them and get them out of here. He now faced a new plateau in his life. He realized that for the first time since he met Alex, he not only loved her, but now he depended on her. He depended on her for his very own life.

57

ALEX LOOKED AT HER WATCH to get a sense of the time following the last meeting of the day for the rescue committee. She estimated that wherever Tom was, it was probably dark by now and there were no reports of any sightings anywhere within the search grid. That meant that the location Tom gave her was not where he was. Within those coordinates there were no sightings of any debris fields. A search airplane can spot a debris field ten miles away, but there still were no reports coming in. There were also no reports from the marine units on the water. Alex began to worry, but quickly got her bearings when she realized that if Tom was south of his coordinates he was alongside South America or the West Coast of Africa. He should be easy to spot there. But, Alex thought, he should have been easy to spot on the Tropic of Cancer also.

"Where are you, Tommy?" Alex said openly as she put her head in her hands and began to cry.

Alex was so caught up in her own thoughts that she was unaware that Ed Drummond had entered the room.

She heard his Zippo lighter click open as he lit a cigarette and then offered her a light as well.

"Let's inhale these deep," Ed said. "If you lose it, I'll lose it. Right now I need you to be strong for me as well as Tom. Jesus, how in the hell could something like this happen? I think he's alive though, Alex. Something in my gut says he's alive. Where in the hell he is, I have no idea, but I truly believe he's alive. And damnit, we're going to find him."

The pressure on Alex was so much that she stood and went to Ed who gave her a long hug. The hug was as beneficial to Alex as it was to Ed who tried to make small talk.

"You know the old saying, no news is good news. Somehow, some way, he is going to find a way out of this. And when he surfaces, we are going to be there, like he has for us so many times before."

"Tomorrow let's go south. I'll ask the French to hit the northwest sector also. We'll fan out and see what we can scrape up. There has to be a debris field somewhere. He could not just have vanished into thin air. If they made it to shore somewhere, we would have gotten reports on that. These are heavily populated shorelines. Why don't you go home? There won't be anymore reports come in tonight. This place is like a tomb when everyone is gone. Go home to your family and draw from their strength, you're going to need it to get through the night. Try and get some rest. If you need to talk, call me. Don't be surprised if I call you."

"Thank you, Ed," Alex said as they hugged each other again. Ed turned and went out the door, obviously upset because he didn't look back at Alex, he just walked quickly out the door.

As he made his way down the corridor he collected himself and thought 'have I inadvertently hurt Alex by an act I undertook professionally? How could I have known that something like this could happen to Tom? How could I have known, although I suspected that Tom and Alex would fall in love?' A mile of thoughts ran through his head as he reached the door to his other appointment and was bombarded by a host of supporters who had heard the news about Tom and wanted to check on his wellbeing.

Alex collected all her reports and decided that she would take them home with her to get a head start on tomorrow's search patterns. As she left the room a feeling of finality came over her. She felt afraid to leave thinking as long as she stayed here in the room dedicated to finding Tom, there was a chance. If she left, she thought, she would be leaving Tom stranded. Alex shook off those feelings and headed for home. The girls would want to know what she had learned today about Tom.

She made her way across the parking lot and got into her car. Looking to her left she recalled the vision yesterday when she dropped Tom off at the gate. She refused to let herself think about that, knowing all too well that the only hope was in a clear head and competent decisions. She drove out of the lot and on to the freeway. When she reached her exit Alex drove past the park where she and Tom had talked yesterday. The farther she drove the more memories flooded her mind. She had never realized before all the things that they had done together in the short time they were together. This drive down memory lane was a little more than she bargained for, but the thoughts of Tom made her feel a little more relieved about what she had to do. She was afraid for Tom, but she knew she was in the best position to help him. She pulled into the driveway and opened the garage door.

58

. . . .

WHEN SHE ENTERED THE HOUSE, Chris and the girls who were eagerly awaiting some positive word of Tom met her. It didn't take long for Alex to change smiley faces to gloomy ones when she related to them that there was no word about Tom. As the conversation went on, a grim picture emerged. Chris asked the girls to go into the living room and watch the movie while she finished supper. With the girls gone they could talk.

"We have no idea where he is or even might be," Alex started. "The coordinates proved to be wrong. He is no where off the coast of South America. Tomorrow we are going further south along the coast of Brazil and search over by Africa. Ed is going to have the French search further north. Right now there is no sign of him anywhere. At least we have no news of him being dead. As long as we have no sign of him, I know he isn't dead. They are going to have to prove to me that he is dead before I give up hope."

Alex rose from her seat at the kitchen table and looked out the window.

"We have to find a way to tell the girls. We may even have to do it tonight," Alex said as she folded her arms around herself.

"I talked to them this afternoon," Chris said. "I thought it would be better coming from me."

"Thank you," Alex returned.

Soon after the conversation, dinner was ready and the girls were called to the table.

"Let's keep this to any subject but Tom," Alex said.

"I understand," Chris said.

Dinner was a quiet affair as everyone fought for an appetite no one had. Rocky even sat quietly by and didn't beg. Things were a harrowing quiet. The air was as thick as the lingering tension, but no one dared begin a conversation.

In about twenty minutes the torturous meal ended, and the girls returned to the television while Chris and Alex did the dishes. That was even a quiet affair as Alex just stared out the window, occasionally drying her hands on her apron and directing her attention to some grid maps she had lying on the table. She would make some notes and go back to the task of the dishes only to be distracted again and make some more notes.

Before long the dishes were done and the two ladies retired to the living room and sat down. Chris wanted to strike up a conversation, but was unsure of what to say.

Finally the silence was broken when Alex said, "We're going farther south tomorrow. Maybe we can pick up something and we can find him by tomorrow afternoon. If we're lucky we can have him home by supper. Who am I trying to kid here? The chances get worse the longer he's out there. I refuse to believe he's gone. He's too ornery to die, too full of shit anyway."

Alex stood and looked out the window as she continued her labored conversation.

"He's tough you know, Chris," Alex went on. "He's no candy ass. He'll beat this thing. We just have to help him out a little. We need to find him before this gets out of hand. The current could move them, believe it or not. And where are all the ships that pass through there? How can they not see anything?"

Alex returned to the couch where she picked up an afghan sat down in the Lazy Boy, and covered up with it.

"Tom's mother made him this. Oh, my God, I forgot to call her!" Alex said excitedly.

"I called her," Chris answered. "I had a nice conversation with her and felt better after talking to her. You should call her in the morning, though. I kind of told her you would."

"Yes, thank you, I will," Alex replied. "She's a special lady. I met her last month. Tom and I flew down over the July 4th weekend and met his whole family. It's kind of ironic, isn't it? We go and see them and now this. Jesus, Chris, I promised his mother I would take care of him."

With that Alex started to cry. Chris came over and put her arms around her.

"This isn't your fault, Mother," Chris said. "Don't take on the guilt. You just try to find him. That's all you can do for him now. Crying won't help either. You have your training, you have your charts and you have the authority. Go out and find him. If anybody can bring him home it's someone who loves him. It's someone like you. That ocean isn't big enough to keep you away from your true love; you'll find him. The girls and I have been praying all day for him. And don't worry, when you get the call, you go to him. Don't worry about us, we can take care of ourselves. You know what, Mother? No matter how bad this sounds or how bad things look right now, your love and life with Tom will forever be solidified. You two will forever be together. No one else in the world would ever get the chance to show such love for her man like you can, now, at this stage of your life. That's why I know Tom will come back to us."

Chris continued to hold her mother in her arms until Alex fell asleep. Chris began to wonder how she could have been so wrong about her. How could she have put the blame on her for her father's drinking and eventual divorce? She began to regret the time they had lost during the two years she and her mother didn't speak. As it turned out in the end her father took off for Italy, and when Chris was in trouble, it was her mother who came to her aid. She never asked why or wanted anything in return, just the love of her family and to be all together. Now Chris sat helplessly by her mother holding her while she slept, unable to bring her lover home to her. She would continue to hold her, she felt she owed her at least that.

59

TOM'S SLEEP WAS INTERRUPTED BY screaming children as well as Mylyn's cry for pain relief. Several of the children were crying, Tom surmised, because of the dark and because they were hungry. He had hoped he could get the children to sleep through the night, so he wouldn't have to worry about how he was going to feed them right away. This meant that he would have to get back in the water again, which he really didn't want to do. He needed to regain some of his strength before he faced another day. He felt that if he stayed in the water all day, he would lose feeling in his legs. Being unable to swim put him at an acute disadvantage.

Tom made his way to the children and tried to console them the best he could, since he didn't speak the language .He took a little Korean girl into his arms and she was very quick to reciprocate. She held tightly onto Tom and before long several of the children had left their rafts and joined them. All the children found a piece of him to hold onto and all was well as the children once again drifted off to sleep.

The little Korean girl that Tom went to first refused to go to sleep. She just stared into Tom's eyes and it seemed liked an eternity between blinks. He looked back into her eyes and could not believe the relief she gave him. She reminded him of Corrie, and thinking of her made him cry. Being careful not to show any emotion to the children, he tried to look away from the girl, but she took his face in her hands and returned his eyes to hers.

Tom fought to regain his composure, even in this lifeless place, so as not to upset the children, but it was no use. He was exhausted, overcome with stress and worry, and found himself slipping into a state of despair. He needed the strength of this child to pull him through, for he knew he was in trouble and could see no way out. The silence of the evening was again torn apart by the cry of pain from Mylyn. Tom leaned forward in the water and kissing the little girl, carefully moved away from the sleeping children. As he left her, the little girl smiled and motioned for him not to be long.

He went to Mylyn's side, but she was more alert now than before due to the pain. It didn't take her long to plea for more medication. Tom was prepared to give her the next injection, but he wasn't prepared for what awaited him when he swam up alongside her. She grabbed him by the hair and pulled him close to her, screaming at him for more morphine. He quickly injected her with the standard dosage he had prepared, but Mylyn wouldn't let go of his hair. She began to beg him to give her the remaining dose and put her out of her misery, but he tried to quiet her so as not to upset the children. He tried to get her grip off his hair, but he had to duck beneath the surface of the water to release her grip. Once he was free he kept away from her hands. He held her arms and tried to console her by talking to her, but it had no effect. The morphine wasn't working, and Mylyn began screaming louder than ever.

Tom went down to her bandage and attempted to change it. But Mylyn kicked him in the face. The blow sent his head spinning as if he were knocked out by a blow from Sonny Liston. For a moment he was adrift from the rest of the raft and it took a few moments to regain his composure. As he did, he reluctantly approached her, this time from the head end. He reached up and took her head in his hands and tried to console her again, but she only thrashed at him. He held onto her head and after about ten minutes she settled down and appeared to fall asleep.

Tom returned to her wounded abdomen and tried to elicit some moonlight to check her wound. In the moonlight blood is black so he received no help in checking Mylyn's condition. It would have to wait until morning..

As he made his way back to the little girl, Irene stopped him and said, "You are going to have to take care of her."

"I'm doing the best I can for her," he answered.

"No, Captain," Irene returned, "you're not listening. You are going to have to take care of her."

"What are you talking about?" Tom said in an exhausted tone.

"Give her the rest of the morphine," Irene answered. "Give her the rest. Let her die with some dignity."

"What the hell's the matter with you?" he asked. "We can't just kill her to shut her up."

"That's exactly what we are going to do," Irene ordered. "When she wakes up in the morning in pain, you give her the rest of it."

"No!" Tom answered. "I'll take my chances on the rescue crew."

"That's easy for you to say," Irene continued. "You're a man with no injuries. She's a woman and she's dying and there's nothing you or any rescue team can do about it. There won't be any more talk about a rescue team. Nobody knows we're out here and no body gives a shit. The quicker you get that through your head the better off we're going to be."

"You don't know that," he said. "I know they're looking for us. I know Alex is looking for us, and they will find us. We just have to be strong and hang on. They will find us."

"In the meantime Mylyn is still dying. What is your phantom rescue team going to do about that?" Irene argued. "You Americans always think someone is coming for you. I tell you, Captain, we are dead out here. It's just a matter of time. You go back and stay with the children and deny all this, you pathetic bastard. Mylyn's the lucky one. She won't have to wait so long. Give her the rest of the morphine, you ass hole, and let her die in peace."

Tom went back to the raft with the little girl and once again all the children came over. He tried to comfort them the best he could, but they were upset, he thought, because of the screaming of Mylyn. Now that she had quieted down maybe they could all get some rest. He tied himself off to the raft so he wouldn't sink, and holding the little Korean girl in his arms, fell asleep.

60

. . . .

ALEX ROSE FROM HER SLEEP and helped put the girls to bed. With all the excitement of the day everyone just seemed to sleep where they fell. Chris said good night to Alex and she too went to bed. For the first time since this morning, Alex was alone in the house. She began to tremble with fear and worry about Tom. She collected Rocky and taking a cigarette and her lighter went out to the beach. Lighting her cigarette she looked up into the heavens and saw a shooting star. She couldn't help but be reminded of the first time she stood out here with Tom, the first night they spent together and watched a meteor storm. He told her that falling stars were the fire in the hearts of loved ones trying to communicate.

She stood on the beach and looked out over the ocean thinking that somewhere out there, Tom was looking back at her. If only she could see him she would reach out and get him and bring him home The longer she stood there the sadder she became and realized that she was tired and should go to bed. But somewhere in her mind she thought that staying out here brought her closer to Tom. Once she went into the house she would be alone and so would he. She lay down in the sand and Rocky came and sat along side of her.

Despite the despair in her mind she felt at peace. She could not put her finger on it, but she wasn't scared, sad or depressed. At this very moment she was relaxed. She continued to lay there and let her mind wander over all the good times she and Tom had on this beach. She couldn't count all the times when they made love here. This was his favorite spot in the world to take her, he told her many times. Of all the places in the world to go and make love, thirty feet out of the back door was his favorite place. What I wouldn't do to have you here right now, she thought to herself. She looked where the divot was left the last time they were here and it brought a smile to her face.

Alex thought back to all the times he would come out here wrapped in a blanket saying he was going swimming with his new bathing suit, though he didn't have a bathing suit on nor did he intend to go swimming. She thought back to their argument yesterday and she became sad. Alex put it out of her mind immediately and went on with her thoughts. It amazed her that Tom could show up with a blanket, pillow, wine, two glasses, shrimp and crackers out of nowhere and get her out her on the beach, get her naked, and seduce her before she even knew there was that kind of food in the house. He was good at that, she thought. He always knew how to give her what she needed and wanted even before she knew what she needed or wanted. That man could come up with more ways to do something out of the ordinary. She felt sorry for those people who were married to conventional men who never did anything different. Those other wives had an advantage over Alex tonight, though. They each had their husband home with them.

Thinking back on some of Tom's exploits was one way Alex knew she would be able to cope with tomorrow. She turned her attention again to where the divot was in the sand. Somehow Alex just rolled into it. She never could figure out how he did that, but she wasn't complaining. When I get him home, she thought, we're going to pick up where we left off. Standing up and cleaning the sand off she turned and walked toward the house. She was hopeful about what tomorrow would bring. Stopping, she turned and looked out over the ocean again.

"I'm coming to get you, you crazy bastard. You better be ready," Alex said.

Looking up to heaven she said, "And you're going to help me."

61

. . . .

TOM WAS AWAKENED BY A scurry of excitement from the children. There was a strange sound coming out over the water. It sounded like people talking and working. A great deal of different noises came across the water but it was impossible to get a bearing on the location or to identify the noises. Tom shook the sleep from his eyes and began to strain his eyes and ears in an attempt to locate the sounds. What appeared to be waves breaking got louder the longer the sound carried across the water.

He untied himself and swam to the raft where the little children were and removed the flare gun. Suddenly there was a large metallic sound in the distance and Tom could see the outline of a large ship in the moonlight as it passed by them about one hundred yards behind the tail section. Knowing it would do no good to holler Tom cocked, aimed and fired the flare gun. The flare flashed out across the sky and in the direction of the bow of the ship, but failed to ignite and deploy its trailing parachute. The flare was a dud. Blowing all common sense to the wind Tom started hollering but the weakness in his body really took its toll and he was soon winded.

Trying to hide his despair from the children was no easy task as the ship clearly continued to distance itself from the survivors. Their very existence clung to this temporary raft in the middle of nowhere. Tom's mind began to wander as he realized that the ship wasn't even on the lookout for them or any sign of any wreck on the ocean. Alex would have seen to it that all marine traffic was on the look out for them. Maybe Irene was right, no one knew where they were or even cared. It became painfully obvious to him that he wasn't where he thought he was.

As he looked one last time across the ocean and saw the last of the ship's light flicker out of view he began to believe Irene. They were doomed. There was no way in hell they would ever get out of this alive. Although he thought that this ship was probably their only chance, he also held onto the hope that Alex would change her search in the daylight to go farther south. She would not stand by and let others tell her he was dead without proof.

His thoughts turned desperately to Alex hoping that the thought of her would give him the strength he needed to get through what was in front of him, but he only found himself being overcome with sadness. Tom looked to heaven in the way a man would look to get any type of help he could. It was desperation that he was slipping into. Despair was something new to him, but the feeling was unmistakable just the same. He swam back to where the children were waiting for him. He would attempt to draw from their strength. It's ironic, Tom thought to himself, a grown man drawing on the strength of the very children the Father had sent him to protect.

It would be light soon, he would have to see to feeding the children, and Mylyn was getting restless again. The problems were mounting as were Tom's physical weakness and fears. He would have to put some form of strength on his face for the children as well as Mylyn. If they were not rescued today she would certainly die and he was sure it would be a slow, horrible death. Tom began to mutter to that very Heavenly Father that he was now depending on, but his prayers were cut off by the screams of Mylyn. He had hoped to have an hour or so before having to deal with her this morning. Everything he had hoped for appeared to fall on deaf ears. As he swam over to see Mylyn, he couldn't help but notice the beautiful sunrise on the horizon and it gave him a moment's hope. He again looked up to the heavens and muttered one phrase before he reached her, "We've got to talk!"

And for a reason Tom could not explain, a feeling of peace came over him and his fears began to leave. When he returned his gaze to the rising sun it appeared to resemble Alex's hair, as it would flow in the warm Texas wind. Raising his head once again to heaven he said, "Thank you, I needed that."

He had reached Mylyn.

62

. . . .

ALEX WAS STIRRED FROM HER sleep by the watchful eyes and ears of Rocky who announced a visitor at the door. She rose and walking to the door asked, "Who's there?

"Father Harris," the voice returned. "I know it's late, but I just called the airline and they gave me the news. I told Tom I would help if anything happened."

Alex opened the door and let the priest in. Rocky backed up into the corner of the kitchen and lightly growled as his hair stood up on his back.

When Father Harris saw Alex, he smiled and extending his hand said, "You're every bit a beautiful as Tom said you were. And I don't say that to just any Presbyterian I meet for the first time either."

"Yes," said Alex. "Tom was right. You've got as much bullshit as he does." And with that she hugged Father Harris tightly and said, "Come on in."

"Where should we start?" Father Harris asked.

Father Harris appeared to be a mild mannered man in his late forties with a beard and a full head of black hair with a hint of gray telling his years. Alex wondered, however, how a Mexican priest would have a name like Harris, but for now it wasn't important. He was a very personable fellow who put you instantly at ease and seemed to make all the pressures associated with the accident fade into nothing.

"Have you been brought up to date?" asked Alex.

"All I know is that I had a funny feeling that Tom was trying to contact me and I had the phone turned off," Father Harris began. "I don't know why, ma'am, I never turn off that phone. I was getting ready to take off for a conference in Phoenix when something told me to call, but your line was busy, so I called the airlines. They told me everything had to come through you, that you were in charge of the search. I knew that word 'search' was not good, so I came over as fast as I could."

"What is your first name?" Alex asked as she made them some coffee.

"Troy," the priest answered. "My friends call me Skip."

"I'm Alex," Alex returned.

She sat back down at the kitchen table and began to fill Father Harris in on what they knew. She played the answering machine tape back to Skip several times as he just sat there appearing to be in shock.

Alex shook him on the shoulder in an attempt to bring him back to reality, when he finally looked up at her and said, "He's alive."

"How do you know that?" asked Alex.

"Did he ever tell you about the dreams?" Skip asked.

"After I nearly beat it out of him!" Alex replied.

"What all do you know?" Skip asked.

"I know about him helping some priest. He has been upset for weeks and that priest really has him screwed up. I've seen him jerk to his right or left as if looking for something. I've seen him looking on the beach for, I don't know, footprints! I've seen Rocky's hair stand on end. Tom has horrible nightmares, and I know he dreamed about his funeral yesterday. He stood in the corner of the bedroom and kept turning and running into it as if he couldn't get out."

"How did he get out?" Skip asked.

"I went to him and walked him back to bed," Alex answered.

"Does he ever say anything to you during these dream?" Skip asked.

"Yesterday after I put him back into bed he looked up at me and told me he couldn't help the priest, why didn't he leave him alone," Alex went on. "And then he put his head down on his pillow. I don't think he was awake. I don't think he was talking to me."

"Tom has told me in great detail about his dreams," Skip said. "Let me tell you what I know and what I have learned. Maybe I can shed some light on this for you and maybe bring you a little less worry."

"I don't know how you could possibly do that," Alex interjected. "Not with him somewhere out there only God knows where."

"That's exactly my point.," Skip said. "God does know where he is, He put him there."

"Wait a minute!" Alex said. "Are you telling me you believe that fashionably challenged wacky priest?"

"Oh, yes," Skip said. "He's the key to all this. You understand, he isn't a priest at all. No, he is someone in Tom's mind. Sometime in Tom's life he saw him, probably in a movie No, Alex. That priest is the Father. That is how I know he is alive. In all of history anytime the Father has called upon a mortal to do His work, that mortal has survived. Sometime a little worse for wear, mind you, but always they survive; and so will Tom. I know this because the Father told him so. That is where his strength will come from, from the Father's guidance and your love. Those two things and those two things alone will sustain him through this."

"And you know this-how?" asked Alex.

As the coffee finished perking Alex rose and poured them a cup, Skip went on about the situations other people have gotten into all in the name of the Father. The stories began with Moses and all the way up to and including Mother Theresa. Alex wasn't too impressed with the outcome of the story of Joan of Arc, however.

"It is rare that this sort of thing happens in our day and age, however," Skip concluded. ""So it is very important that we don't let this out. If we do every miracle-seeking groupie in the Western Hemisphere will hound Tom. No, Alex,. I think once we get him back home, we should hide him."

Alex gave Skip an agreeable nod and the conversation went on to where the search was going to lead in the morning. Alex looked at the clock and noticed that it was only three a.m. She was certain that she would not get back to sleep after all she learned in the two hours she had talked with Father Skip.

After he finished his coffee he said, "I must be getting on. I'll check with you in the morning. Get all the rest you can. Once the Father is done with Tom and he returns him to us, it will be up to us to take care of him. It could be exhausting. Look at Joan of Arc. It took them weeks to do something with her hair."

With that, Father Harris left for home and Alex returned to the bedroom. As she lay on the bed she had an irresistible urge to pray, something she had learned from Tom after the fire. She grabbed her bathrobe and her cigarettes and went out on the beach.

Nothing came to her mind, only the peace that she so desperately sought. She did, however, thank God for sending Father Harris to talk to her despite the time.

Talking with him about Tom was a comfort that she couldn't explain. Sitting on the beach she looked up into the heavens and asked, "How much time do we have? How long can you keep him safe for me? Could you maybe drop a hint where he might be?"

Alex sat still waiting for an answer she really wasn't sure how to hear in the first place when Chris came out and sat next to her.

"Who were you talking to, Mother?" Chris asked.

"Father Harris," Alex answered.

"No," Chris replied. "I mean just now in the kitchen."

"Yes, Chris," Alex answered. "That was Father Harris."

"No, Mother," Chris said excitedly. "Father Harris was here earlier this afternoon."

"So?" Alex asked. "He stopped back on his way home again. I thought it was nice of him. He is a very nice man. Tom does have the neatest friends."

"Mother," said Chris. "It couldn't be. Father Harris is black."

63

. . . .

AS TOM SWAM OVER TO Mylyn he stopped by Irene and asked her if she could feed the children while he administered the morphine injection. Irene was very irate this morning and immediately started an argument with Tom concerning his treatment of Mylyn.

"Why don't you do what has to be done, you spineless bastard?" Irene scolded. "She doesn't have a chance in hell, no more than the rest of us. But we aren't in pain and she is. Why don't you help her?"

"I'm going to prepare her injection now," Tom answered defensively.

"Give her all of it," Irene demanded.

"I can't do that," Tom replied. "Not while we have a chance of rescue."

"You are as stupid as you are proud," Irene retorted. "What did you learn from that boat, genius? You gave them the wrong location. No one knows where we are. And they probably wouldn't give a shit if they did. They damn sure know where we aren't, thanks to you. Why don't you do something right in your pampered life and put her out of her misery? For God sake, you can at least do that right, can't you? You're a big strong man. She's a weak frail woman. Go on, be a man for once and do something that will at least help one of us"

"I won't do that," Tom said as he swam toward Mylyn. "Please feed the kids."

"Feed them yourself," Irene snapped back. "I'm not going to help them suffer any longer than they have to. If you let them stay hungry, they won't hurt so bad when they starve to death. You and your hope, you and your belief that someone will come for you just because your girlfriend works for the same airline. Take a look at Mylyn. There's a lesson in hope for you, you pompous asshole."

Tom swam toward Mylyn to get away from Irene. He knew she was right that he was clinging to a small fragment of impossible hope. He did give them the wrong location. They were easily two hundred miles from where he had reported them to be. He believed this to be true by the light maritime traffic. These waters were way too corrosive for any heavy shipping use. This was why Tom was feeling so weak from dehydration, because the salt was sucking the fluids from his skin and with it his very strength. He was beginning to hate Irene. What a bitch, he thought to himself, when he approached Mylyn's raft.

As he neared her he remembered that he had to approach from the head end and not face to face. As he reached her shoulders he put his hand on her forehead and it was obvious that she had a very high fever. As he began talking to her he noticed that her fingers were all covered with matted blood. She had removed her bandage and had dug at her wound in an apparent desperate act to remove whatever organ it was that was causing the pain. She had chewed the majority of her lips away, and no longer lay in a drugged stupor, but trembled as someone who was freezing to death. Her mouth was covered in dried blood and her inner index fingers were both chewed and gnawed badly.

Tom had thought that she slept well since he didn't hear from her during the night. He went on preparing her injection when she spoke to him.

"How much --do we have-- left?"

"Well, good morning," Tom said in an attempt to lighten her mood. "You must be feeling better if you're talking."

"How...much?" she asked again.

"Enough for today and a little before you go to sleep," he answered. "About five hundred cc's."

"Give it...to me," she said as she gasped for air to cover the pain.

"I can't do that," Tom said.

"Fill the syringe...I'll do it," she reasoned. "Don't...make me suffer... fill it. I'd do...it...for you."

Tom looked into her eyes, but there was no rescue to be found in them, only pain. The sun had come up enough to see that she had ripped open the hole that had lacerated her torso and had managed to pull some of her intestines out of line. She had attempted suicide during the night, but it had failed miserably. It was now obvious to him that there was no way he could sustain her for any length of time and the morphine he had left was not enough to cloud her pain with the recommended doses until help arrived. He desperately searched for an answer that wouldn't come.

He looked back at Mylyn who had put her hand on Tom's shoulder. When Tom looked back into her eyes, she nodded her head and said again, "I'd do…it…for you."

He emptied what appeared to be five hundred ccs into the syringe and it completely filled it. He wondered if this was enough to do the trick, and if not, what then?' But when he finished filling the syringe, Mylyn's hand came up to meet his and together they pushed the needle into her hip and gradually emptied the contents of the drug into her body. She lay motionless for a minute or more and then looked up at him and smiled. Her hand fell helplessly into the water. He retrieved it and placed it over her abdomen as he pitched the syringe into the water in hopeless frustration.

Tom stayed alongside Mylyn for what seemed to be an eternity. In a matter of moments, she quit shivering and her breathing was no longer labored. She lay there peacefully. She reached her hand up again and took his hand in hers and shaking her head, yes, she managed a smile. She turned her head toward him and said, "The sun is shining today."

With a smile on her face she turned her head back onto the pillow Tom had made for her and closed her eyes. He continued to look at her, remembering how beautiful she was yesterday when she met him at the gate and welcomed him aboard the flight with them. The kind of beauty, Tom thought, one only found in a magazine. As he continued to look at her, he could see that she was no longer in pain. She was resting peacefully on her raft. The sun appeared to rise to meet her and a soft ocean breeze came upon them. Tom would later swear he could smell flowers. The grip she had on his hand lessened and he once again caught her hand. He lay it alongside her this time and covered her with the blanket. He looked at her one last time. She had a smile on her face, and she was gone.

Tom searched desperately for a place to go to sort this out, but there wasn't any solace for him now, only more misery. He knew exactly where he was and he knew this was going to get a lot worse before it got better.

He was on his own now. Mylyn was only the beginning of the sacrifices that would be made before they either got out of here or joined her in the hereafter.

As he made his way to the children he remembered the priest and muttered to him aloud, "You bastards said you would help me. I damn sure don't see any of you sons of bitches around here."

Tom took what was left of the jellies and the cookie crumbs and began passing it out to the children. Each child was able to have some cookie crumbs or pretzel crumbs and a small packet of jelly. He passed around what was left of the fresh water. The only meal he could prepare was over as soon as it started. The children seemed to believe that Mylyn was sleeping, because nobody mentioned her this morning.

After breakfast Tom noticed that a few dead passengers had surfaced so he went about his task of procuring all the flotation cushions that he could use. He also didn't like dead people within sight of the children. Besides that, an odor was beginning to form around them and he knew only too well what that could mean with the sun on the rise. As he went about his grizzly task, he couldn't help but think of Mylyn. He would always wonder if he had done the right thing. Trying to think rationally he knew he couldn't help her anymore. He would forever be changed, not only because of helping her end her life, but also because of this whole situation. He knew if he ever survived it he would have to find a way to cope with it. Alex was probably right, he would need to see some people to get through this mess.

As he searched the horizon in all directions, it was clear that there was no one on the water. Soon, he thought, the sun will be up over Houston and Alex will once again begin the search. Despite what Irene had said he was confident that Alex would not rest until she found him. He was convinced he was her soul mate and he believed she would find him. He had to believe it; without that hope he had nothing. And he was dangerously running short of hope right about now.

Tom swam back to the children's raft thinking he would have to cool them with the wet blankets soon because the mid-day sun would be brutal today. Just then a rumble came from the north and it became clear that it would rain soon. Rain was good, but a storm on the water would be bad. He cast a glance at the tail section of the aircraft and it appeared that it had not settled at all. The tail could be their lamp of good luck. In a remote chance it would attract a radar beam. If anyone was even in the general area using sonar, they may get a "ping" back from it.

As he left the area where the casualties had floated to the surface he had to pass by Irene. Looking as sarcastic as ever she asked Tom, "How is she doing? Miserably, I'll bet. Have you thought about what will happen when you run out of morphine, genius?" She was beginning to scream as he approached her.

"Have you figured out what you're going to do then, asshole?" Irene screamed.

He swam over closer to Irene and said, "She's dead, you bitch! Now leave me alone." With that Irene said no more.

The morning chores had exhausted Tom. He went over to his little Korean friend and crawled onto a raft. He needed to get some rest. Looking over his shoulder at the northern sky it was becoming evident that there could be some morning rain. With the accompanying thunder it could be a storm that Tom was not physically up to fighting. All the rafts were made of lightweight material held together by shoestrings. If the storm produced high gales it would rip the rafts apart and the children would be spread over the ocean where he couldn't keep them together before they were drowned. This wasn't good; he was weak and he knew he didn't have the strength to fight the wind and rain.

He took a moment to rid his mind of what had just taken place with Mylyn. He had to get a plan together to deal with the threat of the oncoming storm. The emotional effect of her passing ripped at Tom's conscience. He had never openly aided someone in his or her death. It wasn't as if Tom killed her, but he felt responsible because he did nothing to stop it. He was so exhausted and weakened by the situation, that he never even gave it another thought when Mylyn asked him to help her die. He just wanted to be rid of another problem.

He wanted all this to go away so he could go home. He was in the middle of an unknown ocean and he couldn't swim. He was exhausted and there was no where to go and recuperate. He was hungry and there was no food to eat. Despair was setting in fast as he wondered to himself, where all the people were that he had helped in the past. Where were they now when he needed them most? And where was the Father who was supposed to be here for him to get him through this?

The guarantee that the priest had given him was apparently bullshit also. He wondered if the priest knew Mylyn would get hurt during the plan they had for his great salvation of these children. Where are all you sons of bitches now, now when I need you, Tom thought to himself as despair turned to anger. Why didn't you come in time to help her, you bastards? Why didn't you at least come in time for her?

As he looked helplessly around at the vast ocean for a solution to the oncoming problem, he reached within himself for strength, but he had none. He could feel in his heart that he had no fight left. He thought of Alex, but even now her memory wasn't enough to pull him out of the abyss. He was hungry, tired, and defeated. Tom then made another mistake, one that would turn things around and take him as far as he needed to go to get out of this. He looked into the eyes of that little Korean girl and all of a sudden it was clear this was no place for quitters. The little girl smiled at him and reached her hand out to his. He took it in his and, looking into her eyes for a moment found some peace, enough to muster up a smile. The little courtship between the two friends was soon interrupted however, for it had begun to rain.

64

ALEX ROSE HAVING GOTTEN A minimal amount of sleep after her visit with the priest. As she made coffee, she waited for her daughter so they could talk about who this man who said he was Father Harris, actually was. As Chris entered the kitchen the telephone began ringing signaling a day that was starting out to be very busy at the Jordan household. Alex answered the phone as she waved good morning to Chris and put up one finger indicating that she would be just a minute. On the phone was Tom's friend Bob who had just returned from his flight to Hawaii and was told by the dispatcher about his missing. They had plans tomorrow evening for a dinner celebrating Bob and Sharon's fifteenth wedding anniversary. He had told Alex that this was going to be a dinner that she wouldn't want to miss. The men had a special skit planned for their women. The most interesting part of the conversation, however, was when Bob told Alex that the Korean embassy flights always go midway between Africa and South America and then vector to the west to Chile and then turn north to Houston.

This information told Alex that they weren't searching far enough South. This excited her so much that she dialed Ed Drummond on her cell phone to tell him while she talked with Bob on the other line. Within two minutes the whole day's preplanned search patterns had changed and there was a new exhilaration. Bob was also going to join the team with Alex, freeing up Drummond to do some other coordinating at a higher level which required exchanging favors. The Air Force had agreed to send a couple reconnaissance planes over the area. The new type of camera system these planes were equipped with could take a picture of a debris field even if the pilot couldn't see it. This was a tool that would greatly aid them in their search for the crash site.

Alex hung up both phones and sat down with Chris when the phone rang again. It was a member of the rescue team that Alex headed up. It appeared that an airplane had sighted some debris about thirty miles due north of a South American fishing village. There were boats headed out that way to recover the debris. The man on the other end of the line said they should know something pretty soon.

"What do you think?" Alex asked. "Is it responsible information?"

"Well, being thirty miles off the coast, I would think someone would have seen or heard something," the man replied. "These people don't miss a thing in these villages. I'm thinking it may be trash, but let's check it out just the same. I'd love to be wrong and find a whole bunch of survivors this morning; how about you?"

With that comment Alex hung up the phone and once again joined Chris to try and make some sense of who the man was that had been at the kitchen table if it wasn't Father Harris. They were interrupted once again by the telephone when to the surprise of Alex the voice on the other end of the line identified himself as Father Harris.

"I think it would be nice if you could come over here as soon as possible," Alex said.

"Has the situation gotten worse?" Father Harris asked.

"Well, it appears that someone is masquerading around here using your name," replied Alex. "It would be nice to meet you and talk with you if you could."

"Yes, of course," Father Harris replied. "Give me ten minutes."

"We'll have to get dressed, Chris," Alex said hanging up the phone. "Father Harris is coming over and we damn sure don't want to sit in front of God's emissary in Victoria Secret nightgowns."

Alex and Chris made a hasty retreat to their bedrooms to change their clothes before Father Harris arrived. When Alex opened the closet door on Tom's side, a small box fell to the floor. Breaking its fall with her foot Alex reached down and picked the box up and opened it.

The box obviously held a gift. There was a card that read "Happy six months to the greatest beach partner a guy could ask for." Behind the card was an eleven by fourteen picture of Tom and Alex taken on an afternoon picnic at an abandoned railroad trestle about forty miles away. Alex sat on the bed and a tear immediately came to her eyes. She began to laugh softly to herself when she reminisced about the day they went to that spot and Tom took that picture. She swore that day she would always remember him trying to put his camera on the picnic basket and get the right angle. Being a windy day, he had to anchor the basket so the camera wouldn't sway. All was fine until out of nowhere a squirrel came along and tipped over the basket nearly breaking Tom's prize Minolta. The funniest part was the entire hassle Tom went through to keep that camera still. It was a day to remember as Alex looked at the beautiful picture of them and the beautiful background he had chosen. When Alex looked at the photograph she felt like he wasn't missing at all, only on a trip. She knew for now she could hold this picture of the man she loved and freezing the moment in time, Tom would be with her. She closed the box, putting it back in Tom's closet and continued getting dressed. She could hear Father Harris coming up the front steps.

65

. . . .

TOM WAS BEGINNING TO BECOME very concerned with the magnitude of the wind that had come up with this storm. There was an increase of lightning and the waves were rising into a dangerous roll. He swam over to Irene and told her to tell the children to hold on to one another. Tom then made a swim around the perimeter of the raft to check on the bindings that held it together. He motioned to the children and physically placed their hands together with their partners as lightning crackled loudly overhead. After taking a look around Tom thought that the raft just might hold up as long as these waves didn't begin breaking under the children. The belts might be able to take the strain, but the shoestrings were already weakening under the corrosive nature of the salt water.

He looked into the eastern sky to try to get a fix on the time. If he could at least estimate the time he could estimate the time when Alex would return to the search. Just then he heard a child scream and looking quickly to his left he saw a head go under the water. Tom swam feverishly to the edge of the raft, but the child didn't bob back up to the surface. He knew he would have to lose his life vest and he did so stripping it off quickly and handing it to a child on the raft.

Tom then dove under the water and saw the child just kind of hanging suspended about ten feet below the surface. He swam to the child and coming from underneath her lifted her to the surface and back on the raft. It didn't appear that she had aspirated much water. With a little coughing and heavy slaps on the back the child soon recovered and took a grip on the raft next to her partner.

"God damnit, Irene!" screamed Tom. "I told you to tell the kids to hang on. The next one that goes, you go after them."

In desperation and anger Tom swam over to Irene.

"If this storm gets much worse it'll wash these little shits right off these cushions. Help them, damnit. Without us they don't have a chance."

"We don't have a chance anyhow," Irene hollered. "You're the only fool who can't see that."

"We—are the only chance—they have," Tom returned loudly. "We've already lost one, I'm not losing another one."

"We'll all be dead in an hour," Irene argued back. "This storm is the best thing that ever happened to us. It won't be long now."

"If you want to die so damn bad, then go," Tom ranted. "But as long as I have life I'm not letting these kids go. If you don't want to help, fine. Shut the hell up."

The argument was soon ended when a large bolt of lightning struck nearby and most of the children began screaming and moving about fearfully on their rafts. Tom went around the raft again and tried to calm the children down. With the lightning came more rolling waves and the sea was getting rougher. Tom put the children's feet on the cushion and told them to hang on. He wasn't sure if they knew what he was talking about, but he had to say something to calm them down. As he hung on the raft to rest, another child hollered out to catch Tom's attention. Looking to his left he could see that another child had washed off the edge of the raft and was being carried swiftly away from them. Remembering his poor swimming ability, he grabbed his vest and took off swimming after the child.

When he neared, a wave came from the opposite direction and washed the boy right over the top of Tom forcing him under the surface and ripping his vest off his body. As he thrashed to regain his position on the surface of the water, he noticed how difficult it was to move. He was being pulled down no matter how hard he attempted to get to the surface. He was able to look down and see that the little boy was under him and had a death grip on his leg. Tom curled his body and grabbing the boy pulled him off his leg and alongside of him. He then covered the boy's mouth and using his left arm thrashed his way to the surface.

When they broke the surface, Tom shook the water from his eyes just in time to see another child approach them in the water riding the force of a wave. Tom reached out and grabbed the child and the three of them made their way back to the raft. When they reached it he noticed that a section of string had broken loose and dumped the two children into the water.

Tom had a spare belt and made a quick makeshift repair. The experience had exhausted him. He had taken in some water on that swim and began to vomit heavily. The swim also weakened him so much that he was having trouble holding on to the raft. Both little children were all right and soon were back on the raft hanging on for dear life. The rain had become heavier, but the lightning seemed to dissipate as the storm headed south. Tom figured that was a good sign. The lightning scared the children and why not, he thought; that shit was nasty on the water.

If the raft would hold together in this wind they should be all right. As long as he didn't have to retrieve any more drifting children he could catch his breadth. He was coughing feverishly over that last swim, but the vomiting was beginning to settle down. Tom hollered and made a hand signal to the children to hold on and eventually he joined his little Korean friend. When he got there she again offered him her hand and taking it, Tom fastened himself to the raft. For now he would just float here. He would crawl aboard in a minute. They had won the first round. He lost no children. He looked up to heaven and waving said exhaustedly, "Okay, you win. No more bitchin', but a little help would be nice."

Tom put on a spare life jacket and struggled to climb aboard the raft. The rain felt good. Putting his arms around his friend he closed his eyes and tried to rest. Everyone was quiet. The rolling of the waves had a calming effect. Once on board the raft he got his first look at his body. His shirt was gone and his pants had a bleached effect. His skin was pruned and had a clammy, wrinkled, excessive look to it. It was clear the salt water was taking its effect. He closed his eyes and soon was asleep.

66

. . . .

ALEX MET FATHER HARRIS AT the door. He shook her hand and said, "Tom has told me a great deal about you. He was much too modest. And I hear you are of the Presbyterian persuasion." He then looked over at Chris, winking and greeted her saying, "It's nice to see you again"

With that exchange Father Harris put her at ease. It was clear that Tom was right about his friend. He was a different kind of person who made everyone feel good about themselves and the situation they were in.

"So, tell me about this imposter first," Father Harris said.

"Well, Father," Alex began, but was interrupted.

"Call me Skip," Father Harris said.

Alex went on telling Skip the story of the mild mannered priest who came over at three in the morning and told her that Tom would be safe, that he was doing the Father's work and he would return.

"He said something about historically all servants of the Father fare pretty well except for Joan of Arc," Alex concluded.

"Yes," Skip replied, "she was Presbyterian."

With that, Chris let out a giggle and again the pressure of the situation was eased. Alex rose from her chair and whacked Skip on the shoulder as she took his coffee cup for a refill.

"All right, you," she said. "Tell me what you know."

Father Harris did what he did best; he took control of the situation and diffused it by humor. In his heart he was sure that Tom was alive. How safe he was, however, was another story. The real challenge was to convince Alex that Tom was safe. He was impressed with her, for she was everything Tom had told him she was. He knew now what the spark was in Tom's life. He was happy for him, but Tom was also his very good friend and he was very concerned about his well being.

As he and Alex talked about Tom's dreams and what Ship knew about being called by the Father, the phone rang again, but Chris took a message for her mother. .

"If you are confident that the Father will keep Tom safe, how much time do we have?" Alex asked.

"Well, that's a gray area," Skip replied. "Of course the sooner the better, I assure you. There are reports of survivors hanging on for very long periods of time, like that bunch that crashed in the Andes. Of course, once they got on track with their dining arrangements things worked out quite nicely."

"Oh, my God, you're incorrigible!" Alex said again as she got up and whacked Skip on the shoulder. This time she also gave him a big hug and said, "You are the best thing to come into my life in a long time. I feel better already and I didn't think that was possible today."

As Skip got ready to return to the church he said, "I have a few things to do today. Why don't we meet at the rectory about six for supper? I'll have Rosario fix us a big Mexican dinner and afterward we'll sit around the fireplace and sip Alka-Seltzer. Oh, can that woman cook up a mean batch of beans."

Once again the kitchen filled with laughter. By now the children were awake and came out to greet Skip. Having just seen him the other day they were very excited. They weren't totally aware of the purpose behind his visit, only that Tom's friend had stopped by.

"We can't leave here in the evening, Father," Alex said. "Why don't you bring Rosario and come here for dinner? We will fix you a good Presbyterian dinner."

"Saints preserve us!" Skip said while laughing hysterically. "I'm doomed to the fiery pit. Actually that would be a great idea. I'm out of Alka-Seltzer, come to think of it."

With that Alex, Chris, the girls and Father Harris had a large group hug. Just before Skip left for home he said, "Let's say a prayer together for Tom, shall we?"

With that they all bowed their heads as Skip led the prayer.

"Heavenly Father, we ask that you watch over Tom today, keep him safe until we can find him and bring him home to us where he will once again touch us with his inspirational presence, his laughter and his unending love. Amen!"

"Amen!" all replied. With that Father Harris bid everyone farewell and made plans for their supper date later in the day.

Alex looked at the clock above the sink and remarked at the time and made her way to the bedroom. Midway down the hall she stopped and went to the telephone and called the rescue office hotline telling them she was going to be a little late. But what the heck, she thought, she wanted to talk to Chris first about Skip.

"Do you know what he did, Chris?" Alex asked. "That little Catholic got out of here and never mentioned who the other Father Harris was."

"You're right!" Chris replied. "Those Catholics are all alike."

As Father Harris drove down Sommer Street toward the rectory, he was very much aware that he didn't mention who the other Father Harris may or may not be. He was quite concerned himself as to who the man was. He thought that it might have been the priest that met Tom on the beach on several occasions. This unsettled Skip immensely because it could have been a message to Alex that Tom was in deep trouble and trying to soften the blow. Skip thought he would get the most important issues done first and he would then cancel the rest of his daily activities. Alex needed him and he promised Tom that he would be there for her. For the first time since this ordeal had started, Skip was afraid.

T OM WAS AWAKENED BY A rolling wave that went over his face and into his mouth. The coughing effect of this was exhausting until he could get the water off his gag nerve. He began to vomit forcefully once again and this in itself weakened him more. The action of the waves had gone from soothing to difficult. And it looked like it would be another problem he needed to solve.

The sky was very overcast and would make looking for them difficult to impossible. The average plane would not chance this low an altitude to look for victims for fear of becoming one

Tom wasn't sure if the kids had enough strength to hang on to the raft. He feared he may have to tie them to it, but that had its bad points also. The more he looked at that sky the further the possibility of rescue became. His only hope was another ship. And those were few and far between.

With the weather, Tom couldn't get a fix on the time. He could only estimate it as late afternoon. He made a trip around the raft to make sure the bindings were tight. The waves could rip the raft apart and he knew he didn't have the strength to retrieve the children if they were washed off into the water. As he made his way over to his raft position by his little Korean friend he tried to lift himself out of the water, but couldn't. He had weakened past the point of self- preservation. He would have to float in the water and conserve as much energy as he could.

Looking into the scared eyes of his Korean friend, he reached out and took her hand and smiled. He knew they would not be together much longer. He had done all he could do. Tom; who according to Alex was forever the optimist, was quickly losing hope. His thoughts changed from how long before they were rescued to how long before they were all gone. He tied himself to the raft so he could try and get some sleep. Maybe, Tom thought, he would pass before he woke up. Worse things could happen.

68

AS ALEX MADE HER WAY to the freeway in route to the office she heard the news broadcasting Tom being missing. The news broadcast said that he was the pilot who safely brought the burning airplane into Presque Isle, Maine, six months ago.

The news went on to say quite a bit about Tom and his career and Alex had less of a problem listening to it then she thought she might. However, when the newscaster made the statement—" Captain Tom Jordan was fifty-four years old," that unnerved Alex so bad she had to pull over to the side of the road and get out of the car.

"He's not dead, you son of a bitch!" she screamed to a passing motorist who just kept on going.

Alex stood by the side of the road for a few minutes and cried before returning to the car. We're running out of time. She thought to herself. He has got to be out there somewhere. There are only so many places he could be. Damnit, Tommy, where are you?

She thought to herself of the progress on the amount of area covered on the grid maps. They had covered a great deal more of the area than the standard flight plans usually take. His friend had told her to go deeper South with her search. However, Alex was saddened to hear that the entire area was in a deep overcast. There had to be a way to cover that area.

In a few minutes she would be at the airport and at the center of the rescue operation. Maybe they had heard something in the time it had taken her to get to the office. As Alex made her way down the concourse to the rescue crisis office she was greeted warmly by people she didn't even know. Many said to let them know if there was anything they could do. Many others said inspirational things to build up Alex's hopes. But the one person Alex was taken in by was an elderly pilot who said, "Never count him out. He's a crusty old bastard. The Chinese couldn't get him; no ocean is going to get him either. You just find him. He'll be alive."

Alex shook the man's hand and as she walked away she felt a moment of peace come over her. Being impressed by the man's message, Alex turned and looked back, but he was gone. That's strange, she thought, there are no exits in this corridor. Wow, that Tom has some strange friends. Alex turned the corner and went into her office.

"Good morning, everyone," Alex said. "Do we have any new developments?"

"Nothing good, I'm afraid," answered a man looking at a weather map. "The skies are so overcast to the south we couldn't see a debris field if we were right on top of it."

Alex was somewhat put out by that response. She collected herself professionally and asked, "But we are going to keep looking, right?"

The man looked at Alex and replied, "Oh yes, ma'am. Most assuredly."

Right answer, Alex thought, right answer.

Joining Ed Drummond at the other end of the table Alex said, "I'll bet you he's right here-- what do you think?"

Shaking his head as if confused, Ed lifted up his hands and said, "It's the only place he could be. We've been everywhere else. If they went south like Bob says, the reports from the shipping lanes would have picked him up."

"Those ships wouldn't see him either," said the man reading the weather maps. "If it's raining out there, those guys will get caught up on their sleep. There will be no deck work to speak of on a rainy day. And by the look of the overcast sky, they wouldn't see them even if they nearly ran over them. I'll bet you, Captain Sanders, that is exactly where they are."

"What do you know about that location?" Alex questioned the man with her arms folded and a very serious tone about her.

"The tropic of Capricorn is known for its warm water, high salt content, many whales and rarely any sharks. One could live there for a couple days," the weatherman answered Alex with an air of expertise. "But the salt content of that water will take all the fluids out of his body. It will eat him alive."

Being concerned about this, Alex asked, "Can you explain this a little better?"

"The person looks ashen," the weatherman began, however grizzly. "His skin will decrease nearly half again its size and become white. It will stretch and tear if it is grabbed or pulled on. His eyes will sink into his sockets and he'll take on the look of the reaper himself. The salt will turn his hair a bleached whitish color. It will remove the very pigment from him if he is black. He will prune very heavily and will have no pink under his eyeballs. He will look void of all blood, like a zombie, for lack of a better word. In some cases, I've seen their fingernails dissolve. That salt is bad if they are in Capricorn, the salt is a little less than that in the Dead Sea. If they can get out of the water, they might have a chance. Of course when we find them we will have to deal with that. But, if we find them alive, we can overcome that."

Finishing his explanation Drummond was compelled to ask him, "How do you know this?"

"I came here from air-sea rescue with the Air Force," he answered. "I've seen too many to ever forget what they look like."

"Did you ever find any living men among those you rescued?" Alex asked.

"A few," he said. "A few. We need to get in there soon; they don't have much time. Captain, in my expert opinion I would recommend that we get all we can in that area as soon as possible."

"Thank you…Mister?" Alex said quizzically as she extended her hand.

"Wyatt. Aaron Wyatt," the weatherman said.

When the meeting adjourned and those men went on with their individual tasks for the day, Alex and Ed sat down with a cigarette and began talking.

"How do we get over there and under that soup to even get a look?" Alex asked.

"I don't think we can ask any pilot to risk his life to fly that low, but it would be nice to get a volunteer," Ed replied. "The damn NASA satellites can't even see through this soup."

"What do you think about what Aaron said?" Alex asked.

"I was hoping you wouldn't ask that," Ed said.

"Are there any submarines in that area?" Alex asked." Maybe they could be on the lookout?"

"Submarines don't volunteer when they are where they aren't supposed to be," Ed said. "South America and Africa are independent countries without a submarine fleet. Therefore, there shouldn't be any in the area. It would be nice; however; those subs could find a bug fart in a tornado. I'd give God a hundred dollars if he'd go down there and give us a hint. Well, listen. Call me if you need anything. I have an interview this afternoon and some things to get caught up on. We're meeting again at four, correct?"

"Yes," Alex replied. "I'll see you then. Four o'clock is eleven o'clock his time, right?"

Looking back at Alex, Ed saw a tear forming in her eye and took one more minute to console her. Walking over to her, he hugged her and said, "We'll find him. I feel it in my bones. He's out there and we're going to find him"

"I know. I know we will, Ed," Alex answered. "I'm just a little afraid, that's all."

As he walked down down the concourse his mind drifted back to the day his son Cad died and Tom was there for him and was his only strength when everybody else blamed him for Chad's demise. Ed slipped into the executive washroom, sat on a commode and began to weep uncontrollably. One of the members of the search and rescue team was also in the washroom and heard Ed's weeping. Not having a clue as what to do he returned to the conference room and found Alex.

"Captain Sanders?" the man said.

"Yes," replied Alex.

"Ma'am, could you come down to the men's washroom, please?" the man said. "Mister Drummond is down there and he is in a bad way."

Knowing what the man was talking about Alex put down her paperwork summaries, dried her eyes, and softly said, "Yes."

When Alex and the man entered the washroom, it was obvious Ed had reached that point in a man's life where he was both emotionally and physically drained.

Alex looked at the man and said, "I'll take care of this. Everyone, would you please leave us alone?"

As the men filed out of the washroom, Alex locked the door behind them and going to the corner stall where Ed had locked himself in, sat down on the floor next to him and began talking. Eventually he collected himself and came out and sat next to her on the floor. Alex placed his head on her shoulder and put her arm around him as the two of them began talking about the man they knew and loved who had made such an impact on their lives.

69

. . . .

THE PRIDE OF THE BRITISH Submarine fleet, the H.M.S. Conqueror, was sailing past the tip of South America on its way through the Tropic of Capricorn enroute to the Tropic of Cancer, taking a northern route back to the British Isles. It was a submarine veiled in rich military maritime war history, for it is the only nuclear powered submarine to sink a ship with a conventional torpedo in an act of war. During the Battle of the Falklands, the Argentinean government decided to send the General Belgrano to the Falkland Islands to begin shelling British holdings on that island.

The General Belgrano was a re-commissioned cruiser left over from World War II; given to the Argentinean government for use in the rare event they would ever need border protection. It was a cruiser of the heavy Spanish class and was very well fitted for battle.

When the British War Department received word that the Belgrano was headed for the Falklands to shell the coastal cities, they called upon the H.M.S. Conqueror to apprehend, shadow, and hold a position of about one mile from the battleship and await further instruction. It was still inconceivable to the British that any country would have the gall to attempt an attack on one of the Queen's holdings. They were, however, not taking any chances.

When the Belgrano entered into its third day of steaming toward the Falkland Islands, the Conqueror pulled within torpedo range and began to shadow, completely undetected by the General Belgrano.

It wasn't until the Belgrano turned amidships and presented itself with the most opportunistic firing angle did the British government give the order to fire. Captain Brown fired two torpedoes, scoring two direct broadside hits and the Belgrano sunk within minutes. Three hundred and sixty-eight of its hands were lost. And with that act, innocent civilians on the Falkland Islands were saved and naval war history was written.

But today, all that was just history. The Conqueror was still an attack submarine, but this day it was on a mission into waters shared by the South American and African governments, just to have a look around. It was just a normal fact- finding kind of day until the radar man found something that was not supposed to be there. And that moment of highly trained concentration was to be the beginning of a very important day in the lives of sixty-five children, two adults, and the crew of the Conqueror.

Captain Fletcher Brown, the youngest submarine commander in the British submarine service, was just finishing his dinner in his quarters when he was called to the conning tower by the executive officer, Commander Richard Conner.

"What is it, XO?" Captain Brown asked.

"We have a radar contact off our port beam, sir," Connor replied.

"How far away?" Captain Brown asked. "Everybody look alive."

"Sonar!" Connor barked. "Do you have a fix?"

"Looks to be about eleven miles, sir." Richey, the sonar man replied.

"Can you tell me what it is?" Captain Brown asked. "Are we still at five hundred feet?"

"Yes, sir," the XO replied.

"No sir!" replied the sonar man. "I'm not sure what it is."

"Where did you find this guy, Chief?" Brown asked.

"Poker game, sir," the chief answered. "I've had a string of bad luck."

"Right you are there, ol' boy," Captain Brown replied humorously. "Richey, give me your best guess."

"Well—sir, it looks like a cross," Richey replied, "just sticking up and bobbing with the waves.

"Holy shit," someone said in the rear of the conning tower. "Wouldn't that be something!"

"What was that?" Captain Brown asked. "I said, what did you mean by that?"

Motioning to the young man stationed at the bow plane control to come over to him, the Captain once again asked," What did you mean by that, son?"

"Well, sir, I heard on the news that the Koreans lost an airliner and it was unknown exactly where it was. It could have crashed in this area. They couldn't extend the search in this area today because of the weather," the seaman answered.

"So, what do you make of the sonar man saying it looked like a cross?" Captain Brown asked seriously.

"It could be the tail sticking up, sir," he answered.

"You're Mitchell, right?" Brown asked.

"Yes, sir," Mitchell answered.

"Okay, Mister Mitchell," Captain Brown asked. "Why would the tail section stick up like that if; and I'm only saying if, this thing out there is indeed a tail section of an airliner. Why wouldn't it sink with the rest of the plane?"

"Well, sir," Mitchell went on, "the news said it was an Airbus 300. They store all the passenger oxygen in the rear section of the plane. The tail is heavy and if the plane were to strike the water, the tail would probably break off. With the oxygen tanks in the tail it couldn't sink if it wanted to."

"How do you know all this, Seaman Mitchell?" Brown asked.

"I was once in pilot training school, sir," Mitchell answered.

"Did you wash out?" Brown asked.

"Yes, sir."

"Another bad day at poker, Chief?" the Captain asked.

"Disastrous, sir," the chief answered. "Lost everything! Shirt, pants, everything."

"So tell me, Mitchell, how did you manage to wash out of Her Majesty's Air Force?" Captain Brown asked. "Bring us up to two hundred feet, let's have a closer look at this thing. All ahead two-thirds! Put us on a heading to intercept, Chief. --Go on Mister Mitchell."

"Aye-aye, sir!" the chief replied. "Turn left to a heading of two seven zero."

"You were saying, Mister Mitchell," Captain Brown said to return to the conversation despite the ongoing operational interruptions. "Johnson, my tea!"

"I missed a final written exam, sir," Mitchell replied.

"Did you get drunk and oversleep?" Brown asked.

"No, sir!" Mitchell answered. "My wife came up from London. It was our anniversary and I overslept."

"Chief!" Captain Brown hollered.

"Yes, sir!" the chief replied.

"Teach Mitchell here how to play poker. Another good man lost to that sexual temptress known as a Navy wife, " Brown said as the crew got a good laugh. "All right, let's take a cruise up the straits and see what this is. Good job, Mister Mitchell."

"Thank you, sir," Mitchell replied pleased.

"All right, listen up!" Brown barked. "Everybody on their toes. If either of these countries find us in their side pools, they will have a conniption. Radar, make sure no one comes up on our flank. If we are caught out here your ass is grass and I'll be a lawnmower. Okay, we're going in and getting out just as soon as we clarify what this is."

"Sir, I just want to say that you are an inspiration to the men on duty here today," the chief said in a sarcastic joking manner.

"Don't let the crew shit you, Chief," Captain Brown said. "They know that I know that someone brought a case of porn aboard last month. They are hoping I'll forget about it. The captain sees all and knows all."

"That's how you got your own sub at such a young age, isn't it, sir?" a young seaman asked from the conning tower area.

"No, young man. That had nothing to do with it whatsoever," Captain Brown said.

"Can we not get into this, Captain, at this very moment, if you please?" the chief asked.

"Chief, I believe the crew should be made very aware of the Captain's credentials whenever the need arises," Captain Brown said.

"God help us!" the chief muttered under his breath.

"No son, the reason I got my own sub at such a young age is because my father, at middle age, used to service the Queen in her old age," Captain Brown explained. "I think the Americans call it ' flowing down hill'. I learned to accept my father's misfortune as his good fortune, son, and press on in Her Majesty's Navy. Quite successfully, if you'll note."

As Johnson brought the captain his tea, Brown turned to leave the conning tower. In doing so he had to walk past the chief.

"You couldn't let it go this one time, could you, sir?" the chief asked with a grin on his face.

"No, Chief, I couldn't," Captain Brown answered as he walked away, grinning.

"Your father certainly went the distance for you, sir, that's for sure," the chief said.

"Yes, he did," Captain Brown returned. "North as well as South, on several occasions I'm told. Poor bastard."

"Close your mouth, sailor and get back to work," the chief instructed. "Not all jobs in the Navy are as pleasant as yours.

"Call me when we are a mile out, Chief," Captain Brown ordered. "Note the time and put it in the log."

"Aye-aye, Captain," the chief replied. "Make the time twenty-one hundred hours."

"Aye-aye, Chief!" came from the rear.

70

. . . .

E D AND ALEX FINISHED TALKING in the washroom and eventually rose to leave. Alex had to help him get up off the floor and in doing so, he said, "Thank you, my dear. Any time you need to see me in my office, you just let me know. My secretary will set it up."

"I'll make note of that," she said. "Shall we go to our meeting?"

As Alex unlocked the door there were several people milling about the concourse hallway. However, when they exited the washroom, not a word was spoken.

Ed and Alex entered the meeting room and unofficially called the meeting to order. All the faces of the team were very glum as the weatherman, who had become the spokesman said, "We have absolutely no reports from any station whatsoever. The authorities want to call off the search. The Koreans are ready to write it off as a total loss. South America as well as Africa has come to the same conclusion. That, Captain Sanders, is not unusual for them. They haven't the same value on life as we do."

"Can they do that?" Alex asked.

"Yes, ma'am," Mister Wyatt said. "The search is on their property; their back yards. Most of these smaller countries don't have the resources to handle the financial burden that a search of this magnitude puts on them. And once the Koreans say they are happy, there isn't a lot more to do, since it is indeed a Korean airliner with Korean citizens."

"What became of the debris field thirty miles off the coast of South America?" Alex asked.

"It was the remnants of a boat fire," another man answered.

Alex sat down on a nearby chair, obviously beaten down by the bad news of the day. She remained quiet, empty and void of all emotion and hope.

"How about the Red Cross?" Ed asked. "What is their status on this?"

"They're still in the search as is UNICEF," Aaron Wyatt said. "I have a friend in charge of the air services over there. He said they would do whatever they could, but they may need a little financial help to offset the fuel costs."

"Give them whatever they need," Ed said. "Clear it through Alex first."

"I'll give them my credit card if it'll help," Alex said.

"How about helicopters to comb the area?" Ed asked. "Does your friend have any clout with helicopters?"

"Yes, he does," Aaron replied. "However, the trouble is that by the time they get to the search site, they are low on fuel and need to return. They have a very limited search time. They don't have any heavy duty helicopters."

"Where in the hell are they looking, for Christ's sake, if they're running out of fuel before they can start looking!" Ed asked in a semi rage as he threw down his papers.

"Let's not kill the messenger, Ed," Alex said. "Where exactly on this map are they going?"

"Right here," Aaron said as he pointed to a spot on the map in the middle of the ocean.

"Why there?" Alex asked.

"Because that is where we all agreed he was this morning," Aaron said defensively.

"I didn't mean it like that, Aaron," Alex apologized. "I never realized he was that far out. Can we get any airplanes from any where else?"

"Only the military," Aaron explained. "And only Mister Drummond can work that side of the table."

"The state department turned me down," Ed said. "They're worried about an international incident. What is the weather for tomorrow?"

"Rain tonight," Aaron said looking dejectedly at a map. "But clearing before daybreak and nice for the rest of the week. That will allow the satellite to view them."

"They didn't turn the satellite," Ed said as he looked out the window.

After a few moments it was obvious that the wind was leaving the sails of the rescue team. Someone spoke up and asked the obvious question. As Alex looked down at a stack of papers that read of the demise of the man she loved, a distant quiet, 'why not' was heard.

"I don't know why," Ed said as he continued to look out the window. "Aaron, can you get your friends to make a pass over that area even if only one more time tomorrow? I know he's out there. I know it! Promise them whatever they want. Look! If they look and he's not there we'll pitch a bitch and make the whole world feel sorry for all those poor Koreans and we'll get the whole world interested. Do any of you guys know any corporate pilots who would take a flight over that area?"

Another pause came when a new voice was heard.. The team looked only to see standing there, First Officer Keith Pitts, Tom's best friend, Captain Bob Sheltonhammer, just back from Hawaii, and Ann, Tom's chief flight attendant.

"Why don't we log some flying hours, Alex? We'll take a 747 the long way to Paris ourselves and just fly over there and have a look-see. I'm sure Captain Sanders could benefit from some training and so could my newfound friend, Officer Pitts. Ann here says she needs to check out the new coffee pot," Bob said as he walked over to Alex and gave her a kiss and a hug.

Walking over to Ed Drummond, Bob extended his hand and said, "Good to see you again, Ed. I think you know these two folks. Okay, this is what I'm thinking."

Everyone was so glad to see Bob, that they all rose to hear what he had to say.

"We've been eavesdropping. We look at it like this. Why pay the Africans and South Americans to find what they haven't so far? Nothing personal about your friends, Aaron, but I'm saying let's look for our own, and we can help the Koreans also," Bob continued. "I'm with Alex, that crusty bastard is too tough to get killed. You know he was probably in the rear of the rear of the aircraft like all freebees are. I think he's still out there and I agree with Aaron. He is right there in the middle of that storm front. So, here's what I propose. We take an empty, fully fueled 747 with a few of us on board and go down there and take a look. We can search the whole area and when we get low on fuel we'll duck into South America and refuel. If we can't find him by nightfall, we'll reconsider our position. We have enough qualified pilots here for the flight and Ann to help us through the rough spots. I figure we leave about five a.m. and we should be where we need to be by the time the storm front breaks. Any of you who wants to tag along and see what life in the trenches is all about, you're more than welcome to join us."

"Excuse me for asking, but what interest do you have invested in this?" Ron Pine, executive vice president of aircraft operations, asked.

"Nineteen seventy-two," Bob began. "I'm ass hole deep in a rice paddy in Vietnam, shot down over who knows where and here comes Tom Jordan in a broken down B-52. He calls in my location and begins circling me with every piece of armament shooting. He kept them bastards off of me for nearly forty-five minutes until the choppers came in and picked me up. Yes sir, I have a very important interest invested in Tom Jordan. If he didn't show up that day, I would have died in that prisoner of war camp. I made a commitment that day. I would go to hell for him if he asked and I would look forward to the trip. I'm thinking he's calling and my bags are packed."

With his voice quivering slightly as he ended, Sharon put her arm around her husband in a consoling fashion and added, "And I'd go along with him. I've known Tom Jordan longer than he has."

With that exchange of feelings from Bob and Sharon and several other people in the room, the vice president of operations said, "I don't think I've heard a better idea in a long time. I'll put it together. What time do you want to leave, Bob?"

"Five o'clock, sir," Bob answered.

"I'll see to it," he said as walked out the door with his cell phone in his hand. "I'll be in operations if you need me. Thank you all."

As Mister Pine walked out, Alex was the first to speak "I think this is our last chance." If we can't find them tomorrow, the Koreans won't pay for another day of searching. We will never find them. I think we are all going with Bob in the morning. Everybody here put an assistant on the phones. Find some volunteers for spotters. Ann, if you need any help get what you need. Tomorrow's meeting will be at about five-fifteen after wheels up. I want to thank you for all you've done so far. Aaron, please accept my apologies for all the rudeness I have shown you. You were the unlucky messenger in this outfit. Everybody get some sleep. If you want to bring your wives tomorrow, please do. The more eyes the better off we are. Thanks again, everyone."

With that Alex concluded the last meeting of the rescue and recovery committee. And in doing so she turned away from the eyes of all who were searching deeply for something to say to help her through the night. She was alone now, as was Tom. In their own private thoughts they both stared out into space, Alex through a window facing nowhere and Tom across an ocean which had claimed him as its victim. Nightfall was nearly upon Tom, but Alex still had time for despair before she would be alone in the dark with her own thoughts of the man she loved who was quickly slipping away from her.

Alex composed herself the best she could when Bob called to her. He approached her but could only take her hand, look into her eyes and shake his head. As tears quickly filled his eyes he turned to Ed and taking him by the arm said, "Let's have a look at those charts so we can file a flight plan."

It was obvious that the conference room was becoming the staging area for a wake and Sharon put an end to that quickly.

"Okay everyone!" she said. "We are going to adjourn this meeting in the dining room. The airline is picking up the tab. This is mandatory. We can't search if we're hungry. Really everyone; I think it's time we got out of here."

71

. . . .

"JOHNSON, CONTACT THE SKIPPER." CHIEF ordered. "Tell him we're three miles out and in heavy traffic. Keep it down, guys. Sonar; on your toes!"

When the captain arrived, he took a look at his bearing, depth and speed and asked, "What's the delay?"

"We have a lot of shipping out there, Captain," the XO answered. "I slowed us down a bit."

"Good move," Captain Brown said. "Sonar, give me a fix with a gap on these boats."

"The nearest one is now three miles away at ten knots. Next one is about twenty minutes away at twelve knots," Sonar reported.

"Stern or bow?" Captain Brown asked.

"Bow, sir," the XO answered.

"Bring us up to periscope depth," Captain Brown ordered. "Get me a tracking heading on those two boats, Sonar. All ahead standard. Stop one mile out."

"Aye-aye, sir," the man at the sonar answered.

"All ahead standard, aye, sir," the XO answered.

Captain Brown paused, looking to the bow of the boat, and had the most peculiar look on his face. Since he and the chief had been together for quite awhile, he recognized that look only too well.

"Sir, are you thinking what I think you're thinking?" the chief asked. "Because if you are, sir, I wish you wouldn't even think that, sir."

Captain Brown looked at the chief and only smiled. After a moment he nodded and said, "I'm not going up there without insurance. Torpedo room, load the bow tubes one through four."

"Mary, Mother of God, Captain!" the chief pleaded. "We can't sink these merchant ships just because they might see us. Besides, Captain, the weather is bad out there, they can't see a thing."

"In that case, Chief, let Mary, the mother of God, protect those dumb saps against doing anything stupid," Captain Brown ordered. "I'm not saying it again, load those tubes or I'll load them with you."

"All aft tubes loaded, sir!" came a holler from the rear of the boat.

"Begging the Captain's pardon," the chief said. "What are you so worried about?"

"We aren't supposed to be here," Captain answered. "We're spying on our African brethren because the Admiralty thinks they have that new anti-submarine technology. If they do and it works, we're dog shit at this depth. We were going to run some tests farther down the coast, but certainly we have no business here. I don't like those other ships out there. So, until I'm convinced that we're safe, I'm going to take some precautions. Had you done so earlier in your career you wouldn't have all those kids."

"Thank you, Captain," Chief replied. "I'm glad we had this chance to talk about my family planning short comings."

"I thought you'd find it inspiring," the captain answered.

"Periscope depth, Captain!" the helmsman replied.

"All stop," Captain Brown ordered. "You are my only support here, Chief. If it weren't for you, I'd let these bastards float. Don't get by-the-book on me now."

"Boat is stopped," replied the XO.

Looking at the chief his best friend, he said, "Up scope."

The captain met the periscope at the top of its rise and immediately took a three hundred and sixty-degree rotation to check for any other activity. Bringing the periscope back to the heading of zero degrees he looked at the mass of the sonar contact.

After about a minute the captain pulled his head away from the eyepieces on the periscope and looked down as if he found the need for meditation. Ever so somber, quite unlike him, he put his attention back to the eyepiece of the periscope. After a few tense minutes he again took his gaze off and inviting the chief to have a look, called for Mitchell to come forward. When the chief stepped back with a serious look on his face the captain motioned for Mitchell to look through the scope.

The captain and the chief locked gazes and for a moment just kept their comments to themselves. Finally the captain broke the silence when he said, "What the hell did we get ourselves into?"

"It could only be God's will that we came across them, Captain," the chief answered.

"You better tell God to cover our ass," the captain said. "We don't need this shit, Chief. Dammit! We can't turn away now. Dammit! Mitchell, is that what the ass end of an Airbus Three Hundred looks like?"

"I'd bet my life on it, sir," Mitchell answered.

"What do you make of that to the left?" Captain Brown asked.

"It looks like seat cushions tied together. There are people moving on them and in the water!" Mitchell said excitedly as he stepped back.

The captain looked at the area on the surface again and invited the XO over to have a look saying, "Sorry, Tom, I'm not trying to keep it from you. Mitchell, don't go too far. Chief, let's talk. Sonar! Radar! Talk to me."

Sonar and Radar both cleared the horizon and the ocean depth to satisfy the captain.

"Keep a sharp lookout you two. If some bastard comes up on us and I lose my parking spot at the Officers' Club there will be hell to pay," Captain Brown said as he patted the sonar man on the shoulder.

Looking to the chief, the captain said quietly," What in the hell are we going to do with all those sonsabitches? There must be fifty of them, for shit sake."

"Let's get the doc up here," the chief said.

"Good idea," Brown said. "Call him, would you?"

The XO stepped away from the scope and had the worst look that anyone had. Looking at the captain the XO said as he wiped his chin with the back of his hand, "My God in heaven, those poor bastards won't make it through the night. But, can we get them all on here?"

With a silence from behind him the XO looked back into the scope and repeated his question to the captain. "Can we get them all on here?"

When the XO looked away from the periscope and back at the captain he was met by a blank stare.

"We've come this far off course," the XO began defiantly. "This far without even conferring with me and now you look at me like I'm a flippin' idiot. We are not leaving these poor bastards for the buzzards. Not this time, Brown. Stand down, Chief! This is between me and the captain."

The chief put up his hands defensively and said, "Let's see what the doc says, gentlemen. Please, not in front of the men."

The XO was referring to the refusal of the captain to rescue any of the men from the sinking of the Belgrano. Because of that decision not to attempt a rescue by the Conqueror, over two hundred and sixty-eight men perished on those rough seas. The XO always held the captain responsible thinking he should have disobeyed his orders and rescued them anyhow. All through the years the XO and the captain had been at odds over this issue.

It was apparent that this was about to blow into a public display of anger when the doctor entered the conning tower.

"What is it, Captain?" Doctor Frey asked.

"Take a look and see what you think, Bob," the captain said." Give me your best appraisal of the situation and tell me if you think we can do anything for them. See if you think they'll live until the morning. Helmsman, move within one hundred yards of them."

"One hundred yards! Aye, sir!"

The doctor looked through the scope and suddenly cringed when he brought the viewfinder into focus. He seemed to become more emotional the longer he looked when he asked, "Does anybody know how long they've been out there?"

"Mitchell, when did you hear that news report?" the captain asked.

"Yesterday, sir," Mitchell responded.

"That means they have been in the water for at least two days," the doctor said. "They all appear to be alive, barely though. There is someone in the water. It's a man. He's bigger than the rest."

Just then the helmsman interrupted the doctor saying, "One hundred yards, sir."

The captain looked and nodded affirmatively and said to the doctor, "Can you tell how many there are?"

"Those are kids on that damn raft. Christ, there must be fifty of them at least. There is one large adult also—looks like a woman on the raft. That man in the water is near death. Look at his skin. He's totally pruned. The kids appear to be starving. Put together the salt, the heat, no food or water for two days and I doubt that any of them will live through the night. No longer than that, however. They will probably all die when the night temperature drops."

"Can we do anything for them here?" the captain asked. "Do you have room for them?"

"Oh, yes. Yes, indeed," the doctor responded. "We can put them two to a bed except for the man and woman. We're talking some chicken soup, a de-saline bath, and re-hydration. They should pull through, but we need to get to them soon, though, very soon. That man looks bad. He is probably dying of de-hydration brought on by extended exposure to the salt in this area. He doesn't have long. But, yes. I think we can accommodate them quite nicely. I wonder how they have survived this long. The good Lord is looking out for them, that's for sure."

"Are you sure that we can't call in their position and send someone for them?" Captain Brown asked.

"If we could have gotten to them sooner, they may have had a chance," Doctor Frey said. "But this late in the game they don't have a chance of making it till morning. No, sir, a rescue party will just find corpses tomorrow."

"Are you sure you can save them if we pull them out now?" Captain Brown asked.

"Absolutely!" Doctor Frey said.

"We can put a rescue party together in a minute, sir," the chief said. "It'll be dark soon, Captain. That may help matters a little."

"XO," Captain Brown said. "Do you have anything to add?"

"I think darkness is a good idea. We'll wait until then," the XO returned.

"Okay, Chief," the captain finished. "Put together the rescue crew. Feed the men early. Doc, you do what you have to do. Take what you need for volunteers. Down scope. Make depth fifty feet. We'll lay there until sunset."

72

. . . .

ALEX AND ED SAID THEIR good byes for the evening as did Bob and Sharon following the post meeting dinner. Alex found her way to her car and for a moment had a chance to relax. It was a very disheartening day, she thought to herself. As she left the parking lot she stopped at the stop sign and looked back toward the location of the last place she had seen Tom. She remembered the vision she had, but she fixed her memory on his waving and smiling at her from the step of the air-stair truck.

As she entered the freeway, she again thought of the talk they had in the park after their argument two days ago. Alex strained her memory to hear Tom's voice again, but she was too tired to think. She changed lanes on the freeway and headed for the park.

She parked her car in the same spot as on that day and walked to the bench where they had sat. She came across the same stick she had held in her hand and threatened Tom with. She refused to let reality set in and dampen the very reason she came here, but her mind would not let her rest. In total despair Alex rose from the bench and walked toward the car when she heard a voice call her name.

She turned in the direction of the voice but found no one there. She stood motionless for a moment and listened intently, but there was no one there. For a reason that she could not explain, Alex quietly said, "Tommy. Is that you?"

Just then a breeze blew over her and filled her heart with peace. For the first time in days the tickle left her stomach and a tear of peace came upon her. Recalling the deep faith Tom had, Alex, in an attempt to draw on that faith, looked up to heaven and said, "You know where he is, don't you? Bring him home to me and we'll forget this ever happened. You think Joan of Arc had an attitude, you ain't seen nothin' yet, buddy."

With that exchange of pleasantries, Alex once again got in her car and headed for home.

Upon her arrival Chris and Carrie, who were excited to hear any news of Tom met her at the garage. Learning that there wasn't any news, Chris said, "We have another problem, I'm afraid."

Totally exhausted Alex said, "What now?"

Walking into the house, she saw Corrie sitting in the kitchen holding Rocky's collar with tears streaming down her face. Knowing only too well what had happened she put Corrie on her lap and holding her in her arms began sobbing right along with her.

After a few minutes the two ladies regained their composure and were able to talk about Rocky running off.

"What happened, honey?" Alex asked.

"I took him out to pee and he ran after the priest," Corrie explained. "I couldn't get him to stop."

"What priest?" Alex asked. "What did he look like? Do you mean Father Harris?"

"No!" Corrie answered. "It was the other priest."

"Are you sure, honey?" Alex went on. "Have you seen the other priest?"

"Yes, Grandma," Corrie replied. "I've seen him with Tom on the beach a couple of times. Rocky doesn't like him very much."

"Honey, where did the priest go when Rocky chased him?" Alex asked.

"I don't know, really," Corrie said. "Rocky never caught up with him, he just kept running."

Alex stood up and saying hello hugged Carrie as she excused herself, took a cigarette and walked out on the beach.

She lit the cigarette and took a deep drag that made her cough slightly. When she got to the water's edge, she took off her shoes as she had done so many times with Tom and dropped them in the sand. Looking down the beach in both directions she strained her eyes for a glimpse of Rocky. In desperation she called to him several times with no results. She then said quietly as if in a prayer, "Come on home, baby, you can't help him.

Come home to me where you belong. We'll look for Tom together. I can't lose you too."

Turning around and picking up her shoes she looked skyward and said, "I'm not believing You took his dog too. My patience is wearing thin with You. You don't want to piss me off. I'll expect them both home by morning or we're going to talk. You'll think Joan of Arc was a girl scout if I don't get my men back; both of them and soon.

Venting her frustration, Alex looked down the beach again and returned to the house. Looking at her watch she noticed it was six o'clock. She quickly added the hours and knew it was one o'clock in the area where she thought Tom was.

She was tired, exhausted and emotionally spent and just wanted to go to bed, but as she turned toward the house Father Harris and Rosario met her. It was time for dinner.

73

. . . .

TOM AND THE REST OF the survivors watched the sun set over the western horizon and with that also set most of their hopes for rescue and survival. Tom had made one last trip around the perimeter of the raft checking on the lashings and when finished, tied himself off for the night. The trip around the raft weakened him so much that he had trouble lifting himself up enough to tie the cords onto the raft which kept his torso out of the water.

As he finished the knot he doubted that he would have the strength to survive the night. He was also certain that once he was gone the others would go. Hopefully, he thought, it would be in their sleep.

Dusk turned to darkness and his mind began to wander as he was falling asleep .He had to fight to stay awake. He knew only too well that he was dying. His mind was filled with thoughts of Alex; the evenings they spent making love on the beach, the time when she began moving her things into his house and all the fun they had arranging everything for a lady in a house designed around a man. The walks they took and the subjects of spending forever together filled his mind as if they were walking together at this very moment on the beach where they shared so much of their bodies and their souls.

Thoughts of her seemed to make the final hours seem a little more bearable. He thought of what would have been had he met her years before. Would he be right here, right now? How could this have happened, he thought, as sadness and despair encompassed his mind in an uncontrollable shroud of darkness.

His mind began to wander throughout his life, the choices he made and the people he met. The relationships were few, he thought, too few to count serious. He did remember, however, the pretty blond haired girl named Cherie who sat in front of him in homeroom during high school. Tom wondered what had become of her as he bobbed in the smooth sleep inducing waves of the ocean.

A smile came across his face when he recalled his grammar school bus driver, Herbie Gabel. Now there was a man with the patience of Job. How much trouble he, Dave Hofelich and Jane Nieset gave to ol' Herb and he never raised his voice. And at the end of school the following day, he was back for more. He wondered what happened to all the men who had shaped his life into what he was. If Bill Williamson could only see him now!

The smooth motion of the waves had managed to loosen the now rotten knot that held him to the raft and he began to slip lower and lower into the ocean. Unable to muster up the strength to hold himself to the raft, the water had risen to his neck as he held his head above the water in a desperate attempt to breathe. He glanced over at his little Korean friend when he noticed her grip on his arm loosen. But with a little nudge he was able to awaken her before she too slipped into the water.

With Tom's strength completely drained he was powerless to hold himself up any longer and he slipped into the water stopping at eye level. Holding there for a moment he thought of his family back in Ohio and then he felt nothing. The water covered his head and he felt for the first time in days an indescribable veil of peace. His eyes opened slightly as he looked into the empty nothingness where he was slipping.

As he gazed into the water a vision came of a being walking across the water toward him in a bright glow. As Tom looked he thought it must be Jesus Himself coming to get him and take him home, but the closer the figure came he could see it was a woman. He stared at the figure and concluded it must be Alex. She was walking toward him in her bare feet with her hair floating in the breeze wearing a snow white night gown. She approached him with her right hand out as if to take him out of the water.

With one last desperate burst of strength, Tom jerked himself out of the water and at the same time screamed her name as loudly as he could extending his arm to take her hand in his. He screamed her name a second time and again began slipping into the water.

74

. . . .

DINNER HAD FINALLY ENDED AND Alex was glad to see Father Harris and Rosario get in their car and return to the rectory. She was totally spent. The events of the day had not been good to her and the longer she was awake the worse the torment became. She excused herself and went out on the beach for a cigarette. As she stood in the sand and stared at the darkening sky, all thoughts went to Tom. She knew they had run out of time, knew even as strong as Tom was he couldn't withstand this type of torture any longer and knew he would be dead by morning, if he wasn't already. She looked hopelessly lost into the darkness and began to cry.

"I'm not beyond making a deal, you know," she said as she continued to look into the darkness. "I'm listening. Father Harris told me You're a loving God, so let's see some of that love. Talk Your stuff to a hard core Presbyterian. I'm asking You for help here. Make me a deal I can't refuse, I'm easy to deal with when it comes to Tom."

A few moments passed and Alex stood motionless against the edge of the water when a peace fell upon her unlike anything she had ever felt. She threw her cigarette into the surf and began to talk to the darkness in front of her.

"How do I know You are telling me the truth?" Alex said to an empty black sky. "Tom believes You will do whatever You say You will do. I'm not that easy. What guarantees do I have that You are telling me the truth? How do I know this? My father didn't believe in You so You can understand why I'm a little skeptical. You were never there when he needed

You. So tell me something I want to hear. Convince me that it is You in front of me now and not exhaustion. And just who are You anyway?"

After a few moments the conversation with the dark continued. "You're telling me that I'm going to hear Tom calling for me. And you expect me to take that on faith? All right, all right, I do not doubt You, but he's a thousand miles away. How do You expect me to hear him? You're going to take care of that also, I see! Okay-okay. I get it. But You must remember that I've seen how You take care of things. I wouldn't be in this mess now if it weren't for You. I'm not sure You're the man for the job. Well, hell no, I haven't gotten any better offers today. Do You think there are hundreds of morons standing in line to go out and find him and pick him up? But You're asking me to take a lot on faith here. I've never had to have faith before, Tom always took care of that, and I'm new at this! You've never gotten between us before. So tell me what it is You want because I am very vulnerable right about now. I'm all ears!"

Chris, having heard the conversation her mother was having with the dark came out onto the beach to see Alex. When she arrived she stood behind her and listened to a conversation which appeared to be in a language all its own. The only part of the conversation she understood was the last word Alex said.

"All right, You've got a deal," said Alex. "You produce him and I'll show You mackerel snappers what a good Christian woman looks like on Sunday. I'm holding You to what You said about hearing Tom also. Don't forget that little tidbit, and don't think I don't know his voice. Don't mess with me on this. I'm in no mood to be screwed with. And I am just to have faith and go to bed; that's what You're telling me? I'm going to need my rest, am I? All right, whatever You say, You pull this off and I'll believe You. Bring him back to me and there won't be a day that I won't publicly praise Your name in the courthouse square and give those heathen Baptist bastards twenty minutes to draw a crowd. You've never dealt with a grateful Presbyterian, have You? You know You are my only hope and You have me by the short hairs. Whatever it takes. I'll do anything to get him back."

Alex stood motionless once again and everything was quiet. The only noise was an occasional sniffle because of her crying.

"Mother, are you all right?" asked Chris. "I got a little worried about you."

"Yes, I'm fine, thank you," remarked Alex. "Just a little tired. I feel good about tonight. I think we are going to find Tom tonight."

"It's dark, Mother," Chris said. "How will we find him in the dark? Who were you talking to?"

"Just an old friend of Tom's," Alex replied. "I guess we should be getting off to bed. I think we'll have a busy day tomorrow."

Looking up to heaven one last time she said in a muffled tone, "I'm counting on You. We've got a deal, You know."

As she turned around, she took Chris by the hand and heard a voice very clearly call her by name.

Jerking around Alex screamed, "Tom! Tom!" She ran to the water's edge and dropped to her knees and dropping her head into her lap she said, "You've found him!"

"Mother, are you all right?" Chris asked anxiously.

Going to her mother's aid as if she were injured, Chris dropped down to her knees to help Alex get up.

"Don't touch me right now, Chris," Alex said clearly. "They've found Tom. Did you here him call to me? They've found him"

"I didn't hear anything, Mother," Chris replied.

"You didn't hear that?" she asked. "My God, it was as clear as day."

"We have to go into the house now," Chris said. "It's time for bed and you must be exhausted."

"You go ahead, I'll just be a minute," she replied.

Just then Alex heard the voice calling her again. And reaching out her right arm she screamed," I'm here, Tom. I'm right here."

At that precise moment Chris's two children came out to the beach.

"Did you hear Tom, Grandma?" Corrie screamed hysterically. "I heard him. Is he here, Grandma, where is he? Where is he?"

Corrie joined her grandmother and began screaming Tom's name as if he were in front of them trying to find his way home. Alex and Corrie sat together in an embrace and looked out into the dark abyss of the ocean in a grip of hope and inspiration. Chris and Carrie sat alongside them, in shock at not seeing or hearing anything, just being together as one family ready to console the other two who appeared to be in a world by themselves. Chris was getting scared. She could see where her mother, nearly exhausted, would think she had heard Tom calling, but Corrie was adamant about it.

"ALL RIGHT! LISTEN UP!" CAPTAIN Smith hollered. "Radar and sonar, let's get with the program. I don't want to see one damn fishing boat within fifty miles of us. Is that clear?"

"Aye-aye, sir!" came the reply from the other end of the conning tower.

"We'll be all right, Captain," replied Chief. "We're the best crew on the best boat. It'll be a walk in the park, you'll see."

"How did I get talked into this fiasco?" Captain Smith said as he leaned closer to the chief's face.

"It's the right thing to do, sir," he replied. "They'll put your picture on a cereal box for this, Captain."

"The Admiralty finds out about this little stunt that's exactly what I'll be selling for the rest of my life," Captain replied. "Don't you get too far from me on this one. I'm depending on you. Helmsman! Bring us up to periscope depth slowly; and I do mean slowly. All I want is the deck visible. Chief, arm those two standbys. Put them on the deck."

"Aye-aye, Captain!" the helmsman barked. "Periscope depth, show only the deck and slow as she goes."

"Periscope depth, Captain," the helmsman said. "The deck is clear, sir."

With that announcement the captain looked at the chief and said, "This is it. Anybody want to change their minds?"

Looking over at the XO he received a negative shake of the head. Looking back at the chief he met a grin from his friend who said in a humorous tone, "This will be our finest hour. Let's get it on, sir."

"Take it away, Chief," Captain Brown said. "Make us proud."

"Hatch is clear, sir," the helmsman said.

"Rescue party to the ready!" the chief said. "Surface! Surface."

With that order the helmsman blew the main tanks bringing the Conqueror to the surface.

76

. . . .

IRENE LEFT HER PLACE ON the raft and labored to swim over to where Tom had sunk below the surface. When she arrived, she reached down and grabbed his hair and pulled him back up so he could breathe. Attempting to hook his rope back up to the raft, she heard a strange gurgling noise off to her right. She was able to secure him to the raft once again and bring him back to consciousness. Then she turned her attention to the noise on her right.

"Captain, what the hell is that?" Irene asked.

Tom, struggling to wake himself up, looked at the sub and said, "It looks like a whale."

"I don't think so, Captain," she said in a labored voice. "If it's a whale, some crazy bastard painted numbers on the side of it. And there are people walking on its back."

"Those aren't people!" Tom said. "That's probably that crazy Ahab. How are you feeling, Irene?"

"Hopeful, Captain. Very hopeful!" Irene answered. "Captain, that ain't no whale. That's a goddamn submarine! Wake up, you son of a bitch. That's one big God damn submarine!"

Tom mustered a little more strength and was brought back to reality by the intense beam of light that struck him in the eyes like a dose of smelling salts wakes one from a stupor.

"They've found us, Jordan!" screamed Irene. "You were right, you limey bastard. They've found us. Children! Children! Wake up! We are going home."

As Tom fought to get a handle on what was happening he once again looked over to the whale and saw people get into rafts and make their way over toward them. Their movement was in slow motion as they made their way to the children in a muffled tone. It was now clear that Tom was looking at a submarine. Before he could comprehend what was happening he was looking into the eyes of a man with a mask who spoke English.

As Tom looked he could see divers all around their make shift raft helping the children. They were lifting them most carefully off the raft and putting them into a small raft.

A naval man came to the aid of Irene and asked her if she was hurt. She replied that she was fine, but the captain next to her was in bad shape. As the frogman turned his attention to Tom he shined a light into his face and quickly ran it the length of his body.

"Stay with him, Warner." the frogman said. "I'll come back to help you in a minute. Don't try to lift him, you'll tear him. He's got it bad. Just keep his head above water. I'll alert the doctor."

The frogman turned to Irene and said, "What do you say we swim to the boat? You relax, I'll carry you."

As the frogman swam with Irene he was the first to break the no communication barrier when he shouted out, "Help me with her. Tell the doc I have the one we saw in the scope. He's pretty bad."

When the frogman reached the boat he helped put a harness on Irene to aid them in picking her up to the sub's deck. As she was ready to be lifted she turned to the frogman and said, "That's Captain Jordan from America. He saved us all. Help him."

"America?" the frogman said. "He's not the pilot?"

"No," Irene answered. "He's one of us."

"Give me a sheet!" the frogman answered. "Did you tell the doc? This bloke is in bad shape."

"He said be careful and bring him on," a crewman said. "The doc wants to know what he's looking at."

"Dehydration and starvation!" the frogman answered. "Maximum exposure."

"I'll pass it on," the crewman shouted in reply.

As Tom waited for his turn to be rescued he watched his little Korean friend get put on a raft and waved back to her as they sped to the sub.

When the frogman returned with a wet sheet, Tom heard him shout out, "The captain says five more minutes and we're gone. Let's wrap this up. Leaning his head on the shoulder of the diver Tom watched as all the children were removed from their makeshift haven and put on the deck of the submarine. He watched them lift Irene out of the water with a winch and help her down the stairs. He and a few children were all that was left on the water.

"You weren't the pilot of this ship?" the frogman asked.

"No," Tom said in a labored tone. "I was a passenger."

"Are there any more survivors?" the frogman asked.

"No, but we need to pick up Mylyn," he said.

"Where is she?" the frogman shouted.

"Over there," Tom pointed.

The frogman swam over to Mylyn, and looking at her swam back to Tom and said, "She's dead, for Christ sake. She stays with the rest."

"We can't leave her here," Tom shouted weakly. "We can't leave her here with the rest."

"That's exactly what we're going to do!" the frogman said. "The clean-up crew will get her. We don't have room for corpses, Captain. That's the best she's going to get today. We have to go now, sir. If you want to stay with her until the others get here, that's up to you. But we are leaving and she's not going. What's it going to be?"

The other rescuer said, "Take it easy, he's hysterical. Give me the sheet and let's get out of here."

As they wrapped the sheet around Tom the frogman said, "The clean-up crew will take good care of her, Captain, you're in pretty bad shape. Don't fight us, just relax so we don't hurt your skin. But, we really have to go."

The two men towed Tom away in the harness the sheet provided, He took one more glance at Mylyn and the raft they all lived on for two days. Looking up to heaven he said a silent prayer of thanksgiving, but for the most part he still wasn't alert enough to grasp what was happening. He wasn't sure he was alive, but he was grateful he wasn't in pain. He looked out over the ocean to where he saw Alex walking a short time ago but there was nothing but a ripple on the surface. He could feel himself being pulled through the water and then in an instant saw Alex kneeling on the water with Corrie. As he mustered a wave the frogman once again barking orders to the crew on deck broke his concentration.

"Use the sheet, don't touch his skin, you'll tear him," the frogman ordered. "Where's the doc?"

"I'm right here, Corpsman," the doctor replied. "I'll take him. Good job men, all of you!"

Tom's first grasp of the reality of the situation was the bright red lights inside the submarine. All of a sudden, the words that he was too weak to speak came to his mind. They had been rescued and were safe. Alex had found him. Out in the middle of nowhere, Alex found him and sent a submarine to bring him home. Just like he knew she would. Just like she said she would.

"Wrap a sheet around his legs and put him on the backboard that way," the doctor ordered. "Put the children in the hallway and put him and the woman in the exam room."

"Captain!" the doctor hollered, "we are finished here, sir!"

"Roger that!" Captain Smith returned.

Without giving the chief the ship's orders, the captain looked down from the conning tower into the control room and screamed, "DIVE! DIVE! DIVE! Take us down to one five zero feet! Stay on course. Sonar, watch for debris from that airplane! Up scope!"

Walking down the ladder into the control room, Captain ordered," Clear the deck and dive the boat." Taking the periscope in his hand he made a complete three hundred and sixty-degree circle to look for other ships in the area. Once he was satisfied with the view of the horizon he ordered, "Down scope!"

"Helmsman!" he said. "Get us the hell out of here. Expedite, my boy; and I do mean expedite!"

"Aye-aye sir!" the helmsman replied. "Making for twenty knots, steady as she goes."

"Thank you!" the captain returned. "Sonar, anything?'

"We're cleaner than Kleenex, sir," the man replied. "There's nobody out here, sir. Chief was right. They would have never found those poor bastards. They would have been bait come morning."

"You made us proud, sir," Chief said. "You saved a lot of people today."

"Yes, we did," Captain Smith replied. "Not exactly the mission of this boat though, is it?"

"The Queen will wear a proud crown tomorrow, sir. You can make book on that," the XO said.

"XO, will you put some nice words to the Admiralty for us?" Captain asked. "Let's come up with a transfer point and give them a fix to pick up the victims. Other than that we have no knowledge of the situation for the time being."

"Captain," Chief asked, "do you mind if we secure from torpedo ready status?"

"What's the matter, Chief? Are you afraid to get your torpedo wet?" Captain Smith asked humorously.

"Right you are, sir!"

"Secure torpedo!" Captain ordered. "You should have thought of that before you had all those kids. However, that's a discussion for family planning night, isn't it? All right, good job everyone but that will be enough of that shit from now on. No more Good Samaritan crap. I've got a reputation to keep."

Two levels down in the sub the doctor was giving orders to his corpsman for the treatment of the survivors.

"Watch those IV's. The kids aren't going to like them. Be gentle," Doctor Frey ordered. "Give me a count when you have a chance. Give them all some soup to eat. Open those IV's up. Let's get them all hydrated, but keep an eye on them. Don't leave any of them alone. Nobody leaves! Who's next?"

Making his way into the exam room, Doctor Frey came to Irene and examined her shin, the pigment below her eyeballs, the quick of her fingernails, her gum line, and her inner ear for sediment. The doctor found her to be reasonably healthy for the ordeal she suffered.

"How did you manage to take such good care of yourself?" Doctor Frey asked.

"I didn't, he did. He put us on a raft and we stayed there," Irene answered. "He took care of us and kept us alive until you came. He knew you would come. He said his girlfriend would send you to get us, but he has been in the water too long. The storm damn near killed him. You take care of him, I'll be all right."

Looking at the corpsman the doctor just nodded saying, "Standard IV, watch the needle. Put the cream on her legs and treat her feet for sunburn. Soup also. Keep track of her blood pressure."

"Ma'am, are you diabetic?" Doctor Frey asked.

"No!" Irene answered. "I'm Irish."

As the doctor made his way over to Tom a corpsman stuck his head in the doorway and said, "We have a count, sir."

"Go ahead, please," Doctor Frey said.

"Sixty-five kids, sir. All strong and all healthy," the corpsman advised.

Looking back at Irene the doctor said, "Sixty-five! How did you keep that many kids alive? What did they eat?"

"We didn't really," Irene said. "Just some crumbs. Anything that the captain could scrounge up."

"How many did you start with?" Doctor Frey asked.

"We took one hundred and nine kids and three stewardesses on board," Irene began. "After the crash all we had left was sixty-five kids and three adults. The other stewardess didn't make it. She died yesterday. They were all Korean, from the embassy, except me. I'm their nanny from Gloucester, Massachusetts. The captain is from Aurora Airlines. He was a passenger riding back to Houston."

"So, who cared for you while you were out there?" asked the doctor.

"He did," Irene said as she pointed to Tom. "He saved us all. And by the looks of it he's the worst off."

"We'll take good care of him, don't you worry about that. You get some rest now," Doctor Frey said. "Jim. Shut off these lights and tell the guys not to overfeed the kids. If they keep it down, give them some bread and then some sugar. Keep an eye on them."

"Yes sir!" Jim replied.

Walking over to Tom, the doctor phoned the XO. "Tom? Bob. They're all the property of the Korean Embassy. The captain was a passenger. He's with Aurora Airlines. He was hitching a ride back to Houston."

"Thanks, Bob. I'll pass that on to the Admiralty. I'll bet the Americans are hunting for his happy ass," the XO replied. "How are they doing?"

"All well except for the captain," Bob replied. "He's not doing so hot. I think he has some internal injuries. He has a lot of dried blood in his mouth. Give me a couple of hours with him and we'll know more then."

Looking down at Tom, the doctor said, "Captain, I am Commander Bob Frey, Her Majesties Navy. I'm a doctor. How do you feel?"

"I don't feel nothin," Tom replied in a labored voice.

"Captain, we have to put you in a de-saline solution bath to get that salt off. It's killing you. The IV isn't doing a lot of good right now. And then we are going to coat you with a glycerin balm that we'll take off an hour later. I'm going to start you on a steroid regiment to pick up your strength, all this while you're sleeping. I'm going to give you something to help you sleep now."

"Captain?" Doctor Frey asked. "Would you have any objection if I taped your treatment?"

"Where am I?" Tom asked weakly.

"You are on the nuclear attack submarine, H.M.S. Conqueror. We are midway down the coast of Africa and South America, about sixty miles south of the equator, in the absolute worst salt water next to the Dead Sea. How you survived at all is a miracle."

"I don't suppose you have a phone I can use?" Tom asked in a labored tone.

"The Captain is taking care of that for you, sir," the doctor said. "He will call the Admiralty and they will pass on the word. Your loved ones should know in about two to three hours."

"How am I doing?" Tom muttered.

"Not good, sir," Doctor Frey replied somberly. "You're hurt pretty bad. But, that is why I'm going to put you to sleep awhile and get started on this steroid therapy and this salt problem. Once I get some nourishment in you and you get this shit off, you should fare pretty well. We'll talk again in the morning. We'll know more after reading the x-rays then."

As the doctor motioned to the corpsman to begin Tom's bath and IV therapy, he said, "I've seen what you did for these kids. Now we're going to do the same for you."

Doctor Frey returned to Tom and shaking his hand said, "It will be an honor to treat you, sir. Now get some sleep."

As the doctor walked away he fell fast asleep.

E

D DRUMMOND TURNED OFF THE television and took the phone off the hook and tossed the receiver out of the way of earshot.

Thinking of a time in his life when he had first met Tom Jordan, he opened a cupboard door and stared lustfully at a bottle of Jim Beam whiskey. Prior to Tom Jordan, thiswas his only companion and he had spent many an hour in the company of a friend that showed no morning after remorse.

Taking the bottle in his hand he removed the cap and poured the contents down the drain. Not since Chad had died had he taken a drink and after all the help Tom had given him at that time, Ed thought it a sacrilege to become weak enough to turn to another source of strength.

He closed the cupboard door and turned off the lights, never even bothering to get undressed. He just crawled into bed exhausted, covered up and turned out the lights.

He couldn't put a time frame on how long he had been asleep, but he was awakened by the telephone ringing. He got up with a vulgar expression for being awakened by a disconnected phone when he noticed someone standing at the foot of his bed.

Before he could answer the phone, it stopped ringing and the being at the foot of the bed turned to him and said, "They damn near got him this time. What are you thinking? Why don't you let him alone? Let him live in peace with Alex. Tell him he's going to take the chief pilot's job, don't ask him. Get him out of the air. His time is up. I can't help him anymore."

"My God!" Ed said. "Is it really you? Where have you been, how did you get here?"

"We take cabs, nowadays," John Beck said. "Where the hell do you think I've been? Cleaning up the shit you make out of people's lives. What the hell is the matter with you, putting him on a Korean airliner? What the hell are you thinking? Them damn Koreans couldn't fly a kite let alone an airliner and you put Jordan on the damn thing. And hang up your damn phone, the British are trying to call you."

After a few moments the conversation continued when John said, "No more, Ed. He's done flying. Either you tell him or I will. He's not out of the woods yet either; he's pretty banged up. He may not make it anyway. I can't do anything about that. I found him, now you and Alex go get him and bring him home. You owe him, for Chad. You owe me for him. Get some rest, it won't be long."

As Ed Drummond looked in disbelief at the figure of John Beck he disappeared into a vision of what were better days now forever passed. Ed checked to be sure the phone was hung up and in a stupor crawled back into bed and fell back to sleep.

Alex and Corrie were fast asleep in the master bedroom as Chris looked in on them before going to bed. It was a day she would not soon forget. She had seen so many things that had no explanations to satisfy every question that came to mind. At one time she was convinced she sat at the kitchen table next to the devil himself and at the same time felt certain that Almighty God had a one on one conversation with her mother on the beach. Her mind spun in circles as she tried to make sense of the day. But that was exhausting and she too fell fast asleep.

As Ed Drummond tried to get some sleep, it became apparent there would be no reprieve for the telephone rang waking him up once again. As he stumbled toward it he remembered the conversation he thought he had with John Beck, so he answered it with a great deal of anticipation.

"Yes, hello, hello!" Ed said to the person on the other end of the line.

"Hello. Is this Mister Edward Drummond of Aurora Airlines?" the voice asked in a most sober tone.

"Yes!" Ed said," I am he!"

"Mister Drummond, I am Jonathan Edwards of the British Embassy," the caller identified himself. "We have received word from the Admiralty that we have found and rescued your pilot, a Captain Thomas Jordan. Are you familiar with this gentleman, sir?"

As Ed attempted to answer he was overcome with emotion and couldn't even talk.

"Mister Drummond, are you there?" Mister Edwards asked.

"Yes, yes, I'm here," Ed stuttered. "Yes, I am familiar with Tom Jordan. Yes, he is one of mine. My, God, is he alive?"

"Oh yes, very much so," Mister Edwards answered. "He is however, in a very bad way, although the attending physician did give a very promising prognosis."

"Where is he?" Ed asked.

"I can't tell you that, sir," the man answered. "But if you come to your office we will make all the necessary arrangements to take you to him. Shall we say in two hours then?"

"Yes, I'll be there!" Ed answered.

"Very good, sir. Good bye," Mister Edwards concluded.

Ed hung up the receiver and attempted to get a grip on what to do next. He fumbled for the note that had Tom's phone number on it even though he had committed it to memory years ago. When he attempted to call Alex, he got a busy signal and he remembered she told him she was doing that to get away from the well wishers in the neighborhood.

Exhausted and keyed up he decided to call the airport and get a security vehicle to come and get him; code three. He threw a few things together and waited for his ride. As he sat there in the dark he could feel a presence.

Finally giving in to his intuitions he said to the darkness, "All right, I'll go get him and bring him home and that's the end. No more, I promise."

As he sat there in the dark a being came from behind him and put his hand on his shoulder, "Good-bye, old friend. You two take care of each other. And you take care of your wartime sweetheart. Remember, those were bad times and nobody is perfect. I wanted to have someone. You'll be all right now. She'll get you through the rest of your days. You and Tom have a lot of work to do with the new kids. Show them the way."

"Who are you talking about?" Ed asked.

"Alice," John answered.

"I never mentioned Alice to you," he replied defensively.

"You forget Who I work for," John said. "I asked Him if you could take her home. You earned it. Good-bye, my friend."

And with that John Beck walked visibly away from and out of Ed Drummond's life.

The car had arrived at Ed's house, and it was time to go.

Alex rolled over restlessly in bed and hugging Tom's pillow began to dream of him. She saw him walking with a man in an old uniform down a runway that had no end to it. And although they both walked briskly they got nowhere. Tom stopped mid-stride and bent down to get something. It was Rocky, who had come running up alongside them. As he walked down this runway he was joined by a great deal of little children that all had life jackets on, all in different ever-changing colors. As they walked along, a beautiful lady left them and walked away alone releasing the hold she had on Tom's hand as lovers would when they parted company. There, her own children who were wearing regular clothing joined her. They all stopped and waved good bye and then they all turned and walked in different directions.

Suddenly, Rocky and Tom stopped walking and turned around. Tom held out his hand to Alex saying, "Come along with me, honey. One more walk and we'll never be parted again." As Alex held out her hand Chris woke her saying, "Mother, you better get up. I think Ed Drummond is here."

As Alex got out of bed and went to the front door, several vehicles met her with lights flashing and sirens blaring. The lead car missed the driveway and came to a sliding halt in the front yard of Tom's most proudly manicured, imported Ohio lawn.

As Alex, Chris and the girls stood on the front stoop, Ed Drummond exited the car and stood there in the lawn unable to speak. He could only stare at Alex with tears streaming down his face. Alex walked up to him and taking his hands in hers said ever so softly, "They found him, didn't they?"

Ed could only muster out a weak mutter of the word yes and began sobbing. He and Alex hugged tightly and sank to their knees on the grass.

Chris and the girls came over to them when the driver of the car said, "The British have him somewhere. We need to get you some clothes, and they will take you to him."

"Is he alive?" Chris asked.

"As far as we know, he is very much alive," the driver said.

Taking Ed's face in her hands, Alex looked into his eyes and asked, "Are you ready for one more trip today? One more trip-- let's go get him and bring him home."

With that Alex and Ed stood up and with their arms around each other walked into the house.

"Turning to the officers in the cars Alex said, "You guys come in, we'll make some coffee. Chris, we better call Tom's mother. Ed, you better cancel that morning search flight

Just as Alex had done since she began the operation she gave out this set of orders as she went to the bedroom to pack some clothes.

As she went to the closet to pull out a small valise, the picture of her and Tom fell out on to the floor. She picked it up and kissing Tom's face put the picture in her suitcase. She hurriedly packed the bare necessities and was on her way to the waiting vehicle that would take her and Ed to the airport.

78

. . . .

ABOARD THE CONQUEROR, TOM AWOKE after a few hours sleep as he was being rubbed down with a glycerin balm prior to the x-rays that Doctor Frey had ordered for him.

Doctor Frey approached him and said, "I was hoping you would sleep a little longer. But since you are awake let's do those x-rays, shall we?"

"How am I doing?" asked Tom in a slightly better tone. "Were you able to get in touch with my lady? How are the children?"

"One thing at a time, Captain," the doctor answered. "First, you have a visitor- and then we'll talk."

Tom noticed a beautiful little Korean girl standing alongside his bed grinning from ear to ear. It was the same little girl that had kept Tom going all those times when he wanted to quit. They stayed in that spot, her standing and Tom lying in bed, holding hands and looking into each other's eyes for a long time.

Doctor Frey and the corpsman stepped into the hallway to talk.

"What did you find out?" Frey asked.

"He has blood in his urine and he moaned when I touched his abdomen," the corpsman returned. "I think he has serious injuries in there. The x-ray will tell us more."

"Let's get it started, shall we?" Frey answered.

As Doctor Frey and the corpsman entered the room they noticed that the little Korean girl had crawled in bed alongside Tom who was by now very exhausted. When the little girl came in contact with Tom's side he let out a moan of obvious pain. Doctor Frey carefully grabbed the girl to take her weight off Tom and just held her there momentarily. When he turned his head he had a show of blood oozing from his mouth. It was now obvious that Tom had some serious internal injuries both because of the blood as well as the grimacing of pain.

"Captain, we have to take some ex-rays now," Doctor Frey said. "We have some questions to answer."

Putting down the little Korean girl who went over and gave Tom a kiss, Doctor Frey wheeled the x-ray into position for a closer examination of Tom's abdomen. He once again fell fast asleep even as the x-ray technician began working.

The chief stuck his head in through the infirmary door to get the doctor's attention. When Doctor Frey came back from taking Tom's x-rays, the chief asked, "Can they be ready to travel in-let's say eighteen hours?"

"If he has to be," Doctor Frey answered. "He's hurt bad. I hate to say this, but it would be best if he didn't die on this vessel."

"He doesn't look that bad." the chief returned. "Well, considering all he's gone through. What the hell is the matter with him?"

"He's busted up inside," Doctor Frey replied. "By the blood in his mouth, I'd say pretty badly busted up inside. Eighteen hours is it? I'll get to work."

"We are going to rendezvous with a PBY at sunrise tomorrow. We'll take him out as carefully as we put him in if you can get him ready to travel by then." The chief finished, and excusing himself went back topside.

"Do you feel like burning the midnight oil, Bill?" Doctor Frey asked the corpsman. "I'd really like to finish the work-up on him before we have to send them on their way."

"Whatever you need, sir," the corpsman replied.

"How are the x-rays going?" Doctor Frey asked.

"Good sir. They are coming out now," Bill replied.

It was clear to the two men that they had a long night ahead, but neither of them were complaining. Being a doctor and a medical corpsman on a submarine in peacetime left a great deal of idle time. So when the opportunity presented itself they were only too eager to give it their all. And in order to get Tom ready to travel it would take all they had this night.

"The blood work is back on the captain, sir, and we have all the salt off and the glycerin balm on him. Charlie said his grit is poor and asked that you check on that and advise him. Is there anything else you need on him, Doctor?" an orderly asked.

"Do you have any more samples left?" Doctor Frey asked.

"Yes, sir," the orderly replied.

"Run a liver panel on him, also," Doctor Frey ordered.

"Right away, sir," he answered, taking the order from the doctor and returning to the laboratory.

"What are you thinking, sir?" Bill asked.

"Did you see how black his blood was in that vial?" Bob answered.

"No, sir. Just that it coagulated in his mouth awfully quick," Bill answered.

"I'm thinking liver damage," Doctor Frey said.

"I'm thinking a punctured lung, lower lobe." Bill returned.

"This poor bastard doesn't have a chance," Bob Frey said.

"Only what we can give him in the short amount of time we have him," Bill returned. "Do you think the captain will let us hang on to him until he can safely travel?"

"I'll bet if he died on this vessel he would spit him out a torpedo tube and never look back," Doctor Frey answered. "All right, let's have a look at those x-rays."

As the two men looked at the x-rays, hopeful anticipation was replaced by defeat. Both men looked at each other and could only shake their heads and say, "shit!"

"We were both right," Doctor Frey said.

"Did you figure on a ruptured spleen as well as liver and a punctured lung?" Bill asked.

"No! I never even considered that much damage," Bob said. "He must have taken a hell of a hit. It looks like seat belt damage. He must have been facing the seat."

"Well, at least we know what we're dealing with," Bill said. "Why don't we bring the x-ray unit back in and see if the rib is sticking in the lung?"

"Yeah, good idea," Doctor Frey said and went to the lab to get it. "Why don't we set up a couple of shunts and drain the blood out so it doesn't turn septic. Let's increase the steroids and start an antibiotic drip. If we can stop the bleeding and ward off infection, he might just make the trip. Where are they taking them? What is our nearest port?"

"I'm thinking Granada is their best bet," Bill answered. "We're nowhere close to Korea and the Americans won't turn anyone away. And with the captain being one of their own, it's a good place to go."

"All right, Bill. Let's document everything and maybe they can take it from there. Are you ready for that x-ray? I've got the shunts ready. Let's get started. We can do wonders in seventeen hours."

79

. . . .

E D AND ALEX WERE WELL on their way to the airport in the security cruiser when the car phone rang. The driver answered the call and said, "Yeah, just a moment." Turning a bit in his seat he handed the phone to Ed saying, "It's London."

"Yes, this is Ed Drummond," Ed answered.

"This is Jonathon Edwards, Mister Drummond. We spoke earlier, is that correct?"

"Yes, Mister Edwards, I am that same man," Ed acknowledged. "Please go ahead."

"Your captain is still alive, although we have it on good authority that he has been injured. At this time all I can say is that the reports are of a serious nature," Mr. Edwards continued. "He will be airlifted, as will all the survivors, to the United States hospital in Granada. They should arrive there on or about eight o'clock Eastern time. Do you have any questions?"

"No, I think we have it," Ed answered.

"Very good, sir," Mister Edwards returned. "There is one more thing I think you will be interested in knowing. There were sixty-six other survivors with your Captain Jordan, sixty-five children and one adult. The reports are that your Captain Jordan saved them all. All sixty-five of those children owe him their lives. That's all I have at this time, sir. Good luck and God's speed to Captain Jordan's recovery.

"My God!" Alex replied. "He dreamed about that. In his sleep he kept talking about saving children. Step on it, would you, driver?"

"I'll call the airport and get the Lear prepped," Ed said.

"Are you thinking what I'm thinking?" Alex asked.

"You mean when we get him back we aren't letting him out of our sight again?" Ed replied. "Yep, that's exactly what I'm thinking. His days of flying are over."

"That's scary, Edward," Alex returned. "That was exactly what I was thinking."

80

. . . .

"**B**RING US UP SLOW, SON!" the XO said calmly as he put his hand on the seaman's shoulder. "The captain will shit himself if he sees a native in a dugout standing on the deck. Up scope! What's the ETA on the PBY, Chief?"

"Seven minutes, Commander," the chief answered.

"All right, everybody on their toes. Radar- let me know two miles before he gets here. Helm- let's put the bow under his wing and up against the door and we can walk them over there. Chief, make ready the transfer. Doctor Frey, are we ready?

"Yes sir, Commander," Doctor Frey answered.

"Were you able to do anything for the captain?" the XO asked.

"We clamped off the spleen and crudely mended the perforation in the gut. We drained the old blood and we patched him up for the trip, but he's hurt pretty bad," Doctor Frey answered.

"How did he manage on the water for so long as banged up as he is?" the XO asked.

"The water kept him buoyant and light," Frey answered. "Until we put him on the boat and gravity set in he didn't realize he was hurt that bad. But every swim he took, every ripple that he endured just ripped him open a little more."

"Radar contact off the port beam, sir!" came the bark of the radar operator.

"Very well, let them land and we'll go to them. Someone wake the captain. Bob, do you need any more help back there?" the XO asked as he made ready the exchange.

"I think we're good. Thank you."

"Keep the nose underwater, son," the XO said. "Wait until they stop and we'll go to them."

"How will he know where we are, sir?" the helmsman asked.

"If we're as good as we think we are, he won't," the XO answered. "Sonar, give me a sweep with a wide berth. Torpedo room, are we still loaded?"

"Yes sir!" was the reply.

"Make ready all tubes- fore and aft!" the XO ordered.

"All tubes fore and aft made ready, aye, sir!"

"The PBY is stopping, sir!"

"Okay, keep an eye out. Radar, where's the other one?" the XO asked.

"He's coming in now, sir. A little off course, but he's coming," the radar man answered.

"All right, helm…stick us in his front door," the XO said. Taking the microphone in his hand he barked, "Surface…surface…lookouts on deck. Smooth as silk like a glass of milk, gentlemen. If we get caught off the coast of Africa, you'll wish your mother never met your father. Okay, Doc! Bring em up."

With the de-saline baths, the hydration therapy, and some hot chicken soup the children were well on their way to recovery, evident as they gingerly scaled the ladder to the deck.

Irene was the next to come up the ladder. When she cleared the hatch that led to the deck and the open sea air, she grabbed the handrail and froze in her tracks.

"Let me help you, ma'am," the seaman said. "It only looks like the floor is moving. Just a walk in the park, I believe you Americans say."

Clinging tightly to the man's arm, Irene eventually made it to the plane as the other PBY pulled up to wait its turn at loading. There she was helped to her seat by an attendant and strapped in.

"Sun-up in fifteen, Captain," the XO said.

"How many more?" the captain asked.

"Thirty, sir."

The captain looked at his XO and nodded respectfully. Turning slightly to look along the perimeter of the ship he paused and said, "I wanted to pick up those Argentinean sailors too, but the Admiralty wouldn't let me. I was a prick then and I apologize. But you have to remember, Commander,

I was a spoiled little Londoner who had just killed two hundred sailors the first time out. I didn't know what the hell I was doing. If it weren't for you and the chief I would have blown my brains out. Instead of thanking you like a man, I blamed you for not stopping me. I swear I will never do that again. No one can make me kill ever again."

The last of the children and Tom were brought topside. Getting Tom through the hatch was a bit painful for him as he was hoisted in a standing position through the two-foot diameter hole in the deck, which separates them from the ocean.

As he was again lowered to the prone position, Doctor Frey looked at one of the drainage tubes and watched as a trickle of blood with a grimace of pain on Tom's face revealed another tear in his gut.

"Dammit, my suture tore!" Doctor Frey exclaimed. "Get me my bag!"

"No, Doctor!" the captain overruled. "He goes as he is. We are late for the door and the sun is on the horizon."

"He'll die like that if he keeps bleeding!" Doctor Frey argued.

"Hell, Doctor," the captain answered, "he's already dead. We're just delaying the obvious."

Doctor Frey took offense at the comment and was about to get in his face when the XO came up and said, "Let's clamp him, Bob. We have to get out of here. This is a hell of a lot better than he had."

Doctor Frey bent over Tom and made a twist in the suture to tighten it up. Tom extended his hand to the doctor and said, "Thank you, sir. I will always remember you for all you did for us."

The captain and XO came over and extending their hands to Tom said, "Captain, we were never here and this never happened. Go with God."

With that a pair of seaman came and grabbing the litter carried Tom onto the PBY for his trip home. As he was strapped in, his little Korean friend came alongside and buckled up for the trip home. She held Tom's hand and smiled in a language they both understood.

They were on their way. While the PBY gained speed for a take off to Granada the H.M.S. Conqueror slipped beneath the sea to the security of the deep. They had gone above and beyond the call of duty of destroying humanity to preserving it. The captain felt good about the exchange of fate. He would fight off the demons of that fateful day in the Falklands and for the first time in years he would have his first restful night.

81

. . . .

THE PILOT OF THE LEAR called back to Alex and Ed and said, "They're up and away. We have a window of one-hour lead time. We'll get there ahead of them."

Alex stared out the window in deep thought oblivious to what the pilot had just said. She was caught up in a mood thinking of what Tom had told her when the chips were down. A smile came across her face as she reached her hand out and said, "You reach out and hold on to Him and you don't let go, because He won't."

"Are you all right?" Ed asked.

"Yeah!" Alex replied. "I think I'm going to be just fine now. I was thinking about Tom. I thought we lost him, Ed. Jesus, I was scared. And then I remembered what he would tell me got him through those low level bombing missions: skill and faith, heavy on the faith. Sometimes you just have to pucker and not give up. We're going to owe a lot of debt for this, Edward. I hope your spiritual checkbook is up to date."

Reaching into his pocket, Ed pulled out a small Bible and said, "I never leave home without it."

"Why you ol' sandbagger, I never thought you were a man of the faith."

"Oh, yeah. Tom hooked me when Chad died," Ed admitted.

"I'm going to need a crash course in it and I mean soon," Alex commented.

"Let's both be strong, I don't think we 're out of the woods yet. But, let the Old Man do his job and we'll stand by for instructions," Ed finished as Alex drifted off to sleep.

As Tom lay on his stretcher mounted in the mesh netting that makes up cargo plane seating, he heard the engines change pitch. For a seasoned pilot like him, he knew it meant they were getting close.

As he raised his head he could see his little Korean friend's head on his chest. He held her hand being careful not to jar her awake. His heart was filled with the joy of knowing that he would soon lay again with Alex. It was customary that after they made love she would put her head on his chest and fall asleep. Although he never shared this with Alex, he would just lay still and smell her hair, as it would ride up in his face, because Tom couldn't sleep on his back. Now was no different.

As the plane pitched slightly to his left, Tom knew it was time he made some decisions. Although he was reluctant to admit it, he knew his flying days were over. This was his third strike. He would not survive the fourth one although that was pilot folklore. Tom believed in it. He knew God had saved him three times. He couldn't be so selfish to ask for a fourth. He believed that the good Lord was trying to tell him something when Ed offered him that chief pilot's job. It was time to say good bye to the friendly skies and pilot a desk and maybe, just maybe, he could make a difference in another young pilot's life. Maybe that pilot would come from a peace time Air Force and not have the ghosts that come in the night to plague one into self-condemnation.

Tom thought back to the despair that overtook him while adrift in the ocean. He felt ashamed that he had thought the one person he trusted the most, had betrayed him, when He was actually making arrangements on smooth seas. Tom had given up, even accepted death- because he was weak and in despair. He thought of how he failed the test, and then he looked around and saw all those children eating ice cream and laughing. Newly orphaned, the lot. But they had an air about them. They would go on, because that's what they do. They pick themselves up, brush themselves off and go on to another day whatever it brings. Tom knew they had that "another day" because of him and for that he was proud. He had done what the Father asked and for the most part, the Father had kept His part of the bargain.

Tom knew he had to forgive himself, but he knew Alex would get him through Mylyn's death. Once he came to grips with that, he knew he could go on, but he had to erase that look of desperation on Mylyn's face from his mind before he gave her that fatal overdose of morphine. In time he would, but it was going to take a lot of time.

As Tom lay on that stretcher he realized that all the people who had depended on him in the past would now be his source of support. He knew he could depend on Alex and he knew Ed would be there for him, also. This would be a good time to introduce Alex to his family in Ohio.

As he lay there he could feel his legs again and he seemed to be perking up a bit, but he could feel his abdomen swell, and knew what that meant. It wouldn't be long and he would dump all his cares on Alex. If I can hold out for one more hour I'll be all right. He would pick himself up, heal up, and go on.

The PBY pilot announcing that they were making their final approach into Granada broke Tom's concentration. He also said that the Korean embassy attaché would meet them all.

82

E D STIRRED ALEX AWAKE LIGHTLY to tell her they were landing in Granada. The pilot pointed to the dock where the PBY would land. He advised them that he had arranged for transportation to the receiving dock. A special ambulance from the United States hospital would come for Tom. The rest of the kids were going to other embassy hospitals.

"Touchdown in thirty seconds," the pilot returned.

As Alex put her seat back in the upright position, she reached over and took Ed's hand "You done good, Drummond. I'm proud of you."

"You didn't do too bad yourself, Sanders," Ed returned "for a woman."

The Lear jet rolled to a stop a short distance from a gray Naval van and both Alex and Ed were on their way to the receiving dock in a matter of minutes.

"I'll look for you on the way back!" the pilot screamed over the screech of the jet engines.

As Alex walked to the van she could see the PBY landing on the water. She hollered at Ed and with a pointing motion as she sat down and closed the van door. Several ambulances screamed by the van on the way to the dock.

"I'll drop you off with the ambulances and I'll park in the lot and wait," the driver said.

"Thank you!" Alex replied. "Thank you for everything."

"We knew they would find them," the driver said. "It was just a matter of time. As secretive as it is about who found them tells me it was probably a rogue Russian."

"Don't they know who found them?" Alex asked surprised.

"No, we picked up a blank low frequency transmission," the driver went on. "The British Embassy picked it up on a decoding machine."

Ed reached over and took Alex's hand and whispered, "Let it go."

When Alex looked at him, he just lightly nodded his head and the subject was ended.

"Here's the dock! They will come in at the very end," the driver explained. "They will bring the captain right here. You can wait for him up at the front if you want and meet him when he gets off the plane. He should be on that plane coming in right there."

Ed and Alex joined hands and a quick walk soon became an excited gallop to the end of the dock. Towards the end there was a building where passengers wait for their planes or in this case, arriving passengers.

The entrance to the furthermost part of the dock was roped off to prevent injury to any unsuspecting civilian. The roped off area provided clearance for the PBY wingspan where it unloaded its cargo. There was then a corridor of about fifty feet where no one was allowed entry. There was a step there. How odd, Alex thought, to put a step in the walkway of a boat dock.

The entrance was crowded by a large number of women speaking a foreign language and scurrying about calling out names. There was a great deal of crying and some of the ladies had to be helped to a seat some where in a makeshift lobby. All of a sudden she realized that this was the staging area for a tragedy.

About thirty-five children got off the first plane. Among them was one white lady, a large American with red hair. Most of the children appeared to be met by mothers that were not theirs. The children were not looking for their parents as if they knew they would not be there. The mothers continued to crowd the entrance as the first plane motored away.

As the second PBY drifted to a stop, a man in uniform was barking out orders and a medical technician showed up with a wheelchair. He took the wheelchair around the corner to the door of the plane.

The remainder of the children came around the corner to the waiting women. One little Korean girl stopped at the entrance of the waiting area as if waiting for someone. She held out her hand and was met by a frail, droopy looking man in a wheelchair. At first he was unrecognizable, and then as Alex strained her eyes she could tell that smile a mile away. It was Tom!

She began a controlled walk that quickly turned into a full sprint. As the other ladies saw Tom, they all walked up to him and touched him and then moved aside to give him room to leave. When he got to the step with his wheelchair, the soldier couldn't lift him and some how Tom mustered the strength to get out of the wheelchair, but he couldn't master the step. As Alex approached him, he fell to his knees on the top of the platform. Lifting his head to look into her eyes his arms gave out under the weight of his torso and he fell to his face with a horrific "splatt" sound.

About fifteen feet from Tom, Alex turned and hollered at Ed, and was so fast at Tom's side and in the soldier's face who was trying to get him off the floor.

"Get away from him, you idiot!" Alex screamed. "What the hell's the matter with you? Ed! Ed!"

"I'm right here, Alex! I'm right here," Ed said as he bent down to help her turn Tom over.

Ed looked up at the soldier as the many women huddled around, and said, "Get some help. Get a gurney now!"

As the two of them got Tom turned over, Alex got her first look at his horrible condition. She began crying, saying, "Oh, my God, baby, what did they do to you?"

Even though the pain was evident in Tom's face, he looked into her eyes and said, "It was nothin,' baby. A walk in the park."

"We're taking you home!" Alex said. "Right now. I was so worried about you, baby. Come on, let's go."

Just then a team of medics came on the scene with a gurney and dropped it down to ground level.

"Ma'am, let us have him. We're taking him to the hospital," the medic pleaded. "We've got to go now. We haven't much time."

As the medic grabbed Alex's arm to get her away from Tom, she stood up and pushed him away.

"Get away from him!" Alex said with a tremor and a look that explained exactly what she meant.

"Sir, please help us," the medic pleaded with Ed. "We have to get him to the hospital, he has internal injuries. We have to go now, ma'am; you can come with him, but we have to go…Now!"

Ed went to console her and get her off Tom so they could transport him when he saw blood flowing from the tube in his abdomen.

"Oh, shit!" Ed said. "This is bad. Alex, we're leaving right now. You ride with them and I'll follow in the van. Okay, lets go!"

And with that, they put Tom on the gurney in spite of his painful groans and facial distortions.

Alex took his hand and began walking beside him saying, "It's gonna be okay, baby, it's gonna be okay! Stay with us, baby, we're almost there."

But Tom had slipped into a deep pain induced coma and would not remember the ride to the hospital.

Ed caught up with Alex in the hospital waiting room. She was pacing the floor not to happy that she wasn't in the operating room with Tom. She explained to Ed that the doctor, a young foreign, however pleasant, fellow had explained to her the main points of Tom's trauma. She said that he had a ruptured spleen and a perforation tearing in his gut. The doctor also said Tom might have broken ribs or a fracture in his lower back. Considering what he had been through, he was lucky to be alive. There was also the issue of de-hydration and the excessive exposure to salt water. Tom was being taken to surgery to repair his spleen and to mend the perforation in his gut. It was imperative that they stop the internal bleeding. They would know more when the surgery was completed at which time the doctor would talk to them again.

"I lost it back there," Alex said.

"You had a right to," Ed said. "Jesus, I can't believe that damn fool left him standing there alone. My God, did you hear him hit that concrete floor? Damn, that had to hurt. Okay. Now we wait. This is the easy part. We got him back, we can deal with this."

While the two of them waited for Tom to be returned to his room, Ed made a call to the airlines and brought them up to speed on his condition. Alex, in turn called Chris and briefed her. She asked her to touch base with Tom's mother in Ohio, and as soon as she received any news she would call again.

"Chris," Alex asked, "did Rocky come home yet?"

"No, Mom, we're still looking," Chris answered.

"There's going to be some ugly words if He doesn't bring his dog back!" Alex added.

"Who, Mom?" Chris asked.

"Never mind, I'll explain it later. Give my love to the kids. I'll call again soon. Bye for now," Alex concluded and hung up the phone.

When she turned from the phone she heard Ed say, "She's right here." Turning her attention to Ed, she saw the doctor coming to her with a most serious look on his face.

"Let's go in here where we can talk," he said with a sense of urgency. "We have repaired his spleen, that will heal. We have repaired the perforation in his abdomen, but he has a laceration in his liver and that is serious. He has a fractured rib along the junction of the spine and horrific bruising in the lower back area. It looks like a seat belt injury. He has lost a great deal of blood and has been overexposed to salt water. We are continuing the steroid therapy and have given him three pints of blood. We are going to start a drip of morphine with an antibiotic catalyst. We've got to get that salt out of his body. My best prognosis is that I just don't know. He has been through what three men couldn't take and has survived. The fact that he is alive says a great deal for him, but it's too early to tell. He has a long road ahead of him, and he's pretty badly beaten up. Any questions?"

"Will he live?" Ed asked.

"I don't know," the doctor replied. "If we can get him through the night we have a very good chance."

"Can we see him?" Alex asked.

"Certainly," the doctor added. "He will be in room 1762. They are taking him there now. Please let him sleep if he can. The antibiotic works with the steroids better when he's asleep."

Alex and Ed thanked the doctor and headed for Tom's room.

"Do you feel like you just got the run around, Edward?" Alex asked.

"No, Alex," Ed replied. "No, I don't. I do believe that doctor is scared to death though. I think he's just as afraid as we are. I don't think he knows what to do for him. As soon as Tom is well enough to travel, we should probably get his butt out of here and back to Houston. But I think the doctor is a good man. He'll do the best he can for Tom. Here we go, the room is down this way."

When Alex and Ed entered the room they saw Tom hooked up to more contraptions and wires and monitors than they had ever seen. Alex was glad there wasn't a breathing tube down his throat. As best she could tell Tom was sleeping comfortably.

The nurse walked into the room with a scowl that instantly set the stage for a personality conflict. She was a large woman with an attitude and a frown to match the rough personality that she took no effort to hide.

"I hope you don't intend to spend the night here," she said. "I don't like long term visitors on my floor."

"We won't get in anyone's way, I assure you," Alex said kindly.

"What you don't understand is that you are already in my way." the nurse retorted.

Alex cleared her throat and shuffled in her chair to turn her attention to the nurse and said, "What part of 'I'll stay here as long as I damn well please 'don't you understand, lady?"

The nurse looked at Alex and with a "huff" gathered her things and walked to the door. "I want this door left partially open at all times. I always stay on top of my patients. No exceptions."

When the nurse walked out and adjusted the opening width, Alex looked at Ed and with that ember of fire in her eye, rose from her seat and closed the door so that there was no mistake the door was indeed closed.

"She opens her mouth one more time, Edward, and it's going to be on!" Alex said. "What a bitch. Are we in United States territory?"

83

. . . .

ALEX AND ED KEPT THEIR vigil with pleasure just grateful they had Tom back in their arms again. Alex held his hand while Ed stepped out of the room to make a few calls and for the first time since this ordeal had started she found herself alone with Tom.

She began talking with him as if she hadn't been away from him at all. She told him of the girls and how everyone had come together to help find him. She was, however, reluctant to tell him about the disappearance of Rocky.

As she talked with him and carefully rubbed the palm of his hand, she couldn't help but notice that he was beginning to tremble. A little at first, but now he was at a full tremor and this greatly concerned her. Not wanting to ask the nurse after their original introduction, Alex chose to open the door a crack. She heard the doctor coming down the hall talking with Ed, and she breathed a sigh of relief.

"How's he doing?" the doctor asked.

"He's trembling," Alex answered." It's increasing with time."

The doctor pulled Tom's chart and after studying all his orders reached up and made a slight adjustment on the IV. He also ordered an additional antibiotic saying to Alex, "This should settle that down a bit. You met the nurse, I take it?"

"Yes we did!" Alex returned.

"I'm going home shortly," he said. "If you need anything just check with the nurse. Her bark is much worse than her bite. I shouldn't pay her much attention . You can also call me if you like."

With that, the doctor left and Ed followed him out the door, shutting it behind him. Alex went to the closet and found a blanket to cover up her feet propped up on the edge of his bed. Picking up a *Readers Digest* magazine she humorously asked Tom if he wanted her to read to him. Placing her hand in his again she leaned back in the chair and began.

"Well we have a story here about Herman Melville," Alex said. "This should be interesting to you; didn't you tell me you used to go fishing as a kid? You could really tell some stories if you hooked one of these babies. I sure wish you would quit that quivering, Thomas, that is very nerve racking.

She sat there in her lazy boy chair and looking at Tom, put the magazine down and tightened her grip on his hand. She rubbed his hand and began talking to him in a different time frame, like they hadn't seen each other for years. She told him of her grandchildren and how they couldn't wait for him to come home. The strain of the past few days was taking its toll on her as she rested her head on the back of the chair. She mumbled a few senseless words and was fast asleep.

She held Tom's hand tightly to steady herself against the gusting wind that had mysteriously stirred up on the beach that evening. As Tom fluffed the blanket into position on the sand and poured the wine into glasses, she noticed that she still strangely had his hand in hers. She also noticed that he had poured three glasses of wine. When she asked him what he was doing, he answered her in an unfamiliar language and spoke as if he was speaking with someone else. He looked past her instead of at her and then handed the glass of wine to someone else saying, "Your favorite, John."

When she turned her attention to the man Tom was speaking to, she saw another man dressed in a totally black outfit. His words were soft yet unmistakable. He left no question as to what he was talking about. He put Alex totally at peace. The man was next to Alex although she didn't see him move. As he turned, Alex's attention was directed again to Tom who was lying in his hospital bed sound asleep with a great deal of people standing around him crying and shaking their heads. She felt an arm around her waist and saw it was Tom standing next to her holding her as the man spoke. Soon there was an elderly lady standing next to Tom who was holding him tightly. She spoke to John Beck in an unusual language. Both men were very happy to see the lady they referred to as Mrs. Lewis.

There were many people speaking, but the only one she could understand was the man in the black suit.

"We have a deal, right, Mrs. Sanders?" the man said.

Alex looked in terror at the man she had just come to realize was the man she talked to on the beach the night before. She thought the man was God, but she knew a mortal never saw the face of God unless they were... unless they were dead.

Alex's attention was diverted to the thought of how she died. But the man assured her that all was well with her but she needed to listen to what he had to say. As the man talked to her Tom let loose of her waist and turned his attention to a young Korean lady he referred to as Mylyn.

Alex attempted to make sense of all that was going around her. She couldn't help but notice that Tom was tugging on her sleeve. As she looked over at him she noticed that they were all alone in his room. It was then that she realized she was sleeping. As she woke she realized that Tom's tremors had progressed into convulsions.

Lifting up in the chair she saw the nurse and Ed standing over him. After collecting her wits, she asked, "Why is he shaking like that?"

"Considering what he's been through with the dehydration and the electrolyte imbalance," said the nurse, "I'd say he was dying. It's not surprising. He was near death when they brought him in here. It shouldn't be long now."

It took Alex a few seconds to absorb what the nurse had said, but once it was clear what she meant Alex removed the kid gloves.

Looking over at Ed, their eyes met. He shook his head in agreement as he got up and opened the door.

Alex said to the nurse, "It's time you left, we won't be needing you any more. Now get out!"

"Excuse me!" the nurse retorted. "This is my floor, lady, and not yours. Who do you think you're talking to?"

"Get her out of here now, Edward!" Alex said as she reached for the phone.

While waiting for the connection, Alex said, "Do you want me to show you the way out or can you do that for yourself? He's been through too much to have some negative pompous ass tell me he's dying. No one is going to die here today, you bitch. Is that in any way unclear? Now get the hell out of here!"

When the phone was answered at the nurse's desk Alex said, "Get that doctor down to room 1762 stat."

"Yes ma'am!" was the answer on the other end.

With that, the nurse left and Ed closed the door behind her.

"Jesus, Alex, what the hell's wrong with him?" Ed asked.

"He's allergic to steroids!" Alex said as she closed the valve on the IV tube. "I don't know where my head was. I listened to that doctor tell about his steroid regiment and never gave it a thought."

"How do you know this?" Ed asked.

"Tom's favorite hidden picture is the one with his face transposed on Arnold Schwarzenegger's body." Alex said as she tried to settle Tom down. "He told me he could kick Arny's butt in the court house square to show me what a man he was if he wasn't allergic to steroid's. Worse than penicillin."

When Alex finished talking the doctor reappeared." What's going on? Miss Personality said you threw her butt out."

"I screwed up," Alex said. "He's allergic to steroids."

"Oh shit!" the doctor said. Looking out the door he hollered down the corridor, "Bring me the anti-steroid treatment kit, stat!"

Tom began thrashing terribly. Alex told Ed to take his legs so he wouldn't hurt himself. As Ed did, the nurse burst through the room with the cart. Moving very swiftly they hooked up a new IV bag and the doctor began monitoring a new set of vitals. Stopping to make entries in the chart he noted, "My God, they started giving this to him on the sub. Well, how would they know? I think the initial treatment probably saved his life, but I agree with you, Mrs. Sanders, he's had enough for one lifetime. Who's coming on now?"

"Jean," the nurses' aide answered.

"Okay, that will work. I think you will find the oncoming staff nurse a little more agreeable than Nurse Rachett was. If not, I'm sure you will take care of it," the doctor said extending his hand. "It was a pleasure meeting you, ma'am, and you also, sir. We'll keep a closer look on his vitals. If we're lucky he'll pull out of this. We'll know soon enough. I'll be in touch."

When the doctor left, Alex took off her shoes still holding Tom's hands from hitting the bed or anything else in close proximity. She then pulled back the light covers and crawled in bed with him.

Getting as close as possible, she put her arms completely around him and intertwined her legs with his in a post-coital position. She took her free arm and held his head close to her chest to stop the convulsing. As she was holding him she began to cry and whisper in his ear words that Ed could not hear. This was more than Ed could take, and he asked Alex if she would excuse him.

"He'll be fine now, Ed," Alex said, "We just need some time together for a while, that's all. He needs to know that I am here with him. He probably thinks he's alone in hell and he's trying to crawl out. These allergic reactions are a bitch."

"How do you know all this shit?" Ed asked.

"My husband was an alcoholic. I've been through this before. We've crawled out of many an abyss, believe me," Alex answered. "Go get some air, I've got him now.

Alex continued to hold Tom tightly as she glanced up at the IV solution to speed it up a little. As she continued to whisper to him, the other staff nurse came in and looked at the IV and took his vitals. Alex thought she would say something to her because she was in bed with Tom, but the nurse looked at her and smiled saying, "My husband is a Vietnam vet who has some doosies for nightmares. That's what I do, I hold him until he stops. He told me once that he feels secure when I hold him even though in his dream he is running for his life. Stay there with him as long as you like. It can't hurt anything. Do you have everything you need?"

"Yes, thank-you," Alex said. "What is your name?"

"Jean. My friends call me Jeanie, "she said. "I'll be right down the hall if you need anything. Feel free to ring me."

"Thanks, Jeanie," Alex said.

And with a casual "Your welcome, hun," Jean smiled broadly and was out the door to look in on another patient. She intentionally closed the door behind her leaving Tom and Alex alone.

Alex held him tightly against her body and talked softly to him while stroking his hair. She would repeat things like, "I'll take you home soon, honey, just as soon as you wake up, we can go home. We'll lie on the beach like we used to. You'll see, Tommy, everything will be all right"

She looked up and noticed he had settled down quite a bit. He was only slightly shaking and his breathing had returned to normal. As she continued talking to him her words began running together and she found herself talking to the man in the black suit.

Alex had her arms around Tom, but he was over by John Beck and Mrs. Lewis. There was a white bridge crossing a minute ground level fog and a gate on the other side of the bridge.

There was Tom, John Beck, Mrs. Lewis, a Korean lady with a bunch of children, and the man in the black suit. They all held hands together and were very happy, each in his language and culture. Alex loosened her grip on Tom and noticed he wasn't there at all. As she walked to the bridge she was stopped by the man in the black suit who said only," You can't come to this side, it's not your time yet. You have so much to do yet, but don't be frightened, I will be alongside you."

Alex looked down at her feet and realized she couldn't see them, they appeared to be covered by the fog. As she looked back at the people on the bridge she noticed they had crossed over to the other side and were standing at the gate. Alex screamed out Tom's name but hr only looked at her, smiled, and looked away again, caught up in the conversation he was having. Alex tried desperately to get closer to him but was unable to cross over the bridge. No matter how she struggled she could not get any closer to him. Ever when she reached out her arm she couldn't grab him.

Finally, the man in the black suit put out a reassuring hand to Alex and opened the gate. As he did so, Alex noticed that thousands of flowers bloomed in a circular collage. As they started to go through the gate the man in the black suit put out his hand and rested it on Tom's shoulder and said, "You have done what the Father has asked of you. Your work is done here but there is much more for you to do on the other side. This is as far as you go."

Sadness appeared on Tom's face as he took one last look at his friends and then back to Alex and then back to his friends again. The girl they called Mylyn came and hugged Tom, kissing him lightly on the cheek and speaking in an unrecognizable language. Mrs. Lewis said to Alex, "Don't you worry, Alex, I'll see my granddaughter soon enough. We've got the rest of their lives."

The man in the black suit extended an open hand to Alex inviting her to cross the bridge. When she did so, the man put her hand in Tom's and said. "Go and live the rest of the life that I have planned for you in peace and love. You shall be tested no further."

The three of them turned and walked across the bridge together and immediately the man in the black suit was gone. As Alex looked into Tom's eyes the vision of him became faded. When she twisted to look over her shoulder she woke Tom out of his steroid induced sleep and he found himself lying in bed with Alex lying next to him.

He could feel the warmth of her body against his. He could smell her hair. He could smell her perfume and recognized it as *Beautiful,* from *Estee Lauder.* He had given her a bottle for Christmas. This was the first time Tom realized he was alive. When he put his fingers in Alex's hair and smelled her perfume, he knew the ordeal was over. He knew that no dream could imitate the reality that gave him the hope he needed to stay alive on the sea. He adjusted himself up a little higher in the bed and held her in his arms running his fingers through her hair. It was a sensation he thought he would never experience again. Lying with Alex, in bed, running his fingers through her hair while she slept was an answer to his prayers.

Tom looked up to the ceiling to thank God just as Jean came into the room.

"Hey, look at you, you're awake," Jean said. "Welcome back to reality. How are you feeling?"

"Not bad," Tom said. "Look what I found in my bed."

"Yes, I see that," Jean answered.

"Can I keep her?" Tom asked.

"Well," Jean mused. "Only if she follows you home."

Shortly after, Ed walked into the room and seeing Tom awake sitting half way up was too much for him to cope with and he started to cry. He couldn't find the words to say, he could only pace and cry. Jean became concerned about Ed and taking him by the arm led him to a chair on the left side of Tom's bed and sat him down there. Ed and Tom put their hands together as they had done many times and with Jean's hands on Ed's shoulders, they managed to quiet him down. Neither man spoke, they just looked at each other and with a nod of their heads all was right with both of them.

"I'll leave you two alone. I'll stop back in a little bit," Jean said. "You going to be okay, Edward?"

"Yeah, thanks," Ed replied.

"All right," Jean said as she patted Ed on the shoulders and left.

"Do you remember anything? Anything at all?" Ed asked Tom

"I remember everything," Tom replied. "And I don't think I'll ever forget it. But let me tell you about it some other time in some other place. Just take me home, will you, please? I'll be fine when I get home. I remember you got me in a world of shit over that job offer. How did you find me here?"

"The British found you and brought you here. They called us...hell, when did they call us? What day is it?" Ed asked.

"You're asking me, for heaven sake?" Tom returned. "Hell, I've been asleep for two weeks. How long have I been here, speaking of two weeks?"

"They brought you in here this morning," Ed answered. "You were one sorry son of a gun, let me tell you. So, tell me true. How are you feeling?"

"Weak and tired," Tom replied. "But I tell you, if she gets to feeling any better against my leg, I'll muster up some strength in a heartbeat."

"I don't think Nurse Jean is going to sit still for any tom foolery on her watch," Ed said.

"You watch the hallway for me, won't you Ed?" Tom chided. "What are friends for?"

About this time Alex woke up from her nap and said, "Watch the hallway for what?"

"Tom wants to jump your bones!" Ed said.

"Okay!" Alex said. "But, Ed, can you watch the hallway from the other side of the door?"

Having said this Alex got up and leaned over giving Tom a kiss.

"Good morning, sailor," Alex said. "Damn it's good to see you!"

"It's good to be seen, let me tell you," Tom replied. "You two never gave up on me. I knew you wouldn't. It's what kept me alive. I knew you would come. And here you are. How are you? I have so much to tell you. So much to thank you for and so much love to share with you. Would you please take me home soon? I never want to be alone without you again."

Alex sat down on the bed, wiped away a tear and gently kissed him on the lips. "Whenever you're ready, I'll take you home," she said. "We've got a lot of love to share with each other. A lot of people can't wait to see you, but first you have to get well. You've gone through hell and it damn near killed you. One day at a time if we have to, but I nearly lost you. I can't deal with that again. I won't hurry with your life ever again."

"Have you seen the kids?" Tom asked. "I lost track of them in the boat."

"There were sixty-five kids and one woman," Alex answered. "They were on the first floor. They may have gone home by now."

"Oh, damn!" Tom said. "I wanted to say good-bye."

"Well, listen," Ed said. "I want to go look at that admitting nurse's butt before she goes home, I'll see where the kids went. You two need to be alone for a while anyhow."

84

W HEN ED WALKED OUT THE door, Alex crawled back in bed with Tom and put her arm around him.

"Just let me hold you," Alex said. "I'm so tired. And I'm afraid if I fall asleep you'll be gone when I wake up."

"You go right to sleep," Tom returned. "I'm not going anywhere. I'm not leaving your side ever again."

With that they both fell asleep.

When Jean entered the room a short time later, she found them both fast asleep, so she covered Alex up. After changing Tom's IV bag she was gone leaving the two of them alone. As Jean closed the door behind her she chuckled at the sight of them and was warmed by their love.

As Ed walked down the hall to the nurse's station in search of the nurse whose posterior he sought, he passed a doctor who was talking with a nurse. He looked up as he walked past them, and their eyes met. Ed forgot his search for the endowed nurse as he realized he knew that lady from somewhere. His gait slowed considerably. Likewise the lady doctor had lost her concentration and she also slowed her gait. Ed stopped walking and turned around. The doctor had stopped her conversation and also turned around. Both just looked at each other for what appeared to be an eternity.

The doctor spoke first as she looked at Ed, and with a strange look, merely said his name. Ed returned the greeting in the same manner saying her name." Alice? It can't be! Can it? Ed and Alice walked toward each other and when they met they gazed into each other's eyes.

"My, God, how long has it been?" asked Ed.

"Too long, too very long, "Alice returned. "I haven't seen you since Saigon. I turned around and you were gone. I never saw you leave, you were just gone. We made love that afternoon and then you were gone."

"They told me you were gone. That the blast took out the triage room and everything in it. They told me the parts they found looked like you. I didn't learn until 1990, that you were still alive. I saw your name in a listing of medical crews published by the outfit for some kind of reunion. Kind of like a 'where are they now' kind of thing. I saw your name on that list and damn near had a heart attack. My God, look at you, you're all grown up. Come here."

Alice handed her papers to the nurse standing beside her and gave Ed a hug.

"I've kept track of you over the years, Edward," Alice returned. "I got the same publication you did. I'm sorry to hear about Chad. I know how alone you must have felt. And your divorce. Have you remarried as yet?"

"No," Ed said. "Once is enough."

"Maybe I can change your mind on that," Alice said as she looked into Ed's eyes.

"Are you alone too?" Ed returned surprisingly.

"Yes," replied Alice. "He ran off with some preppy from a medical school conference. I went to work one day and when I came home the house was dark, everything he owned was gone, and a sweet little letter about my standing in the way of his happiness. I saw him in court for a pathetic ten minutes about five years ago now, and that was that. Edward, what are you doing here? Was that one of your pilots? Don't just stand there, you big galoot...say something. Where are you staying? Don't worry about a hotel, you can stay with me. How long are you staying? Damn, it's good to see you!"

"You haven't changed a bit," Ed said while he hugged her again. "You're still a motor mouth! I'm here about a pilot! Yes, that's my pilot. No, I haven't a hotel yet, but I'd rather stay with you, and for as long as you can put up with me. And oh, yes... it's good to see you too!"

"Have you eaten today? You're wilting away to nothing," Alice concluded.

"Not yet, but I figured we could take care of that at your house," Ed replied.

"My God, Edward, we've got some serious catching up to do," Alice started. "I hope you brought your mouth with you."

"I never leave home without it," Ed replied. "Shall we go, my dear?"

"Please put those on my desk, if you would, Catherine, and I'll get them in the morning," Alice said.

"Yes, Doctor Lewis," Catherine returned.

"You took back your maiden name!" Ed exclaimed.

"Yes, I did it for my grandmother," Alice replied. "She was the sweetest thing. I owe her a lot. I was proud to take her name."

"You said...was," Ed returned. "Is she gone?"

"She was on that airplane that burned up in Maine. The stress was too much for her. She died in her sleep," Alice answered. "God, I loved that woman. My information is sketchy, but I hear that the pilot got her off all right although he got burned in the process. She was taken to the hospital and released, but she died in the hotel overnight."

"My God, Alice!" Ed said as he stopped walking and took her by the arm. "Have I got someone for you to meet, but later, all right?"

"Much later," replied Alice. "One good memory a day is all I allow myself. Come along, Edward, maybe we can walk out of this hospital before it explodes. You always did leave me with a bang."

As they walked out, they were met by the valet driver. He brought up Alice's Mercedes and opened the door for her.

"What do you think, Edward? This is a far cry from that beat up old Army jeep you used to court me in, wouldn't you say?"

"Quite a far cry, at that," Ed returned. "You've done quite well for yourself."

"A girl has to do what a girl has to do," Alice answered as she took her seat and closed the door behind her.

Ed walked around to his side of the car and his mind began to sort out what was happening at this minute. Looking up to heaven he said, "You ol' son of a gun, you were listening, weren't you? I had all but given up, and You had this planned all along. You knew this was going to happen years ago, didn't You? Even though I believed her to be dead, I always knew You were up to something. This is really worth the wait. You can have the pain back, but I owe you for this. Now I know where Jordan gets it."

Ed stopped at the door and took a look around. He knew he would never pass this way again and he wanted to cherish the moment with this lady he had said good-bye to such a long time ago.

It was nineteen seventy-five in the base hospital in Saigon, Vietnam, and things were quickly getting out of control. Ed was a medi-vac helicopter pilot and Alice was a young intern. They had met there on a typical hot steamy Vietnam afternoon when Alice was called over to the Navy side to do a procedure on a sailor, and Ed provided the transportation. They were young, exciting and idealistic and fell in love immediately as do so many war time romantics.

Both Ed and Alice were no strangers to danger and destruction and the last day of the South Vietnamese Regime stronghold in Saigon was no different.

The evacuations were not going well and there were so many wounded to be tended to and made ready for travel that the rescue choppers could not keep up with the demand. Then, to add insult to injury, a C-131 Starlifter carrying about four-hundred children from a Red Cross orphanage, crashed and exploded at the end of the runway killing all aboard and making takeoffs impossible.

Civilian as well as wounded refugees were being boarded on the roofs of the embassy as well as the hospital. Landings were made between the barrage of Huey Gunship Mini-gun cover and things were very dicey.

The last landing Ed saw Alice on the roof signaling him one finger, a twirl of her hand around her head and a hand edge across her throat. Ed knew this meant one more trip around and we are out of here. She then blew him a kiss as he lifted off the roof en-route to the harbor to land on the aircraft carrier Oriskiny and return to pick up the last of the doctors. It would all be over soon as the enemy troops were advancing uncontested now. All remnants of the Vietnamese Army had retreated to the safety of the boats in the harbors leaving their loved ones and families at the mercy of the conquering army.

As Ed waited for the gunship to chew up the enemy troops piecemeal, one of them was hit by a rocket. It dropped through the roof exploding in the triage unit where Alice was working. The explosion had such force that it sent up slivers through the skin of Ed's helicopter causing it to pitch side to side. The heat wave from the exploding chopper had driven Ed to an altitude of about one hundred where he saw too clearly the carnage of the spot where Alice would have been standing. Ed circled the roof area until the flames and smoke cleared and went back in to pick up any survivors. Only two people came out of the inferno. One was an obstetrician who worked alongside Alice. When Ed hollered to her, she could only scream back hysterically, "Dead...they're all dead!"

Ed made another sweep in toward the roof where he saw a Viet-Cong aiming a rocket at him, and he squeezed off his twenty millimeter cannons shredding the soldier and pulled away looking back at what was left of the woman he loved.

That was the last time he saw Alice, on the roof of that hospital and he never forgot the kiss she blew him as he pulled away that afternoon. As he flew away without her, the dreams of an entire lifetime went with him. And now thirty-one years later, she was sitting in her car waiting on him, to take him to a safe haven out of harm's way; home to her house.

As he opened the door and got in the car, she looked at him and said, "You were logging a memory, weren't you? You always said that every day would bring you something to remember. I can assure you, Edward, that this is only the beginning of the memorable events of this day."

Alice reached over and took his hand, and picking up her cell phone, said, "I've got to tell my daughter. I don't want any interruptions tonight. She is so not going to believe this."

Ed was humored by her use of the younger slang. He attributed it to talking to her grandchildren. He rarely talked to anyone who wasn't close to geriatric counseling.

When her daughter answered the phone, Alice said," Do you remember that big handsome hunk of a man you saw in that picture you found snooping through my scrapbook about ten years ago? Well, he's sitting right here next to me and I am bringing him home to feed him before he wilts away to nothing. Could we get together tomorrow?"

"Oh, yes, tomorrow would be a great time to meet him...say eight o'clock?"

"No, he's the boss. I don't think he has to run away too quickly. Do you, Ed?"

"Not at all," Ed returned.

"Wait until you see him. He hasn't changed a bit. He is still the adorable hunk he was in the seventies. I saw his cute butt strutting down the hallway. What was he doing walking down the hallway, you ask? He was in pursuit of a young nurse, no doubt. What do you mean how did I get to him first?" Alice said as she winked at Ed. "I used the feminine wiles on him. I still got it. That or he's awfully easy. Well, he's probably a little tired and hungry, but what has that got to do with it? Yeah, right. I do intend to charm him. I'll talk to you later. I'm busy. No, sweetheart, I don't need any help. Thank you. Good bye."

Alice closed her cell phone and looked back at Ed saying, "Ashley is a great kid. You'll love her when you meet her. Hopefully she won't let herself in without knocking."

"Where do you live?" Ed asked.

"By the ocean!" Alice said excitedly. "After living with you by the sea, I couldn't imagine living away from the water. See the big impression you made on me? We'll be there momentarily. Just around the bend here."

"Why didn't you get hold of me before you left the country?" asked Ed. "God, if I only knew you were alive...could you imagine how different our lives could have been, the things we could have done together? There wouldn't have been any of the bullshit we went through or anything like that. Why didn't you call me, Alice?"

"Well, Edward," Alice returned. "Bullshit is really the word for it. I wasn't entirely honest with you in Saigon. I was married then to a urologist who remained in private practice when I went overseas. Of course, nothing about his sex life was private as I was to learn when he failed to pick me up at the airport. I walked in the front door and found several pair of blue jeans of varying sizes on the floor. When I went upstairs I found all the owners of them in our bed. Did I mention that they were all men? He always was a little strange, but even I didn't think he was that far gone. You would think a urologist would have his fill of dicks, but not in this case.

So, at the time, I thought I was after the same thing you were, a little fun and security. You have no idea how lonely a war zone can be when you're sleeping alone. I apologize for not realizing it was more to you than that. Had I known then I would have gone about it in a different way. I was very fond of you, Edward, and I would not have hesitated to lure you away from your helicopter seat and into my bed on a permanent basis."

"Well," Ed replied. "How do you feel about a little fishing with that lure right now?"

"Very lucky!" Alice replied. "Do you have any reservations about being hooked?"

"Not by you," Ed returned. "I'll bet we can make good fishing partners. Where would we live, your place or mine?"

"Do you have anything you can't leave behind in Houston?" Alice asked.

"Just Tom Jordan," Ed said. "I have to get him home. I promised John I would see him to the end. And when he is able I am giving him my job. I was going elsewhere, but I am prepared to retire just the same. But I have to see him home. After that I am free, Alice. Completely free."

"How do you feel about life on a Caribbean Island?" she asked with a smile on her face.

"As long as you're there," he said returning a smile.

"Well, Edward, I promise that I will be there and will not leave behind a fiery explosion without prior notice," Alice chided. "And speaking of being there, we are here. What do you think?"

Ed leaned forward to get a better look out the windshield of her car. He was very impressed with what he saw. The yard was immaculate for a busy physician in a teaching hospital. There were two palm trees adorning the two ends of the front lot. There were three pillars that appeared to reach into the sky, but in actuality only went to the red tiled roof that displayed a grand front entrance with a large chandelier hanging over the front door. The front of the house was a very warm white stucco finish with several windows reflecting a lush green tobacco plantation across the street. The windows were open and one could see the flowing sheer curtains behind the French window panes. These supported hanging baskets with festive colored flowers. Its appearance suggested a plush hotel entrance instead of a private residence. It was as if Ed stepped out of his world into a magazine.

The upper floors held guest rooms, each graced with their own balcony. They also had sheer curtains flowing in the late afternoon Caribbean breeze. The house was as amazingly meticulous as was Alice. They were a tribute to each other, Ed thought to himself, very well kept.

"How do you keep this up, Alice?" Ed asked quizzically. "With your schedule and all."

"One requirement about living here, Edward, is that if you're an American making a good living, you share the wealth with the locals," Alice explained. "Except for the plantations, there isn't a lot of work here. When it became an American holding and the hospital was built, it was agreed that Americans who worked here would hire some of the locals to look after the places they owned. The hospital employs a great deal of orderlies and janitorial types, but other than that there are more people here than there are jobs. So, I enjoy the employ of three local residents with a fourth from time to time. Come inside and you can meet them."

When Alice and Ed approached the front door it opened from the inside and they were met by a lovely, friendly lady with a smile from ear to ear greeting them as if she hadn't seen them for years.

Ed 's first impression was that of the lady on the *Sangria* wine bottles. She had long black hair tied back, a large flowing white blouse and a very sultry red skirt that hid the beautiful figure of a middle aged lady from the islands.

"Good afternoon, Mrs. Alice!" the maid said. "How are you today, sir?"

"Teresa, this is Ed Drummond," Alice said. "He'll be having dinner with us tonight and may be staying awhile also."

As Ed extended his hand in the customary greeting, Teresa couldn't help but stare deeply into Ed's eyes. Finally Alice broke the ice when she said, "Yes, Teresa. He is the man in the picture."

With that Teresa smiled at Ed and said, "Welcome, Mister Drummond."

"Come, Edward, let me show you around," Alice said as she took him by the hand and began the grand tour of the house. As Alice and Teresa tried to make him feel at home an airplane flew over the house at a low level catching Ed's attention.

"The airport is just down the way a bit, "said Alice, "you 'll quickly get used to it. At least I did."

"What is all that back there?" Ed asked.

"Wine vineyards," explained Alice as she pointed in a semi circle around the perimeter of her back yard. "We butt up against a large plantation on the far reaches of the property."

"Your flowers?" asked Ed.

"Oh, yeah. Have to have my roses," she said as she hugged and kissed him lightly on the lips.

"What do you do for fun back there in Texas, Edward?" Alice asked.

"Never took the time for it actually," he said. "I guess I've learned to live without it."

"Do you fly anymore?" she asked. "They're always looking for good pilots around here. Most of them are military pilots and the government doesn't allow them to do social work. We have a boat also if you're into fishing."

"Wait a minute here, Alice!" Ed exclaimed. "Let me get my feet wet first, will you please? This is still a shock for me seeing you. Give me a minute to absorb all this."

"I'm sorry, Ed," returned Alice. "I'm just afraid you're going to get away, and you know what they say about first impressions."

She put her arms around him again and gave him a hug that more than made up the time they were away from each other.

"Do you ever feel you've been given a second chance at life, Ed?" Alice said as she looked into his eyes. "This is my second chance. I couldn't plan this any better if I had a week's notice you were coming. But now that I have you here, I don't want you to get away. These are the things that dreams are made of. If you only knew how many times I dreamed of you, where you must be, what you were doing, and where life took you. If you only knew, then you would know what this moment means to me. I've never stopped loving you, Ed. I only lost track of where the love was going. We've always been straightforward with each other, we've never had to fake it. I'm not about to start now."

"Dinner is ready, ma'am," Teresa announced and broke the mood. Kissing Ed again, Alice took his hand and led him to the dining room.

"We'll talk more after dinner," she said in an excited tone. "We have so much to talk about and get caught up on. Do you have vacation time left for the year, Edward? I'm planning on taking next week off; we could spend quite a bit of time together. Do you think you can still handle me after all these years?"

"I'm sure we'll find out, won't we?" answered Ed as he sat down to dinner. "As soon as they release Tom I'll be taking him back to Houston. There will be loose ends to tie up and then after that I'm free as long as you want me. There is another issue about a job offer I have been looking into. I was hoping to groom Tom into my present position so I could leave it to a responsible pilot. Now, he's almost a shoo-in for the job. I don't think Alex will let him fly anymore. But we can talk about that."

"Aren't you close to retirement, Edward?" Alice asked.

"Give or take, I suppose," he replied. "I never thought of it since I don't have anyone to retire with. I've really no plans. Are you thinking along those lines, Alice?"

"I'm not sure, actually," Alice said. "I sometimes think of a sabbatical for a year just to get away and see what I may be missing. I've been blessed in my career, but it makes more demands on me than it's worth. I'd like to spend some time where I don't have to deal with the possibility of someone dying on me every day. Sometimes the burden of being someone's only hope is too much to bear. I don't want to quit, mind you, I just need to get away for awhile; just a little rest. Just to catch up. Am I making any sense here, Edward?"

"Oh, yes, perfect sense," replied Ed. "I've felt that way for years. But I'm afraid if I got away I wouldn't ever come back."

"Really, Edward," Alice remarked. "Where does your heart lead you?"

"A quiet little fishing village in Alaska, where there are real life Eskimos and no traffic." he answered with a gleam in his eye.

"It gets cold up there, you know. I'm going to need to be kept warm. Are there any plans for a hot blooded doctor to keep you healthy and satisfied, not to mention well loved?" Alice queried.

"I think we can work something out on that subject," he replied." Maybe we can check your resume after supper."

"I wouldn't have it any other way, Edward," Alice said. "Let's get started, shall we?"

Ed and Alice rose from the dinner table and as he walked towards her he felt as if his world was spinning so fast he wasn't sure he could get off if he wanted to. He was afraid he would wake up and find himself alone and Tom still lost somewhere in the great abyss of the ocean. But as he and Alice met in the dining room, he knew this feeling was too true to be a dream.

As he held her he couldn't comprehend all the things that had happened these past forty-eight hours. He had lost his best friend only to find him alive again, and he found the one true love of his life. He had both in his grip and believed that they would never get away again. How could this be happening to him? It was beyond his understanding and he felt now was not the time to question it.

When Ed and Alice arrived at the bedroom, and Alice shut the door behind them, a new chapter in the life of Edward Drummond was about to start. He knew he would have to learn as he went, but he felt secure in the feeling that Alice was going to prove a fine teacher. He held her tightly in his arms and kissed her. His life was about to change and he wasn't about to be late this time. Nothing would be left to chance. He knew he would never pass this way again.

He turned around and shut off the light.

85

· ·

ALEX STIRRED EVER SO SLIGHTLY and woke Tom from a light sleep. He still lay with Alex in his arms, very reluctant to let her go. Looking at her he brushed a lock of hair from her eyes and was met by a most loving smile.

"Hi," Alex said.

"Hi back," Tom said with a smile as he stretched over and kissed her on the lips.

"You appear to be quite feisty for a man who spent three days afloat on a raft, Thomas." she remarked.

"Hey, babe," Tom returned. "I was with the British Navy. They are one wild bunch, let me tell you. You better look out, I'm feeling my strength returning with every passing minute."

"Uh-huh... I hear ya," Alex chided as she nuzzled closer to him and put the covers over them both.

Just then the nurse came into the room and looking at Tom's IV said, "Well, I think you've had enough to eat for now. Why don't you try and get up and see how those legs are recovering? We can take this out now. You had a good dinner, Captain."

"Did you serve the wine in with everything else in there?" Tom asked.

"Oh, for sure," Jean returned. "This had Don Perigon in it. Didn't you taste that?"

"No, sure didn't," he replied "I think the strong salmon taste covered it up."

"Don't you hate it when that happens?" Jean said.

"Yeah," he said. "What were you saying, Alex?"

"There were a lot of strange happenings around the house while you were gone. The place isn't haunted, is it"?

"No, why do you say that?" Tom asked." Ouch! That needle wasn't rusty, was it?"

"Probably," Jean said. "The Japanese left them at the end of the war."

"Frugal little bastards, weren't they?" Tom said as he shook the sting off his arm.

"Go take a walk and get some blood flow going. If you're gone in the morning, you two take care of yourselves. It was nice to meet you both," Jean said as she exited the room and went on down the hallway.

"Some other place at some other time, we'll talk about this, okay, Tommy?" Alex said.

"Well, Alex, I can't think of anything around the house that our trusty hound dog couldn't handle," Tom returned.

"Tom, can we please talk about this later?" Alex pleaded as she looked away.

Tom reached out his hand and a tear streaked down her face.

"What's the matter, baby?" Tom asked. "Come here, honey. Let me hold you. What happened, honey?"

"Rocky took off after the priest and never came back," Alex began. "Corrie took him out to pee and she said the priest came on the beach and Rocky chased him as far as she could see and we haven't seen him since."

"What did he look like?" Tom asked as he adjusted himself in bed.

"Tall, skinny, needs a shave. Black robe and a rose colored sash. Spanish mission vintage, I'd say," she described.

"No kidding?" he said as he looked away. You saw him too?"

"I fed the son of a bitch breakfast!" Alex answered.

"I'll be damn," Tom said. "I'm gone two days and you're hustling a collar. Have you no shame, Alex?"

"Tom, don't make fun of this," she said. "This is serious. I'm very worried and he wasn't back yet this morning. Corrie is pretty shook up about it. This is just not a good thing to be happening along with everything else."

"Along with what else?" Tom asked.

"Well, you-- dummy! That took all the wind out of us when you didn't show up at that airport, " Alex continued. "I may be selfish, because I know you didn't have it so great either, but have you any idea how it feels to have the best thing that ever happened to you get ripped away in the middle of the night without a trace? We learned that the Koreans were giving up the search after another day of bad weather only to come home and find out that Rocky had taken off. I'm sorry to whine, Tommy, but this hasn't been a good week. That crazy dog was the only one I could talk too. And I couldn't figure out how I was going to tell you this on the way down here. I just want everything to get back to normal, but I'm afraid it's too late for that."

"It's not too late. He'll come back. Maybe he needed to get away for awhile and sort things out his own way. He's probably horny," Tom explained in a comforting way. "We just need to go home and everything will be fine. You'll see. This will all work out."

"You make it sound like Rocky is a people," Alex remarked.

"He is," Tom returned. "He's my people. He'll be back. He probably went a few blocks to that collie's house to watch old Lassie episodes. He'll be back. As soon as we get home he'll come around for supper. What time of day is it, honey?"

"It's nine p.m., Tommy," Alex answered. "Are you tired or hungry?"

"No, honey," Tom replied. "My butt is asleep. Let's go for a walk. I smell water. There must be a beach nearby. Grab that blanket. You know what they always say about standing on a new beach."

"No, I'm afraid that one escapes me," she said.

"When you go to a beach for the first time you should make love in the sand. That way your love is sealed all over the world," he explained.

"I never heard that one, Tommy," Alex answered. "Are you sure you didn't just make that up to get in my pants?"

"Alex!" Tom blurted out with a snicker on his face. "What kind of a low down scheming hound dog do you take me for? I'm appalled that you would even think that about yours truly. That hurt, Alex."

"Cut it out and close your gown," Alex said as she swatted Tom on the backside. "Your bare butt is sticking out."

"Ouch!" Tom said. "Do you realize that you're abusing an injured man here?"

"Yeah, right. You're so injured you want to jump my bones in the dark on a beach that is known for it's shark mating ground of choice," Alex ranted on.

"Are you kidding me? No shit! We'll be shark bait?" Tom rambled as he buttoned his pants and put on a bathrobe.

"No!" Alex chided. "Not we...you!"

"Oh... true love emerges," Tom said. "See how you are? Help me with my skivvies."

"Are you sure you can walk out of here? "Alex asked.

"Yeah, piece of cake," he said. "Give me a hand here, will you?"

"The nurse is gonna have kittens if she catches you outside walking around," Alex remarked. "Are you sure you're up to this, Tommy?"

"Yes, trust me," he said. "And grab that blanket. Take a look out the door. We need to case the hallways."

"You need therapy, Thomas," she said.

"No, what I need is out there on the beach," Tom returned. "Grab that blanket and put a move on it, would you?"

When he stood up from the bed he wavered just a bit and then sat back down. He wiggled his legs and made a stretching motion and said, "Let's try that again." He held out his arm to Alex to help him to his feet and he stood there motionless for a moment, "Let's try a step, shall we?"

Trying desperately to get control of his balance, Tom held tightly to Alex for support. He took one step at a time until he was at the door to the room. Taking a "scooting" type of step, he cleared the threshold and was out in the hall. Before long he had walked about twenty feet and was getting the feeling back in his legs and feet.

"Let me go for a second," Tom said as he continued on down the hall without help from Alex. "Don't get to far, honey. I like leaning on you. I tell you, by the time I get you on that beach, you're gonna be in a heap of trouble."

"You're doing just fine, Tommy," Alex said. "But I don't think you can run yet to catch me. Okay, here's the elevator. Watch the balance when it goes down."

"Okay, babe," he said. "I'm ready. Let 'er rip."

As the elevator started down, Tom started to wobble and reached for Alex. She was right there steadying him for the descent to the ground floor.

"I never did like elevators much," Tom said.

"I know, you told me that a long time ago," Alex replied.

"Isn't that amazing-the things you remember about someone?" Tom asked. "All the time I was on that raft, I kept thinking about how you hold your mouth when you're trying so hard not to tell me that I am a dip shit. And I could just imagine you standing there, looking at me and thinking; how the hell did you get your sorry ass in a mess like this? I felt that water go over my head and there wasn't anything I could do about it, I was so weak. I resigned myself to the fact that I was going to die, but the worst part was that I was going to die alone-without you. I thought I owed some Great Spirit a debt for surviving the fire and finding you. I never dreamed the price would be so high. I thought maybe it was retribution for giving in to Mylyn, but even God knew there was nothing I could do for her no matter how hard I tried. None of us, especially the children, could take listening to her scream in pain any more. She wouldn't die on her own. Why did God make me do that? Why couldn't she just die? I slipped under that water and for the first time in a week I wasn't tired, I wasn't hungry, I felt no pain – only peace. I wasn't afraid. I was done puking and coughing and tasting my own blood. My arms floated effortlessly in the water, because I could no longer hold them up. I could see everything as if I was watching it on a movie. It all became very clear. And do you know what, Alex? I was all right with it. I welcomed the relief. I had finally gotten out of this shit hole I was asked to go in, and I was all right with it.

I understood what they mean when they say we are going to a better place. Shit, Alex, I thought I was back in Kansas with Auntie Em and that little scrawny barking dog. I thought this isn't so bad. Nice mellow colors, no monsters, nothing biting at my feet, just an endless abyss of solitude. The only think wrong was that I couldn't find the light. I always wanted to walk toward the light but I couldn't find it. I even remembered to look for the thirteen virgins in case I had any Muslim blood in me, but no luck there."

Tom stopped talking at the front door of the hospital and paused to look down the street before crossing it and walking on the sand of the beach in front of the hospital.

Alex just looked at him with a fixed gaze as if to say, "My God, Tommy, what happened to you out there?"

They walked very slowly out onto the sand as Alex assisted him with every step for fear that he might lose his balance in the sand.

"Let's go over there and spread out the blanket, okay, honey?" Tom asked. "My legs just aren't up to any long strolls tonight, I'm afraid."

A slight breeze over the ocean helped in spreading out the blanket. Even though it was dark and the hospital lights were on, it was very easy to see the stars.

Looking up, Tom said, "You have no idea how lonely the stars are at night when you're all alone. The loneliness leads to despair and that leads to memories. Do you have any idea how many times I re-lived making love to you under the stars? It was all I had to keep me holding on to that damn raft. If I concentrated on it hard enough, I could almost feel your body next to mine. Then someone would cry or cough and I would be swept back to reality. All day long that's all I had to hang on to- you. When I slipped below the surface I knew it was over until I saw you walking on the water in your white nightgown and your hair flowing in the wind like an angel. Had you not reached out your hand for me, I would have surely died. I had no reason to leave the serenity of death. I couldn't fight it, I didn't have the strength and I wasn't sure I wanted to start over again just to return here. When the sub came along, you were gone. I looked for you, but you weren't there, only a glow of where you had stood. It took me the longest time to figure out what happened. One minute I was at peace, the next I was in pain again, but I knew I wasn't alone this time. There were people everywhere, and they were all in a hurry. I remember they wouldn't go back for Mylyn and I couldn't understand why. We couldn't just leave her there, but we did. Maybe it was best – best to leave the regretful memories in the water that claimed her. Maybe the boat was only for the living, for those who were chosen to go on. But the children had nothing to go on with. Their parents were in the front of the aircraft and were killed instantly. Their corpses bobbed up in front of their own children, still strapped in their seats. Nobody should have to go through that. And what did I do for them, Alex? I could only keep them alive so they could see that. Why would such a loving God ask someone to keep a child alive just so they could endure such pain? We would all have been better off if we had died instantly.

For the longest time, I thought that the only true proof of my survival would be to come and sit in the sand with you once again. I knew that would be my testament, my salvation. And here I am. I can feel your warmth, smell your hair and look into your eyes. I don't have any more doubts now, only gratitude. And if I never see that priest again, it will still be too soon for me. We'll go home, find Rocky, hug the girls and get on with our lives. We owe that to each other- I owe that to myself."

Tom lay down on the blanket, because he did not have the strength to hold himself up. Alex lay right beside him cradling his head against her chest. He continued to hold her as tightly as he could as he continued talking.

"I'd like to make you a deal, a promise, if you will," Tom said as he snuggled even closer to Alex who caressed him even tighter.:" I'll fly no more overnighters, no more alone when the sun goes down. I can't take the chance of being away from you ever again. I won't survive another one of these ' three day passes'. No more good-byes, no more 'see you tomorrows'. I'm going to live everyday with you and for you like it was my last day on earth. And believe me, Alex, I know what that feels like. The man upstairs owes me. I trust Him. He'll take care of us, all of us. And my little dog too."

With that Alex started laughing and said, "I've never felt more confident that that crazy dog will be coming home soon. How you can joke about that at a time like this is beyond me."

"What do you mean a time like this?" Tom returned. "Did you forget how I spent yesterday?"

"Point taken," said Alex. "Tell me, do you think you can open that gown just a little more in the front? I have something here I think you're going to like."

"By God, Alex!" Tom said. "I thought you were going to make me beg for it, but right now, I don't think I could deliver. Give me until tomorrow. Just let me lay here with you awhile. I'll deliver tomorrow, I promise."

"That's okay, Tommy, I thought that's why you brought me out here, to jump my bones." Alex said.

"No, honey. I actually wanted to come out here for closure," replied Tom. "All the time I was on that raft, all I could think about was you and me on that beach. If I could feel it, I would know in my mind that I was safe. I've never been so sure of my mortality before in my life. I actually thought I was a dead man. I gave up, Alex. I was too tired to fight. All I could do was think of meeting you on the other side. And I saw the other side; and it was beautiful— unbelievably beautiful. I wanted to go there. I wanted to be free. I could feel the sand under my body and I knew you were there with me, but I couldn't hold on to you any longer. I just wanted to die. And now I have to get back into living again. Because I don't believe I'm here. I want to forget this ever happened, but I don't think Mylyn will let me. I'll never forget her face."

"I'll help you forget, Tommy," Alex said reassuringly. "We'll start living again, just the two of us. Let me help you get through this."

As Alex talked to Tom he became limp in her arms. When she looked down at him she could see that he had fallen asleep and she cradled him tighter to her chest rocking him back and forth.

"My, God, Tommy," Alex whispered. "What has happened to you?"

As she looked at him he appeared lifeless in her arms and she began to cry. The man who was always her strength was helplessly weak in her arms. There was no laughter in his face, nor the usual banter that separated him from other men Alex had known, just a strained drawn appearance to his face. Probably the salt water, Alex thought, but it was obviously painful. As he slept in her arms he called out and jerked about. This was unlike Tom. It was clear he was reliving every wave that had tossed him endlessly on that raft of total despair. And who, Alex thought, was Mylyn? She wasn't on the survivor's list. What, or rather who, was she and what part did she play in this epic struggle that Tom still fought against? She would ask sometime, but now just wasn't the time. She thought it might be time to get back to the room and that was the last thought she had. In her mind as she drifted off, she wanted to take Tom home where she could take care of him. She knew that he would be safe there and this nightmare would end. In her mind she would take care of Tom and make him as good as new. But Tom had some mental issues from near death stress and she may need some help for them. Normally, she would contact the priest that Tom knew, but right now she wasn't sure how that was going to work out. She never felt the soft salty breeze blow over her. She was already asleep.

86

. . . .

E D WOKE EARLY TO THE smell of freshly brewed coffee and the view of Alice scurrying around the bedroom getting ready for a task that appeared to be important. Alice wasn't one to waste motion. How beautiful she looked, Ed thought, for a lady her age. She was as beautiful as the last time he had seen her on the roof of that Saigon military hospital.

He cleared his throat slightly to get her attention as she breezed by.

"Well, you're awake. Good morning," she said as she gave him a kiss. "Are you ready for some breakfast?"

"I'm not a breakfast person," Ed said. "But I will take some coffee."

"Oh, contra re'!" Alice remarked. "You'll need your strength today. You have to see your friend back to Houston and take me to your house for a little R & R. You need all the strength and nourishment you can get. You've got another long day ahead of you."

"Are you serious?" Ed asked

"Top shelf," Alice replied. "I was planning on starting my vacation today with no commitments on my slate. So it's just you and me for a while. If you'll have me, that is."

"I wouldn't have it any other way," Ed said as he reached up and pulled her back into bed. "Let's not rush this, shall we?

A police officer on his morning beat came across two bodies lying together in the sand and became a bit unnerved. Being careful not to sound an alert he walked up to the two people and touched Alex. "Are you all right, Madam?" the police officer asked.

"Good morning, Officer," Alex said. "Yes, we're perfectly fine. Thank you for checking on us. I think we had better get back inside. As she stood up, Tom woke also. She reached out her hand to the policeman wishing him a good day, and he in turn tipped his hat and walked away. What a pleasant person, he thought. It is very rare to see that in the early morning.

Alex looked down at Tom and said, "Are you going to get up with the rest of the world this morning, Thomas or would you like me to order beach front room service?"

Tom looked up at Alex and smiled coyly. "Don't you feel that? Can't you see this? This is what it's all about. This is life. This is what I never thought I'd wake up to. I am alive. I am here with you and I am alive. And now I'm ready to go home. Beach front room service, you say. Do they have that here? Help me up, would you?"

"How are you doing today?" Alex asked.

"Good, thanks," he replied. "I think all I needed was a good night's rest. And I certainly got it with you here. So, what do you say we go see the good doctor and get ourselves checked out of here? What day is it, honey? I had a dinner date set for your birthday, but I think I may have messed that up with my little detour."

"Not to worry...having you back is all the gift I need," Alex said.

"I was hoping you'd say that, I'm a little short on cash this week," he replied as he cracked her on the butt.

"You're going to have a hard time getting into my pants when we get home if you don't come up with something to insure me how much you care," Alex said as she returned the swat. "After all, we women need to be pampered once in a while."

"Let me assure you, I'll do anything to get into your pants when we get home. What ever happened to love?" asked Tom. "That always worked before."

"I'm sure that will be just fine this time also," Alex said as she steadied Tom when he rose from the ground. "Let's go get you checked out and go home," she said with a great deal of enthusiasm.

"Lead on," Tom returned as he wobbled a little on the sand.

When they reached the front door they were met by a very pleasant surprise. There were sixty-five children and Irene standing in the vestibule. There were some other dignitaries standing there too. They held up flowers to Alex, and a gift was given to Tom. It was an hourglass on a piece of wood with all the children's names signed on it. Tom was unprepared for anything like this and he fought back tears. He was doing a pretty good job of it until the little Korean girl came up to him and handed him the gift. When she did this she reached up to give him a hug. Tom bent down to meet her, picked her up and held her in his arms. Nothing was said but there was no mistaking the love between them as a result of the ordeal they had shared.

They held each other, and looking into each other's eyes, they kissed, and smiling Tom put her down. They all clapped and Irene, as their spokesman said, "As the only English speaking person here, we would like to thank you, Captain Jordan, for our very lives. Had it not been for you we would all have died out there. When we arrive back at the school, a tree of life will be placed in your honor to signify the gift of life and growth you have given to all of us here. Please accept this gift on behalf of the grateful nation of The Peoples Republic of Korea.

As Tom accepted the gift, he still held the little Korean girl's hand. Looking at Alex, Tom said, "Please help me. I can't do this right now," as tears began to flow from his eyes.

Alex stepped up to Tom and took the little girl's other hand and said, "On behalf of Captain Jordan and myself it is a great honor to receive this gift. I am very grateful to all of you for bringing him home to me. It is my hope that we will all live to be old and to share with our grandchildren this time in our lives when God's love shown down on all of us. Let us also remember those who died during this ordeal so that those lives were not lost in vain. They will forever be held close in our minds and our hearts. Thank you from the bottom of my heart."

There were several men who came up to Tom, smiled broadly and said something in Korean and in a short time the whole crowd except for Irene and the little Korean girl had gone. Irene and Tom talked, and then she translated for the little girl. Alex shook Irene's hand and hugged the little girl as they too were off to catch the plane back to Korea. Tom watched until the little girl was out of sight. He turned to look at Alex who put her arm around him and said, "Are you all right?"

"Yes. Thank you for holding me up. I couldn't have done that without you," Tom said wiping his eyes. "Get me out of here before I embarrass myself some more."

"I know what you mean," Alex replied. "That was a little tough for me and I wasn't even there. I'm here anytime you want to talk about it."

"I don't know where I'd start, honey," Tom said as he kissed and held her obviously starting to cry again.

She held him close and at that moment began to feel that the man she loved was actually mortal. Her heart welled up with the feelings a wife would have for her man at this moment more than she had ever felt for anyone in her life. She held Tom even tighter and looked up toward the ceiling and said a quiet, "Thank you for this."

While Alex was still embracing Tom, the doctor came up to them and said, "I hear you spent the night on the beach. Are you ready to go home? Your tests all check out. All you need is some rest and you can get that better at home. I have signed you out. Have a safe trip and good luck to both of you."

"Thanks for everything, Doctor," Alex said. Tom turned from Alex's shoulder, shook the Doctor's hand, thanked him for everything and invited him to their house if he ever got to Houston.

The doctor accepted their invitation and smiling, turned and walked away in a hurry with probably more to do than visit.

As they made their way down the corridor they heard the familiar voice of Ed Drummond behind them. When they turned around they were met, not only by Ed, but also by a radiant looking lady holding his hand.

It was unfamiliar to have someone with Ed, but Tom extended his hand and raising his finger said, "I've seen your picture someplace, haven't I?"

"Yes, you have," Ed said. "Alex and Tom, this is Alice. She 's coming home with us."

"Why you old hound dog, you," Tom kidded Ed. "You done good! You're the girl from Saigon, aren't you?"

"Yes, I am," she said.

"You're a doctor too, right?" Tom asked.

"Yes, I am," she said again.

"This lovely lady is Alex," Tom said. "We live in sin together, but I couldn't live without her. I hope you and Ed have the same love for each other. However, I hope it is never tested like ours was a few days ago."

"I heard you had quite an ordeal," Alice said. "Were you able to meet with the children before they left?

"They just left," Tom answered. "It was nice to see them, but I could have done without the fanfare."

"I heard you are going to be a Korean national hero," replied Alice proudly. "They are going to plant a tree in your honor. I don't mean to lecture, but that is right up there with Ghandi and Schnidler. This is a big deal to these people. You should be proud, Captain. I must tell you that just knowing someone who has been bestowed with this honor gives me goose bumps."

"Are you serious?" Alex asked. "It's that big of a deal?"

"Absolutely!" Alice exclaimed. "To them the tree grows forever. And with that your memory. To them, it is an eternal gift. A thank you that lasts forever."

"I like her, Ed," Tom said.

"Yeah...me too," Ed returned. "I do believe we have a plane to catch.

"Alex and I are taking a bus if you don't mind," Tom added.

"Ah...no!" said Ed.

The four of them made their way back to Tom's room and collected the new clothes Ed had brought him. After that Tom signed out of the hospital and even though he stopped and shook a few hands they were out of there quite quickly. They all crawled into the limo that Ed had secured for the ride to the airport. After the car began moving, Ed turned and looked at Alex and said, "You done good, ma'am...you done good. And you, sir, are grounded!"

87

TOM FOUND THE TRIP BACK to Houston very relaxing. There were many times that he just closed his eyes and relived the days he spent in the water and tried to come to grips with what had happened. Alex could sense his discomfort as she leaned over and said quietly, "Just let it go. Let it out there where it belongs. Let it go."

He knew if he could just come to some form of closure within over the death of Mylyn, he could learn to live and go on. But he could not shake her last words, the look on her face, and the gratitude in her eyes when he gave her the lethal dose of morphine. A constant battle of guilt raged in his head. In his heart he knew it the best thing he could have done for her, but in his conscience he knew he had killed her. Call it mercy...call it kindness...call it whatever...it was murder and he was right in the middle of it. And it had cut a hole deep within his very soul.

All his life Tom believed in another human's right to die in peace, why couldn't he accept that now? Was it that he was not as comfortably secure in his convictions as he thought, or was it the fact that euthanasia was all right as long as he didn't share the responsibility. As he pondered the thought of it, he could feel Alex's hand tighten on his and thought if there was ever a time in his life he needed somebody else it was now and it was Alex. He would have to let her in and maybe, just maybe, she could bring him out of this.

Tom opened his eyes and sat up in his seat when he heard the landing gear drop and lock. *One more formality and then I can go home,* he thought to himself. He thought about how Tom Hanks must have felt in the movie *Castaway.* All he wanted to do was go home with no more fanfare. Just take me home and put me in my own bed and I'll work this out in my own way. But he could not do that, at least not just yet. There was one more stop.

Tom began to feel like he was the most ungrateful person on the planet. These are the people that saved your very life. Granted someone in a submarine picked you up, but these are the people who gave up all their spare time for your existence. Show a little respect, you asshole.

Alex reached over to him and said, "Let's make an appearance and I promise I'll get you out of here quickly."

"You know something that I just realized?" Tom said. "I owe these people my life. They are my dream come true. Without them and especially without you I would still be out there. Let's make more than an appearance. I want them to know how grateful I truly am to them all. And you...I'll give you a personal exhibition later. Lead on, my dear."

As the air stair was moved into place, Ed came up to him and said, "Are you ready for this?"

He looked at Ed and said, "Damn, it's good to be home." And as he stood up he fell back into his chair still a little weak.

"Maybe I'll celebrate a little slower. Would you lend a hand to a weary old traveler, my dear?"

As Tom reached out his hand to Alex, she and Ed were both crying.

"Come on you guys, I'm not that weary." Tom said.

"You have no idea. We thought this day would never come," Ed said. "So bear with us. I'll embarrass myself if I want to."

Tom got a grip on their arms and was lifted back up to his feet. All four of them hugged in the aisle of the small commuter jet.

"I've got a lot of people in there to thank," Tom said. "Let's not keep them waiting."

When the four of them cleared the threshold of the gate entrance Tom was amazed at the number of well wishers that had come to greet him. There was the usual food and refreshments available and a large banner that read, "Welcome home, Tom!"

Many of Tom's friends were there as well as some people he had never known. There was a great deal of clapping and cheering as they came in to the room. Tom's friend Bob, First Officer Pitts, Tom's new co-pilot, and Emily were there as well as Ann with her husband and the remainder of the crew. Off in the corner of the group to his surprise, he spied Beth.

There was a great deal of hugs, pats on the back, and shaking hands going around. They knew they had a part in this and were entitled to the celebration to honor one of their own that was lost and returned.

One of the company's top executives had a podium set up in the center of the room and as the fanfare seemed to slow down a bit he came up to the podium and tapping lightly on the microphone got everyone's attention.

"Ladies and gentlemen," he began officially. "It gives great pleasure to be here with you today to honor not only Captain Jordan for surviving, but to honor all of you who worked so unselfishly to find him. This is a blessed day for all of us at Aurora Airlines. And if I can offer a bit of a prayer of thanksgiving...Thank you, Lord, for returning our son, Tom, to us. He was lost and now he is found. Let this be a reminder of Your eternal blessing on all of us in time of trial, not to lose hope but to continue to the prize of Your eternal salvation. Amen!"

The 'Amens' came from every direction of the room. Some were smiling and some were wiping tears from their eyes at the conclusion of the executive's words.

Everyone expected Tom to say something, but he was very hesitant to move forward. Finally with the help of Alex and Keith, he moved up to the podium. Having no idea what to say and doing everything in his power not to break down, he cleared his throat and said in a moronic tone... "Ah...hello." And then he started laughing and everyone else laughed and clapped again with him. Those that knew Tom knew what he meant, but he did go on.

"I heard that on *Beavis and Butthead* once, and always wanted to say it. Nothing I could say would ever match the feelings I have in my heart for you. But I assure you that every morning when I wake up I will remember all of you who went above and beyond to bring me back home. I promise you that you will never be forgotten. As I was out on that raft I knew you were my only hope. I knew that you would never quit. And I was right. That is why I'm here today. Thank you...thank you...thank you all."

Before Tom began to break down, he turned to Alex who was right there with a shoulder. Keith took the cue also and began clapping and that spread throughout the room. Finally someone hollered, "Let's eat," and that was the end of the official fanfare.

Tom heard Alex say hello to someone and when he turned, he was greeted by Chris and the girls, Carrie and Corrie. Working his way over to a chair he hugged the girls. There the company physician greeted him and seemed quite concerned that Tom was so weak and tired. He advised him that if there was anything he needed, not to hesitate to call. Tom shook his hand, thanked him and watched him walk away. Corrie tried to sit on Tom's lap, but he was too weak to support her. So she stood next to him as a sentinel for his very strength.

Bob, Tom's long time friend, instrumental in the search grid plans, came up to him and jokingly said, "Korean Airlines has offered you a refund on your ticket and a free pass for any future flights you may be interested in."

"I'll look into that," Tom returned. "Thank you, Bob."

"Don't mention it," Bob replied. "You'd do the same for me."

Sharon, Bob's wife, and also long time friend leaned down and kissed Tom on the cheek and said, "Welcome back."

The celebration went on for nearly an hour and things were breaking up when Tom felt a tap on his shoulder. When he looked to his right he was shocked. Standing next to him was Caroline. Tom left the security of his chair and standing up hugged and kissed her. They looked into each other's eyes for a brief moment and then shaking their heads in total agreement, Caroline turned and walked away.

Keith took him by the arm and said, "I've seen her someplace before."

He looked at Keith and said, "We used to fly together a long time ago."

Alex took Tom's hand again, and said, "Flying as you and I do?"

"Not quite that high," Tom replied.

Shortly after Caroline's visit the party broke up.. Bob and Sharon came once again and reminded Tom and Alex that their anniversary dinner was still on whenever Tom felt up to it. Chris and Carrie went out and got the van and brought it around so Tom didn't have to walk too far. It was obvious he would never make it, because he had to stop and rest before he could get through the concourse. Alex was concerned about his weakness, but took it all in stride. She would strengthen him up when she got him home, she thought. Once she had him home everything would be better again. The only difference at home was that Rocky was not there to greet them. That hadn't been mentioned yet and she hoped it wouldn't.

It wasn't long after Tom and Alex made their way to the front door after bumping elbows with a great deal of well wishers, that Chris made it through the traffic to the entrance. Alex opened the door and got Tom situated. As he put on his seatbelt he looked at her with an evil grin and said, "Once I'm back on my feet, honey, I would like you to continue this chivalry. I can get used to this."

"I've got your chivalry," Alex said. "Wait till I get you home."

When Alex turned to walk around the other side of the car, she glanced up at the sky and said a quiet thank-you and got into the car. It was time to go home.

The trip home was very interesting to Tom to say the least. He passed the sign where he saw the priest turn into a glass of orange juice. The car that the old lady nearly drove into Tom was sitting along the side of the road with grass grown up around it. And as he looked out the window at what was plush landscape last week, Alex commented on what an eyesore that property was.

The church seemed to remain as beautiful as it was the day Tom and the girls visited Father Harris. Thankfully, Tom thought to himself, some things never change.

"Almost home," Corrie said to Tom as she snuggled up closer to his arm.

"Yep," Chris returned. "There's our street."

As she turned the van down the street she drove in front of the house. Tom instantly had an attack of 'rubber neck' when he turned and looked saying, "What happened to my front yard?"

"We were hoping you wouldn't see that so soon, hon," Alex said laughing.

"My God in heaven!" Tom screamed. "I'm gone for a weekend and you guys turn my yard into a parking lot for the county fair. Corrie, couldn't you keep a closer eye on these two characters?"

"I think it was the policemen who did that, Tom," Corrie explained.

"The policemen!" Tom ranted. "My God, you had the law here also? Where was the watchdog during all this? I can't believe the place went downhill so quick. My God, don't let my poor mother see this yard. She'll have a stroke. Alex, I'll need to see you out on the beach for a moment, please."

"Right, honey, I'll be sure to get right out there," chided Alex. "I don't think you're in any condition for a beach rendezvous at this juncture of your day, Thomas. Besides, it's still daylight. Come on, get out of the car before you get in trouble."

When Tom exited the car he reached up and took Alex by the arm for support. In doing so Alex could see that he was still weak. Maybe some supper would give him some strength. And if he spent the night in his own bed that might help also. But the issue of Rocky was still left untouched and she wasn't sure how to approach that. His sense of humor was in full gear though, and she knew that was a good sign.

When she opened the door leading from the garage to the kitchen, Tom smiled at her and motioned to the beach.

"I think Corrie and I will take a stroll before dinner, "Tom said as he let his hand drift away from Alex's waist. "Let's go and see if we can find our wayward dog, honey."

"Well, good luck to you," Alex said. "But if you come back with him, I'm going to start to really worry about you."

As he turned and walked out the back door with Corrie in tow, Alex had a strange feeling about him. She felt there was a different gait, a different aura. She almost felt like there was much more to Tom than Tom. Get hold of yourself, for God sake. You're getting as looney as he is. She went into the house.

Tom and Corrie went to the beach, not for their usual run as was Corrie's way of getting there, but in a slow deliberate walk. Corrie began telling Tom the story of the priest coming and Rocky attempting to run him off but never catching him and never returning. Tom held her hand and continued to explain and console her that it wasn't her fault and that if they saw the priest again, he was sure that Rocky would be in hot pursuit.

As they stood on the beach overlooking the ocean, Corrie said, "This is where Grandma and I heard you call the other night."

Taken aback, Tom said, "What do you mean, honey?"

"The night we were all out here," Corrie said. "Carrie and Mommy and I heard Grandma talking to someone and we came out to see what was going on. Grandma and I heard you, but just Grandma and me, no one else. After that Mommy made me go to bed."

"Who was Grandma talking to?" Tom asked.

"I don't know, there was no one here," Corrie explained. "It was dark and cold. I was scared. But when you called, it warmed up a lot and Grandma and I listened for you again, but we only heard you twice. I think the water quit moving. Mommy tried to get Grandma into the house but she wouldn't come in. After that Mister Drummond came in the middle of the night and said they found you. It was scary. But we knew you'd come back. When you called, we knew you were all right."

As Tom listened to her he began thinking back when he had drifted off the raft and into the water. That was when he saw Alex walking on the water and extending her hand. He remembered screaming her name then as Irene pulled him back onto the raft because the submarine had surfaced. Tom wondered if that was at the same time. He began to feel a chill as he stood on the beach on that hot afternoon and noticed a cloudy vision in front of him. He felt Corrie's hand tighten on his and heard Corrie say, "Where is my dog?"

Standing in front of them along the edge of the water was the priest. He hadn't changed a bit. He still had the need for a shave, the faded plum sash, and the worn out brownish robe.

"Where is my dog?" Corrie asked again.

"You needn't be afraid, little one," the priest answered. "He will be coming along shortly."

Looking at Tom the priest said, "You have served the Father well, my son. Go and live a good life. It will be filled with promise and the beauty of children. The favors of the fathers will never pass you by. You will find peace and happiness all the days of your long healthy life. You will go to the Father together in the peace of your sleep.

"Where will you go now?" Tom asked as he extended his hand in a gesture of friendship.

"I will leave this place," the pries answered. "That is why I can't touch you. I am not of this world."

"Are there any more like you?" Tom asked. "Will any of you stop by again?"

"There are many who serve the Father that walk in the sun with mortal man," the priest answered. "But you will not be called on again. You have fulfilled the destiny put you to complete. You, little one, are a witness to the presence of all those who live in the faith of the Father and serve him unselfishly. You also will be blessed with a long life and many children. Now I must go. Tell no one of this. As you would say, my son; "they would lock you up and throw away the key. I enjoyed your dog."

It seemed like only a split second before the image of the priest faded away down the sun glazed beach. Tom and Corrie stood there holding each other's hand and felt the gulf breeze blow on them.

He looked over at Corrie and said, "Did you see anything or am I just tired?"

"I saw something, Tom," Corrie said. "But he told us not to talk about it."

As the two friends turned toward the house, Alex hollered out the window to come in for supper. It didn't seem that long to Tom and Corrie that they were standing on the beach talking to the priest, but Tom did notice that the sun had moved around the corner of the boat dock. As they neared the house they heard a dog barking off in the distance.

They looked at each other and at the same time said, "Rocky?" They turned and ran back to the water's edge. At about the same time Alex heard it also.

Turning toward Chris she said, "Oh, my God. This is getting too freaky for me!"

Chris came and looked out the window just as Tom and Corrie made their way to the water. They had crouched down and were clapping and coaxing something to come to them.

Chris followed her mother out the door saying, "I know what you mean!"

On the waterfront they could see Rocky making his way in a labored gallop down the beach, barking, tongue hanging out and stopping to pay his respects to the neighbor's poodle, and then he was again on his way to the waiting arms of his family.

Alex couldn't help but comment that Rocky was a typical man; he was probably starving to death and he still had to stop and sniff a crotch. Tom looked over and gave her an evil grin and continued cheering Rocky on home saying, "That's my boy."

Eventually Rocky found his way home and for being gone two days was remarkably clean. He came up to Corrie and flopped down in front of her whining and moaning and begging to have his belly rubbed. Tom looked up at Alex with a look like...'see, I told you he'd be back.'

Alex looked around making sure that no one else thought she was talking to a dog and decided to join everyone celebrating his homecoming.

The celebration for Rocky was not nearly as exuberant as it was for Tom, but Rocky did get more touches and rubs than Tom did.

Not to let the moment pass he said, "Gosh, Alex, nobody rubbed my belly."

"That's because you don't have abs, Porky," Alex replied.

"Oh, that was low," Tom blurted out. "Why do you do me like that?"

"Come on in everybody," Chris interjected. "Dinner's getting cold."

As everybody moved from Rocky's belly rub, Tom held out his arm and Alex helped him up. He swatted her on the butt as they walked to the house.

Something caught Alex's attention and she looked away from Tom. When she did so she saw the priest that she recognized from the house that night standing in front of her by the waters edge. He said nothing, only smiled as he stood motionless in front of her. Alex looked at the priest as if waiting for him to speak, but he only nodded his head, then turning he was gone.

When Alex turned around Tom was about to put his arm around her. Laughingly he pointed to a spot in the sand and said, "See, I told you the mark would stay a while. Let's come back and re-size it tonight."

"Thomas Jordan, you can hardly stand," Alex said emphatically. "Tonight, young man, I am going to hold you and you are not getting anywhere near the water. Tomorrow we'll consider a beach party."

"Kick a guy when he's down, why don't you?" said Tom as he continued on to the house. "I thought you loved me."

"I do love you, but this is just not the time for bullshit!" Alex corrected. "Tom, stop where you are and look at me! We know that was no picnic for you. But, please don't make light of it. You have no idea of what things were here either. Trying to laugh this off is only going to make it worse. Your body and your spirit are hurt, and you want to put this behind you as much as we do, but this is not the way. Please don't cover it with humor when it is obviously painful to you. Whether or not you can see it, the girls are beside themselves with misunderstanding, guilt over the dog, and the real fear that you were not coming back. They need your help to get them over this. They need you serious for awhile, and so do I. You were gone, Tom, and no one gave you much chance of coming back. So, please, let's get serious for now and get things back to normal."

"Normal for who?" Tom asked. "I'm sorry I offended you."

Tom turned and walked to the house, noticeably upset as he put his hands in his pockets. As she reached up to take his hand he squirmed away from her saying, "Leave me be, I can make it on my own."

Tom had hoped to deal with this in his own way, but Alex made it very clear he was not going to laugh it off. As he sat down to the dinner, he felt that he was dining with strangers. He passed the serving plates around the table and picking up his coffee cup, excused himself and went outside.

As he stood on the beach he couldn't help but remember the days spent on the raft, the terror of the screams of the children and the pain of the crash. He couldn't get the pleading face of Mylyn out of his mind. He remembered the waves that damn near drowned him as he swam to save those children who were washed off the raft by the waves. He was all right, he thought, until Alex scolded him for not being serious. Now he had to take it seriously whether he wanted to or not. And he did not. Damn her, he thought, for doing this.

He continued standing at the beach and looking out over the water, his mind going a mile a minute over everything that happened the past three days. He turned and looked at his boat resting on the dock and walked over to it, cup in hand. He was overwhelmed with a feeling of aloneness. Surrounded by people, he felt he was alone against the world and the world wanted an answer to a question he hadn't a clue to. He was confused, alone and afraid and he did not know where to turn. He thought Alex would make everything right, but now he felt betrayed by the very person he looked to for strength.

As he reached the ramp to the dock he finished his coffee and laid the cup on the railing. He stepped onto the boat and through the door to the cabin. He could hide here and no one would find him. He would be alone with his problems and here, in peace he could find the answers he so desperately sought.

His mind raced uncontrollably through the events of the three days. The day he met Mylyn at the gate and how great and welcomed she made him feel. All those people who died in the initial crash and their children left in the rear of the airplane alone. What a horrible way to die, Tom thought, with your children being protected by a stranger. He had trouble accepting that a single God would put him on this one airplane to save these children. Why me? Tom began to talk aloud. Why not just let the plane land someplace and prevent all this crap in the first place? What the hell were you thinking, Man? So explain this to me, I save these kids and send them home safe and sound. Who the hell is going to send me home safe and sound? I'm so screwed up I'm talking to myself on a damn boat tied to a dock. And I'm supposed to be rational. Go figure! Did you check my resume' while you were at it? Hell, I can't even swim! I damn near drowned twice. Did you notice that?

"Yeah, he noticed. We all noticed." a voice behind Tom said. "But you didn't! Did you notice that? I never took you for such a whiner, Jordan. You sound like a kid whose batteries went dead on Christmas in his brand new fire truck. Grow a dick! Do you think it was easy for those kids and how about Mylyn? That had to hurt. You were lucky; you walked away! So you're a little scared and confused. Who isn't? You're sitting here on your boat, bitching. Hell, at least you got a boat. Half those poor slobs you pass every day don't even have a flush toilet. And you got a little wet and got into a situation that you couldn't control and found yourself depending on someone else. So how does it feel? Even Superman had to answer to Lex Luthor and that kryptonite shit to get through the day. What about me? Did you ever wonder how I felt when my plane crashed and the windshield took my freakin' head off? You think that was a walk in the park? I even knew my ass was grass. Did you ever hear me bitch? Hell, no! I said my usual cuss words and got my shit together real quick. And that's what you need to do".

"Are you going to take this boat out in the water or are you afraid of it, too? Captain Ahab would shit himself if he saw you right now. So, you didn't like Alex telling you to grow up and deal with this like a man, is that it? What do you want her to say, let's laugh it up and pretend this never happened? Well it did happen, you dumb ass! And it damn near killed her trying to find you. She even asked me where you were. Of course, I couldn't tell her, but she even threatened to kiss my ass if anything happened to you. And then she went to the Man Himself and made some kind of arrangement for your sorry ass. And where are YOU right now? Sitting in a boat, bitching at Him demanding an answer. Well, there are no answers, Bucko! There's just shit that's got to be done. And if you're lucky, you'll come out of it unstained with all your parts attached. Looking at you, I'd say you're shitting in some pretty high cotton! You're lucky you weren't that priest. That sorry son of a bitch got his ass locked up by Poncho Villa and left to starve to death with a bunch of other sorry smucks. Every time I see that skinny bastard I want to feed him a Big Mac and Fries to fatten him up so he quits looking like he fell out of a hearse. And quit beating yourself up over Mylyn. That couldn't be helped. That's a chance she takes every time she flies. Do you see what I'm getting at? Shit Happens! We do what we can and move on. Just because of you it happened with a little more survivors. You'll be taken care of, so quit feeling sorry for yourself and get out there and make someone proud they know you."

"You mean get back out there and fly again?" Tom asked.

"No, your flying days are over. Take Ed's desk job offer. You will be of much more value there than you will be in the sky from now on. And I won't be around to bail your sorry ass out of the crap you get into. Take Ed's offer, get your strength back and screw Alex's brains out until even Viagra fails you. And quit your bitching...He hates cry babies. My lord, Peter is still complaining about that little water issue he got into during that storm. Who cares? Get over it."

"What do you mean you won't be around here?" Tom asked. "Where are you going?"

"I don't know," John said "Hopefully someplace where it's warm. But I'll never be back here again. I came to say good-bye, Thomas, my boy. You'll be all right, now. Everybody has this little complaint session when they get back. That's the trouble with mortals. We're never happy. Once you get upstairs, life is good, except for Peter. He's never happy. Well, it's getting late. You had better get back to the house, Alex is waiting for you. We've been out here for quite awhile," John said as he motioned toward the sunset. "It's been a hell of a ride, man. Thanks for all the times you were there for me. We are even now."

Tom turned and looked out the boathouse window and noticed it was dark. When he turned back around John Beck was gone. He opened the boathouse door and began to laugh-- Saint Peter complaining about a wet tunic, after all he'd been through. That poor shit!

He closed the door and made his way to the house As Tom walked he ran his feet through the sand and realized all his questions had been answered. He was all right again. He was no longer scared, no longer confused and no longer alone. He had found the peace that he had searched for to answer the questions of those three days. He looked up to the stars and shook his head and said, "Thanks for everything, glad I could help, sorry about the bitching," and walked into the house.

When he got in the house he found Rocky asleep at the foot of the couch and Alex lying on the couch with an afghan watching a movie.

"Did you have a nice walk?" Alex asked as she moved her position and patted the cushion for Tom to lie down next to her.

"Yeah, I did. Thanks," Tom replied as he took off his shoes and slid in next to Alex. "Ooh...you're nice and warm. I think I could lay and dream like this all night long."

"You go ahead and dream," Alex replied as she pulled the afghan close to Tom's chin. "I'm going to stay awake so your dreams don't take you anywhere away from me."

"You awake and me dreaming," Tom commented. "In dreams awake. That's sounds kind of neat, doesn't it? Didn't some writer say that about being away in his dreams and yet still awake. That he saw all the beauty and pain of the world...in dreams awake?"

"That could be," Alex said. "But my pilot needs his rest and he has seen enough pain for one lifetime."

THE END

www.ingramcontent.com/pod-product-compliance
Lightning Source LLC
Chambersburg PA
CBHW030912300726
48970CB00001B/131